THE
BOOK
OF
NUMBERS

THE
BOOK
OF
NUMBERS

by Robert Deane Pharr

Doubleday & Company, Inc.
Garden City, New York
1969

1

In the beginning there was only Dave and Blueboy. They came to town during the Easter season of 1935, and the first thing they did was to search for a man like Eggy Manone.

Now Eggy was a womanless clod and a drunkard who was every gambler's meat. But Eggy could count and Eggy could fry eggs and the Good Lord in His Infinite Wisdom had deemed these two talents sufficient unto Eggy's needs. Each morning at five the man arose from a deep stupor and went to work in the cavernous kitchen of the Cavalier Hotel.

White people who really understood Negroes always said that Eggy was a sober, dependable, colored boy; a credit to his race. Negroes who knew Eggy maintained that he was the sloppiest-drinking, dumbest damn fool in the Ward, even if he was the fastest egg cook in the United States. Still, they generally added a gracious footnote: "He never done nothin' to nobody but hisself."

At ten each morning, Eggy would lean on the serving counter for a breather. The breakfast rush was over, but he could not leave his station for another half hour. This morning, as he idled, he noticed one of the extra waiters coming over. Eggy took a deep breath and snorted, "Floatin' waiter, this one!"

The object of Eggy's scorn was a tall, bronzed rather than brown youth. Because the young man was walking too slowly to be bringing a breakfast order, Eggy grew as alert as an old maid on a hay ride. The egg cook instinctively distrusted this waiter for no other reason save that he was a stranger. Eggy liked to lump all out-of-town waiters into one disparaging catchall, "floatin' waiters." He got angry when one of them insisted that he was a *traveling* waiter, because Eggy and everyone else with good sense knew better. "Here today and gone tomorrow with somebody else's wife or daughter." This one would be gone, too, as soon as this here convention was over.

The waiter came up to the range and smiled. Eggy glowered. The fella's age was uncertain, twenty-one, perhaps. But after looking at those somber eyes, Eggy revised his guess. This floater could be ten years older than that.

"You gonna take a break before lunch, Eggy?"

The unnecessary question was an added irritant; that smile had already rubbed Eggy the wrong way. It was a white-folks smile, the kind they used to butter you up with just before they asked you for something for nothing. It was, in fact, a something-for-nothing smile, and Eggy swore no colored man had a right to use it on another colored man.

"Wuffo you wanna know?"

"I got a nice little proposition for you," the waiter said. "It's right down your alley and it won't cost you a cent. I'm gonna wait for you in the locker room, tell you all about it." He went away without waiting for a reply.

Eggy watched the waiter's receding back, and his lips curled. This floater wanted to borrow money. Eggy had none—he was always broke, even on payday—but he began to frame a refusal that would make this wise guy think that he did have the money to loan, if only he thought that the prospective borrower was trustworthy.

Now if this young fellow was like that other waiter he came here with, things would be different. (Or so Eggy thought, although he still would have been broke.) But Eggy did have to laugh every time he thought of that other waiter. His name was Blueboy and you just had to like his little black self. Eggy lazed on the counter and recalled Blueboy's first morning on the job with this other waiter—he never did know that one's name and nobody else did either. Which just went to show . . . But anyhow, it was only three, four

2

days ago, and this Blueboy had rushed up to the range with his face all screwed up fit to kill.

"Now hear this!" Blueboy had barked. "I kills me a fry cook every season, but I ain't mean! They makes me do it every time. Now you happen to look like a likely youngster and so I promises not to do you in lessen you diddle with my orders. Now scramble two with bacon and let me go on the double track where the boss ain't mean and the work ain't hard."

It wasn't that it was so funny; it just made you feel nice and good. Like as if he had took a long, long trip just to come here and kid with you. You could tell that Blueboy was a gentleman who'd been around, floater or no.

A cloud intruded on Eggy's thoughts. That young waiter hadn't acted *too* much like he wanted to beg a loan. There hadn't been no gums in that smile. Teeth? Yes, but not enough gums showing that said, "Loan me." Still, some of these waiters had a whole lot of crust.

At ten-thirty Eggy rushed into the colored employees' locker room and headed for the lavatory. He nodded genially at the uniformed back of a waiter standing at the adjacent urinal.

"Mawn, fren," he said. "That was a lovely brefust, wasn't it? Course the roof could pop off and us cooks wouldn't git one cent more, but ah likes to see my waiters make them tips. Sometimes they buys ole Eggy a drink." He adjusted his clothes and moved over to the washbasin. "We got us three thousand teachers here at this national convention, and don't you know that them white teachers is the only ones got money these here hard times? Chillun gotta larn and so them teachers gotta git paid. Depreshun or no. T'aint like colored. They gotta take what the county gives 'em or quit."

Grinning hugely to himself Eggy turned to face his colleague and was chagrined to find that it was the young floater. "Oh. It's you," he said. "You new heah, ain't you?"

The waiter ignored the slur, if it was one. "Yeah," he said slowly. "I'm Dave Greene. Everybody knows who you are, Eggy."

Eggy grinned. "Yeah. Heh. Heh. Guess everybody knows ole Eggy." Then he remembered that he was talking to a beggar, and frowned. "Floatin' waiter, eh?"

"You mean, do I travel?" Dave paused and then appeared to be reflecting aloud. "I follow the money. Money don't follow me, and so I goes where the water and the horses are."

"What's wattah got to do with it?" Eggy demanded.

"Hot Springs, Cold Springs, Lithia Springs, salt water, sulphur

3

water, piss water, makes no difference. If there's water or a race track, you gonna find rich white people there too." Dave Greene said it carelessly, singsong. His air of indifference was more convincing than his words. Eggy was an instant convert.

"Ain't it the trute," he exclaimed. "Now that's what ah allus say: White folks scared of dying and effen dey heah 'bout some mysteruss wattah, den—whoey! Dey done gone to lap up some of it."

And Eggy chattered on. Dave had not realized that the man was so stupid. But listening to Eggy's inanities made Dave restless. "Look here, Eggy," he said suddenly. "I got a scheme that can make us all rich. And I need you bad as hell. So I'm gonna let you in on the ground floor. And it won't cost you one red cent."

Dismay wrote its name on Eggy's face. "Races? Horses? Shucks man, I'm busted. Ah can't bet on nothing."

Now Dave was magnetic, a man with a dream. "This is business," he cried. "Damn some gambling when you got a sure fire business deal going for you."

One could see that Eggy liked that word "business." It was white-folks language. He poked out his lips, trying to look business-like.

"You meet me and Blueboy in Booker's at ten o'clock tonight. All the drinks will be on me," Dave said.

"Wal . . ."

Eggy hated to say yes to this floater who definitely wanted something for nothing, but the only thing Eggy loved more than whiskey was free whiskey. And it would be a pleasure to drink up this dicty boogie's likker and then turn him down cold. "Okay," he muttered, waving his hand in a vague gesture of good-by as he left the lavatory.

Dave grinned with satisfaction and went back into the locker room. He dressed slowly. There was a long afternoon ahead; extra waiters did not work lunch. The teachers ate their noontime meals in the convention-hall area, further downtown.

"Davey-boy, how you doin'?"

With a smile, Dave glanced up from the bench—and in came Blueboy.

Short and round-headed, Blueboy Harris was twice as old as Dave Greene, but most people never noticed, because Blueboy acted younger than Dave. Making himself comfortable on the bench, Blueboy wasted no time. "I just got through beatin' my gums with a coupla ham-fat local waiters and they tells me that I've seen all there is to see of this town already—and I ain't seen nothin' *yet* to write Maw about. They say the Block is the only place for spooks in this burg. And we livin' in the middle of the Block now." Blueboy stopped to marvel at his own information. "Thirty thousand

4

coons in this city and only one lousy block for them to fuss and fight on. You sure this is the town you is looking for?"

As far as Dave was concerned, Blueboy had just said that this town was anybody's oyster and an easy one to open at that. "There's only one section of this city for a man in the sportin' life and that section is called the Ward," Dave said. "The main drag of the Ward is a cutthroat lane of joy called Vessey Street—and, you're right, the wildest stretch of Vessey Street is the part everybody just calls the Block. That's where we landed and that is where we shall rule. Man, I'm telling you, it's a *perfect* setup. We can operate out of the Block and get to everyone worth gettin' to in the whole city."

"Well put, maybe. But one block equals one horse. And about the only thing that happens to folks in this here town is when they dies and they gets their first pair of real shoes."

"Blueboy, stop trying to talk my ear off. Listen. I just got through talking to Eggy Manone. I'm goin' to finish selling him tonight at Booker's."

"Eggy's popular." Blueboy was suddenly thoughtful. "Yes," he said, nodding his head, "leastways, everybody knows who he is. Yeah. He's got to do for now."

"You sound temporary."

"Everybody loves that guy," Blueboy said, "but I bet my bottom dollar that he ain't got a friend to his name. And I'll tell you why. He is stupid. Every damned body is so sure that he is stupider than they are that they just naturally love the cluck for it—but you take my word, nobody wants him for a friend."

Dave thought that Blueboy might be at least halfway right. But he didn't bother to defend his choice of Eggy. Instead he said, "We'll be in a position to do his thinking for him. Makes it kind of nice."

"True enough. That *is* true," Blueboy said vigorously. "But don't you ever forget for one minute that that boy ain't bright. A damn fool is always trouble in the long run and we ain't here for the season, we come for a *reason.*"

"I know. But we got to go with him. We let him go for us in the first race, if you know what I mean."

"So long as you don't forget," said Blueboy.

The two friends smiled at each other, slammed their lockers shut in unison, and headed for the Block.

2

In 1935 the old city was still gently southern and beautiful. It was a town of the cavalier, not the cracker. Because it had long been the regional center of insurance, banking, and food and tobacco processing, the national depression had decreased wages, but unemployment was minimal. The basics of daily life, especially for the Negroes, whose wages had began low to begin with, remained the same through good times and bad.

The city boasted five colleges. Three were white and two were for colored. One of the Negro schools was a respected college and was always referred to as the "University" or the "Campus"; the other was a decrepit normal school, eventually absorbed by the University in 1939.

Two thirds of the city's Negro population lived in the Ward. Originally this sector had been the First Ward in both name and historical fact, but it had been gerrymandered during the 1920s into appendages of four all-white city wards. It now had no political identity, and the name meant simply the colored neighborhood.

The Block was the Ward's focal point, and the busiest place in the Block was Booker's Hotel and Restaurant. Booker's at this time

6

may well have been the only American business property owned and operated by one colored family for more than two generations.

In all probability, Booker's began as a Negro-owned bawdyhouse that catered to white only. Time has dimmed the Ward's memory, but it is a certainty that Booker's never catered to Negroes until after the "shooting."

At the time of the shooting Booker's was tantamount to a private club for the city's white hotbloods. There had been a street-level taproom with four private dining rooms upstairs. Handsome mulatto girls were smuggled upstairs after dark. It was a bitter cold day in 1912 when a young white man, evidently a gentleman, strode into Booker's taproom and fired one shot from his .44. He turned and walked back into the oblivion from which he had come. He left one of Booker's three colored waiters, Arthur Joyce, dead on the floor. It was whispered about that Arthur's wife and his assassin were lovers. It was also rumored that Arthur had been the lover of the white man's wife. The only facts ever uncovered were that a white man had shot a colored waiter in the back of the head.

There was much talk, but little activity on the part of the police, who felt strongly that Arthur had no business getting himself shot by a white man. One month later the police department announced that the case was closed since no dependable witnesses were to be found.

And Booker's was closed.

Two years later it was reopened to the Negro trade and had prospered haphazardly through the years. The four dining rooms upstairs had become hotel rooms and catered to Negro tourists, and although Booker's sold illegal corn whiskey, it had remained the social center for the Ward's best citizens.

Booker's still clung to some of its former glory in a way that was ritualistic and nostalgic. Every Christmas, the city's best white families sent their holiday hams to Booker's to be cooked in wine. Sportsmen still sent their game to be prepared and delivered hot from the oven. These circumstances made it a Negro, Booker, who was the final social arbiter of the city's white society; there was no more damning censure than for Booker's to be "too busy" to cook a white family's holiday ham.

This background of Booker's had always beguiled Dave, and he had fallen in love with the place long before he reached town. It was now 9:30 that night, and he sat in Booker's, enjoying his gentle daydreams, sifting through the ashes of history. Jack Johnson, Howard Drew, Booker T. Washington, Langston Hughes, and James Weldon Johnson had slept here. The whites Embree and Spingarn had eaten here and created local history while passing through town on their way to write important pages of Negro history. Booker's Hotel had seen more great Negroes, including Marcus Garvey and the Reverend Jasper, than any Negro church in America.

Booker's, then, was a concrete heritage to Dave. It was his personal Plymouth Rock. And as he sifted these ashes in his mind his flesh pebbled with pride. For Dave, despite his muted tone, was above all else a race man.

"I ate here once. Maybe ten, twelve years ago," he murmured to Blueboy.

"You gonna tell me that you picked out this town when you was eleven or twelve years old?"

"Hell, no," Dave said absently. "But I never forgot this place and Old Man Booker up there." He used his head to gesture at the proprietor perched on a high stool near the entrance. The man was guarding the cash register behind him and a showcase of sweet potato pies in front of him.

Suddenly Dave leaned forward. His voice was warm and uneven with an emotion that Blueboy would always refuse to share. "This place is one of the few things that the Negro has to be proud of," he said earnestly, his face a blend of pride and regret.

"This dump?" Blueboy exclaimed. He made an exaggerated survey of his surroundings. "I suppose Small's Paradise don't really count," he murmured politely. He sat absolutely still, but his stocky torso seemed to increase in height. "Are you a complete damn fool?" he burst out in a shrill voice. "This is a lousy, black-ass restaurant with four lousy bedrooms upstairs. And you gonna make history outa that?"

"Okay. Okay. Don't get excited now. But you don't know the history."

"And I don't want to know. They got bedbugs upstairs, that's enough."

"But this place is history . . . our history, Blueboy." Dave's voice was a plea. For like only one or two other things in Dave Greene's world, Booker's was an emotion.

"*My* history ain't got nothing to do with bedbugs and whether or not you ate here once when you was a kid. They got a plaque on the wall? You get indigestion?"

Dave grinned sheepishly, but he really was not ashamed at all. "My father once brought me here to a convention. It was an NAACP thing, or something like that." He laughed. "Everybody was talking about 'The New Negro'; I thought they was getting ready to produce a brand-new kind of human. Like a robot or something.

8

And where the hell is a waitress? We supposed to live in this booth the rest of our lives?"

"Wave some money."

A waitress materialized before them and they both gaped in astonishment. It was more than the girl's instant appearance. Black as coal, she was undeniably beautiful. There was no posturing or grimacing to detract from her looks. The girl was not sullen, but there was certainly no friendliness in her lovely features. Her beauty reminded Dave of his childhood when he would take an unblemished horse chestnut from its pod and hold it to catch the sun's rays. The girl was much darker than that, but somehow that was the only sight that Dave could think of that compared to the flawless face. Nor could he recall ever seeing a girl so dark with hair like hers. A glittering cascade of black diamond ripples that flowed to her shoulders.

"Yassuh?" The two syllables dribbled sloppily, profanely from her lips, filling Dave with a white-hot anger. He felt betrayed by her. To Dave, the flat voice, with an accent so thick that it was a caricature of a Negro dialect, desecrated her pretty mouth and perfect teeth. Only a second ago he had vowed to make her his girl friend.

"Bring us a half-pint setup," he snapped, and was glad that the girl did not so much as nod her head before she disappeared.

"Now if that wasn't the prettiest little thing I've ever laid eyes on," Blueboy exclaimed. "Prettier'n a speckled pup running long 'neath a watermelon wagon." He paused in careful deliberation and then came to a decision of moment. "Of course I don't much hold with black gals, but then she ain't really black." He looked defiantly at Dave, begging for contradiction. It came promptly.

"I never want to see nothing blacker," Dave snorted.

Blueboy bristled and grew taller in his seat. "For shame," he bellowed.

The two words filled the dining room and halted all conversation among the guests. Dave shrank visibly under the curious glances of the other diners, but Blueboy was unconcerned.

"That little girl got more *red* in her skin than you got," Blueboy said, "even if she is somewhat darker. And it makes no difference anyhow. When they comes that pretty, blackness don't really count."

Dave dearly wished that the subject now be closed, but Blueboy was of another mind. He took a deep breath, blew through his lips and sallied forth to do battle. "When you ever see a gal that color before and her nose ain't squashed all over her face like some elephant stomped on it?" he demanded loudly. "And when they

9

comes that black, they's usually born with the razor scars already in place on their ugly faces. And she got the tiniest little mouth; it's smaller than most white gals' . . ." He paused to glare at Dave. "And what in hell is you all swoll up about? You looks like she insulted you personally."

That was exactly what she had done, Dave thought, but he dared not say so now. "The way she talks. It's an insult to herself," he muttered. "Nobody's got a right to talk that sloven."

"She ain't said a damn word hardly!"

"But did she have to say it like a black . . . a black . . ."

Blueboy was the only living creature on earth who could remain stark still and yet create the illusion that he was in the throes of an epileptic fit.

"You should be proud for the race. She's neat. She's clean. That little white uniform is spotless, and it highlights her lovely coloring." Blueboy stopped talking to savor his words as if they were a mint in his mouth. "Now there's a happy phrase. Lovely words, those: Highlights her lovely coloring."

"Nerts."

The waitress returned with a tray which held a cream pitcher containing eight ounces of colorless corn whiskey, two empty fruit-juice glasses, a heavy china soup bowl of chipped ice, and a five-cent bottle of sweet ginger ale.

Blueboy became paternally courteous. Dave always called this his "kind daddy approach," and it always worked.

"What's your name, little miss?"

"Ah name Delilah."

Dave winced. It came from her lips as "Ah-nay-yum-dee-lie-uh."

Blueboy radiated true happiness. "Beautiful, beautiful," he exclaimed like some connoisseur sampling fine wine. "And now you must tell us what church you attend." Delilah gazed at him. It was the flat, wide-eyed, and unfeeling stare of the three-year-old who must leave his play to come and listen to the gushings of a stranger.

Blueboy jibed on, and a begrudging smile began to play in the corners of Delilah's lovely mouth. "But you never told us where your home is . . ." Blueboy scolded.

"Ah born right neah heah . . . Jonesville."

Dave bolted up in the booth. "What?" It was not just an exclamation of surprise, but of disbelief. Delilah leveled clear eyes upon him, and he squirmed with embarrassment. All at once his entire body was damp with sweat. He felt those eyes still upon him, evaluating him.

10

"You frum Jonesville, Mistah Greene?" And she did not really seem to care.

Too distracted to wonder how the girl knew his name, he retorted, "Do I look like it?" Under the circumstances it was a boorish sort of reply, and he knew it, but he just wanted her to go away and stop worrying him.

Delilah either ignored the innuendo or failed to grasp it. But she did continue to measure him until, apparently having come to a conclusion, she turned and rapidly walked away. Her walk, Dave saw, was stiffly controlled; there was no movement of her hips. That made him even angrier.

Blueboy saw his duty and said so. He said that Dave was still a child who sat and sulked at the feet of true beauty instead of sitting up and saying something about it. He also wanted to know how Dave had become an expert on the "native heaths of strange little girls." After he took a sip of corn to revive his flagging tongue he continued to flay Dave. ". . . and here we is after traveling the length and breath of this land, you gotta pick a one-horse town to play the fool in . . ."

"I didn't say anything," Dave mumbled in a form of apology, hoping that Blueboy would shut up so that he could enjoy his lovely pique at Delilah in peace.

"You called her a liar."

"She *was* lying."

"How do you know? Was you there? She's sixteen, about, so you was seven when she was born. You gonna tell me that you was a seven-year-old midwife?" Suddenly Blueboy smiled, all graciousness and reason. "But of course you do have an explanation . . . ?"

"I've never been to Jonesville, and neither has she . . . or she'd know better . . ."

Blueboy gasped. "You . . . are . . . crazy."

"Please shut up for a minute and I'll explain," Dave pleaded. "That girl's not from Jonesville . . . she's too dark."

"How is hell can a person be too black to be born?" Blueboy shouted at the top of his lungs.

The crowd laughed, causing Mr. Booker to get up from his seat by the cash register. Arms akimbo, he stared at the two strangers. He had his doubts about waiters who rented his expensive rooms by the week. He never had known what to make of them, but if they thought . . . Well, just one more time, he decided.

A group of boys, evidently from the campus, were packed in a booth directly across the room from Dave and Blueboy. "Easy pal

11

. . . thass real easy," one of them said. He had an infectious drawl that drew more titters from Mr. Booker's guests.

"Shut up, Cokey," another student said, chuckling.

Dave was scared. Old Man Booker might ask them to leave the dining room. How in hell would that look and they were just getting ready to start operating in the Ward? And he had to wait for that damn fool Eggy Manone. Eggy wouldn't have enough sense to ask for them if he didn't see them sitting downstairs here.

Since there was only one way to silence Blueboy, Dave began quietly to outtalk him. "Jonesville is between here and Marceau Beach. Say about twenty miles. So whenever I ran across a waiter who had worked the beach I would naturally ask him about this here town . . ."

Blueboy folded his arms and sat in judgment.

"But none of them knew anything about this town," Dave continued. "Because whenever guys go to work the beach they never bother to come here. They go to Jonesville for their kicks . . ."

"Jonesville's got *two* Blocks, mebbe."

Dave ignored the interruption. "Jonesville's got the most beautiful women in the world."

Blueboy tittered. With courteous prudery he covered his mouth with his hand so as to not actually be laughing in Dave's face.

"Everybody says the same thing, Blueboy. There's no reason for everybody to lie."

"You, of course, took a good look at Delilah?" His tone was kind and helpful.

Dave saw defeat looming ominously behind those sweet words. Experience had taught him that they were merely an introduction to more fireworks. Sure enough, Blueboy's round happy face became an avenging cloud, and his stocky body grew taller.

"Even her tits are pretty, you fool!" Blueboy roared.

Perspiration dotted Dave's brow. Now, the diners were silent, watching. "I know she's pretty," he said. "Any damn fool can see that, but everybody in Jonesville is red . . . yellow. Damn near white. You catch hell trying to find somebody my color there, much less hers. And everybody there is related. Practically everybody there is named either Jones or Dennis."

Majestically silent now, Blueboy seemed only half awake; far too intelligent to contribute to this imbecilic conversation.

"Maybe folks exaggerate some," Dave said, "but the way I heard it was when you went to the colored church there, the usher took a good look at you and if you are my color he puts you in the last pew. If you're red with nappy hair you sits in the very next pew

12

from me. The yeller ones with good hair sits next. And the light-haired ones with blue eyes sits on the front row, right up with God."

"What about my color?" asked Blueboy indignantly.

"You ain't supposed to go."

"I can't believe it. And from my very own people." His voice wept immeasurable tears. "My very own people."

"They ain't no people of yours, Blueboy, and they ain't no relatives of Delilah's either."

"Evenin' gennlemuns."

They both looked up to see Eggy Manone standing before them, a shabby outsider in this respectable place.

"Whatcha say, man? Sit down and have a drink." Dave's geniality increased Eggy's discomfort and sense of guilt. Without his cook's uniform, Eggy was minus all aspects of human dignity.

Dave managed to catch Delilah's eye, and though she did not acknowledge his glance, she turned to a sideboard and picked up a glass. When she came to the booth, she stared at Dave. "You owe sebenty-fi cent."

Dave's temper flared; she might very well have used the same tone to accuse him of theft. "You ask for it?"

Her perfectly formed features were expressionless, and yet, Dave was acutely conscious of her cold hostility.

"Ever' budda no de likkuh setup sebenty-fi cent. How muchum you tink?"

With studied malice, he silently handed her two one-dollar bills.

Delilah looked at the money as if it were poisoned. "Whuffo?" she finally asked.

Dave thought it was a weak attempt to be insulting. "Scram," he said sharply.

As if she had been waiting for his command, she walked away. Out of the corner of his eye he soon saw her talking rapidly to another waitress. It was rather odd; he could not conceive of Delilah speaking fluently to anyone. He noticed that the other waitress was pretty, but in a different way than Delilah, who was beautiful.

He returned his attention to Eggy. The cook was sitting in the position that many Negro males assumed when they felt they were in surroundings that are above their social level. Eggy's shiny bald head was bowed as if he were scanning something written on the top of the table. Shoulders hunched protectively, he sat with his knees pressed together. In cupped hands, like a child would hold an egg, he held his hat in his lap.

Keeping his head bowed, he rolled his eyes up to look at Dave. "You gennlemuns got bizniss?"

Dave plunged to the heart of things. No sense wasting time; opening remarks would only confuse the fool. "You know anything about numbers?" he said.

Again the eyes shifted upward. "Policy? Numbers?"

"Yeah, policy, numbers, boleda, lottery." Dave felt waspish.

"I been to Philly," Eggy said, as if it excused him of something. He looked hungrily at Blueboy, wishing he would start talking. Then everybody could laugh and feel like folks.

"We are going to start a numbers bank here in the Ward," Dave said.

Eggy's eyes shifted wildly. It was evident that he thought Dave insane and wished that Blueboy would take him away. "Heah? Heah?" he muttered.

Blueboy pounced. "And why not here?"

"Dis-dis heah a funny town. Nice-nasty ah calls it."

The expression was already familiar to Dave. It was a localism for hypocrisy. "Nice-nasty or not," he countered, "people are gonna jump at the chance to win money at six hundred-to-one odds."

"Mebbe." Eggy remained in his duncelike position, but now his gaze was fixed on the ceiling.

"Damn," Blueboy murmured.

Still looking at the ceiling, Eggy said, "We got preachers."

"He got preachers," Blueboy echoed.

"Now you take dem preachers . . ." said Eggy.

"What in hell you keep talking about preachers for?" Blueboy shouted. "We don't need no preachers!"

That was enough. Dave rose abruptly. "Let's go upstairs," he suggested.

A curvy waitress came over to them, the girl Dave had noticed Delilah talking to. He sat down again, and beautiful white teeth smiled happily at all three of them in turn. Dave was convinced that the girl was happy.

"Hello, fellas. I guess you don't know me, but my name's Althea Goins, but mostly everybody calls me Pigmeat, or just plain Pig . . . I don't mind."

"And why should you?" Blueboy gushed. "Pigmeat is sweet—tender—juicy. Oh, I loves pork, I do."

Pigmeat smiled at Blueboy and then put a friendly hand on Dave's shoulder. Her sparkling eyes grew very sad, and Dave was sure that she was really sad.

"It's about Lila . . . you know . . . Delilah. Ain't she pretty?"

14

A fact she seemed to be observing for the first time. Dave smiled his bewilderment; all in all, the girl's bubbling speech had a pleasantly intoxicating effect. "Well, anyhow, poor lil Lila doesn't know what to do." She paused expectantly, awaiting an answer. "Now Lila and me are from the same home town, Jonesville. You know, cousins. Only Lila was just born there, she never really lived there at all, but she *is* pretty, ain't she? And she's so innocent." Her voice dropped to a stage whisper, and she leaned conspiratorily over the table. "She needs a man; but she won't. But anyways, she doesn't know what to do." She looked at Dave and waited.

Dave sweated.

Evidently she felt sorry for Dave, who could not speak much English, and so she said, "I mean about the two dollars . . . You meant for her to keep the change for a tip because she's so pretty, didn't you?"

"No," Dave blurted. He hadn't given it to her because she was pretty, but he suddenly saw his mistake. "Yes . . . she knows," he added petulantly.

"You tell that little girl that she ain't pretty just for change," Blueboy cried. "Pretty as she is, I'm gonna give her every penny I makes for the rest of my life. Now I know how to treat pretty gals . . . ugly ones too for that matter."

"I don't think Lila believes in tipping much," Pigmeat confided. "Now you take these schoolboys that always come in here. Lots of times Lila tells 'em to take their money back 'cause she don't want them to hafta walk back to the campus late at night. Ain't that cute?"

"Ain't no cuter than you, Little Miss Pigfoot," Blueboy replied, beaming.

Pigmeat dimpled. Suddenly she pointed an accusing finger. "You're Blueboy," she exclaimed. Dave was positive that she could not have sounded any happier if she had suddenly been presented with a million dollars. And Blueboy was just as elated . . . you could see him puffing up.

"Guilty, mam, guilty. In fact you makes me feel guilty just for looking at you. Reckless eyeballing, they calls it. And you're guilty as all get-out yourself. In fragrant delicious, as we say in Latin. How come you keeps all that highbrown yaller all to yourself? Why don't you pass out some of it to all these ugly gals I see running around this Ward here? Yassuh! They sure named you righ, Miss Pigmeat."

"You mean that I'm too fat?"

"Gal, I should whup your pretty haid. Destruction of righteous

15

beauty . . . that's what you done. Every delicious ounce of you is in exactly the prettiest place, and I loves it. Why some of them curves is bold enough to wink at me and if they don't stop I'm gonna do something terrible nice to them one of these days."

Dave was slightly bored. Blueboy and Pigmeat were two of a kind. They both cast words into the air for no other reason than to make cheerful sounds, and both of them talked so fast that they couldn't possibly hear all that they were saying. But he was proud of Blueboy. The little guy was a black-faced Peter Pan. In five minutes Blueboy had risen from a rank outsider to happy host. Dave wondered why he had bothered to worry about being asked out of Mr. Booker's dining room. Everybody was now Blueboy's guest, hanging onto every word as his voice filled the place.

The guy had no secret, anybody could do it. It was a matter of question and praise . . . or was it praise and question? In no time at all Pigmeat was giving him a complete synopsis of her life, loves, and early childhood.

After learning all there was to know about the pretty girl, Blueboy evidently decided to repay her by giving an exhibition of outright clowning. He was standing now and his voice continued to fill the dining room in a tirade. Blueboy accused Pigmeat of unfeeling cruelty. She had no right coming to their booth and getting them upset like this, he said.

Pigmeat stopped laughing long enough to gasp. "If you don't stop embarrassing me, I'm gonna leave."

"You do, and I'll start whooping and hollering all over this place."

"You are already," Dave said mildly.

Doctor Blueboy immediately diagnosed Dave's problem. "The trouble with you is you don't appreciate the good things in life. Especially if pretty wimmin got 'em."

"Blueboy," Pigmeat said, "how come I've never seen you before? Looks like if you are staying with us you should eat. And it makes me feel real bad cause we got the bestest home cooking and politest girls and everything . . ." The really bizarre part of that statement was that she meant every syllable of it.

"We eats on the job. We're waiters," Blueboy said.

"Ooooh. We're all in the same profession," Pigmeat gurgled.

Dave looked cross-eyed at Blueboy and Pigmeat, but the pair were too far engrossed in discussing the pros and cons of their profession to pay him any heed.

Then Blueboy told a tale about a rapscallion baby stork that

16

scared the hell out of two little waitresses. Pigmeat raised her hands in mock surrender as she slowly took her provocative hips away.

Dave watched the swaying walk in open admiration. "That's the friendliest pretty girl I've ever seen," he said. "And she really is happy."

"She's a Vessey Street chick," Eggy said.

"That girl is the most flagrantly sexy wench that ever walked away from the farm," Blueboy said slowly. "She's got a kind of lewdness about her."

Dave was shocked, "You're drunk. She ain't lewd."

"It's funny," Blueboy said dreamily, "but if you took that gal and togged her down from the skin out, put the finest silk lingerie on that fine chassis, and the sheerest stockings on them legs, and I. Miller shoes, and then you puts her in fine Saks cloth, and over her shoulders you drape a lovely mink scarf down to her knees . . ." He looked up sharply. "Do you know what every man who saw her would be thinking?"

"He wouldn't have to think," Dave said.

"Every single man is gonna have the same thought: Underneath all them clothes she's nekkid as hell."

Dave laughed in agreement. "And some really weak-minded guy would actually grab a sheet to cover her," Blueboy declared.

At Dave's insistence, they left the booth to go upstairs. "What's a Vessey Street chick?" Dave asked Eggy.

"Nuthin'. Only there's some gals won't work no place except in the Ward here. And they won't go with anybody but these slicked up guys what won't work and hangs out in de Block alla time," Eggy said. "Now a hardworkin' man like me couldn't make 'em even look at me if ah wanted 'em to."

"They got them in every town," Blueboy said quietly.

As they left the dining room Dave almost collided with Delilah. After offering an awkward apology he asked her to send a pint of whiskey to his room.

Delilah's gaze was flat, implacably reserved, but no longer hostile. "Ah suxteen. Mist' Booky don't 'low me upstah wait."

Dave was pricked by an angry frustration. Anybody would think he was trying to lure this black clown to his room. When he reminded himself that it was his error (he should have given the order to Mr. Booker) he was more upset. With a great show of patience he glared at her. "I said to *send* it, not bring it." He turned, but added over his shoulder: "And ice water."

"Waal . . ."

Dave pondered that "Waal." Was she accepting his order or

17

admitting that he had not invited her to his room? Muttering, he vaulted up the stairs after Blueboy and Eggy.

The plainly furnished room inspired Eggy with awe. "Now dis heah's somepin," he exclaimed. "Only doctors and lawyers kin afford dis heah. Tourist like, overnight. Can't nobody 'ford dis reglar."

Blueboy had flopped across the bed while Dave took a perch atop a wooden kitchen table that was intended for a writing desk. Something told him to let Eggy stand if he didn't have enough gumption to take a seat.

"Now hear this, you grease burner," Blueboy said. "We traveling waiters are cosmopolites, and the Ward's best is none too good for us. Seems like you would be cognizant of that by now."

Eggy grinned in bewildered appreciation. Blueboy's fine talk went right nice with this fine room. The only thing that really disturbed Eggy now was what in the wide world these men needed with the likes of him. His wonder grew until he was apprehensive. He felt mighty glad when he recalled that they had not locked the door.

Dave extracted a huge roll of money from his pocket. Eggy was horrified as he watched the young man peel off a ten and a twenty. Then, in apparent disgust, he leafed through the remainder of the roll. He turned to Blueboy. "Gimme a five-spot," he said, and Eggy could plainly see that Dave was much put out because he had nothing as small as a five dollar bill in that roll. And when Blueboy was more careless than Dave, extracting a roll of money that was just as fat as Dave's, Eggy embraced the awful truth. There could be no doubt that these men were bank robbers, or worse, and that they planned to use Eggy as a fall guy. Eggy had no intention of letting them do it. He was going to tell them that just as soon as he got his mouth shut so that he could talk.

At last Blueboy found a lowly five and tossed it to Dave. The money fell short and Dave had to pick it up off the floor. Then he handed all three bills to Eggy.

"Put it in your pocket," he said.

Eggy's senses swirled way out into numbness. Temporarily a deaf mute, he tried to shake his head, but he didn't think it was shaking, because Dave was continuing to press the money into his hand just as if he didn't know that Eggy didn't want no money at all.

Eggy gawked at the door, a door no longer friendly, because somebody like the police was knocking at it. It seemed like his whole body had turned to glue, and Eggy couldn't move to hide nowhere.

18

"Come in," Blueboy yelled. "Entrez-vous."

"Evening gentlemen," Mr. Booker said. He placed a tray containing three heavy glasses and a pitcher of water on the dresser. From his pocket he pulled a pint of corn whiskey, putting it beside the water. "That will be two dollars, gentlemen," he said, and then in righteous explanation added, "that's including room service."

Blueboy bounced up from the bed. "Mine dearest host," he cried, "it does this old heart good to meet a boniface who demands good service for his guests. My friend Emily says never to tip your wealthy host so whatever change there is you give it to the sable child of beauty who told you we were dying of thirst."

Already Dave had begun to grin because he knew that his friend was about to do his half-pirouette. It was a gesture that made Blueboy look as if he was going into a buck and wing dance, only he would turn with his knees slightly bent and thrust his hand deep into his pocket, miming an illusion that he was reaching into a bottomless cornucopia. The end of the routine would have Blueboy airily waving a bill under Mr. Booker's nose.

Old Man Booker responded with arthritic vim and vigor. He stepped over to the window and adjusted it. He took Eggy's hat away from him and hung it on a nail in the door. After that he uncorked the whiskey bottle with a flourish, accepted the bill, and then gracefully bowed out the door.

It was all too scary for Eggy. This was like a nightmare, with all these white folks suddenly turning black like Eggy, and the worstest part about it was that they didn't know they wasn't white no more. They kept on talking all proper and handling money just like they was still white, and it just plain scared Eggy. He wished that he had the courage to tell them . . . but maybe it was better not to, he decided.

Dave pierced Eggy with a look. "We need you," he said sharply. "People gonna trust you. They know where you work, where to find you." Eggy shuddered. "And so they won't be afraid to trust you with their nickels and dimes. Blueboy and me are strangers, they wouldn't trust us, but everybody knows where to find you every morning at six o'clock. Right?"

Eggy nodded glumly. "Thass right. Seben days a week."

"So naturally you can introduce the fellows at the hotel to numbers playing better than we can. And word of mouth advertising will have us doing a big business in no time . . ."

"Every waiter in the world is a town crier . . . a human black dispatch," Blueboy added.

"Writing numbers is about the easiest thing a man can find to

19

do," Dave said. "You just let somebody pick out any number from zero to nine hundred and ninety-nine and place any amount of money they wants on it to come out that day. Everyday but Sunday a new number comes out. Ya understand? Take, for instance, a guy likes two hundred and forty-seven and plays it with you. Now if two hunded and forty-seven comes out, he gets paid at six hundred to one odds."

"That's six hundred pennies to every penny he plays on it," Blueboy added.

Dave nodded his head and continued. "That's right. He wins thirty bucks for a nickel. Three hundred bucks on a fifty-cent hit. Not bad, eh? You won't have to beg people to try to win money like that. Once people hears that you are writing numbers they will come to you."

"And out of every hit you takes a ten per cent commission," Blueboy said. "A guy hits for a dollar, that's six hundred bucks, you gets sixty right off the top. He hits for a nickel, that's thirty dollars, you get three bucks right there. You only pays the winner twenty-seven bucks. You get yours before he gets his. You can't miss."

"And the guy who hits will probably lay a couple of bucks on you. Even for a ten-cent hit," Dave pointed out. "And we pay you fifteen per cent commission on all you write a day. Everyday you get fifteen cents out of every dollar's worth of numbers you write. That means you got money in your pocket every day . . ."

"And you gets that right off the top too," Blueboy said. "You write twenty bucks' worth of numbers tomorrow, you'll take three bucks out before you even hands the money over to us. And you should write more than twenty bucks' worth in the locker room alone. You got damn near fifty waiters and cooks, counting the extra banquet waiters."

Eggy was determined not to succumb to these heavenly blandishments. "Wheah de numbah coming from?" he whined. Again hope flared. "Ah would be paying off eveybuddy . . ."

"Oh, Jesus," Blueboy prayed softly.

"Eveybuddy gonna come say dey play de winnin' numbah. Dey gonna say ah forget, and you knows ah knows mah counting. Ah's de bestest egg man . . ."

"And eggs," Blueboy snarled.

Seeking to forestall more of Blueboy's sarcasm, Dave went to the dresser and pulled open a drawer. The drawer was jam packed with small pads. Eggy did not have the slightest idea of what they were for, but there were too many of them there to suit him.

20

Dave took one of the pads, threw it on top of the dresser, and picked up a newspaper. He came to Eggy's side and pointed to the front page.

"See this box of figgers here?" He was pointing to the upper right hand corner of the paper. "Don't ask me what they're for, but these totals are in this space everyday. Got something to do with the Mint or the Treasury, makes no difference. We are gonna use these figgers for a while until we get a better system. Now here's today's number."

He took a pencil and drew an elliptical circle around the last three figures in the box.

"Today's number is five-eight-seven," Dave said. "If anybody played five hundred and eighty-seven with you, all you'd have to do is come to us and we give you the money to pay the hit. You want anything simpler than that?"

"Whooey," Eggy said reverently. "Ah seed dem numbahs in de paper all de time, but ah nevah thought dey were dere for just you all . . ."

Blueboy raised his eyes in piteous admonition. "This ain't right!" he rebuked the heavens. "Ain't right at all!"

Dave reached for the pad off the dresser. "Now here's your numbers pad," he said, leafing through it. The pad was not much larger than a package of cigarettes, and much thinner. "See how you got three different colored sheets here? You got a pink, a white tissue one, and a yellow one. You gotta be careful and get your carbon paper right."

"That pad writes in triplicate," Blueboy informed the room at large.

"That's right. Now this pink slip you give to the guy who plays the numbers. The yellow one you tears out and saves for me, and the tissue one you leave right in the book. That is your receipt."

Eggy became quite animated. "Now dat dere is biznuss." He employed the stern tones he thought appropriate to the subject. "Dey got a ruh-ceet, ah got and you got."

"All God's chillun got ceets," Blueboy grumbled.

Eggy had a sudden thought: "Ah still doan trust dem preachers . . ."

"You ain't goina ask no goddam preachers to play numbers," Blueboy yelled.

For once Eggy stood his ground. "Y'all doan understan de kinda preachers we got . . ."

"Preachers he got," Blueboy whispered.

21

"Dey hates all sin and gamblin'."

"Dey hates sin and gamblin'," Blueboy croaked.

"Dey is greedy. Just like sinnin' cost dem money. If you go to a dance dey figger dat you is using money dat rightly belongs in de collection plate . . ."

Blueboy stood up. "They still got dances in this town, don't they?" He turned his back and walked away. "If you got any sense at all, will you please get off that gospel train of yours?"

Dave spoke quickly. "Don't bother to ask any church folks to play," he said, knowing full well that once somebody in the Ward hit for a few hundred dollars the church members would beat a path to their door.

The immutable determination of stupidity forced Eggy to hold out. ". . . but dem greedy preachers gonna kick," he insisted.

Blueboy answered him like a child. "I've sailed the Seven Seas plus the Great Lakes. I've been in every corner of God's green earth. I've walked from Chicago to San Francisco, carrying a tray . . ."

"Ah doan believe it," Eggy said flatly.

"I was in a dining car, but I was still walking and carrying that damn tray," Blueboy shouted. "I been everywhere and done everything and one thing I know is true: A greedy man is a natural-born sucker. The first thing a professional con-man does when he hits town is to go looking for a greedy-ass preacher."

Eggy would not be moved. "All our preachers is colletch folks."

"Reading, writing, and 'rithmetic!" Blueboy screamed. "That's just three more ways you can make a sucker out of a man. You can read it for him, you can write it for him, and you can add it for him. An educated sucker is the best kind; he's open to all attacks. But a damn fool like you . . . hell. I got only one chance and that is to shove it inta you as hard as I can. But if I shove hard enough you'll take it."

Dave poured three drinks, like oil on troubled water. "Look, Eggy," he said easily, "we've talked enough for the first night. Now tomorrow night you meet us at the same time and we'll practice writing numbers. Okay?"

"Sho' thing," Eggy replied with some enthusiasm. Writing numbers, he figured, was a lot easier than trying to outtalk Blueboy. Besides, he had thirty-five dollars.

After Eggy had left the room, Blueboy announced he was going to his room to go to bed. Dave said that he thought he could use a sandwich and a bottle of beer.

"And I'm gonna get that naked waitress to wait on me," he told Blueboy.

3

The next morning Dave awoke with a start and glared at the shafts of sunlight that striped his bed. Bright sunlight meant that he was late for work, and in the depression no new waiter showed up for work at the Cavalier or any other hotel after sunrise. If he did, he was fired.

He and Blueboy had purposely showed up late for work all over the United States so that they would be fired and paid off immediately. They did it rather than quit and have to wait until payday for their pay, but neither one of them had ever been fired unless they wanted to be fired. In this case, Dave was mad as hell.

Then he glimpsed the fine hand of Blueboy. The little runt had purposely allowed him to oversleep. So, in his way, Blueboy had coolly tossed Dave into the sea of chance.

Dave grinned. This, then, was his moment to get started. He was filled with exultation. The one dark cloud in the future had turned bright. That cloud had been Blueboy's steadfast refusal to be his partner in the operation of his numbers bank. But Dave now knew that Blueboy was not only behind him one hundred

23

per cent, he had precipitated this moment when Dave no longer had an excuse *not* to start the bank immediately.

He lay back, closed his eyes, and enjoyed the luxury of his thoughts. He tried to fathom Blueboy's refusal to be his partner. After a spell he gave it up with a sigh and a chuckle. Why worry about the caprices of Blueboy? The guy himself was a caprice.

So Dave Greene, waiter, was dead.

Long live Dave Greene, Numbers King!

For only a moment he was abashed at the flamboyant way his mind was functioning but he knew that was exactly what he had come to the Ward to be. The One and Only Numbers Banker in the Ward.

Awash in a sea of optimism, he had one regret. He should have told Eggy that white gangsters were backing the numbers bank. That must be the first thing he drilled into Eggy's head tonight. All Negroes denied it, but the fact remained: Boogies don't like for Boogies to handle their cash. And the first law of commerce was to know your customer and treat him likewise.

Lie and Deny, the Negro National Anthem.

In the noise of thoughts that buzzed in his head, one had a special urgency. He had to look at the Ward in daylight. To look around, to meet some people, and to plan.

While dressing he made a vow to never shave himself again. A man in his position should have a live-wire barbershop as his unofficial headquarters. As soon as he reached the street in search of a barber, his thought turned to the wonderfully compatible Pigmeat.

"If two young people like each other," Pigmeat had firmly stated, "they should enjoy accommodating each other . . ."

Where the hell was this battle between the sexes?

She *had been* naked underneath her clothes. Creamy and warm and softly naked. With body and brains.

Pigmeat could be standing at your table, talking a mile a minute, and all at once dart off to wait on a guest, jiving and kidding with him all the time, but when she returned to you, she would pick up the conversation exactly where she had left it. She talked dizzy, but she had brains with the best of them.

And she was nobody's gossip. Pigmeat talked about everything and everybody, but never with malice. That little girl could find something nice to say about the landlord of hell.

But how could any girl like Pigmeat stay single?

Why look gift whores in the mouth? Cut it. Pigmeat was no whore . . . she just happens to know the score. Shakespeare! And

24

she was all that a guy just starting up a racket needed. No lying. No denying.

There are no strings, no charges for accommodation. Wives are for titty pimps and losers. Dave Greene's lucky break.

No love. No arguments. No regrets.

No lying, no denying, just accommodation.

Dave entered the first shop he passed and immediately began to regret it. It was as morbidly spotless as a clinic, unfriendly, and empty. The lone barber on duty looked as cold and reserved as the steel-rimmed glasses he wore. This was definitely not the type of shop that catered to potential numbers players. No barbershop had a right to be as sterile as this one, Dave thought. He was angry at his own reluctance to hurt the barber's feelings by walking out. Closing his eyes, he fervently prayed that this barber was as silent as his shop.

He was not. The barber's name was Tom Ellis. He had been in town nine years. Dave ignored the open invitation to say who *he* was, and where from, and how long. He matched no conversation for conversation, and only half listened while barber Ellis started in on what Dave could only think of as a prepared text. Like barbers the world over, Tom Ellis had just a few staples of conversation, and today he was ready with one of his favorites. He was disgusted with the town, the Ward, and the Block.

"We got no sporting life here," Tom told him. Now, Atlanta, Richmond, Memphis, all them kinda towns, had a sporting element in them that went to make barbering a good profession. Tom was willing to concede that he made a living, but he would never retire to a rich old age if he stayed on in this town. He stropped his razor.

Tom said that he had heard that two international gamblers had been staying at Booker's, but to show you how slow this town was, Tom said, they did not even try to find any sport on the Block. And Tom wondered where they got their barbering services from, because nobody of an international description had been in his place of business because Tom would have spotted them a mile away. He could tell them kind of operators a mile away. He had once owned a shop in Norfolk, but he had to give it up to come and live here with his wife's folks, who were ailing, but there was a big difference all right. Everybody knew that, Tom said. Now in Norfolk, he had four numbers men; pickup men, they calls them there. They was like foremen. Well, anyhow, these here four pickups came in every morning before they starts to hustle, and gets a shave and a shine. Now you take this here

25

Block here, Tom said. Why a man couldn't get a *shine* in a barber-shop weekdays. Tom said it didn't pay to keep a shine boy any day except Saturdays. And that only went to prove that this town had no sporting life.

Course, now Colonel Eldrege runs a pretty fair crap game over across the street in the back room of the Lil Savoy, but even so, a guy gotta be mighty lucky to take a hundred dollars out of that game on a Friday night. And any town where a man can't win a hundred dollars in the biggest crap game running ain't got no sporting life, Tom said.

Tom pointed out that he could look at Dave and tell that he was worldly and all and that he wanted a shine with his shave, but on this chintzy street, Dave would have to go to a shoeshine stand near the corner.

Dave wondered how much poison was in this cup that was so much to his liking, and he was thankful that lather covered his face. But Tom Ellis was so fascinating an oracle that Dave protracted his visit by ordering a Boncilla massage.

On an impulse, Dave asked Tom if he was positive that there was no numbers playing in the Ward because he thought he had overheard some waiters discussing numbers in Booker's last night.

Tom thought that Dave might have misunderstood the waiters' conversation, but he did not wish to contradict a man who might become a steady customer. However, Tom did say that his brother-in-law was a banquet captain at the Hotel Lee, and if there was any numbers playing going on, his brother-in-law would be the first to know of it because that brother-in-law was a gambling fiend just like all the rest of the waiters in this town.

Dave considered his dollar tip well invested. Still mesmerized by the intimations of his oracle, he proceeded through the Ward.

4

He wanted to share the life of his would-be subjects, and so King David took to the side streets and alleys. He soon viewed the Ward with at least three minds.

He gazed in horror at the once beautiful yellowstone mansions that here and there dotted the Ward, and pondered the sanity of a man who would build a fine town house in the midst of such squalor. This mind informed him that wealthy black fools had feared that no one would be able to see and envy their homes if they were built away from the beaten path. He refused to face the fact that the fine houses had been built by whites long before the Ward had become a Negro neighborhood. With one mind he preferred to be amazed at the nigger-rich conceit of the man who would brazenly erect a home in such surroundings.

Another mind believed that these homes represented the hopes and ideals of his forefathers. And Dave convinced himself that Negro pioneers had erected these homes many years before to light the way for lesser men, hoping that others would take heart and build equally well. Who, he wondered, were the builders of these houses, and their children, and their children's children? What had they been like? How could recently emancipated slaves have afforded such homes, now so subdivided and indifferently prostituted into rooming houses, lodge halls, and mortuary establishments?

His thought veering in another direction, he began to romanticize, and conjectured that these homes had been built by wealthy white men for their mulatto mistresses. And this too, he wanted to know: Where are they now? Where are the love-babies of these clandestine affairs? They would be grandparents, he realized with a pang. But where had they gone, these children who had had one taste of the silver spoon?

Unannounced, a sense of ownership came over Dave. Every home in the Ward, large and small, rich or poor, housed future numbers players. And they all would belong to him. All his.

And he would be King.

The benevolence of the liege lord rather than fellowship prompted Dave to approach three men standing near a corner. At times, the taciturn Dave could be charming. After all, Blueboy was his mentor.

"Good morning, gentlemen." Dave's smile was shy, friendseeking. "Seems like you are gentlemen who've been around and won't take offense if a stranger asks where he might find a drink this time of day . . ."

The three were silent, watchful, but not hostile. Dave thought he imagined that he saw quiet admiration in the glances of the two who were facing him. The third young man had stood with his back to Dave, but when he turned, Dave broke into a huge grin and said impulsively, "Who the hell are *you?*"

The man bore an unholy resemblance to Blueboy. It was far more eerie than a case of look alikes; this little guy was Blueboy when Blueboy was twenty-four years of age.

The young image grinned slyly. "Blip-Blip, but you can call me Blip for short, if you wants," he said. "The kid here is Flick, or Flick the Kid for short, or even Kid Flick. Nobody knows for sure." He turned to introduce the third man. "But this here is jest plain Randy Jones." Blip-Blip paused for effect in the approved Blueboy manner, and then said, offhandedly, "This here's Dave Greene, Pigmeat Goins' latest victim."

This guy was born to be his friend. Dave had not the slightest doubt of that, but it was a minute before he could get his tongue untied. "How come you know so much? We never saw each other before in life."

Blip-Blip ignored him and addressed his companions. "Pig went and rolled them boudoir eyes at this stiff, and he jest naturally

28

laid down and fainted. Then she picked him up, slung him over her shoulder, and toted him up to the Lil Savoy last night."

"You call that answering my question?" The four men had begun to walk slowly up the street. "Is Pig so glamorous that you guys keep tabs on every move she makes?"

"In a way, kinda. But that don't go for you," said Blip, who was leading the way. "If you think that two strangers is gonna start living in Booker's by the week and the whole Block ain't watching to see when they spit you got a whole lot more thinks coming . . ."

He turned in at a house with a newly painted wrought-iron fence, a neat patch of lawn, and a worn hammock on the porch. All in all, everything about the house seemed to cry aloud its fervent accord with Mr. Volstead's proposition.

Blip-Blip opened the front door and bellowed, "Who dar, I say?"

A rich contralto voice drifted back from the rear of the house. "That you, Blip? You got company? Nemmine, I can tell. You all go in and set in the front room. I be there directly."

Dave instinctively disliked this house; he had always disliked parlors anyway. From early childhood, parlors and funerals had been synonymous. And this parlor Blip led them into was the essence of all parlors. Mirthless and stuffy, it was dedicated to the dead, and openly defied any living thing to be comfortable. It had been created with the sole purpose of laying out the various members of the family whenever their appointed time came.

It was, above all else, a negroid parlor with its half-dozen faded brown photographs of kinky-headed, mustachioed males in frock coats and wing collars. These men were all dead, Dave assumed, for they came from a period when all colored men invariably posed either of two ways for commercial photographers. One hand rested on a massive Bible, or on the back of a barbaric throne of an armchair. Dave wondered if any Negro man of that day had ever been caught, dead or alive, in any other pose. And why, he wondered, were colored people constantly accused of being imaginative?

Bizarre imaginations? Only when they were telling lies, he reflected. Otherwise, his people tended to be as cruelly conservative as pre-adolescents. His mind wandered. Where did all the starving Negroes get the wherewithal to purchase pump organs? The damn things were always in these parlors with sheet music opened at the ready, but rarely with anyone in the house who could play them. He had never heard one played except by a stranger hired for the occasion. He tried to estimate how many kids could have been college-trained by all the senseless money that was paid out for one million pump organs that no one ever played.

The room had stolen Dave's lightheartedness. He felt trapped in this place that was both stuffed and stuffy. An upholstered "suit" of furniture challenged all comers. China, glass, and tarnished metal dust-catching gee-gaws were scattered over every level surface, including the floor. Dave cordially hated it. Parlors were for sad times; kitchens were for fun. He observed that his companions were of the same mind. They stood uncomfortably and talked in funeral whispers. All that was needed was the corpse.

"Don't get up. Jes keep setting." A giantess stood in the doorway. This room belonged to a shriveled little widow, and Dave had been totally unprepared to see this female warrior staring down at him. Her pleasant voice was at odds with her fierce eyes, which were cruel as a hawk's.

Those eyes caused Dave to reappraise her entrance speech. It had not been a meaningless courtesy, but a sharp command to sit down and enjoy her parlor. He knew he was correct when his three companions guiltily took awkward perches on the edge of the uncomfortable-looking furniture.

Her eyes met Dave's. "You are a stranger."

Blip jumped to his feet. "This here's Mist Greene. He's staying at Booker's for a visit." Then he turned to Dave and winked. "This here's Ophelia, and she run *the* most high-class pad in the Ward."

The fierce, dark eyes acknowledged Dave's affluence. Dave's hunch was confirmed. Stopping at Booker's had prestige value. He must not move until he was able to rent a proper house and he vowed that it must be within a stone's throw of the Block.

"How do, Mr. Greene. Proud to make your acquaintance," Ophelia said dutifully. "Welcome and be comfortable, and don't you be listening to Blip-Blip, cause this ain't no pad. It's just what you see. This here's my home, and I keeps it respectable all the time." She paused to stare at Blip who was wiggling on the davenport with delight.

Randy had been nodding his head in reverent agreement. ". . . And that's the honest truth," he said in amen. "Nothing but professional men like doctors and postmen and such. Ophelia don't run no pad. She just serve only her friends, sociable like. We all got a few quarters," he said, looking at Dave.

"But I asked you to be my guest," Dave replied.

"We ain't no hustlers," Randy said.

Blip chuckled, pop-eyes dancing mischievously. "Ole Randy's

scared you'll think we is po' boys jest because we don't live in Booker's, too."

"No such thing. I just said . . ."

After telling Ophelia to bring them a pint, and to put it on his bill, Blip returned to Dave. "That settles who's gonna pay for the poison. I owe you a drink anyhow. My turn; you bought first."

"Cut it out," Dave said. "Anytime I buy a drink for a gate that is the spitting image of my best friend, I'd know it."

"You set up the house in the Lil Savoy last night, didn't you?" Blip asked.

"So that's where you get that jive?" Dave exclaimed triumphantly. "But you only heard; you weren't there. If you was, like I say: I wouldn't forget it."

Blip smiled jovially. "I was there, Sonny-boy. I was right there. I come in from the back room where the game is, and the barkeep pours me a drink on you; and I raises my glass to you and Pig, and you raises your'n back at me. Of course I had me on an eyeshade, and mebbe you and Pigmeat was so took up with each other you didn't bother to give me a good look. But, anyhow, it's my turn to buy."

"I remember the guy in the visor, but damn if I thought he looked like you do now. Even with the shade I should've noticed. By rights I should've jumped up and come over and asked you what the hell you was doing with that visor on, thinking you was Blueboy . . ."

"Well, that was me all right."

"You like craps, eh?"

"Nope, never shoots," Blip said, and Dave was sure that he was as crazy as Blueboy. "I'm the stickman for the Colonel though," Blip added, a little too carelessly.

Dave carefully lit a cigarette. Who would make a better numbers writer than the man who operated a professional dice table?

"So you're the Colonel's stickman?"

"Going on two years now. It's the best-run game in town. We get's lotsa action Friday, Saturday nights."

"I never dreamed one of you guys was in the sporting life when I stopped to talk to you," Dave said respectfully.

"Alla us are in the life, so to speak," Blip said. Dave found himself holding his breath while Blip continued. "Flick here, just opened a newsstand-smokeshop, and Randy here is the night barkeep at the Elk's rest. Alla us are pretty well known on the Block."

"Goddam," Dave muttered, thankful that he was sitting. No horse race, no woman had ever made his knees quiver as they were doing now, and those were the two most exciting things he had ever known.

Randy was nodding his head, grinning proudly. "You s'pose to be a member to get in, but any time after eight, you come by and tell the guy on the door that you are my personal guest, and you won't have no trouble at all getting in."

"Me and Blueboy will be there at eight sharp tonight," Dave promised. Then he began to fret over this manna from heaven. It was too much too fast and he forced himself to search for flaws in what he felt was too impeccable a coincidence. Although he derided superstition in others, he was not without superstitions of his own, and one was that too much good luck was merely the post-ponement of bad luck.

Blip, Dave almost knew, would hardly be a problem when it came to enlisting him as a writer; he was already engaged in illegal gambling. But Flick and Randy were something else again. Local Negroes probably did not look down on their means of livelihood. They were probably highly respected men in the community and wished to preserve that status, but then, Blip had said that they were all a part of the Ward's sporting life. He wondered if Blip really knew what sporting life meant.

As he inspected Randy, Dave saw that here was one of the most unremarkable men he had ever seen. In truth, he was nothing. He was not handsome or ugly, well-dressed or poorly dressed. Neither was Randy short nor tall, stout nor slim; he could not even boast of a definite complexion; it would most likely be described as medium muddy brown. Randy was about as invisible as any man operating outside the law could ever hope to be. A perfect man to pick up numbers, Dave reflected.

Flick was the very opposite of Randy. He was far more than just noticeable. He was a striking-looking lad in his late teens. But since he was a familiar of Blip and Randy, Dave decided he had to be a little older than that. Tall and well built, Flick had large, innocent eyes; his skin was the creamy beige coloring often seen in Latins. He had dark brown wavy hair like a white person's, and his right hand and arm were afflicted, apparently from birth. He either habitually held his right arm to his chest or it was rigidly crooked that way, so that his lifeless hand dangled down across his abdomen. Here, too, was a perfect numbers operator, because, although Flick was remarkable-looking he was undeniably innocent-looking. Virginal. He was not a character the police would stop and search without good reason. He even had the ideal front for writing numbers . . . a newsstand.

32

In the midst of this plenty Dave was haunted by a persistent doubt. By happenstance he had met the three most promising aides a beginning numbers banker could hope to employ. And yet, he found himself believing that they were beyond his reach. He doubted that these men would give up the good money and respectability they now enjoyed to enter a racket that was just getting on its feet.

He countered this with anger at his own weakness and a blind determination to make the jobs in his operation the best jobs a Negro could get in the city. No small-time stuff for him. He made a vow that the whole Ward would come to admire his pickup men.

"Is Pigmeat the prettiest girl in the ward?" he asked naïvely.

"Purtiest on the Block and the friendliest," Blip assured him.

"And the smartest," Randy added. "She got herself a penny or two saved away."

"But she take and give you the clothes off her back," said Flick. "You only gotta ask." His voice was as pleasant as his appearance. He spoke in a guileless manner, and yet, it was a confiding type of voice.

"You allus can bet your bottom dollar on Pig," Randy asserted. "She don't change. She regular as a old shoe and make you feel twice as comfortable."

The three buddies continued to sing praises unto Pigmeat Goins. They did it so unctuously that Dave began to feel like he was present at a memorial service for some long-dead saint; the services being led by three professional mourners.

Pure deviltry caused him to say, "But she's a Vessey Street chick, ain't she?"

"No she ain't either," said Randy. "She don't even have to work; but she does."

Dave looked askance to Blip, but Randy explained his own statement. "She could go with any bigtime bootlegger in town and other racket guys and never have to do a lick of work, but she go with who she want and work like she want."

"In a way though, she gotta work in the Ward . . . on the Block," Flick said. "She can't work for no white folks, the men wouldn't leave her alone. She can't work in service cause she would drive her boss nuts and his ugly wife would end up accusing her of stealing and have her sent to jail like they allus do. Pig gotta work in the Ward, and that's what really makes a Vessey Street chick . . ."

"No it ain't," Randy said heatedly, and Dave realized that he had inadvertently precipitated an argument that should turn out to be very enlightening for him. In no time at all the discussion had broadened to include all the pros and cons of life on Vessey Street.

33

Dave's feeling that all was well with the world returned. With it came an insight. As the men talked, Dave saw that he had overlooked a most important thing. He was smarter than these men; and they knew it. He was already their boss, all else was up to him.

"Naw she ain't," Randy was repeating vigorously as Dave emerged from his thoughts. "Pigmeat ain't lowdown. Can't anybody say she is, and you knows it. Why that gal ain't never two-timed a man since she came to the Ward. She's straight as an arrer and you know it."

Blip was glad that the conversation had returned to Pigmeat. "And she wouldn't cut butter, much less a hard-assed nigger. She don't never carry no weapons." He frowned at Dave. "She's my baby sister, you know."

Dave followed the counsel of Blueboy. The best answer to anything odd is a smile. It was very probable that Blip was kidding, but dark as he was, it was still possible for him to have a near-white sister. It was all very confusing. No black people came from Jonesville, and yet Pig had said she was related to that pretty black waitress who also claimed that Jonesville was her birthplace.

Flick solved his quandrary. "Any chick you can't screw," he said to Blip, "you wanna take and call your sister. Some jive."

"I've screwed more waitresses outa Booker's than you've had to wait on you, boy," Blip said equably. "You just don't know."

"Take and prove it," Flick retorted. The lad also had a beautiful smile, Dave noted. The snowy white teeth were well shaped. And it occurred to Dave that "beautiful" was the only word that did Flick justice. There was nothing feminine about Kid Flick, but he was far more than handsome. He was beautiful. And Dave was tempted to believe that the withered arm was a godsend, for without it Flick would have been too perfect, unreal, a freak. That arm served only to make him equal to lesser mortals.

Dave resolved to enlist these men. It only needed the right time for the doing. Like a litany of joy, he kept turning over in his mind all the assets of the three. Each dealt with the public; each was required to count money and make change; each was a self-described member of the sporting life.

His meeting with them had made Eggy Manone expendable, and now Dave regretted his rash generosity of the night before. It had been a silly grandstand play from the start. Only a damn fool nigger gives presents of cash to new employees, Dave reminded himself. Showing off was a luxury that he must learn to forego. From now on he had to dodge the limelight. Personal gossip would be his greatest enemy. There were no colored cops in the Ward; theoretically it was possible to bank numbers forever in the Ward without the white man's law interfering.

His showboating crime loomed larger. He couldn't even afford it. After all, a four-dollar hit would destroy his bank before they got off the ground. There was no joy in *that* thought. Of course, Blueboy would come to his rescue with all he had, but that did not excuse Dave for giving away money.

His dark thought begat blacker ones. Suppose every damn fool in the Ward played the same number? These small town folks might decide to all play 711, and nothing but 711 until it came out. He was sweating now as he thought. He sought to re-enter the conversation as a damper to his own thoughts.

And now the topic was Blueboy.

"Goddamit, I was here first," Blip exploded. "Looks like at least one person would say he looks like me, instead of telling me I looks like him."

"You don't have his color," Flick said gently.

Blip glared. "Whut you mean, color?"

"Personality," Flip said, grinning.

Dave laughed. "Haven't you seen him?"

"Naw, I ain't had time," Blip said moodily. "I been running in and outa Booker's every chance I gets away from the game, but I ain't seen him . . . I only heard."

"Don't worry. I'll see that you meet him tonight. Mebbe I'll bring him up to the game tonight way late. He can get pretty happy-handed with those dice at times."

"Tell me every waitress in Booker's breaks their neck to wait on Blueboy," Randy ventured.

"That ain't all," Flick said excitedly. "They claim that Old Man Booker raised hell, and told Blueboy that he couldn't have but *one* waitress in his room at a time from now on."

"All you can hear at the Rest is Blueboy this and Blueboy that. Damn if some of them drunks don't argue about him more than they do Joe Louis."

It always happens, Dave mused. Blueboy carried the limelight around with him at all times; sheer magic it was. How could one dark little man, who had not spent ten waking hours, all told, on the Block be the subject of any conversation, much less *all* the conversation?

Just like this business about the waitresses coming to Blueboy's room. Now, Dave knew that hadn't happened. Who started these fables? And why? Certainly Blueboy didn't start them, and Dave doubted very much that the waitresses had. Of the two of them, *he* was the one that had dated a waitress; but evidently few people knew that Dave Greene existed.

Not that it mattered, but why did people insist upon making a legend of the guy, Dave wondered? Blueboy was pretty fabulous without the added dressing.

As for himself, Dave was sure that he was only tolerated, never quite fully accepted. These men and their acceptance of him was a case in point to Dave. They readily accepted his hospitality, but at the last moment had tried mighty hard not to let him pay for the drinks. It worried him. These men would have been honored to have Blueboy buy them a drink, and would have boasted of it long afterward. So why did they insist upon buying Dave a drink? So they could let him know that although he was not a Blueboy, they did not really dislike him? Yes. He was present and accepted now in this pad simply and only because of his relationship to Blueboy and Pigmeat.

And these guys had never even seen Blueboy.

"Hey, Dave!" Blip sought his attention.

He looked up, startled. "Yeah, what?"

"Is it true that Blueboy is an international gambler?"

Dave shrugged. "What's an international gambler?"

His listeners were silent, and with one look at their disappointed faces, Dave was all too aware of the difference between him and Blueboy. He was the crassest of fools, and he despised his obtusity with all his might. Why was he, a Negro, so incapable of being a Negro, Dave wondered? Why could he never recognize his people's needs? Negroes must have their games, and he knew it. So why had he not taken the part they had asked him to play in their game? Blueboy did it; and that was his secret.

He wasn't mean, only dumb as hell. He had been given twenty-three years of experience in the fine art of being a Negro, and yet he thought, he could act more stupid among Negroes than any white man.

Here were three young men, intelligent, fully aware of the fact that it was impossible for a colored man to be an international gambler. Who the hell could a goddam nigger gamble internationally with? A Negro couldn't get into a hundred-dollar-limit poker game in a Harlem after-hours joint that slumming Italian mobsters and Irish cops had started on the spur of the moment. These men well knew that.

And it was because they knew this that they had asked their question.

A Negro's social and recreational life is so limited that at times

36

he has a yen, as avid as a junkie's, for a tale of make believe to satisfy his need.

Dave knew that only a fool asks: What is green cheese? What makes you think that rabbits lay eggs? Is Blueboy an international gambler?

Childlike, these men had handed Dave a worthless bauble, and requested him to weave a fable around it. They were like a crippled child who, knowing that he cannot go on the Sunday school hike, asks to be told a fairy tale about a trip to the moon. Does that make the child stupid?

Suddenly it dawned upon him. This was the crucial hour when he must prove whether he was a fool, or the superior of these men. And he knew how he had to proceed. He leaned forward, and by his very intensity, made Flick, Blip, and Randy into members of the underworld.

"We've been casing this town," Dave stated evenly, "and now we are ready to go on with our plans . . ." He cleared his throat. Three heads nodded in unison. Gravely they awaited the telling of the fable. "Me and Blueboy are starting a numbers bank here in the Ward, and you three guys are gonna be key men in the operation of it, if you want."

"Lawdee," Blip shouted, and flung his arms wide as he collapsed back on the davenport, prostrate with joy. A rapturous smile creased his face.

"Thass it! Thass it! . . ." Randy chanted.

Damned if Kid Flick's soft eyes didn't hold luminous tears of gratitude. His withered hand became palsied, and he held it still with his good left hand.

Dave viewed all this with dispassion. Without a doubt, these three jubilant men believed that he was lying. But they didn't care; they needed this lie in the same way they needed Blueboy to be an international gambler. Now that they had swallowed their shot they were high and enraptured. They would not be half as exhilarated if they knew that they had just been told the truth, Dave reflected with fatherly despair.

"There it is, short and sweet. As of this minute you men are in the numbers racket." In his throat the words seemed harsh, but they came from his lips like a sigh.

"Blueboy done started a numbers bank in de Ward!" Blip announced ecstatically, his pop eyes commanded his friends to shout hosannas to Blueboy.

"I know all about numbers," Randy gurgled. "I went up to Norfolk last summer, and thass all folks talked 'bout up there. Numbers!"

37

"Me too," Flick whispered. "I got me two uncles in Philly . . ."

Suddenly Randy was heartbroken. "We has no money to bank numbers with. Blueboy ain't gonna want us!"

Dave wondered if he should be annoyed or amused; actually he felt neither, and he wondered if he was reacting normally. Dave knew that he could no more be jealous of Blueboy than he could the King of Sweden. However, it did seem to him that these part-time children could at least have granted him the courtesy of being a partner with Blueboy in the bank.

"Blueboy is only . . . he's my adviser. I'm banking these numbers on my own. I pay you; you don't need money."

"Den Blueboy won't need our money." This desolate remark came from Blip. Intimations of suicide and worse were couched in it.

A nervous laugh escaped Dave. Things were becoming much too much, he felt. These child-men preferred their narcotic figments to the truth. Blip knew damn well that he had no money to invest, but there he sat, bemoaning the fact that since Blueboy was not running the bank he was being denied co-ownership in this proposed numbers bank. It made Dave feel as if he had just been doomed to be a kindergarten teacher for the rest of his days.

For the sake of clarity, he repeated: "I'm hiring you men to write numbers, you know. You will go around in the Ward and solicit people to bet money on any number they like as long as it's only got three digits."

All at once Dave was empty and weary. The die was finally cast, but he was almost too tired to be interested in the outcome. In a bizarre fashion, these three had stolen the essence of the occasion from him. The moment lacked both nobility and intelligence.

"Come by my room in Booker's tomorrow morning about eleven," he said heavily. "I'll explain the whole setup to you then."

" 'Leven sharp!" Blip chortled.

"We'll be there. 'Leven sharp," Randy said.

Dave grunted, and thought he might be catching the flu. There was a searing ache of tiredness between his shoulder blades. He was sure his new pickup men did not yet realize the reality of the bank. They still seemed to cling to the idea as a fiction, not knowing that for the first time in their lives, a fable had a strong chance of becoming reality.

"Somebody go tell Ophelia to bring us a whole lot of whiskey," he ordered.

38

5

"Three nights in a row we been making these dry runs. And now there ain't gonna be another dry run ever. Do you know what that means?" Blueboy cleared his throat. "It means that the very next figgers you write are goin' down in history. What you been doin' so far don't mean doodly-squat."

"Gee!" Pig made it sound as if Blueboy had conferred a great honor upon all of them. Then her eyes sought out the figure of Dave. Blueboy did more than his share of the talking, but it was the moody presence of Dave that got you, she was thinking. Dave was smoking and soberly talking to Blip, who was all smiles and grins. Then Dave looked up. "Somebody go out in the hall and ring that button for room service."

Pigmeat thought that Dave looked more bored than ever when the whiskey came and everyone started bragging about how much they were going to write tomorrow. Eggy Manone was a perfect fool, and now that he was one of the boys, he was worse than that. She was just as glad as Dave to see everyone finally go home.

It was 8 A.M. when Pig answered the knock on the door to admit Blip. Dave yawned awake. "Hiya Blip. What's the matter? Things isn't jumping enough for you? You want people to get out of bed just to play the numbers with you? Take it easy . . ."

"I ruint the three books you gimme, Dave . . ." Blip began.

"What?" Dave jumped out of bed. "Fer chrissakes, man. You can't do this to me. Eggy Manone is more use to me than you, and he is a horse's ass."

"Couldn't help it, Dave. Everyone comes running to me on their way to work and keeps giving me numbers faster than I can write 'em, but I tried. I got three books just ruint with folks' figgers, though. Effen I had more pads I'da wrote more figgers and ruint them, too . . ."

"You crazy sonofabitch. Stop making like Blueboy. One Blueboy is enough in my world. Whoopee!"

The two young men danced like savages all over the room, then locked arms and did a cakewalk over to Blueboy's room. Still cake-walking, they kicked in unison on his door.

"Three numbers pads never made or broke a numbers bank," Blueboy said irritably. "Furthermore, I am the factotum. Next time bring *me* the slips and the money. Dave can't count."

At 9 A.M. Flick stepped into McSally's fish store. "Morning, Mister McSally."

"Mawn, boy. How's your paw and the white folks' bank doing?"

"Fine, sir. But we got a new kinda bank in the Ward here now. I'm working for it. You get a six-hundred-dollar return on a dollar if you're lucky. The return on one cent will pay your gas and light bill for two months. It beats the Benevolent Savings Society every time . . ."

"Hush, boy. Don't you know us cullud ain't suppose to know they got more than one bank in this man's town? Ain't no bank on earth loan to cullud like your Daddy's bank."

"Daddy's just the custodian for them white folks. And there's ten more white banks in town just as good."

"'Tain't so, and you knows it, boy. What's this new bank anyhow? Marcus Garvey again?"

"No. Dave Greene."

"Never heard of him. But don't you know that nobody can pay six hundred interest."

"We can, because only the winners get paid. It's a lottery bank." Flick grinned mischievously. "You take and play one cent on a number and we pays you five dollars and forty cents if you hits. How's that?"

"Why in hell didn't you say you was trying to write numbers? I sends my brother in Deetroit three dollars a week to keep this address in every day for six days. Yessir. Four-eleven for fifty cents a day. Now you don't think I'm gonna stop and start trusting you with the money, do you, Flick?"

"Why not? You'd be saving postage, and you gotta give your brother a little taste of your hit too, ain't you?"

"I'm gonna tell your paw, boy. You fixing to get kilt! I don't believe Cuhnel Eldrege got that kind of money to throw away on numbers. And he's the richest man in the Ward, I reckon. Takin' folks' money and not being able to pay off is dangerous, boy. Where you git thet idea in the fust place? You needs talking to, boy."

"Dave Greene can pay off just as quick as them Detroit gangsters."

"Hush, boy. You don't know how sinful you sound, talking about cullud men got as much money as white. 'Tain't right."

Flick gave up. After which he went to every female pad owner in the Ward and after explaining his proposition, got them to solicit their customers for him. Flick finally turned in just as much money as Blip.

Randy's brother Elks were determined to a man to show him that they were worldly gamblers.

"Hear you is writing numbers, Randy."

"Yeah, Moe. What you want?"

"I wants seven-eleven, but first off I wants proof I'm gonna git paid. I wants to know all about this Dave Greene. Where he get so much more money than everybody else? Dutch Schultz ain't never had enough money to take on the Ward. How come Dave Greene can? Now where's the proof I gets paid?"

"I'm the proof! I own my own home, don't I?"

"Fair enough. You putting up your house on Dave Greene's name; I'll trust him with seventy-five cents."

And there was Jimmy Adams, who staggered up with his own idea. "Randy, I come to you time I heard that you was trying to write the daily number. Now my cousin is a policeman in Harlem, and I knows all about numbers first hands. Can't nobody tell me nothing 'bout numbers. And so I'm gonna tell you how to write *single action!* Now my way you don't have to turn hardly no money

41

at all in to this Dave Greene, and me and you is gonna split the difference . . ."

Randy got so much advice that he did not know where much of it came from.

"The boleda is easier to write and to figger out than the American numbers. You sell the sheets with all these numbers on it and if the lucky person shows you that his slip got the winnin' number then . . ."

"Effen there was money in banking numbers the white man would be banking them!"

And then there was Roy Desaint: "Randy, I wants me six-eight-two just like Ames here. Only I wants mine in the box."

"Box? What damn box? Box of what, man?"

"Now we always combinates in Richmond, Randy, and effen you don't know how to combinate in the box you don't know nothing about writing digits. So gimme your book and I'll write my own numbers . . ."

"Is you crazee, Roy?" Randy howled. "I took lessons writing numbers three nights straight. I don't need any damn fool help from you." Randy glared around the bar triumphantly, knowing that he was due applause for that sally. But everyone's face seemed to say that Roy had a right to demand his numbers in a box. "How you write 'em in a box?" Randy said cautiously.

"Gimme your book then."

"No."

"Well I ain't gonna waste my own time *and* paper showing you how to write figures."

"Gimme a piece of paper," Randy said to the day bartender.

With a flourish Roy showed Randy how to combinate in a box:

$$6 \quad 8 \quad 2 - 5\phi$$

"Now that is the way to write it in your pad, and it means that I win if six-eight-two comes out in any of the five other combinations it can come out in:

$$6 \quad 8 \quad 2$$

$$2 \quad 6 \quad 8$$

$$8 \quad 2 \quad 6$$

"Now if any of them numbers comes out, readin' any way you please, I wins at a four hundred to one for every penny I bets you in the box."

"You means you wants to play a number six different ways and I gotta give you four-hundred-to-one odds?" Randy squeaked.

"Why not?"

Randy went to Tom Ellis' barbershop. Blueboy had set up temporary headquarters there. Tom was writing numbers between snips at his customers' heads, and Blueboy was giving a kind of campaign oration upon the happy arrival of numbers in the Ward.

Randy told Blueboy not only of his plight with the box, but of all the dozens of minor harassments fostered upon him by Elks who wanted to play all sorts of foreign ways.

Blueboy was silent for ten seconds. "Bring that Roy to me."

Roy swaggered in a few minutes later. "You wants me, Mr. Blueboy?"

"Don't Mister Blueboy me. I only allows pretty women to do that so they can remember their places. Now what goddam right you got to be teachin' my mule new tricks? You on my payroll? You got a good idea? If it's so good whyn't you bring it to me and get paid for it? Why hide talents under other people's bushels? Now here is a pad, and any more fool ideas you get, bring 'em to me."

Roy rushed out of the shop without even thanking Blueboy. He ran out into the middle of Vesscy Street and stopped the first car that passed by (the driver was a Negro, thank God!) and proceeded to put one foot on the running board like a traffic cop, while he insisted that the man pick any number he choose for a free ten-cent play on Roy Desaint, since it would be the first figger in his first pad.

"Randy, you are something like Dave," Blueboy said. "You never show any evidence of intelligence, but you always manage to do the intelligent thing. I bet Blip or Flick wouldn't have come to me about some damn fool new way to write numbers . . . and they'd have left a good man like Roy there out in the cold. Now that man crystallized for me the fact that numbers is a universal game. Everybody can play. Ain't nobody gonna be too poor to bet with Dave Greene's bank. Tomorrow we starts taking half-cent bets: two numbers for a penny, and if they wins they gets two dollars and seventy cents which will buy twenty-seven pounds of fat meat, a half year's supply. Not a damn soul on the block pays more than three bucks a week room rent. After a half-cent hit he needs only thirty cents. A penny hit will buy a ton of soft coal, and nobody in the Ward burns hard coal. I want all my men to impress on folks what a hit will buy. A dollar hit will pay almost half the price of one of these clapboard houses some folks live in around here. We is gonna take all bets no matter how small. As long as we operate like that,

43

we is gonna remain in business as long as the Ward remains in business."

A little later Dave strolled in. "Where you been?" Blueboy asked him.

"Nowheres. Just walking. The whole Ward knows that numbers is here to stay and I mean stay. Maybe only a few will put their money on a figger today, but the introductions are over."

"You haven't tried to write any, have you?"

"Naw. Why?"

"Like I told you: We are bankers. If me and you never write, then our writers will never bank. Okay?"

"I went in a coupla pads," Dave said. "Kid Flick's got a corner on them. Pad owners sure like that kid especially for him to be a teetotaler. Never saw anything like it before . . ."

"That Kid Flick is a likable kid. All-American kind. It's a damn shame that his only path to riches is in writing numbers. But that's the white man's problem, not mine."

"I oughta be mad at Pigmeat, though . . ."

"What in the world could she do wrong?"

"It just ain't right for a girl to be going from store to store writing numbers like she is selling tickets to a chitlin supper given by the Missionary Society of the First Baptist Church . . ."

That night it was a gathering of the new clan. Two booths in Booker's were occupied by Dave and his men. Only Blueboy was conspicuous by his absence. The clan would have probably taken the big square table in the back of the room, but the Omegas were having some kind of a dinner at it.

Pigmeat's brow creased. She was sure that she would get slapped for her pains should she now suggest that she and Dave go upstairs for a little bit. But he did look like he needed something. It occurred to Pigmeat that this was the reason why she liked Dave so very much. Dave was not like other men; he always seemed in need of something that only you could give him. Pig had been in love many times, but Dave was the first lover that she had ever really liked. Pig also decided that she and Dave never had any arguments because there really wasn't anything with Dave to argue about. She'd had a lot of misunderstandings with all of her other boy friends, but not Dave. He was different.

Pig was inordinately proud of Dave. All the girls liked his style. He was the best all-around man she had ever had. This, too, was strange, Pig thought. Of all her former boy friends, Dave was not the best-looking by a long shot, but he was the handsomest just the

44

same. She did not have the slightest idea why this was so, but it was so. He was not much over five ten, and weighed about 170, but he looked much bigger and soft kinda, but his lean hard body was fun, she remembered. Dave looked so much like everybody else that he really didn't look like anybody. He had pretty good hair with a sort of wave to it, and it stayed shiny all day after he used a little vaseline in the morning. It didn't have to be caked down with NuNile or any other waxy goo like most fellas in the Life used. And he kept his hair short, although not nearly as short as Blueboy's.

But it was Dave's skin that Pig really loved. She was always thinking about his pretty color, that copper brown. Like a real old penny that was still shiny. And there was something about Dave that was very much like Abraham Lincoln in a way. Dave's features were all rounded but his nose was not flat. It was big and sharp like Lincoln's. She stealthily took a penny out of her pocket, and with her thumbnail she covered the point of Abe's beard.

"Why the hell should I have expected Blueboy to make me blow my top today?" Dave said. "All my life . . . since I've known him, he has never let me down," he went on. "I figgered him to do it today by talking me silly. How come?"

Pigmeat laughed. "You was worried because the bank wouldn't be a success and then Blueboy would be upset on account of you. That's what you was worried about, honey. Blueboy didn't have time to talk anybody out of their wits today anyhow. He was too busy to be worried. Keeping track of all that money and slips. How much money, honey?"

Dave shrugged irritably, but he tried to make his voice gentle, companionable; Pig deserved it, he thought. "A little over four hundred bucks. And we'll show a profit even if seven-eleven comes out, and it won't. But you'd think Blueboy's been banking numbers all his life, wouldn't you . . . ?"

Pigmeat instantly slapped at the faint self-doubt in his question. "You sound like you think you didn't do nothing."

Dave grinned. "I didn't."

"We just obeyed orders. Who do you think masterminded it all, honey?"

Yes. Who *had* masterminded it all? Dave wondered. It had all been so easy. Too easy. Making money should be harder work than this, but who was he going to complain to?

Blueboy eased into the booth beside Pig and Flick. "Why ain't you drunk, Davey-boy?" he hollered, and all of Mr. Booker's guests looked on in delight.

Dave smiled sarcastically. "And when we buy a paper at midnight, who is gonna decide who gets paid? The betters?"

"We ain't paying off nobody at midnight. We is bankers with bankers hours. We will pay the writer of the winning number tomorrow afternoon at four P.M., when he brings in his take for tomorrow. Every cent we took in today goes into the regular savings bank tomorrow, soon's it opens. We pay today's hits outa tomorrow's receipts.

Pigmeat impulsively grabbed Blueboy's hand and squeezed it.

"Got more sense than I thought you had," Dave mumbled. "When you get that bright idea?"

"Genius cannot be dated, son," Blueboy said sweetly. Then he hollered. "Waitress. Oh, Miss Pretty Waitress! Please bring Blueboy his special bottle."

6

_____

A Vessey Street chick is all kinds
of things. There are also a good many things that she is not.

She is not very well educated.

She is not a prostitute.

She is not in the Life, but sporting life would be very dull without
her.

She is not a churchgoer.

She is a native of neither the City nor the Ward.

She does not ride motorcycles.

She does not work in any other part of town save the Ward. It
just isn't any fun working anyplace else.

She does not fight with a razor, but, once she loses her temper,
she will throw anything that comes to hand, be it a vessel of boiling
water or a bunch of magnolia blossoms.

On the positive side it may be stated that a Vessey Street chick
is very good-looking, with luxurious hair and a sexy torso that
dwindles down to bowed, rachitic, or just plain skinny legs.

She has big feet and pretty teeth, and she smiles constantly.

She likes to wear motorcycling togs on many occasions.

A Vessey Street chick considers it to be her civic duty to welcome all strangers. All strangers being a select group, such as musicians, gamblers, ministers, and the like. Any male that can afford an overnight room in Booker's is a welcome stranger.

A Vessey Street chick professes ignorance of the existence of any and all Vessey Street chicks, and she hates them.

Vessey Street chicks stick together.

She prefers a skilled husband or boy friend. Said skills may be put to any type of endeavor, save honest toil.

Although she is of college age, the chick considers all male undergraduates "schoolboys." She would rather not be caught in bed with one of them.

An undergraduate named Cokey Louis once stated: "Every single one of these chicks is born with their eyes pointing toward N'Yawk." Mr. Louis' assertion remains unchallenged.

She never gets any nearer to her Promised Land than ". . . buying a ticket next week . . ."

She never becomes quite pregnant, and she is the only female in America that *likes* to be pinched.

She is a country girl that is deathly afraid of the country.

She hates and fears housework, leaving all domestic situations to her darker unfortunates.

A Vessey Street chick would starve before she sold her body, but she has never been in dire financial straits.

The chick is a perennial child engrossed in playing house. Her playmate-husbands constantly change, but the game goes on until she nears thirty years of age. Then, she quietly fades away.

Pigmeat Goins was a Vessey Street chick, and she was always the first to deny it. When Pigmeat was serious, her dimples deepened and became more pronounced.

"I think," she said to Dave, her dimples deepening, "that young people should have their own things and make do."

Dave silently translated her words and winced.

"I don't think it looks very nice for me to come sneaking up here every night," she added as she snuggled closer to him in the bed.

It was not only Pigmeat who thought Dave needed new quarters, Old Man Booker was becoming restive too, and Dave could not blame him. Like all respectable restaurateurs, Mr. Booker had obtained a permit to dispense beer and light wines to his guests, but such a permit could be revoked at the whim of the state. Consumption of hard liquor, gambling, or other immoral acts on the premises could bring about cancellation of the license. While it is true that Mr. Booker had no intention of ceasing to sell whiskey to his guests and was willing to take other chances, he did not think it his part to try and harbor a now thriving numbers bank on the premises. Dave was like-minded, but Dave was a procrastinator. He also had a maudlin attachment for Booker's. It was his original base and he was reluctant to move. Not until Blueboy convinced Dave of the utter senselessness of leaving the numbers operation open to a raid by a bumbling group of liquor agents, did he finally move.

Dave rented the first floor of a two-family house on Macon Avenue, and Pigmeat immediately moved in with him. He ran his numbers activities from the kitchen.

"That is just about the stupidest arrangement a man could think up," Blueboy declared with profound admiration. "You not only gonna get yourself arrested, but your lady friend too. Plus, you might even manage to get yourself charged with adultery, fornication, dubious morals, and plain stupidity." Blueboy refused to give up his room at Booker's, but every morning at eight o'clock he cheerfully woke up everyone at the Macon Avenue address.

Dave tried to explain: "It ain't like we was in love . . ."

And it was convenient.

And it didn't cost much . . .

Blueboy was more succinct. "It's a two-bit setup, and you and me ain't never been two-bit operators since the very beginning."

Blueboy resolved the issue. He walked into the house one afternoon and announced, "I've leased us a fine house on Gay Street. And I'm gonna stand in the backyard and throw rocks at Old Man Booker all day long . . ."

The house on Gay Street was the former residence of the late Dr. M. M. Mason, one of the Ward's wealthiest M.D.s. It was a modern two-storied home with spacious rooms and hardwood floors.

"With things breaking like they is, the problem of where to put it is gonna be more important than making money," Blueboy advised Dave. "You want to run up all the bills you can. Big bills. You are gonna buy the white merchants' friendship. I don't mean the clerks . . . They're gonna be jealous and hate you—like poor trash should. But respectable debts is more important than money in the bank. No southern white man wants a nigger who owes him a thousand dollars to be setting in jail."

"Paying bills everyday is gonna be as noticeable as putting money in the bank every day," Dave replied.

"You don't pay the same goddam bills over every day," Blueboy said. "Owe and pay! Make the white bastards love you. I keep telling

49

you that white business people don't give a damn about how a jigaboo makes his living. All they wants to know is: Does he pay sooner or later? You just do that and they'll all be saying that you is a good black boy."

"You'd just love that too, wouldn't you?"

"You're damn tootin'," Blueboy said, with a catch of sincerity in his throat. "I think you is a damn good black boy myself."

Laughing in spite of himself, Dave thought that now was as good a time as any to drop his bombshell. "I guess you already know that I'm gonna let Pig stay on at Macon Avenue," he said tentatively. "I'm gonna still pay the rent," he added. He gazed expectantly at the ceiling.

"Well, now. That's nice."

"You ain't got a few words of protest?" Dave asked.

"You owe her plenty."

"Me?"

"The bank would have never taken a holt if Pig hadn't a talked it up in Booker's and all through the Ward twenty-five hours a day. And you forget that she wrote more numbers than anyone else the first two weeks, and wouldn't take a cent commission . . ."

"Yeah, but . . ."

"But what?"

"I dunno," Dave foundered. "I guess I thought . . . Damn it. I don't know what I thought . . ."

"You thought she owed it to you because you was generous enough to share your bed with her?"

"Why the hell you gotta get things all twisted ass backwards?"

"I ain't twisting nothing. Untwisting mebbe."

"Nerts."

"That Pig's the best good-will ambassador any numbers man could have, and it ain't never been no sin to pay a pretty gal's rent anyways. And besides that, you raised her manner of living. You ain't got no right to lower it back. Not when she ain't done you nothing but good . . ."

"You mean I owe her more than rent?"

"Never try to repay a pretty woman, Davey-boy," he said softly. Before Dave could interrupt he continued. "Pigmeat's a lily of the field. She was born one of them and yet she toils. Jesus Christ didn't even ask that much of her . . ."

"Now what the hell does that mean?"

"No smart man ever tries to repay a pretty woman for anything. You might just as well ask the sun and the moon and the rain how much they wants back. So you can suit yourself," Blueboy snapped.

After a brief silence he said, "If you didn't do a damn thing for her she would still be the prettiest and kindest girl in the Ward."

Dave sighed. What was there to say?

"You two call it quits?"

"Nooo . . ." Dave said. "Nothing like that, only sometimes it seems that we're such good friends that it don't make sense to spoil it with romance, if you know what I mean . . ."

"Wondered when you was gonna find that out," Blueboy said kindly. "You got the sharpest delayed-action mind in the business."

"Okay," Dave said. "And so we always take care of Pig like a mascot, a good-luck piece?"

"Something like that. Only, don't bother to worry about Pig. She's too busy doing unto others to miss what you ain't doing unto her."

And so it came about that Miss Althea Goins became the proud possessor of the only bachelor girl apartment in the Ward. Honors were immediately heaped upon her. She became the undisputed social arbiter of the Block, the leader of the Vessey Street chicks, and Dave's official hostess. This was a far juicier role than just being Dave Greene's woman and she graciously relinquished that title.

She enjoyed herself immensely, and continued to enjoy other people as well. She and Dave remained the best of friends until parted by death, and on occasion, they still accommodated each other.

7

When Dave and Blueboy started the bank, they had only one bureau drawer full of the peculiarly made pads that were so indispensable to writing numbers. Many was the time Dave had promised himself to canvas the local printers and stationery manufacturers for estimates on large lots of the pads, but he always put it off. One day, Blueboy warned him that there was less than a ten-day supply of the pads left. By this time, the bank had been operating for over a month, and Dave had managed to increase his cash reserves to $6000.

The printers in town did not tell Dave that he was crazy; they just acted as though he was. All claimed that they did not have the facilities for making the pads; but Dave believed that these men simply refused to take him seriously. And he was afraid to take these white men any further into his confidence. All but one of the stationery men were the same. The latter claimed that he would not stoop to the manufacturing of the devil's needs.

Even so, Dave was not dismayed; there were a dozen numbers bankers within a 120-mile radius of the Ward, and he was convinced that he could fall back upon professional courtesy to fill his needs. But Dave had not reckoned on the effect of the movies. James Cagney, Edward G. Robinson, Paul Muni, George Raft (and Scram!), were the ideals of the Sporting Life all over America. Every numbers banker from whom Dave had hoped to obtain help had cast himself in a role that ran counter to the hopes and plans of David Greene.

The nearest numbers operator played the Cagney role to the hilt twenty-four hours a day. His name was Joe Sneef, and it was to him that Dave and Blueboy first turned for aid. Joe owned a poolroom from which he openly operated in a town not much larger than the area occupied by the Ward. Sneef sat in a glass enclosed office in the rear of the poolroom, and, when Dave and Blueboy were ushered in by a splowheaded lackey who imagined himself to be a torpedo and bodyguard, they were startled to find Sneef speaking into three different telephones, to three different women. He apparently was giving each of them exact instructions to be standing on separate street corners so that he could drive up and offer them a lift in his new car. At least that is the way it sounded to Dave and Blueboy.

The Cagney character yelled, "Good-by, ya skunk," into the telephones and hung them up. He turned to his visitors. "So what's your story?"

"This is Dave Greene and I'm Blueboy Harris. Mebbe you heard of us . . ."

"I heard. I knows everything that goes on in this state."

Blueboy nodded respectfully. "Sorry to come barging in to ask a favor before we even met, but this is what fate decreed. As it is, we happen to be clean outa numbers pads, and our jobber suddenly shut down. And so . . ."

"You come to me to wipe your ass."

Blueboy's usually strident voice was muted, schoolmarmish. "I wouldn't say that exactly."

"You went and horned yourself into a dog-eat-dog racket, buster. I was wondering when you two's dumb luck was gonna run out. You was so dumb you started a racket in the Ward, and you was lucky enough for Bishop Wesley to die the same week you opened or you wouldn't be standing here trying to bum a favor of pads . . ."

"Never even heard of the good Bishop," Blueboy allowed.

"The holy bastard loved colored wimmin so much he hated the nuts off nigger men. He'd a closed yer bank the first day an' a half. And you fairies never heard of him. It's dummies like you make it tough for smart guys like me. And I doan play . . ."

"We only want to know where we can buy some pads," Dave said sharply, unable to take the man's act any longer.

53

"Tough, baby, tough. Now I got me a white boy to supply me mines, and I gives him strict orders to sell to nobody but me. Unnerstan? Nobody. Cause I doan play. I ain't in the favor-doing business."

Sneef's grin sickened Dave. That grin was, in a way, the curse of the colored race; and Dave had an almost uncontrollable urge to smack it off the face of the wearer every time he saw it. He flashed a look at Blueboy, who was surprisingly calm.

"You mean we gotta pay? Okay. We pay. No harm done," Blueboy said.

"What part you play, man? You ain't right bright. I tole you I ain't in the favor-doing business, didn't I? And since you ain't got no sense to unnerstan with, I just might as well come down and take that bank of yours for myself."

Dave picked up one of the telephones and bashed it against the man's skull.

"This ain't no movie. Stay as far away from me as you can, but keep your eyes on me at times," Blueboy cautioned Dave as they made their way out through the poolroom. Several of the fallen king's henchmen were closing in on them with murder in their eyes.

"You don't have to tell me that." Dave knew that Blueboy was right. Only two fools would stand back to back and let themselves be surrounded. Dave knew he would have to play it by ear until he caught Blueboy's rhythm.

Blueboy was the only man present who was a skilled pool-hall fighter. He ignored the cue sticks and made for the pool tables, scrabbling as many of the balls together as he could. This gave him nine ivory missiles. He was a moving target, while the attackers formed one massive target.

The smallest man, who led the attack, chose Dave because he was closest. Dave hit him so hard that his nose split wide open and blood spewed everywhere. After that three men rushed Dave, and he went down under their flailing cue sticks, but Dave fought on in an attempt to destroy all three of his attackers. At this time no one had pulled a knife, probably because for a minute everyone was dead certain that Dave and Blueboy had come armed with pistols. And it was this moment's hesitation before the weapons came out that gave Dave and Blueboy the time they needed.

When Dave went down, Blueboy did not hesitate. He had no choice but to risk hurting Dave to save him. From his vantage point atop a pool table, he fired pool balls with all his might at the struggling men on the floor. He never hit Dave, but one pool ball did crack the wrist of the first man who flashed a knife, and the speed of the ball carried the knife to Dave's cheek, leaving an ugly gash, while breaking the man's bone. Another of Dave's assailants collapsed with an eight ball to the right ear, and when the third turned to surrender he received the nine ball squarely in the mouth.

Dave tried to get up off the floor to rush Joe Sneef, who was staggering out of the office with a huge forty-five in his hand. When Blueboy saw the pistol he sent his two remaining balls through the green-painted plate glass windows of the place. Sounds of the shattering glass could be heard for blocks away. In no time at all one captain and two patrolmen had arrived on the scene.

"These two niggers come in here to try to muscle me outa what is mine, Captun Brown," Sneef whined.

The unscathed Blueboy humbly motioned Captain Brown aside. "See that?" he whispered, "that boy ain't to be trusted, Captain. He all but done said you is protectin' him, and you know that ain't right. All we did was to ask him to stop calling up long distance a certain real yaller gal that one of my good white friends is right taken with. Now what was wrong with that, Captain?"

All the while that Blueboy was talking, he was backing the captain of police into a secluded corner. And Blueboy's derby was held in hand and in that derby was one of the fattest little bankrolls that Captain Brown had ever seen.

That expedition cost over three hundred dollars, including hospital bills and the payoff to Captain Brown. And two precious days had gone to waste.

The curiously made pads were now down to a four-day supply. The two friends were rebuffed wherever they had turned for help. Several bankers had heard in advance of Dave's skull-damaging prowess, and refused to meet them at all.

Another nearby banker, who had once been referred to in his local colored paper as "a local sportsman," believed his clippings, and spent all his spare time hunting and fishing in the company of wealthy professional men whom he showered with expensive favors and gifts. He hated poor people and said so. Dave did not bother to try him.

The banker in Chattanooga was bewitched by his newspaper title of "mystery man," and could not be contacted.

Several bankers simply denied that they were in the numbers racket, and displayed the same attitude to Dave that Miss Pigmeat Goins had for Vessey Street chicks.

"By nineteen forty-five there will not be a nigger numbers banker in the whole United States," Blueboy thundered on the morning the pads had dwindled to one day's supply. "For the past week we have been running around watching them sign their own death warrants. And what makes it worse is that Negroes have been hung separately since the beginning of time. Seems like now they should be afraid not to stick together. Just suppose fifty Negro numbers bankers were to be even loosely associated. Hell, we could *buy* a factory of our own just to make pads, and in time we could do the printing for every Negro organization in the world."

And it was not until that very moment that Dave remembered Billy Bowlegs from Gator City. That the man was shorter, louder, and blacker than Blueboy was enough to make him unforgettable, but both Dave and Blueboy had forgotten the bumptious racketeer.

It was on a Sunday morning, when the bank was only a week old, that Billy Bowlegs had entered Booker's and announced to one and all that he was "Jes plain 'long Billy Bowlegs from Gator City," come to welcome these two men Dave and Blueboy he had heard about into the numbers business. Everyone, from the out-of-town guests to Mr. Booker himself, fell in love with the ridiculous little mite. Everything about him was so uncouth and impossible that you simply had to take the braggart to your heart. And the man was so down to earth, everyone agreed. So genuine. From the twenty-dollar gold piece that dangled from his watch chain, to the sixteen-cylinder limousine, complete with chauffeur and bodyguard, he was a genuine man of the sporting life.

It was to be a meeting of kings, and Mr. Booker had made the most of it. He sent a dishwasher to waken Dave and Blueboy and rushed to the phone to summon the Ward's photographer. Meanwhile Billy Bowlegs was hopping from table to table, introducing himself and ordering seventy-five-cent pitchers of whiskey for each table.

"Ah is Billy Bowlegs," he yelped. "The numbers boss of the bestest numbers town in the United States, and my greates' pleasure is to buy all good folks a drink."

Blueboy came down first, and, sizing him up, he went straight to the stranger and handed him a ten-dollar bill: "The reward for being born blacker and shorter than me!"

Billy Bowlegs jumped up and down like a jack in the box. Waving the ten-dollar bill aloft, he fondly embraced Blueboy and screamed for the waitresses to serve whiskey until the money was spent.

"Ah earned it fair and square," he boasted to his listeners.

Dave came down a few minutes before the photographer arrived, and Mr. Booker proudly posed between the two hand-clasping monarchs for what was the picture of the century, at least, in the Ward.

It was a wonderfully drunken day. A traveling party progressed from pad to pad all over the Ward. Blueboy and Bill Bowlegs were two dark clouds of joy who kept the cavalcade in an uproar for ten tumultuous hours.

When Billy was about to depart, he had grasped Dave's hand and refused to let it go until young Dave promised him faithfully, that whenever he needed anything he would let Billy know first. Yessir! Anything he needed for the business, be it lawyers, money, armed killers, or loose women, Dave promised to let Billy Bowlegs know first.

And this was the man who Dave forgot.

Dave made for the telephone, but stopped. He needed the pads immediately. Why call when he simply had to go and pick them up? Summoning Flick the Kid, they made a mad overnight dash to see Billy. At the end of the one hundred and seventy-five mile trip they were both hungry and sleepy. As soon as they reached the colored section they stopped in an all-night joint for a cup of coffee.

Dave mentioned the name of Billy Bowlegs to the counterman.

"He's as regular as they come," Dave added. "Nobody would dream he was the richest colored man in this town just to look at him . . ."

The restaurant owner sniffed.

Dave wondered what was wrong with him.

"He musta tole you dat," the man said. "Nobuddy else woulda . . ."

"Everybody says so."

"Numbah King!" He took a pitying look at Dave. "Everybuddy knows that loud mouf fool git twenty bucks a week from dem Eyetalians tuh make believe he own de policy bank in dis town, and mebbe they lets him use one of them rich cars once in a dog's age."

"What?" Dave, sick, realized the truth. He grasped at a last straw. Billy was at least a part of the numbers racket in this town; he would be able to direct him to the man who supplied his bosses with pads. He asked the owner the best way to reach Billy's address.

"He's doing ninety days in de wukhouse. Whuffo? You want his job? It open now."

Dave did not join the man in laughter. Neither did he go berserk; he merely refused to talk to anyone for the next three days.

Blueboy tried several schemes for writing numbers, but none were as satisfactory as the triplicate pads. He and Dave were deluged with errors and falsifications. In just three days, their reserve of cash began to dwindle dangerously. To keep up the reputation of the bank, they knew they had to keep paying off even questionable hits—but they knew they could not keep doing it for long.

Blueboy decided on heroic treatment for Dave. "Since you ain't talking to a damn soul, you might just as well be somewhere else. Like Chicago, mebbe."

Dave took the next plane to Chicago, and once there, found that he could purchase all the pads he wanted as long as he bought them in lots of ten thousand or more.

So now it was question of storage space, Dave explained to Blueboy by long-distance telephone.

"You want a vacant store that don't leak, is fireproof, burglar and cop-proof, no rats, and someplace where people aren't too nosey?"

Dave admitted that Blueboy had stated the problem correctly.

"Then you better buy it there and bring it back with you!" Blueboy slammed the phone down and said to his recent acquaintance, the college student Cokey Louis, "C'mon, boy, let's go drink on this matter."

After Blueboy and Cokey had drunk upon the matter for several hours, Blueboy jumped up from the table and marched out of Booker's. Cokey was too drunk not to follow Blueboy who went straightway into the florist shop located between Booker's and Macon Avenue. The shop was a bedraggled place that was not a florist shop at all but rather a sort of buying agency for citizens of the Ward. It took orders for flowers and then relayed the order to a white florist to be filled. A penny ante enterprise at best.

"This place don't do enuff business to pay the rent, so I'm gonna give you three hundred dollars for it. Lock, stock, and barrel," Blueboy said.

The florist-shop proprietor knew a crazy man when he saw one and immediately closed the deal.

The befogged Mr. Louis continued to follow in Blueboy's wake. They re-entered Booker's and went back to the big square table in the rear of the dining room and sat down to drink some more solutions.

Much later Blueboy went to the phone booth near the table, and Cokey heard him calling Chicago. Later, much later, Cokey heard Blueboy screaming into the phone, "I said, you are now the owner of a daisy shop, and a professional plucker of sweet violets."

8

The Square Table in Booker's
was a mighty contraption. It looked like it had been stolen, and, on
top of that, it certainly had no business being were it was. And
although it was a massive, oblong thing, the Block insisted upon
calling it square.

Booker's was a pleasantly arranged dining room with four wooden
booths along each side. In the center, between the booths, were
four medium-sized tables. Just behind these tables, near the kitchen
door, stood the monstrous square table with its ten matching chairs.
That is, the wood seemed to match, and this made the whole
thing interesting, for it would have taken four able-bodied men
hours to transport this monstrosity and its heavy chairs any distance
whatsoever. When one considered the fact that the table could not
possibly have been maneuvered through either the front or back
door of Booker's, the thing ceased to be interesting; it became
downright hysterical.

Blueboy and Cokey were of the opinion that the table, like
Topsy, just growed there. Dave, who at times feared and hated
the table, never tired of telling its "true history."

"Right after the Ward got emancipated," he would say, "some of the boogies decided to form an insurance company, and the first order of business was to send away for this damn thing for the board of directors to sit at. But when the mule train arrived with it, the fools found out that it was too big for any of their cabins . . . including Uncle Tom's . . . and so Old Man Booker's grandpaw tole them that he would take it in outa the rain until they got around to building a cabin big enough. But the company went busted after they paid the freight charges and so the ugly bastid has just stood here waiting for some black fool to come and take it away."

Dave could elaborate further if only Blueboy would let him, but Blueboy loved the table as much as Dave despised it. To Dave, the table personified everything that conspired to keep the Negro downtrodden. It symbolized, even jeered at, all the Negro's shortcomings. In time Dave expanded his loathing to include the group of men that Blueboy gathered around it nightly.

It was the week before Dave went to Chicago when Blueboy had sauntered into Booker's one evening to find every booth and table filled save the square table. Undaunted, he made his way to the contraption and took a seat. The chair was amazingly comfortable.

"The only chairs in the whole damn Ward that were designed with thought and loving care for the human posterior." So said the founding father of the Knights of the Square Table. It was a cruel twist of fate that made Pigmeat his only audience. She laughed merrily.

Blueboy ordered a bottle of beer and reveled in the comfort of his newly found throne. And throne it was, for each massive chair was built like one, and from where he sat, Blueboy commanded an excellent view of the entire dining room and its entrance. With regal indolence he observed a tall, rather homely youth enter the restaurant and look about for a place to sit. Blueboy beckon to the lad, and Cokey Louis nodded and came over to the Square Table.

"Evening, Mister Blueboy," Cokey drawled. He had an infectious grin that somehow made his homely features handsome, even a little dashing. "What may I do for you?"

"Sit."

Cokey pulled out a chair and sat. He waved at the table's broad top. "I see that you like the wide open spaces. I'll take the same. I'm from down Texas way."

Blueboy nodded equably. "Yeah, all good men needs space to holler in if they takes the notion." He paused to study Cokey.

60

Finally he said, "Fact is, schoolboy, I see you around quite a bit. I kinda like the way you carry yourself. You should have a nice future ahead of you."

Cokey's grin was more puckish than ever. "You must write and let Reverend Louis in on your secret."

"Pop's a minister, eh?"

"In Houston," Cokey replied.

"Good leave town, Houston."

"You lived among us?"

"Nope. In the Navy. Just on leave."

"Tar?"

Blueboy glared. "Boy, is you trying to double talk me?"

"Isn't that what they call you sailors?" Cokey asked, feigning innocence. "That where you got the name Blueboy?"

"Nope, not exactly. Always had it. Seems like my Maw liked to deck me out in them little blue velvet suits. Then later on it was blue serge."

"You must have looked right cute in the blue velvet."

"You're goddam right I did."

"I knew there was some reason other than your complexion for your name." Blueboy bristled, but Cokey continued. "After all, you are only a shade or two darker than I am, and there is no earthly reason for people to call you blue."

"That's a black lie. I ain't as dark as you," Blueboy shrieked, stung to joyous indignation.

"I thought you called me over to put a little light on the subject, but . . ." Cokey rose as if to leave.

"Siddown you little coward!" Blueboy yelled. "Is that the way they teach you to talk in college?"

Cokey grinned. "The Nigra youth of today has already learned to talk by the time he reaches college."

"What you screaming for, Blueboy?" Pigmeat stood over them with her hands placed on Cokey's shoulders. "You stop picking on Cokey. He's my boy friend sometimes . . ."

Cokey clasped Pigmeat's hands. "You're all I got to protect me, li'l Miss Tater Pie. Please don't let this Blueboy bite me again and I'll marry you in the morning. And when you gets time, bring me a seventy-five cent pitcher of likker."

"Sure, Cokey." Then she gave him a quick and faintly dimpled look. "You got money, honey?"

"Pretty is as pretty does," Cokey said. "She wants to know if I need any money."

61

"You got that message all wrong, son," Blueboy said, "but since you are supposed to be my guest, I will pay for the stupid juice."

Pigmeat switched away, and Blueboy looked at Cokey. His feelings were those of a collector who has suddenly come across a rare specimen.

"Damn," he murmured. "Me, you and Davey shoulda been in the Navy together."

"That would make a rather odd threesome, wouldn't it? Dave's not so much on fun, is he?"

"How you come to ask that? You ain't stupid for real, are you?" Cokey smiled apologetically. "Well, I really don't know him."

"I've seen you talking to him once or twice in the bar across the street," Blueboy countered.

"The Lil Savoy?" Cokey spoke uncertainly. "I know . . . s'funny. He speaks, offers me a drink and talks even, but somehow the guy ain't there. Or maybe I'm not there as far as he's concerned. You know . . . like the furniture. So I know him or not? Nobody ever introduced us. We never shook hands . . . I doubt if he knows my name."

"If he personally bought you a drink like that, well, you can say you know him and that he likes you. There's nothing phony about Dave. Right now he might seem a little preoccupied. What with these numbers and things just getting started. We are still in our infancy so to speak, but you just wait; Davey-boy loves wine, women, and a nickel in the piccolo better'n most. You just wait and see."

"Well, that's news to me," Cokey said. "I thought he was a pretty cold fish. I did kinda figger that he didn't dislike me, but I tabbed him as a guy that doesn't want any close friends except one, maybe."

"You got it completely backwards. But Dave *is* bashful."

"Bashful? Cool, calm, and collective Dave Greene is bashful?"

Blueboy nodded. "Mebbe it's different from most kinds of bashfulness, but that's what he is. He is socially awkward because he is overly sensitive about what people think about him. That make any sense to you?"

"I guess it does," Cokey said doubtfully. He was more interested in his next question. "You trust him completely, don't you?"

"We're friends and buddies, what's trust got to do with it?"

"Everybody says so. Just like he was your own son."

Blueboy squinted. "You mean that I own the bank and Dave fronts for me?"

"That's the way the story goes."

"The Ward is not only a big liar. It believes in its lies. Dave wouldn't front for the devil. He is the one boogie, on this earth, that refuses to be a phony. He even hates the temporary. That's one reason he's where he is today, 'stead of still waiting on tables, dreaming about being a big shot."

"I'll be damned," Cokey murmured. "He can't be much older than I am and I haven't even picked out a career yet . . ."

"I'm gonna make believe that you never said what you did about Dave. Dave would cut his throat before he claimed to be one iota more than he is."

"And I thought he was a young punk trying to make people believe he was a big-shot gambler," Cokey muttered.

"I understand," Blueboy said. "But I want you two to be friends, and so, like I say, I'm not gonna mention this conversation to him. Dave is too broody at times. He needs a lighthearted guy like you for a pal."

Cokey's features chilled, but he said nothing.

"Whatsa matter?" Blueboy demanded. "I say something wrong?"

Cokey's voice was a shrug. "I like fun and games, but I'm nobody's court jester."

"Why, you can just go to hell, I don't give a damn if you two never speak again in life. I merely said that you two oughta make pretty good buddies. In fact, I know you will, but I ain't never bought no friends and neither has Dave. Do you know that you are a goddam fool and you ain't got no sense either?"

And thus the first nightly meeting of the Knights of the Square Table came to chaotic order. Time passed. Blueboy ordered several more pitchers of whiskey and they sat and talked at each other for a couple of hours. Then Blueboy saw two men standing near the front door. Both men were apparently seeking a table. One was a pale, tweedy Caucasian with a dreamy, almost drunken expression on his face. The other was a dark Negro, a stocky bulldog of a man with veiled eyes. His ugly face was stamped with character, but he was so unhandsome that only the discerning could see more than his homeliness.

"Go get that man." Blueboy pointed to the one occupant of Booker's dining room who was unquestionably darker than he. "I owe him a drink."

Cokey looked at him, startled. "That's Dr. White and Professor Blake from the Campus," he said. "You want me to invite them over?"

"Yass. I wanna buy that black man a drink," Blueboy said impatiently.

63

For the life of him Cokey never knew why he docilely obeyed Blueboy's command. When the three arrived at the table, Cokey made the introductions, and Blueboy politely invited the two men to sit down and have a drink.

No sooner had the teachers settled in their seats when Blueboy scowled and demanded: "If you two are professors, how come I never saw you before?"

The professors exchanged professorial glances. The black one smiled and said, "But you are well known to us, Mr. Harris."

"Well, anyhow, I invited you over for a drink and you know why," Blueboy said meaningfully.

Cokey was seized with a fit of choking.

"I'm afraid I don't," Dr. White said. Although black, he had a proper Boston accent which was genuine. His definitely negroid features made people expect a southern accent, and so the proper speech was disconcerting; one of his pupils had said: "It's like watching a baboon with perfect diction." This, plus an air of condescension, put the doctor at a disadvantage in every initial encounter with colored strangers. His manner was one of constantly trying too hard to understand the black race.

Blueboy instantly perceived that here was a man who was unfamiliar with Negro life.

"Are you gentlemen planning a party?" Dr. White asked, motioning at the large table top.

"We are having a seminar, Doc," Blueboy said offhandedly.

"A seminar?" The perplexity was both genuine and pedantic.

"Yeah." Blueboy snarled. "Topic A being: The Nigger Prof and the People Problem."

Dr. White's laugh was forced. "I don't quite get you," he said. "You are joking, are you not?" Involuntarily he became more pedantic, hence, uglier. Professor Blake remained pale and silent. "But speaking of seminars," the doctor said, "that is exactly what I had in mind for the last few weeks. As an economist I should get to know you people better. You and your colleague interest me greatly."

"Who dat?" Blueboy asked.

"This Mr. Greene, Dave Greene. I am told that he is the new ganglord of the Ward. I definitely must get to meet him."

"Where'd you get this ganglord business?" Blueboy asked.

The teacher showed surprise at Blueboy's coldness. "It's common knowledge here in the Ward."

"Common knowledge of a common bastard," Blueboy said in the same cold voice. "You're a Ph.D., aren't you?"

64

"Yes, Columbia, thirty-four! Why do you ask?"

"Because you talk like you went to the movies to get your education."

Cokey dully pondered suicide and/or murder. He was sure as God made little green apples that he was going to be expelled in the morning.

Dr. White included Cokey and Professor Blake in his bewildered smile. "Why do you say that?" he asked Blueboy.

"First you state that you have a scholarly interest in Mr. Greene and then you turn right around and say that he is a ganglord. Why would a doctor of economics be interested in a fictitious character? There is not a nigger gangster in the entire U.S.A. You talk like a damn fool, or else you think I'm one."

"Oh, come, Mr. Harris. Everybody boasts of the man being a gangboss as if he was a credit to the race and the Ward."

Blueboy was not angry, only bitter. "You are a fool and a liar," he said to the doctor. Then to no one in particular he said, "Here we got a black-assed Ph.D. who earned his degree watching *Little Caesar,* and I'm supposed to respect him. Witch doctor is what he is . . ."

"I resent that!" Dr. White snapped.

"Folks as black as you resent every damn thing anyhow," Blueboy said. "And you never heard anyone call Dave a ganglord. Those are your words, Doctor."

"What difference does that make? We are all aware of what the term denotes," Dr. White said.

Blueboy leaned forward. "The term denotes that after years of struggle you got yourself a doctor's degree and now the grapes are sour as hell in your mouth."

The doctor laughed harshly. "Don't be silly. I'm not jealous of those Jones brothers in Chicago, with their reputed millions, much less an ignorant numbers banker here in the Ward."

"Dave's not ignorant," Blueboy said, stung.

"How much schooling has Greene got?" Cokey asked. He also wanted to know how much education Blueboy had, but he resisted the impulse to ask.

"Dave Greene is a lawyer's son," Blueboy said heavily, "with three semesters of college work to his credit. Any more questions?" His listeners were silent. "He majored in football, hell raising, and a little bit of waiting on tables. And he makes more money in one day than a bullshit prof makes in a month, meals and lodging included. Which makes him a ganglord . . . academically speaking, of course."

"Nonsense," the doctor said rather desperately. "I don't think . . ."

"How the hell can you think anything?" Blueboy asked. "You don't know him. Never saw him."

"Dave Greene is a notorious character here in the Ward. He is known to be a professional gambler, hence a habitual lawbreaker, a felon. I base my opinion on these facts."

"Why, you really are a stupid sonofabitch. The man has not lived in this Ward for three months hardly, and yet you claim he's notorious. He's never been to jail, never arrested, never even charged with a crime, and yet you got him being a felon. Do you *honestly* think you got a right to teach?"

Cokey now considered himself expelled, and so he pondered the most intelligent course. The smartest thing to do would be to jump up, slug Dr. White, and then beg Blueboy for a job. But, like the sons of all Baptist ministers, his revolt against Calvinism was only vocal; he had no desire to lead the life of a racketeer. In view of this, he wondered if it would not be best to slug Blueboy and apologize to Dr. White. After all, the doctor was known as a man's man on the campus. Of course Cokey would regret losing Blueboy's friendship so quickly, but college and later, perhaps, law school, meant more to him than any friendship. Even if he was not the studious type.

Meanwhile Dr. White had half risen from his chair. "I don't have to stand for this," he grated through his teeth.

"Then siddown and shut up," Blueboy barked.

The stocky doctor sat back down. "Why?" he asked more to himself than to anyone else. It was not fear that caused him to heed Blueboy. Dr. White was younger and looked to be a great deal stronger than Blueboy. Moreover he was used to violence; in college he had been one of the first New England scatbacks.

"Now I invited you over here to have a drink because you're blacker than me," Blueboy said in the most reasonable of tones, completely ignoring the presence of the Nordic-looking Professor Blake. "And what happens? You start telling me that my best friend . . . my son, practically . . . is a cutthroat and worse. And you admit that you don't even know the guy. And then in apology you say that you thought we would like the names you called us. Now if that ain't the truth, I'll eat my hat."

Dr. White looked at the empty pitcher on the table and muttered, "Where is this drink you keep talking about? I did not mean to be patronizing. I'm sorry if it seems that way to you, but I honestly believed that no one would take umbrage."

66

The word umbrage softened Blueboy's heart; he forgave the man, but at the same time he decided that a little more chastisement would do no harm. "Are you a member of the Negro race?" he asked abruptly.

"That is a silly question," the doctor replied.

Blueboy's nod of agreement was friendly. "Well, damn if you don't act like you never saw a colored man before tonight. You teach at a nigger college. Don't you ever look at or converse with your students? You say 'you people' like you was a damn foreigner or something."

Dr. White's chin jutted. "Since there is no Negro race in America, I don't see how I could very well belong to it."

Blueboy signaled to Pigmeat to bring two pitchers of liquor and then leaned forward. "Now what the hell does that mean?" he asked the doctor.

"If we are not Negroes, what are we?" Cokey asked.

Once again Dr. White became pedantic, but this time he looked less repulsive. "There is a group of people in America who do have a variable and unascertainable amount of Negro, Afric, Arabic, and Mongoloid genes in their hereditary make-up, which, I might add, now includes also a good deal of Anglo-Saxon blood. For varied unscientific and un-Christian reasons these people have been the victims of much adverse legislation. The Negro is a political entity. Nothing more. I am one of these legislative unfortunates, but political misfortunes cannot create a race. I must admit, however, that I do seek political asylum among like unfortunates."

Blueboy jeered out of sheer jealousy of all those pretty words. Pigmeat brought the whiskey, and Cokey poured everyone a drink.

"I think that St. Paul was correct when he said that all men were of one blood and created by God to dwell on the face of this earth," Dr. White went on. "Statesmen have ruled otherwise, but it is well nigh impossible to find a group of humans more idiotic than any given body of law-makers."

"Very good. Very good," Cokey said softly. Blueboy's eyes shone, but he made no comment.

"I claim to be a Negro, but I also insist that there is no Negro race in America," Dr. White added.

"I believe that a race can be bred and that America has bred a Negro race," Blueboy said at last.

Dr. White laughed. "If we followed your statement to its logical conclusion we would have a world peopled with a democratic race, a Republican ethnic group, people of divorced blood, half-blooded criminals . . ." The doctor paused for emphasis. "I tell you that

67

laws cannot create a racial group. I repeat. The Negro is a member of a political group. He is a political and ethnic bastard. And so declared by the various bodies politic."

"A race of dogs can be bred," Blueboy said slowly. "You gonna tell me that a human is a lower mammal than a dog?"

"Rubbish," Dr. White exclaimed.

"Okay," Blueboy said cheerfully. "These genes you talk about; they tell a dachshund to crawl into a hollow log after game, and to back out instead to trying to turn around; they made a Bloodhound able to catch your blackass; a pointer to point. All these traits and things were bred into these dogs. How come no Negro traits was bred into me? I'm less than a dog? Unable to be bred for survival in a white man's world?"

The economist took Blueboy seriously. "The Negro . . . if he is anything . . . is God's denial of heredity."

"Come again?" Blueboy said.

"You can say what you will about any Negro's ancestors, but you will find that they had nothing to do with that particular Negro's social, economic, or moral status."

"How about Booker T. Washington, George Washington Carver and Langston Hughes?" Cokey said.

The professor smiled. "These men all had white ancestors. Lowdown, lascivious white men who slept with filthy and depraved slave women. The laws of heredity should have doomed these men before birth."

Blueboy gave the teacher a sort of noncommittal glare. "How about St. Louis Kelly, Youngblood, and Llewellyn Harris," he asked.

"Who's Harris?" Cokey asked.

"Me," Blueboy said.

"That makes three tough thugs," Cokey drawled.

Dr. White cleared his throat and said, "These three all carry genes of the superior white man. And although you have bucketsful of degenerate black blood in your veins, it goes without saying that the white man's blood is so superior that you could hardly be anything but the highest type of citizens."

"I think you are the first faculty member I ever talked to that was not a bug on family," Cokey said.

"I guess I am an environmental bug if anything," Dr. White said.

"Why you just called a college-bred lawyer's son a Vessey Street rat," Blueboy yelled. Angry all over again.

The two professors rose to leave. "And I apologized," Dr. White said.

68

"Most every night from now on I'll be sitting here at this Square Table," Blueboy said genially. "C'mon by and be welcome. The drinks will always be on me."

Cokey watched the two men leave the restaurant. "Whew," he said. "Did you have to try to get me expelled with every breath you took?"

"That I'm-so-educated-that-I-didn't-know-you-was-alive-son-of-a-bitch got on my nerves at first," Blueboy said pleasantly. "But they'll know next time."

"What next time? You don't think they'll be back for some more of your insults, do you?"

"I didn't insult nobody. No such thing," Blueboy said. "What that Dr. White guy needed was to be shown the right pew. We merely had a slight difference of opinion. What the hell was the matter with that white man? He didn't say a mumbling word. He was drunk, wasn't he?"

"I love the way your mind circles straight to the point," Cokey said. "But, yeah, I guess he was drunk. High anyhow. I think he's one of those all-day secret drinkers. I smelled it on him in class several times. Blake is not a white man though."

"I got eyes. I can see."

"Well, you see wrong. He's colored. He's from my home town."

"I don't care if he's from Zanzibar. That is a full-blooded white boy if there ever was one. Fact is, he's whiter than most. And that black hair and black spot, I bet his friends call him Blacky."

"I guess you might be right at that. That birthmark makes him look like he's got a black eye at first. But what makes you think that Doc White is ever coming back for more of your brand of hospitality?"

"He don't sit on his high hoss for nothing. Nobody wants to let him get down. He's too black mebbe."

Cokey's drawl was dreamy. "Do you know what you're talking about?"

"He's never been around any real people. Colored, I mean. Black as he is, he ain't no real nigger. We are oddities to that guy," Blueboy said. "I bet he ain't got a colored friend to his name. He is the world's blackest bastard living in the world's whitest tower."

Cokey stared in amazement. "I honestly never considered it before, but you just might be correct."

"I know I'm correct. So what's his story?"

"Doc White was born and raised in a tiny New England village. All white except for his family. Went to a tiny college up there. Probably the only dinge on the campus, but he was the star on a losing football team. He was good for a sixty-yard broken field run every game, even if they did lose sixty to six. So he was a big man on the campus, which for a black boy is a euphemism for freak."

Blueboy grunted with satisfaction. "Had no love life either, I bet."

"He went to Columbia," Cokey continued, "for his graduate work and neither had the time or the money for any socializing. So it's just possible that the guy never had a colored friend. I never considered his social life until a dark little gypsy mentioned it a few moments ago."

"Lots of times real dark people like him don't have many colored friends," Blueboy said. "Niggers are ashamed of him."

"You ever seen a group picture of some Negro college presidents and deans?" Cokey asked.

"Nope. Why?"

"Them that ain't white looks white and don't ask me why, but that's the way it is."

"Moton, down at Tuskegee, don't look white."

"Name another."

"You trying to say what, schoolboy?"

"Doc White don't have too much future in Negro education, and when you stop to think of it, the fault is entirely the Negro's. Makes you kind of disgusted. I think you're right, Blueboy, the doc is a lonely soul . . . with a hard on."

"That white sonofabitch is more lonely than he is though."

"Prof. Blake? I dunno . . ."

"Thought you said you knew him?"

"I said we were from the same home town."

"What was he drunk for?"

Cokey was momentarily nonplussed. Blueboy had an ability to ask the most unreasonable questions in the most reasonable tones. "Well, what are we doing drunk?" he said at last.

"That is different. We ain't college professors."

"That's right. I forgot. We are ganglords."

"I'm gonna kick your butt, boy."

"Short as you are you couldn't kick a duck in the ass."

"Shaddap and tell me about this white man. This full-blooded white one."

"How can I shut up and tell you about him?"

"Trouble with you schoolboys is that you don't comprehend logical English. Now tell me about that fay boy. He don't set right on my mind. Somehow he ain't right."

"He was born in Houston, but nobody to my knowledge has ever

70

seen him there. His mother is well known and still lives there, so everybody knows of him, but nobody knows him."

"What the hell kind of language is that?" Blueboy exclaimed.

"Dammit, he's never lived in Houston since he was a kid. His mother put him in boarding school when he was a baby almost. Maybe before I was born. He must be ten years older than I am. Then he goes to prep school, then college. All white schools upstate. I never even heard of him visiting Houston."

"Think she wanted him to be a white boy? How she feel now?"

"You mean that she sent him away to be raised and educated as a white boy, and then he comes back down South here and joins a Negro faculty? I dunno, Blueboy. I dunno. Could be she's disappointed. He don't ever come to Houston that I know of."

"Well, at least you got my message," Blueboy grumbled. "You ain't as dumb as when you first sat down here."

Cokey accepted the left-handed compliment. "She is kinda mysterious, too. His mother, I mean."

"How's that?"

"She is the subject of much gossip in Houston," Cokey said before changing the subject. "But I can't see Doc White coming back to this table. I think you goofed."

"You kick a lonely whore in the butt, she won't like it, but if she's lonely she's gotta return."

"Sort of breaks the monotony, eh?"

"You'd be surprised," Blueboy said.

Dave stood over them critically measuring the expanse of table top with his eye. "Why don't you guys use the floor and be through with it? You wouldn't have as far to fall."

"Siddown and shaddap, you goddam ganglord," Blueboy said.

"I wish you would shut up," Dave said wearily. "I got a headache." He signaled Pigmeat to bring whiskey. "Big as this table is, a guy feels funny just ordering one pitcher. What the hell you guys sitting here for anyhow? There's empty booths."

"We don't mind it, Lord," Blueboy said.

"You're drunk. And what's this ganglord business?"

"The University's department of economics has so decreed," Blueboy said.

Dave glared at Cokey, but Cokey anticipated him. "You are looking at the wrong windmill," he drawled.

Dave turned to Blueboy. "It ain't funny, you know. Some jerks here in the Ward are gonna pick that up and keep repeating it until some cop hears it, and they just might start thinking that I believe it and start jumping on me with both feet. Cut it out, willya?"

"It came direct from the ass's mouth . . . a prof named White," Blueboy said.

"He said it in here? In Booker's?"

"That he did, but don't worry. I squelched him."

"*You* squelched him?" Dave moaned. "You cussed him? Did you threaten him, too? I bet you made him so mad he writes a letter to the editor or something."

"I got more sense in my little finger than you got in your whole watermelon-eating head."

"Okay, okay. Stop screaming. I told you I got a headache." Dave's manner changed. "I'm sorry, Blue. I should have known better. I need a drink. And where the hell is Pigmeat?"

"Why didn't the bastard talk?" Blueboy demanded.

Dave started. "What in *hell* are you talking about?"

"Not you. I'm talking to the schoolboy here. For some reason a white bastard is passing for colored and he sat right here talking and never opened his mouth. I don't like it."

Dave stared at his friend. "You're not drunk, you're crazy."

Blueboy swelled angrily. "If people didn't know you was ignorant they'd swear you was crazy yourself," he said. "And that's what familiarity breeds," he told Cokey. "When I first met up with this cornpone nigger he would rather break up a Georgia lynching bee with a slingshot than talk to me that way." He glared at Dave. "I treats you like my halfwit son. I gives you knowledge which you sorely needed. And now look at the gratitude I gets."

"A thankful receiver is just another damn beggar," Dave said.

Cokey thought to change the subject before Blueboy suffered an attack of apoplexy. "A guy that color is kinda leery of jumping into just any conversation," he said. "Professor Blake gotta watch every word he says around Negroes."

"You are crazy, too," Blueboy said.

"Suppose he called you a black bastard like you called Doc White?"

"I'd hit him in the mouth. What the hell you think?" Blueboy exclaimed. "I don't let red niggers get too cute with me just because they got a little bit of color."

"Nuff sed," Cokey replied.

Dave smiled thoughtfully. "So this guy wasn't like the day and nothing like the night? Them people I don't feel sorry for. They got no guts. You look white? Okay. Be white. Why the hell do people like that want to hang around niggers who are jealous as hell of their skins?"

"Not me," Blueboy said. "I wouldn't pass if I could. I hate white

72

people too much. Every damn one of them is rotten. Believe me, I was gladder than you were to stop waiting on them and start doing something a man can have some self-respect doing."

Dave hooted. "The bank go busted tomorrow; you go back to waiting tables tomorrow night."

"That's a lie," Blueboy declared. "I'm psychologically unable to serve a white man now. I'd commit murder in the dining room in a week. I'd be dumping scalding coffee down those crackers' necks all day long."

"You're fooling yourself, Blueboy," Dave said.

"Not me. And let me tell you there is only one thing lower than an American white man and that is a damn foreigner. Everytime a starving immigrant hits Ellis Island a nigger loses a job. Soon's the bastard gets off the boat he heads for somebody's kitchen and three months later he's got a tux on and giving colored waiters orders. He's led a life of starvation in a starving land until he landed here, but now all of a sudden he's a food expert."

"But there are lots of good white people," Cokey said. "I wouldn't be in school if it wasn't for my father's rich white friends."

Blueboy glared at Cokey. "You just don't know yet. But you gotta learn to ask yourself one question before you take any white man to be your friend."

"And what's that?"

"How would I like to have this bastard for a father-in-law," Blueboy said coldly.

9

Easter Monday 1937, and here was El Dorado. A golden land after twenty years' search.

Last night Makepeace Johnson had arrived in the Ward with twenty dollars and twenty years of waiting on tables to his credit. This morning, in the glittering sunlight, he was walking toward the Block on streets paved with gold.

"This here is Davey-boy's town," Blueboy informed Makepeace.

"Do?" This one word was the huge man's masterpiece of a catchall. It served as an exclamation and assent, epithet and word of encouragement. The tall and deceptively soft-looking man had the blandly majestic air of a butler or the governor of a large state. Whenever anyone engaged Makepeace in a conversation, they would later recall only one thing the man had said, "Do."

"In less than two years Dave has scaled the heights in this man's town and there's no looking back," Blueboy went on. "That's why we sent for you. The season looks like forever."

"Do?"

"Yep. Never in the last eighteen months have we taken in less than eight hundred bucks' worth of bets a day. And mind you, that is on the very worst days. Ordinarily we takes in thirteen to fourteen hundred a day, and we're growing all the time."

Makepeace politely widened his eyes. "Doooo?" he murmured.

"Davey-boy is the Ward's savior. Believe me when I tell you. He brought new life to the Ward. He gave the economy a shot in the arm. Pump priming! Just like FDR, he did. If Dave was a white boy they would be running him for senator instead of trying to run him off to jail."

"Dave's been to jail right often?" Makepeace exclaimed, aghast.

"No, no. Not that exactly, but we do run an illegal gambling operation. But I gotta admit that the cops in this town ain't too hard to get along with. Five bucks here, ten bucks there. Turkeys for everybody Thanksgiving. Twenty bucks for Christmas. You know how it is."

Makepeace nodded. "Do." He had been in many towns and resorts where numbers playing had been a religion, and he himself had plunged on the digits, but never had he been in a position to see the wealth a numbers banker could accumulate so rapidly.

Blueboy came to a halt before a shotgun clapboard house built flush to the brick pavement. Reaching up he rapped loudly on a window pane.

A round dark face beamed down at him from an upper window. "Go long and stop that fuss, Blueboy, you."

"Stop that fussing yourself and gimme my morning's lovin' since you ain't gonna gimme coffee, you toasted slab of pound cake. Meet Makepeace Johnson, Miss Emma. He's gonna be our comptroller from now on."

Miss Emma did not have the slightest idea of what a comptroller was, but she was quite sure that the huge and handsome Makepeace would make a lovely comptroller and so she said so . . . several times. She also wished him luck. Then she arranged a scowl of outrage on her cheerful face and grumbled, "Gittin' so a body can't get a wink of sleep around here nights. Wasn't that you out here just a hollerin' and carrying on somethin' turbul about two this morning?"

"Mebbe," Blueboy cheerfully admitted. "Ole Blip got took drunk and so naturally his boys had to see him home okay."

"Whyn't you put him in a cab? Wonder the man didn't lock you all up. All the ruckus you was raising. Sound like you was commandin' a regiment. 'Walk straight! Lean on me!' 'Raise your foots . . . de curb ain't comin' down to you!' Oughta be ashamed, waking people like that . . ."

Blueboy grinned. "Wal . . . from now on I'm gonna see that

75

you gets something for your nerves at night. A little something to sleep with."

"Go long, you dirty dog," Miss Emma screamed. "I already got me a little somethin' to sleep with, and it ain't Blue neither."

The window banged shut, and Blueboy continued his victory march toward the Block, the seaman's rolling gait becoming cockier.

Makepeace kept pace in the two-man procession, but his thoughts were not on the delighted hellos Blueboy bestowed to the right and left as he progressed like some all-conquering warlord. Last night Makepeace had alighted from a Greyhound bus with exactly twenty dollars in his pocket. Twenty years and twenty dollars. It was not a rewarding thought. A traveling waiter's life was not so grand when you stood still and looked back on it. After twenty years, every resort had a dog-eared sameness. Same job, same gal, same poker game, and the same whiskey.

Twenty years, twenty bucks. A million years, a million bucks. And nothing ever changed any more. That is, until last night, when he arrived in this golden land of opportunity.

Dave Greene was hardly twenty years old. Less than thirty anyhow. And here he was living like a millionaire after less than two years of banking numbers. Fine brick mansion, fine car, fine women. And all because he quit waiting on tables before he got too old. Everything the boy had was brand new and top quality, with money rolling in like waves on top of waves.

At the corner of Vessey and Macon, Blueboy came to a parade rest before the handsomest Negro man Makepeace had seen in a long time. He was a strapping giant, almost as massive as Makepeace, but after that the resemblance ended. The ex-waiter was a light café-au-lait complexioned man, whereas the stranger was a handsomely burnished mahogany. His noble head was topped with a luxurious mane of steel-gray waves. Strong white teeth shone in a beneficent smile.

"Reverend Taylor, Mr. Johnson," Blueboy intoned.

"My pleasure, Mr. Johnson," the clergyman boomed, in a voice as vibrant as the man. "Are you a business associate of my friend, Mr. Harris here?" Makepeace hesitated. The minister evidently did not know of Blueboy's profession. "Brother Harris is one of our foremost businessmen," the churchman added. "An astute business leader."

"Astute," Blueboy echoed in proud amen.

"A credit to the race," said Reverend Taylor.

"Do?"

76

The minister extended his hand and touched Blueboy lightly on the chin. "Cut yourself, son?"

"Yeah, Reverend. Guess I shaved too fast this morning."

Reverend Taylor nodded gravely. "They make those blades too sharp nowadays," he said. "Now next time I want you to do this for me." He used his hands to illustrate as he spoke. "I want you to take that blade and rub it around inside of a heavy water glass with your finger like this. It will hone down those rough edges, and you'll get a lovely shave."

"Live and learn," Blueboy exclaimed. "Now who'd a thought that a simple little trick like that would save you a world of trouble and bloodshed? Now that's one thing I didn't know and I'm gonna try it tomorrow morning," said Blueboy, who shaved once a week. Then he performed that inimitable dip and turn, with his hand coming out of his pocket with paper money between his fingers. "Can't forget the fare on the Gospel Train, can we, Mr. Conductor?"

"Bless you, my friend. Bless you." And the blessings rang out in organ tones. "And you, Brother Johnson. Let me say to you that the doors of the Macon Street Baptist Church are always open. And I want you to make it your home away from home." So saying, the good reverend tipped his hat and proceeded along the Block. A noble ship of Zion.

"Now there's a penny-pincher for you," Blueboy exclaimed as soon as the preacher was out of earshot. "Who else would stand in front of a looking glass and spend an hour trying to rub a new edge on a two-cent razor blade?"

"It does seem right silly, don't it?" Makepeace said.

"Oh well. I thanked the holy bastard for it. And he's rich, too. The church sisters just love that beautiful black stud."

"Do? And he's got the voice for it."

"Like an organ. He used to ride Dave like a hobby-horse in his sermons until I started to butter him up. He's as vain as a woman and just as easy to handle if you oil him slow and gentle like. I bet he even plays numbers now; and the guy who writes 'em is probably on his deacon board."

Blueboy suddenly wheeled into the doorway of a small florist shop. A pretty girl was watering the plants on the counter. "Good morning, Mr. Harris," she trilled.

"You know my name, gal. And this ain't company. This is folks. Meet ole Makepeace Johnson, and that's his real moniker, too. And we got him to kinda keep order around here, so to speak. So whenever a white man comes in here and starts asking questions you just tell him that you'll have to find out from Mr. Johnson. Furthermore, you is pretty enough to get plucked this morning."

The girl giggled. "That's just lovely, Mr. Johnson. You're going to like it here. Everybody is so jolly and nice."

Makepeace was charmed by the gentle little girl, but Blueboy gave him no time to linger, leading him into the back room. This was a large, crude-looking office. Makepeace looked around while Blueboy chattered. The office contained three battered desks and four telephones, plus three filing cabinets. There was a huge safe which was open and looked as if it had never been locked.

There was still another room beyond this office, but Makepeace assumed that it was unused because the sole piece of furniture in it was a decrepit billiard table.

Blueboy waved his arm to include both rooms. "This is the heart of the operation, the nerve center," he told Makepeace. "Here is where the money comes, and so naturally it is the most important, but first let me tell you once and for all that I don't own this racket. Dave does. Lock, stock, and barrel. I am his right arm, his first lieutenant, but I owns nothing. Dave's word is the law and after that, mine is. So there ain't no use to run to Dave about nothing. What I say goes. So when you don't like what I say, don't grumble and stay—"

"—Grumble and be on your goddam way," Makepeace finished the familiar waiters' maxim.

Blueboy nodded. "But the season here is for the life of the bank and right now the bank looks a damn sight healthier than we do."

"Do? And I know that you are mighty proud of Dave. You brought that boy along like he was your own flesh and blood."

"Couldn't feel no prouder if I'd a spit him out my mouth," Blueboy said. "Now listen close, and let me tell you all about the writers and pickups. Every numbers bank has got to have writers, runners, or whatever you want to call them. Now these writers go around in their neighborhood or on their job and solicit bets from the public. At eleven or so in the morning we send out this crew of fifteen pickup men. Each pickup man has a car and a certain amount of territory to cover before three P.M. He collects the work— money and slips—from every writer in his territory."

Makepeace nodded, adding a perfunctory, "Do."

"When the pickup finishes his rounds he brings all his money here to me. And then I give him a slip showing how much dough he turned in. Then he takes his bet slips down the street to the counting-house. This here place we call 'the bank.'"

Blueboy plumped down in a chair at one of the desks and continued. "As comptroller, you will be in charge of the countinghouse. I run the bank here. I pay off. You determines who gets paid off. Plus you listens to the pickups' beefs and the problems of their writers. And everyday we expect more and more police problems. But you are no fall guy. You are gonna be our liaison man. We needs a born diplomat like you around because me and Dave both talk too short at times."

"Dave explained that already," Makepeace said.

"That he did. That he did. And so this morning I want you to ride with one of our top pickups, a kid named Flick."

When Makepeace met Kid Flick he was pleasantly surprised, for Makepeace was a man acutely aware of beauty. The young pickup was an almost perfect physical specimen, and it was with sadness that Makepeace noted the withered hand and arm. The afflicted kid? A flick of the wrist?

But once in the sleek new Ford, Makepeace was glad to see that Flick was an excellent driver in spite of the helpless arm. They sped out of the Ward and on past the southside. The houses began to deteriorate as they drove, and soon they were in a mean neighborhood where the residents looked even meaner. Makepeace had often heard of these southern slums, but he had never seen one. Resort towns did not have outright slums. This was a corn-likker, knife-fighting territory with more than its share of rachitic babies underfoot.

Then Makepeace spotted the paradox. It was a new service station. It could not have been more than four months old and probably much less. To Makepeace its modern equipment and jauntily uniformed attendant served one purpose, to taunt the surrounding poverty.

Since the attendant was colored and there was no white man about to watch the cash register, Makepeace knew that this was a Negro-owned business. But the idiocy of this venture filled Makepeace with a shame that soon turned to anger.

Kid Flick parked in front of one of the pumps and jumped out of the car. The attendant tipped his cap to Makepeace and went about servicing the Ford without any instructions from Flick, who had gone inside the station.

When Flick returned he started the motor and handed Makepeace an envelope. "You hold the money and I'll hold the slips. Count it; you should have seven dollars and a nickel there."

Makepeace checked the envelope, announced that the money was correct, and then the pent-up question exploded from his lips. "What's that service station doing back there?"

"That station belongs to our boss. Dave built it."

"Don't believe it. No sir, I don't. Blueboy would never let him," Makepeace said. "Why that station is an insult to the intelligence of our race."

"Just the same, Dave built it." Flick looked at him curiously. "What's so wrong with it? It's brand new."

"That station's got no more right to be there than I have. It couldn't possibly show a profit in that neighborhood. Those folks back there can't even afford a bicycle even, much less a car."

Flick dismissed it all. "Shucks, they do a right good business there. They got to. Where else you gonna drive in, play your numbers, and get gas and oil on your way to work?"

" 'Tain't enuff," Makepeace grunted.

"Well, I don't know the gas and oil business enough to argue about profits, but they got plenty of steady customers. And besides, that station has every sort of potential you can think of. There's plenty of reasons for it to be where it is."

"No there ain't!" Makepeace said.

"Do you realize that a colored man can't take and buy a gas station just so?" Flick asked. "Nobody will sell him one." The youth grinned impishly as if this was a very good joke on someone. "Next off, Dave had already bought the property and the house burned down, and I guess he just decided that he wanted a station of his own so he took and built hisself one. They won't sell him one? Okay. He takes and builds one anyhow. And he takes and pays out hundreds of dollars to bribe these crackers to let him build it. Building inspectors, firemen, even the people who furnish him with the gas and oil he sells."

"But why right there in that neighborhood? Just because he owned the property there is no excuse."

"Makepeace, that whole section of town is finished, so that means the beginning of something else. Maybe a housing project. Maybe the new bypass will go through there. It makes no difference, Dave can't lose. New project? Okay. There's a new station to go with it. Bypass? Better yet, maybe. He either has a gas station on a new highway or he sells at a profit. Something's got to be built out there soon. One more hurricane and the whole place is leveled."

"Umm . . . guess so," Makepeace mumbled.

Flick's impish grin reappeared. "Dave's his own best customer," he said. "He's got thirty automobiles."

"Ain't no colored man on earth own thirty cars. White folks would have a fit even in Harlem. And in this town they'd shut him down in thirty minutes and don't you forget it. Do! Thirty cars. He couldn't use thirty automobiles."

Flick grinned harder. "Every pickup has a car. That makes fifteen right there. Dave got for his personal use a Cord, a Zephyr, and a LaSalle. Blueboy's got a Chrysler he never uses. And that flower shop got a delivery wagon. The gas station got a tow truck plus a pickup. Dave's got three limousines he rents out to undertakers by the funeral. Okay, how many is that? And I ain't finished naming them yet . . ."

"It ain't right," Makepeace moaned. "That boy ain't thirty years old yet."

"He ain't been in the Ward thirty months yet," Flick said.

"Do. And does he keep it a secret?"

"The cars? I doubt if a single one is registered in his name. I got an idea that some of them is in Pigmeat's name, but I ain't for sure. Me and Blip are the only ones Dave allows to register the cars in our own names. You see, the cars is part of our salary. Twenty-five a week and a brand-new Ford every year for your personal use, plus fifteen gallons of gas a week. Not bad, eh?"

"Do," Makepeace said, agreeing.

Flick parked in front of a shabby dwelling and got out. "C'mon. You want a drink of splow? That's pure corn likker."

Makepeace clambered out of the car and followed Flick up the littered path and onto the front porch of the house. They entered without knocking, although Makepeace was not sure if the dump had a front door. His nostrils quivered with disdain for this hovel; the smells of poverty and corn likker mingled with the smell of frying food.

A drunk was seated before an upturned orange crate, trying to assort and count a sizable hoard of money. A bloody hunting knife lay on the floor beside him. He had a three-day growth of beard.

"Tried to get that lazy no good woman of mine to hep," the drunkard mumbled in apology to Flick.

"Flick. Kid Flick? Flick, you hear me, don't you?" a woman's voice called from behind a curtained doorway. When she entered the room, Makepeace saw why the hunting knife was bloodied. The woman's head was bound with a stained towel. Blood trickled from beneath the towel down her cheeks to drip from her chin. Her left arm had two superficial cuts. The blood on her arm was congealing, but Makepeace was sure that the head wounds needed stitching.

"It ain't like that atall," she cried to Flick.

"Git back thar," the man snarled, reaching down for his knife.

"Now you jes' go ahead and let that meat burn and see what happens. Ah done tole you ah needs something in mah stommick."

The woman's eyes were awash in tears, but Makepeace's pity was tempered with revulsion. This woman was beyond true pity. She had purple, razor-scarred slabs of liver for lips. Nor was she entirely sober. Her body was misshapened rather than shapeless. It was hideously formed of misplaced blubber. Protruding fat vied with bulbous breasts in a competition for grotesquery.

"Ah gits mah work done before ah goes to bed evey night," the man mumbled. "Eveybuddy know thet. Fore ah goes to sleep ah gits mah money and slips straight. Now lookit."

Makepeace stared coldly at the man. Suddenly, he shoved the man's chair away from the crate. Bending over he began to deftly count the money. Finally he looked up at Flick. "Twenty-three-eighty here." Flick nodded and began to go through the slips.

The presence of Makepeace gave the woman courage. "You and John messed up that money last night. You went in it twice to buy likker with. You know you did, and I ain't touched your money." She turned to Flick and her face was more obscenely ugly, more grieved. "Jackie daid," she said softly.

Kid Flick's body flinched, but he continued to leaf through the numbers slips, silently counting. It was not until he placed them in an envelope that he looked at the woman. "Dead, eh?"

"She took Lysol. Suffered something turbul, Flick. And she jes a chile, po thing."

"Twenty-two. Same as me," Flick said. "What happened? Why'd she do it?"

"Nothing, I guess." The woman shrugged her shoulders. "Jes plain sick and tired of living mebbe. If it hadda been me I'da killed that no good John, but not me. Nosiree, not me. I got too much to live for."

"Jackie and I started first grade together," Flick said to Makepeace. "All the way to high school we was together. And pretty. Always, from the beginning she was the prettiest girl in the class, but that's the way it goes, I guess." He looked at Makepeace. "Let's go, Make. See you folks later."

Once the car was in motion the Kid Flick began to talk in a monotone. From far away, out of a hellish revery, his words came to Makepeace. "Every now and then there is a girl like Jackie," the kid said. "They takes their first drink, and they ain't like other people because they never get sober again as long as they live . . ."

Makepeace laughed uncertainly. He felt as if he had stumbled across two lovers in the midst of a whispered promise.

82

"This kid, Jackie, was real pretty." The way Flick smiled brought a lump to Makepeace's throat. "They said me and her looked like brother and sister. Twins even, but I could never see it. She was pretty."

"Do?" Makepeace whispered, shaken.

"Her father was a postman and her mother was a schoolteacher."

"Makes them well off for colored," Makepeace said.

"That's right. Good looks, good family, good brains, and right nice spending change. She was an only child. And like I say, she had everything until she got high that night."

Flick was silent for a few minutes before he said, "We were juniors, and it was some kind of winter prom. I took her, but she went home with somebody else. Mebbe I wasn't lively enough for her, and mebbe she really didn't know what she was doing, but she didn't look or act drunk. Just real happy and gay. And she was beautiful that night. I guess that was the prettiest she ever looked."

Makepeace suffered with the boy.

"After that there was always likker on her breath. Never drunk then, but never sober either, I guess. Anybody offer her a drink, she takes it, no matter from who. Girls used to say she took and kept a medicine bottle of whiskey in her locker at school. I dunno, but I guess mebbe it's true. She quit high school in her senior year and went to work. She wasn't knocked up or anything. She just wanted more money and time to drink. She worked pretty hard, too. And regular. Waitress in Booker's, maid in a department store, and once she sold tickets at that movie theater on Vessey Street."

The Kid's face was chill. The car was going at a breakneck speed, but he handled it with efficient ease.

"One day, she just wasn't pretty any more. She used to have clean, sharp features and a square little chin with a dimple. Then, all at once, her face was round and she had blotches and there were sores inside her nose she kept picking at. Then she just took and went down to nothing." The Kid paused to reflect, but he was almost through now. "Five years ago she didn't know those people back there in that house. Didn't even know that kind existed. Now I guess that's the only kind that'll be at her funeral, 'cepting me, I guess."

"Do?" Makepeace felt easier now that it was over.

"Yeah. Excepting me. Her mother and father died last year. One right after the other. Seems like there oughta be some money around somewheres. Insurance, pensions, and stuff, but I dunno," Flick said wearily. "Wonder why God does that to us? It don't happen to white girls like that."

Makepeace glanced at him. "Why do you say that?"

"I dunno, but I just know it don't. It couldn't."

They had come to a white residential neighborhood, and Flick stopped the car and went into one of the houses by the back door. When he came out he said, "That's the only white writer I got, but don't tell Dave, because Dave don't understand white people. But this white guy writes up a whole gang of numbers. Fays don't think nothing of putting a whole dollar on just one figger."

A little later they came to a respectable colored neighborhood, but it did not have the ancient and lovable rakishness of the Ward. Flick made a number of stops at luncheonettes and barbershops, each time giving Makepeace the money to count and hold. The envelopes usually held less than five dollars but sometimes much more.

One stop was a beauty parlor. When Flick returned he remarked: "That girl in there makes more money writing figgers than she does frying hair."

Soon after that they were headed for the suburbs and then past the suburbs into a new district. These were the mansions of the very rich. Homes of the true southern gentlefolk, only the surrounding plantations were missing.

Flick turned into a country lane, and after driving a short distance he braked to a stop but let the motor idle. He said nothing, merely drumming an absent-minded tattoo on the steering wheel. A cute little girl in a maid's uniform darted out from a bush-covered path. She smiled fleetingly before she tossed two envelopes in Makepeace's lap and disappeared back into the bushes.

Flick smiled. "Cute li'l trick. Scary as hell, but she ain't too scared to write a damn good book."

"She wrote a book?"

"Not that kind," Flick said. "The amount of money a writer takes in a day is called his book. You write five bucks' worth of numbers a day . . . you got a five-dollar book. Fifteen or over you got a good book. She's got a damn good book. Take and count it and see for yourself."

Later Flick said, "That was Washington Heights back there. You got to be a blueblood and a millionaire to live out there. It's the most exclusive place to live in the state."

"Do?"

"Yup. And the colored people that work in service out there can take and put every penny that they earn on the numbers if they want."

"But of course that ain't right," Makepeace said primly.

"Why not? What they got to lose? Ten? Twelve dollars a week?

They gets their room and board and hand-me-down clothes. S'posen a chauffeur plays four dollars on a certain number every payday. Same number every payday, year in year out. If he ever hits he got over two thousand dollars. Heck, I bet the principal of our high school don't have two thousand cash dollars to his name after twenty years of saving."

Twenty years, twenty dollars.

It was a pounding warning in Makepeace's brain. And it told him that numbers was his only way out.

"Or you take life insurance," Flick said. "What does the average person in the Ward carry? A couple of hundred? Enough to get him buried? Okay. He can take that twenty or thirty cents a week and play a four or five cent number every day, and if he hits he's got hisself twenty dollars or so. And he didn't have to die to get it."

Twenty years, twenty dollars. Makepeace shifted in his seat.

"That's why some people call numbers 'policy.' They take and play up the money they use ta save to pay their policies with."

The huge ex-waiter laughed. "You know, I clean forgot the peanuts some folks get paid in these southern towns. Seems impossible that they lives as good as they do."

"Where you been living at, Make?"

"Resorts mostly. Traveling. Just like Dave and Blueboy used to do. Only they got smarter two years earlier than me." Makepeace smiled oddly. "Sure. We made at least a pound a day, maybe seven dollars even. Depression or no. And we could make two pounds a day or more at a good convention. Of course, don't no season last over three months, but there was always another resort opening up we could go to. We followed the gilt."

"That's the life for me." Flick's youthful enthusiasm amused Makepeace. "Wish I could get around some."

The diplomatic Makepeace refused to offer condolences to the wistful Flick. Instead he said, "There's something wrong about going from place to place. Traveling ain't broadening. You shrinks, if anything. You get so you look down on local people. Make fun of them and shun them, but local people is what the world is made of. Gets so you ain't fitten company for nobody but another floater like yourself. 'Tain't right somehow."

"You think Blueboy shrunk? Or Dave even?"

"There's only one Blueboy in the world, son. And Dave's his shadow like."

"Well, at least you always had money in your pocket and your life didn't end if you got fired."

"How's that, son?"

"Well, you take my pop, for instance. Pop's been porter at the Merchants Market Bank over twenty years. He can't quit and he only makes twenty-seven-fifty a week, but white folks tell him he got the best job in town and that he's a good nigger. But if he should ever do something to get fired, his name would be mud. He'd never find another job in this man's town. And even if he could, I don't think he'd be able to hold it," Flick said. "And he's so proud of that job. He thinks he's socially higher than the president of the colored bank. If the day ever comes when Pop can't go down and open the door on those white folks' money, why he'd just naturally take and die."

"I know what you mean, son. Too many of our people put their heart and soul in jobs that ain't worth it. That's one thing about Dave, especially Dave. He ain't gonna let no white folks' job ever make a fool outa him. That's the secret of Dave's success, mostly."

Flick was still wistful. "But you guys had fun. Plenty of fun. I've heard Dave and Blueboy talking."

Makepeace smiled. "It did seem like right good fun. At least until recently. There's some crazy things we used to do that I'll never forget. Like Saturday night before Palm Sunday in French Lick."

"What'd you do?"

"A bunch of us waiters would all get high and go down and sit on the curb in front of the drugstore. The drugstore was the Greyhound bus stop, and as sure as shootin', old Blueboy would be on that bus. Guess folks thought we was crazy for real. And here comes Blueboy, stepping off the bus, and posing, and waving his hat, and shaking hands like he was some fool senator or something. Saturday night before Palm Sunday was like New Year's Eve in Babylon."

Flick glanced at Makepeace. "Babylon?" he echoed.

"That's the name of the waiters' quarters. It was a regular resort hotel itself. The boss owned it. Old Tom. It had a bar, poker room, horse room with a regular bookie wire—everything just like white. And the boss had it all there for his waiters and bellboys. Guess you're right, son. We did have fun, I guess."

But it had only been *Twenty years, twenty dollars.*

"Was Dave on that bus too?"

"Yeah, Dave was there. The last four or five years anyhow, but nobody much noticed Dave then. He was just a young kid that followed Blueboy around. Of course everbody liked Dave, but Blueboy made so much noise that nobody really noticed Dave."

"Well, how come Dave saved up so much money and Blueboy didn't?"

"Wal, son," Makepeace said slowly. "Every man is different in

86

the way he handles money. Now as far as Blueboy is concerned, I'll bet you there wasn't five dollars difference in his bankroll and Dave's when they hit this town."

"You mean to say that Blueboy could have banked the figgers hisself? Only he didn't want to? That don't make much sense to me."

"Exactly. And that's the question you should have asked in the first place. Dave Greene is a born banker. Me and you and Blueboy ain't."

"You mean Dave's a born gambler?"

"Numbers bankers don't gamble, son."

"Then what do you mean?"

"Well, going back to what I said before, nobody paid much attention to Dave because he was always with Blueboy. It was like Dave wasn't even there sometimes. If he was a white boy, folks would say that he was too busy, keeping his eye peeled for the main chance, but since he's colored, I guess folks want to call him greedy and worse even."

"Dave ain't greedy. That's for sure."

"Do. And personally I'd say it was a kinda fear that makes Dave different."

"Dave's no coward," Flick said stoutly, "You oughta know that. He'll take and fight his ass off if you get him mad enough."

Makepeace nodded. "I see what you mean, but this here thing I'm talking about is got no other name I can think of." He paused to think and then said, "Dave's as scared of being poor as the average man is scared of not being able to raise a hard some day."

"I don't care what you say. Dave's not yellow," Flick said.

"I ain't saying he's yellow, son. I'm merely stating a fact that Dave's got something inside of him that won't let him be a lot of things that most Negro men just naturally be. Like poor."

"I don't get you."

"Like the gas station back there," Makepeace said. "White folks said that he couldn't build one. Right? But Dave was scared not to build one. He had to build one even if it broke him and turned all the white folks against him and his bank."

"You're trying to say that Dave's nigger-rich, aren't you?"

"Well, do!" Makepeace exploded. "I just got through telling you that Dave ain't able to act like a nigger. He built that station to prove to himself that he ain't half-ass-nigger-rich. He had to prove to himself that he was white folks rich. Jewfolks rich! Now you understand, boy. I can't make it no plainer."

"You sure know how to get involved in psychology." Flick grinned, and Makepeace was once again impressed by the boy's smoothness. "All I wanted to know is how a young guy like Dave got aholt of so much money so quick. I figger he had over two thousand dollars when he came here."

"Well, Flick," Makepeace sighed, "all I can say is that you keep looking at the wrong end of the question. It really don't matter where Dave got his dough from because if he didn't get it in one place he would have got it in another. Dave's kind always gits. You can't stop them. Besides, I heard that his dad was rich and left him a good bit of property, but I really dunno."

"Mebbe so," Flick said.

"But, Kid, you are still missing my point." Makepeace sighed, realizing at last that he could never make Flick understand. He made one more try. "The point is that Dave come to the Ward and set up a numbers bank. Nobody else did."

It was well after two o'clock when Flick brought the Ford to stop in front of the flower shop. Inside, Makepeace met a thrilling sight. It was not only Blueboy issuing orders, but all the young men he had around him, busy, active, using their intelligence. His legs, so much like tree trunks, quivered with the pride of participation. Never had he witnessed such orderly yet hectic industry by Negroes.

The mystery of the billiard table was solved: it was for counting. Three men stood at it sorting, counting, and packaging money that was heaped high on the table. Each man had a cue-stick weapon handy at his side.

Flick asked Makepeace for all the envelopes of money he had in his pocket and Flick in turn handed the money over to Blueboy who gave them a receipt for it.

"Don't ask me what Blue Monday is," Blueboy said to Makepeace. "Just you and Flick come up to Booker's private dining rooms after the figger comes out." Then he turned to Flick. "Now take Make down to the countinghouse so he can get the picture all the way through."

In the street Kid Flick said, "Let's take and walk. I always do."

The countinghouse was exactly two blocks down the street from the flower shop. It was a nondescript frame dwelling, behind a rickety picket fence and a scruffy patch of lawn. Flick led the way around to the back door, which was remarkably concealed from all directions, partly because of a high board fence that enclosed the back yard. An old man sat on the porch enjoying a doze in the sun, but when Makepeace and Flick stepped up on the porch he was wide awake. He produced a key and unlocked the door, allowing them to enter the kitchen of the house.

88

For the second time in the hour the sight of Negro intelligence in action pebbled Makepeace's flesh. Three chattering electric adding machines were manned by a trio of young men. Deep concentration produced a stonily handsome cast to their profiles. Reams and reams of numbers slips were all about them. Their fingers danced over the keys of the machines.

Flick explained that the men were transcribing bets onto the ribbons of the machines. Thus the bets of each writer of each pickup were recorded on separate ribbons. If a slip played 241 for twenty-five cents and 865 for twelve cents, the ribbon would read:

241.25

865.12

When all the slips of a given writer were recorded on one ribbon, that ribbon was torn off and given to the writer's pickup man who marked it with an identifying symbol. The adding machine ribbons constituted the pickups' receipt. The countinghouse retained the orginal bet slips for forty-eight hours before destroying them.

Flick took Makepeace aside to a small hand-operated adding machine. He began to check every single numbers slip for errors, sometimes using the machine.

"This is where we get the real screw-ups," Flick said. "So far we have taken the writers' totals at word value. Now we check and see if he added any slips wrong. If it's wrong all bets on that slip are off. You see, the writer only turned in to us the amount of money the total of the slip came to. Now there might be a dollar's worth of bets listed on a slip, but when the writer totaled it he put down eighty-five cents, and all we collected from him was eighty-five cents. So the bets on that slip are off, and we notifies the writer PDQ that that particular slip is off. And it's up to him to let the player know that his bets are off before the number comes out."

"Do. But don't the better get mighty mad if one of them numbers on that slip comes out today?"

"Don't matter if he does. We can't give somebody a dollar's worth of bets for eighty-five cents. This is a percentage racket all the way from the git go. And nobody what can't add should take and play the numbers."

"What if the slips are over?"

"That's part of my salary. Say the slip is totaled for ten cents more than necessary. Well, I just play any number that comes into my head for a dime on that slip. And if it comes out I got me sixty dollars."

"Do?"

"I do mean do. All I got to remember is what I played and on whose slip."

Makepeace began to help Flick check the totals of the slips. When they finished they found that they had only two off slips, and since they were only a nickel off Flick said that he would make up the difference rather than go chasing around town trying to find the writers. Then he took all of his slips to one of the three ribbon men at the big adding machines.

After he had received his ribbons Flick went to still another machine and began to add the total of all his ribbons together. He finished with a sigh of satisfaction. He showed Makepeace that the grand total of all his ribbons came to the exact amount he had turned over to Blueboy at the bank, less the ten cents he had made up himself.

"Well, that's that, Make. All we got to do now is to wait around for the figger to come out."

The big calculators clattered one by one into silence. An ominous silence, Makepeace thought. The twenty men in the house now spoke only in monosyllables as they smoked and lounged. Their air of expectancy was a little different from any Makepeace had witnessed in connection with gambling. He had a fleeting impression that these men were waiting for the cops to break into the house. Suddenly an unseen telephone smashed the silence.

As ugly, hard-faced little man with freckles went into the next room to answer it. "I'm here," Makepeace heard him say. "Nine-four-three," the man said slowly into the telephone. Then the man came back into the room and said, "Nine-four-three. We're paying nine-four-three, boys."

All fifteen of the pickups began to talk at once.

"That sonofabitching nine has led all week."

"Seven-four-three I been playing for a year now."

"Hell, I work here. I ain't suppose to be trying to catch no damn number."

"I know I got it on one of these ribbons. I was just looking at it a minute ago."

Proud, awestruck, Makepeace watched the pickup men unroll their ribbons and search for the elusive 943.

10

In the two years since the innovation of numbers playing in the Ward, the pickup men had become the Block's glamour boys. Each pickup had a car, a steady income, and a higher than average intelligence. It was inevitable that they became the leading celebrities of the Ward. Around this nucleus of fun-loving, hard-living young men was a galaxy of pad and kiff owners, ribbon men, a few writers with very good books, gamblers and con men, and a few other figures of ill will, who together comprised the sporting life which was the Ward's nearest approach to an underworld during the 1930s.

Since most members of the sporting life earned their living by catering to weekend gamblers and drinkers, it was only natural that Mondays became their day of rest and relaxation.

Blue Monday parties had always flourished in the Ward, but the numbers had given them a new identity and impetus. The best party of all was always given in one place. Booker's Blue Monday it was called, and it was the pickups' very own.

Booker's fortunes had paralled those of Dave's numbers bank in the past two years. He had annexed the adjoining building and converted it into a hotel. The four bedrooms over the dining room had been reconverted into private dining rooms and it was here that the cream of the Ward's sporting life assembled for their gala.

The affair was usually started by a handful of hungover sports on Monday morning and lasted until nightfall. The revelers came and went all day long, sometimes returning again and again. This was particularly true of the numbers men who had to work on Mondays, and so the crowd ebbed and flowed.

As the Ward's numbers royalty, it was standard for Dave and Blueboy to put in their appearance at Booker's Blue Monday. These affairs fed Dave's vanity. Monday was his day of triumph, the day he appeared among his loyal subjects in his role as King.

With Pigmeat as their leader, the Vessey Street chicks comprised the greater part of the female contingent present in Booker's, but there were always two or more girls from the campus. These coeds were the sort of mavericks you could find on every campus in the country. They all laid claim to some kind of social or economic prominence in their home towns. They liked to think of themselves as slumming; they came to rub torsos with gangsters. Dave cordially disliked them and went out of his way to avoid them at Booker's.

At his first party, the daughter of a midwestern undertaker had grabbed him and insisted that he dance with her. She was tall and skinny with juicy lips. Aided by corn liquor, she had attained a degree of self-hypnosis.

"Hold me tighter, you dirty brute," she had gritted in Dave's ear between bite-sized nibbles.

The stilted words would have been laughable if she had not rived and thrashed against Dave as if in orgasm. After that, Dave was barely able to stand the sight of these "dizzy bitches."

Blueboy loved to hear Dave. "Here's a dizzy bitch only seventy years out of slavery and now she's so bored and rich, she's got to go slumming with a black-assed Little Caesar to get her kicks. A bored cotton-picking-society-darling. How do you like that batshit?"

Dave was standing in Booker's private dining room on this Easter Blue Monday, brooding upon the sins of dizzy bitches when Pigmeat came over to him. "Honey," Pigmeat pouted, "anybody would think we was strangers instead of old flames. I never see you any more."

Dave grinned. "You look too young and pretty to be anything old," he said. "And they tell me you're so rich now you only work when you want. So how'm I gonna see you?"

Blue Monday conversations were stupid, he reflected. He could even go further and say that all the Ward's conversations were pointless, but fixed in an idiotic, yet polite, pattern. In a few moments the pickups whom he had been seeing off and on all day would be coming in and shaking his hand as if they had not met in years. And this small talk between him and Pig had previously been scripted by the Ward's set rules of conduct. He and Pigmeat saw each other constantly. He still payed her rent and probably always would. Whenever he got very high in Booker's or the Lil Savoy it was Pig who showed up and insisted upon taking him to her house for the night in case he felt sick in the morning. It amused Dave that Pigmeat always insisted upon taking him to her place when both of their homes were the same distance from the Block. Some of these times, they accommodated each other, and on other occasions they preferred merely to bundle.

Pretty dimples signified deep concentration by Pigmeat. "Dave, honey," she said tentatively, "I been thinkin', and it's time for you to be settlin' down. You should have a girl friend . . ."

"I got me plenty of women."

"Not like what I mean, honey. I'm gonna try and find you a nice girl that's interested in your future."

"Stop it," Dave growled. "You know you already got her picked out and that I don't want her."

"You talking about Lila? Why I never thought of her, but now you mention it, I think she's just the type for you. She's so sweet and innocent. Ain't she? And she's the prettiest girl in the whole Ward. Gee, you're lucky, Dave. And I'm gonna tell her you said so."

"Cut it out, Pig," Dave said. "You don't believe that crap yourself. What would I do with a sorry little chick like Delilah?"

"You're no gentleman, Dave Greene. Lila is a lady. That's why you're scared to talk to her. But she's kind and good and wouldn't care. And if there wasn't smoke, there'd be fire, and you're not fooling me one bit."

"Do you know what you're talking about?" Dave asked.

The doyenne of Vessey St. knew how a lady acted on such occasions; she turned and slowly walked away.

But Dave did not know she had gone. He stood staring at a girl who had just stepped into the room.

Barely able to breathe, Dave watched the girl, waiting for her to move, but she didn't. Somehow he felt that if she moved, she would no longer be inhuman. But she remained still as her dark eyes coolly searched the room. When she finally turned her head, Dave stared at the purity of her profile and fell in love.

With both hands, she clasped a purse in such a way as to beckon

93

the eye to her breasts, sheathed in mannish sharkskin. Her hair was amazing: black, but silken. And although her boyishly bobbed hair was carefully combed and parted, a loose curl dangled outrageously across her right eyebrow.

Her complexion was ecru wax, smooth and clear. The fact that she was upstairs in Booker's precluded her being white, but there was no trace of Africa in her beauty. Yet Dave felt she was a singularly un-Nordic-looking person.

The coeds in the room gave a little scream, and then engulfed her, blocking Dave's view; but, he recalled every nuance of her strange beauty as if he still saw her. Never before had a girl affected him like this.

There seemed to be a negative quality about this girl. She was unattainable, therefore, fruitless; her beauty, a cold rebuff.

Dave assumed that when her icy eyes had swept over him and past him, they had also dismissed him. He wondered irritably why this stranger to Vessey Street had come to Booker's.

With no visible gesture of good-by, the girl abruptly turned away from the cluster of coeds and began to walk in Dave's direction. Dave was surprised to find that she did not walk seductively. She had a clearly slicing, toed-in stride that was beyond all arrogance. Her every step had regal self-assurance; all upon which she trod she possessed.

She stopped in front of Dave.

"I am Kelly Simms." Her voice was a bell of clarity, without accent. "Kelly. Like in Kelly Miller. My mother, I think, was a pixy." She said no more before she walked away, leaving Dave slack-jawed.

He did not have time to regain any of his senses before he was further confounded by the sight of Kelly greeting Blip-Blip with a kiss. Dave was absolutely positive that Kelly Simms and Blip-Blip were inhabitants of two separate and hostile worlds—and, yet his eyes were telling him that the two were dear friends.

Dave needed another drink, and he headed for the kitchen table in the corner of the room that served as a bar. Someone pressed a drink in his hand, and in no time at all he was dancing and talking and accepting the Ward's hospitality as if Kelly Simms had never happened to him. Then a crash of glass caused everyone in the room to fall silent. A few people rushed to the connecting doors to see what had happened in the next room.

Meanly, Dave was happy to see that Delilah had caused the disturbance. She had dropped a trayload of ice, 7-Up, whiskey, and glasses. Like an ebony statue, she impassively held her tray while

94

a good half dozen men scrabbled around her feet, gathering up the shards and debris. Particularly reprehensible was the sight of Blueboy and Blip stuffing paper money into Lila's pockets as if they sought to atone for some injustice done to her. This outrageous tableau was all Dave thought he could stand until a tiny voice in his ear whispered. "God, she's beautiful. Just look how she stands there. I don't believe that child even knows she's beautiful."

Dave turned to stare this unseen fool into oblivion. It was Kelly Simms. And Miss Simms was evidently a human chameleon. She now was a wide-eyed schoolgirl with voice to match. The sex goddess had vanished.

Dave gawked at her until his powers of speech returned. "You think she's beautiful?" With matchless unreasonableness, Dave always expected aid and comfort in his secret vendetta with Delilah. One look at Kelly Simms's face told him that he was at present without an ally.

"Does that mean that you don't deal in coal, Mr. Greene?"

Kelly's accusation had disarmed him and he could only stare at her. And he was guilty. Lila *was* pretty; only her accent was ugly.

"I didn't say anything about her color," he managed to say.

"That child is beautiful and you know it. Only the color upsets you, Mr. Greene. I suppose it's to be held against her that her mother was a good little girl when she went to work for the white folks?" Kelly Simms's voice did not become louder, it just seemed to transmit more venom. "That young lady is the *proper* shade, if you know what I mean."

And now the chameleon was an Irish bantamweight as she angrily brushed the cowlick back from her brow. "She is, isn't she? Isn't she?" Kelly kept repeating, but Dave was afraid to open his mouth. He had not the slightest doubt that the lady would slug him if he said one word. One look at her told him that she was not the slapping kind. In view of this fact she seemed to grow tiny. How does a grown man defend himself from a female midget?

But she would not let the matter drop. She continued to berate Dave. And a vast love for Miss Pigmeat Goins welled in his soul; he fondly recalled how that lovely lady would slowly walk away from all that displeased her.

"I wish I was black. I'd show you then," she grumbled.

Dave's mouth flew open. "What would you do?"

Kelly verbally swung from the floor. "See that? And you tried to say you weren't color-conscious. I hope some half-white bitch steals all your millions."

She was crazier than Blueboy.

"Shut up!" she barked.

"I didn't say anything."

"You were thinking. And I hope you choke on your black thoughts." She whirled around and left him. He was still not breathing properly when he saw her pause briefly and say something to Blip-Blip.

To clear his mind Dave decided to think about Delilah. It was less disquieting to contemplate her. And he found it was easy to hate Delilah; this was all her fault anyhow. She was the one who had dropped the tray and started Kelly off to war. And since she had thrown away a trayful of whiskey and chasers, the least she could do was to hurry it up. He needed a drink. From where he stood he could see that the makeshift bar was bare.

"Whatsa matter, Chiefy? Ain't nobody tole you that this ain't no wake?" It was Blip-Blip, and he was feeling very ready. He was holding two highballs and he offered one to Dave, who accepted it, although he did not care for any conversation at the moment. It had been pleasant hating Delilah and her whole dizzy sex; Blip was intruding on his miserable pleasure.

But Blip was beyond the heeding of any signs. "What you and my Baby Sister feuding about, Chiefy?"

Dave was taken aback. He secretly prided himself on his inscrutability. "Lila?" he muttered sheepishly.

"You fussin with her too?" Blip exclaimed. "Naw. I mean Kelly."

"Oh. Her. Yeah, I saw you talking to her."

"Bossman, I asts about you and Kelly fussin at each other. I ain't said nothing about me and her having a polite conversation."

"*She* was fussin at me. I didn't say a damn word to her."

"Damn Sam. Who woulda thought that? Kelly ain't s'posed to care enough about any man alive to waste her lovely breath like that. I didn't think you knew her even."

"*You* know her well enough to kiss her."

"She my Baby Sister."

"Well, I don't know her. She's crazy, isn't she?"

"Kelly Simms? Hell de damn, no. And don't let anybody from the Campus hear you say that."

"Why not? She *is* crazy."

"I jest tole you no! Kelly Simms is the smartest chemistry major that ever hit the Campus. She is a black Madame Koo-rie. Thass whut my Baby Sister is."

"You're drunk. That gal is so batty she's still got my head going round and round just from listening to her."

96

"Like hell I'm drunk. You're drunk. Ast Cokey. Ast anybody. Kelly Simms is a genius."

"Well, who's she go with?"

"What the hell has that got to do with it? Nobody."

"She live in the Barn?"

"You know damn well she ain't no local product. She don't look like it, she don't smell like it, talk like it, or dress like it. So where's an outa town chick gonna live except in the Barn? So that let's you out; you wouldn't even spit on a Barn chick."

"Somehow she just don't carry herself like a Barn chick. How come she's so much smoother-looking?"

Blip grinned possessively. "Kelly is one in a million. After they made her, they called it quits. She drives everybody nuts. Nobody on Campus could get a tumble out of her. When the hustlers here on the Block heard about her, they went up to look her over. Thass all they did was look her over. She didn't look at them at all."

"So she's a bulldiker, eh?"

"She look it?"

"She ain't too feminine-looking. Look at her suit, her hair."

"Kelly Simms is sex with a capital F! Take another look, Boss."

"So're all them Hollywood stars. But look what they say 'bout them."

"Sour grapes, Boss," Blip said disgustedly. "Now some guys figger that when they pats a chick on the head, her legs is s'pose to automatically fly open, or else she's queer. But me? I figger that a gal got a right to screw who she wants and that ain't necessarily me. After all, I ain't the only stud in the world. Fact is, be a hell of a situation if I was."

Dave smiled weakly. There was a small solace in learning that the girl was as unattainable as she looked.

Blip took a long meditative sip and then said, "I slept with her once."

Dave was seized with a fit of choking. Blip-Blip enthusiastically pummeled his back. "Went down the wrong way, Boss?"

Dave wiped tears from his eyes. "I'm okay," he gasped.

"It's hell when it goes down your windpipe like that."

For no reason at all Dave began to doubt Blip's sincerity. "Yeah. I'm okay now," he muttered doggedly. "So what about you sleeping with this chick?"

"Oh, yeah. That was last Christmastime. We was coming back from Cleveland together."

Dave was shocked. "You took her over a state line?"

"Hell no. Remember I had to go bury my brother in Cleveland last Christmas?"

"Oh. That's right. I forgot. I'm sorry."

"Thass okay. No harm done. So anyhow, after the funeral, I'm coming home here, see? I'm on the train, see? And this here Kelly is in the seat right behind me, but to tell the truth, she could have been sitting on the ceiling and I wouldna noticed her. I was that sick and blue and hungover. All I wants is to be left alone so I can sleep all the way to Washington. But anyhow she musta taken me for Blueboy cause thass what she calls me when she starts this conversation."

"She starts it? You don't?"

"Thass whut I said, ain't it? I already tole you I was sick and all. And the last thing I wants to do is have to beat up my gums with some strange chick. I got my back to her, see? I don't see her gorgeous face."

"So just like that you slept with her?"

Blip gave Dave a pained look. "Thass not whut I calls sleeping with a chick. We just sat and talked, and didn't even know each other then. Like I tole you, she thought I was Blueboy at first, but then later she says that she didn't know Blueboy. She just thought I was Blueboy, if you see what I mean."

"So just because she thinks you're Blueboy she lets you pick her up?" Dave laughed. "Is that all you're trying to tell me?"

"Right now I am trying to get you to shut up so I can tell you like it was."

"Okay. Okay. So you picks her up."

"Not exactly. That ain't the way it was exactly. I didn't pick her up, and Blueboy ain't got nothing to do with it. She only thought I was Blueboy." Blip paused to sort of catalogue his facts. He brightened. "You see this car we was in was loaded with college kids coming back from the holidays. You know, Lincoln, Howard, Union, State. Here, there, everywhere. But they don't faze her a bit. Seems like I'm the only roughneck hustler on the train and I'm the only one she wants to talk to. Don't ast me why. I dunno."

Dave tried to appear not too interested.

"And like I say: I've been lushing it up all the week without ever feeling the whiskey. But now I'm all hanged over although I ain't never really been drunk. In fact, I feels so low that I don't even bother to bring a bottle on the train with me. I'm planning to sleep. See?"

"Yeah. I know."

"Thass right. And like I say, she's in back of me, and so she leans over and asts what's the matter. Then she starts jiving that I'm s'pose to be the friendliest guy in the Ward, and ain't I afraid of ruinin' my reputation, and stuff like that there. Now all this is while she thinks I'm Blueboy. But when I tells her I ain't, she keeps right on talking. And pretty soon I'm telling her about my brother."

"Just like that?"

"Whadya mean, Just like that? He weren't hung or electrocuted, or nothing to be ashamed of."

Dave was apologetic. "I was asking about her, not you. I just can't picture this particular chick starting up a conversation with a stranger on a train. That's all I meant." Dave believed what he was saying although he knew perfectly well from experience that the aloof young lady in question was exceedingly partial to starting weird conversations with strangers.

"Oh well then," Blip said. "I see what you mean, but you're wrong. Kelly don't operate by other people's rules. She is what you call unpredictable always."

Dave heartily agreed with Blip. "Looks are sure deceiving."

"So any how, I tells her about the funeral and all that. And she sure acted funny like."

"Funny? How?"

"Well, damn if she don't act like it's her brother 'stead of mine. And then she starts going on about how at least I could go to the funeral. 'Twasn't as if he had died unwept and unknown, them's her words, not mine."

A string of curses came from Dave's lips. "That's a dizzy bitch for you everytime," he grated. "They just gotta figger the worst of you. Just because you are in numbers your brother is supposed to be lucky to have a decent funeral. To her we are nothing but dirt. Thieves and murderers, social outcasts. And why she come here today? I hate 'em all, the dizzy bitches."

"But she don't know I'm in numbers," Blip said. "After she finds out I ain't Blueboy, she still don't know who I am. Though mebbe I did tell her that I works for Blueboy. I musta."

"It don't smooth out no matter how you stomp on it."

"I dunno," Blip said dubiously. "But we was pretty high by then. Mebbe we just had a crying jag on. Though, when you come right down to it, looks as if she was crying more for herself than for me, but thass not important anyhow. What I wants to tell you is that when she first joins me on my seat we talks for a while. And then she gets up and goes back to her seat and when she comes back she's got a shoebox which you know is a darky's natural-born lunch pail."

99

"You lie."

"Man, you know I was shook, but it's the Gawd's honest truth. I jest know that this chick is too rich and sophisticated to be totin' a shoebox fulla fried chicken, but she got it, and I'm kinda disgusted, but I don't say nothing. Although I sure in hell don't feel like smellin' any cold greasy chicken."

"You can't guess a dizzy bitch no way, shape or form," Dave said. "Except you can depend on them to louse things up every time. Just to look at that chick you would swear that she rather drop dead and go to hell than be seen carrying a shoebox even if it had shoes in it."

Blip grinned. "I tole you that you can't guess Kelly. But, any-how, she smiled this crooked smile of hers—that chick can give a dead saint hotpants with that crazy kind of grin she got—and she opens this here lunchbox and what she's got in it is two pints of Cream of Kentucky in newspaper to keep 'em from rattling."

"Why you bother to tell a lie like that?"

Blip's bug eyes begged to be believed. "Honest to God, Dave. Thass all that was in that shoebox; two pints of whiskey. And don't ast me why she got it in a shoebox. I was scared to ast."

"So you two got drunk and went to bed, eh?"

"Bed. Hell, no. We was on the train, I tell ya. But later on I did go to sleep with them pretty tits damn near in my mouth."

"Gawaan," Dave blurted, wondering why he was frightened.

"I ain't lying. She cradle my head in her arms like a baby and—oh hell—you wouldn't understand."

"I understand English."

"But you gotta do more than that. You gotta see them wet eyes. She wasn't bawling and making a fuss, it was just her eyes was soaking wet and, well, merciful like. She was the saddest and pret-tiest sight I ever saw. In fact, it wasn't until then that I started crying like a fool. Dave, that girl was so beautiful and lonely looking that I almost ask her to marry me, but I knew that no matter how lonely she was she wouldn't want no clown like me to take care a her. But jest because I seen that look in her eyes before I went to sleep, there is nothing in this world Kelly Simms can't get from me even if I gotta go steal it."

"She could get all *I* got," Dave said.

"So when we gets to D.C., we gotta change," Blip said. "And I buys more likker because hers is all gone."

"And that's when you got her in bed?"

"Damn it, can't you wait? You're worse than a damn whore-master. I'm gonna get her in bed fast enough. Can't you wait?"

100

"I'm sorry, Mr. Blueboy."

"Okay then," Blip said, mollified. "It's almost midnight when we gets to town here, and . . ."

"You are one longwinded liar," Dave exclaimed. His words were a mixture of taunting and relief. "Time you hits town you had to shoot her straight to the Barn."

"That's how much you know about it," Blip retorted. "They locks the Barn door at eleven-fifteen every night, and nobody can get in or out until the night watchman unlocks it at seven in the morning. Satisfied?"

"Suppose the joint catches on fire?"

"A whole lot of lovely black pussy would get burnt up, I guess. Lessen they jump out the windows. The windows on the first floor are barred."

"Nigger education," Dave snarled.

"Don't they lock up white gals too?"

"Anything an educated nigger does, white folks can't do. So what did this chick do?"

"So me and my whiskey invites her up to my place and she looks me dead in the eye and sez, 'I already invited myself; this depot is cold as hell.' We takes a cab to my house, but I'm not sure how to play this chick now, she being so cool and tack. So I jest relaxes real drunk like, and lets her take the play. And as it turns out, that was the smartest thing I ever done. So then she pays the taxi and rassles me up the steps, and takes my key and lets us in and everything. I'm still playing drunk although I am damn near drunk, but I know what is happening all the time. See? She undresses me and throws me inna bed."

"Throws?"

Blip nodded vigorously. "Thass whut I said and thass whut I mean. Kelly's strong as a ox. Fact is, if you weren't such a cunt hound you'da noticed her walk instead of her butt. That gal is built like a champ. You can tell that by that easy-walking way she got. Her li'l foot kicks out and comes down where she wants it to. Now you take most dames; they lifts one foot and prays it comes down near the other, but not Kelly."

"Yeah," Dave agreed. "That's one of the first things I noticed about her. She walks like a fighter—real easy."

"Thass right. She does kinda," Blip said. "And then after she tosses me in bed she takes off her dress and hangs it up . . ."

"Hangs it up?"

"Wrinkles, stupid. Look at her now. I bet she ain't even got a wrinkle in her panties."

"So that's when she slept with you?"

"Yep. Thass it. She crawled in the bed like a little puppy."

"Like a puppy? Can't you look at that gal and see different?"

Unexpectedly, Blip grew angry. "I'm telling you like it was so you can know Kelly Simms. I can't help it. There ain't no other way to explain how she done it, but like a friendly li'l puppy dog. There wasn't a goddam bit of sex about it. And then she starts giggling, and then she's sitting straight up in bed and laffing down at me and sez, 'I orta give you a li'l bit, but you so drunk you wouldn't know what to do with it if I did.' And then she laffs fit to kill. And I hadda laff, too. It was the way she said it. It was pure friendship. Ain't no other gal on earth coulda said that to a drunk man and made him laff with her. And after that we was so . . . I dunno, but it wouldna been any fun if we had. So we jest goes off to sleep."

"What about in the morning? You wasn't drunk then."

"In the morning she wakes me up and she's all dressed like she stepped outa a bandbox. And she hands me this thing she calls a whiskey sour, and it hit the spot. Ice cold."

Dave hooted. "A beautiful chick like that brings you a drink to your own bed and nothing happens? Don't even bother to try to tell that lie on the Block."

"I know how it sounds, but it's the truth. If you knew Kelly you wouldn't have no trouble believing it."

Dave did not know Kelly, yet he did believe it. But he had no intention of letting Blip-Blip know that; he couldn't.

Blip smiled. "After that I started calling her Baby Sis and she loved it."

"Anything to keep you outa them pants."

"Dave," Blip said, sighing, "the whole thing was queer. I ain't denying that. I don't even claim to understand Kelly, but I wouldn't trade her friendship for all the pussy on Vessey Street. Now I coulda said that I screwed her and you couldn't prove I was lying even if Kelly denied it. But I don't feel like lying about it. But you can't understand that," he added bitterly.

Dave did understand it and felt sorry for Blip, even as he felt sorry himself. "How come I've never seen her before? She can't be no freshman. I been to games and things on the Campus. I'da spotted her in any crowd."

"No particular reason you shoulda seen her. Kelly ain't no sports fan. And she's a junior. And I already tole you she was a black Madame Koo-rie; she ain't looking for no husband at all. Much less one of these Block hustlers that ain't got no future, other than getting his throat cut ina Gawja skin game."

102

"Well, what future has a black Madame Curie got?"

"Ain't you got no foresight at all?" Blip exclaimed. "Her future's unlimited."

"Not if she's black, it ain't," Dave said. "She looks like a suntanned white gal. If she's so smart why doesn't she go up North and pass? And what she's doing here at a Block hustlers' party?"

"This is Easter Monday, stupid. No classes. And I hadda get on my knees and beg before she would even think about coming. And I don't know why she suddenly changed her mind and come. It ain't like her. But don't worry. She won't get all screwed up with none of these two-bit slicksters. 'Pend on that."

"Nerts." And Dave hardly realized he was saying it. He was busy wondering for the first time since he came to the Ward if he was nothing but a Block hustler. Kelly sure could make everything look cheap. Then, he tried to attack Kelly's evident superiority.

"She said something about her mother being a pixy. You mean that's her real name?"

"Yass. She's really Kelly," Blip said. "At first I thought they called her that because she drinks like a Irisher, but that ain't it. That's her given name."

"She's a rummy?"

"You sure are hellbent on running her inta the ground, ain't you? Well, Kelly's got no mercy on a bottle when she's in the mood and with friends, but she drinks like a gentleman. She don't ever forget who she is."

"Any dame that don't have mercy on a bottle's got something wrong with them," Dave said flatly.

Blip gestured toward the lissome Kelly, now dancing eccentrically with a schoolboy. "There she is. Does she look like a rummy? Like she got problems to drown? Ain't nothing wrong with that gal except she's got too much brains for the average nigger."

Soon after that Blip walked away, a little miffed. Dave stayed where he was and let his imagination toy with all he had heard about Kelly Simms.

"Well, Mr. Greene. I see that you deign to talk to black men." It was Kelly standing beside him.

"He . . . he works for me," Dave explained, hating the way his words sounded.

"Now that was awfully white of you to hire Blip-Blip," Kelly said heartily, and Dave feared once again that she was about to punch him, and so he said nothing, hoping against hope that she would soon go away and leave him in peace.

Kelly suddenly grinned. She did not smile, she grinned, and Dave

103

thought that there was derision in that grin. "Well, I'm glad to hear that you don't mind us working for you."

"I meant we've known each other a long time. You know what I meant," Dave said peevishly.

"Oh, come on," she said and marched out of the room. Dave followed her into the hallway and then down the stairs to the main dining room. Kelly led the way to an empty booth and imperiously indicated that they would sit in it. They sat facing each other. Kelly silently studied Dave for a long time. He was sure that she was pondering the joys of vivisection.

She frowned. "Long shall I rue this day," she muttered. Then she said, "Go home."

"Home?"

"I'll be there in five minutes." Her voice was full of amazement. "I guess you think," she said slowly. Then she got angry. "Oh, go on!" she snapped. "Hurry up."

Kelly had acted so possessive that it did not occur to Dave to ask her why they were going to meet at his house. As he walked home he wondered if she was going to play some kind of trick on him as she had played on Blip. And it had been a trick she had played on Blip, he decided. In one way he did not care; the girl was a goddess, and he wanted to screw her, but not unless she fell for him and wanted to be his. And he knew that was out of the question.

Dave didn't want Kelly Simms for a girl friend. Going with a campus chick was like being an animal; especially if you weren't a schoolboy yourself. Friday nights—maybe Saturday, too—she got a pass off the Campus to go to the movies. But instead of going, she takes a fast taxi to meet you in a kiff unless you got a room or something. The two of you have a fast drink and then the kiff owner shows you to a bedroom for a fast hour or so, and then you shoots her back to the Barn. And then you don't see her no more until the next Friday night if you are a Block hustler because the Dean of Women don't let the girls to fool with them.

Going with a Barn chick was for fast studs, and Dave Greene was no stud. Dave appreciated a chick's company just as much as he appreciated her body. All at once he began to yearn for the lady-like accommodation of Pigmeat Goins even if he was madly in love with Kelly Simms.

He let himself into the house and went into the parlor and sat down. Everyone said it was a lovely room; so expensive-looking. He was glad that he and Blueboy had spent a lot of money on the furniture. No matter what Kelly did when she got here, he wanted her to see how well he and Blueboy lived.

Kelly walked into the room. He wondered where he had found the sense to leave the front door unlocked. He looked at her shape and once more he was filled with a lust for her.

"Gluu'uck!" she made a weird sound in her throat and Dave raised his eyes to her face. He had never seen such an expression before.

Kelly began to chuckle, but she sounded bitter to Dave. And yet, she was still chuckling way down deep in her stomach. Then she began to laugh. She threw herself back into a chair directly facing Dave. Actually she was lying in the chair with her legs stretched out and apart so that he had to see the delicately tanned thighs. And he almost retched with desire.

But in a minute or two the weird sounds of Kelly's laughter drove lust from his mind. Her laughter subsided and once more she was chuckling but this time it sounded as if she was crying at the same time. Actually, the girl was hysterical, Dave thought.

Kelly stopped and sat up. "You cheap-ignorant-nigger-rich-son-of-a-bitch." It was as if she was reading from a prepared text. And suddenly Dave knew exactly what she meant.

The parlor was no longer expensive-looking, and Dave saw it as Kelly saw it. The room was a nightmare, something that had been jampacked by two drunken pack rats. After the drunkards had tired of stuffing the room, it would seem that someone's maiden aunt, myopic and tipsy, had tried to create order out of the chaos by shoving everything against the wall. There was an old gramophone with its big horn that Blueboy had decreed was an antique. He had dropped it in one corner and left it there. There were the Spanish shawls that the little world traveler had deliriously flung over the furniture to keep off the dust. Dave wondered why they had never bothered to take the price tag off the clock on the mantelpiece. There was a carton of pots and pans in the middle of the floor. There were four or five vacuum cleaners of different makes and styles. And boxes. Unopened boxes on top of boxes.

It was funny. Before Kelly had walked into this room everyone had always said how rich and lovely it looked. Dave looked at the shambles for the first time. He spied another price tag and shuddered . . .

Kelly got up and began a tour of the first floor. Every time she inspected a room she would come back and stare at Dave, saying nothing, her thoughts unreadable. Once more she was chill and un-

105

touchable, just as she had been when she walked into Booker's private dining room.

For the third time Kelly came back and silently looked at Dave. Then she went out of the room again and Dave knew that this time she had to be going to inspect the kitchen, and that was the one room for which he would not have to apologize. It was the only room on the first floor that he and Blueboy actually used. They did all of their entertaining in the kitchen and it was there that Blueboy brewed and drank his coffee every morning while they discussed the day's plans. No, there was nothing wrong with the kitchen.

Dave left the front room to join Kelly. In the doorway of the kitchen he paused and leaned with one hand on the door frame, waiting for a compliment. But Dave had forgotten about the two massive coffee urns that belonged in some hotel kitchen.

And Kelly stared at those two urns in disbelief. She clearly had not known what to expect, but this was too much. She seemed terrified.

"No you don't," she gritted and eeled beneath Dave's arm and fled for the front door. The amazed Dave followed her. With her hand safely on the door knob, her terror abated, and she turned. "Why?" she whimpered. "Why, Dave? You can't be that small."

Dave would have been angry if it were not for those wet eyes that Blip-Blip had described so well. And Kelly's lovely face tortured him; it was clear that she thought he had deceived her. Then it dawned upon him that Kelly was both frightened and disgusted because of all the stolen property in the house. "I'm nobody's crook," he said.

But in a moment he realized that Kelly never dreamed that most of the piles that looked like junk were stolen. She thought everything had been legally bought and paid for by Dave.

But even if Kelly did not know she was surrounded by stolen things, Dave knew and was ashamed; although, he thought of himself as more of a victim than a perpetrator. Soon after the bank started in operation the Ward's thieves learned that Dave and Blueboy always had ready cash. They constantly came to the house with their plunder and Dave and Blueboy thoughtlessly bought the hot bargains.

In a way, Dave was far more guilty than Blueboy because he had spinelessly believed that if he refused a bargain the thieves would go about the Ward saying that the bank was busted. The urns, however, were Blueboy's masterpiece. He had bought them and spoken vaguely of opening an all-night coffee shop but had progressed no further than allowing the thieves to dump the things in a corner of the kitchen.

"Why, Dave? Why?" Kelly asked again in a moaning voice.

"Why what?"

"Those stinking coffee urns in that kitchen."

"Well, they were dirt cheap, and neither me or Blueboy could ever say no."

Kelly was so disappointed to find Dave a man like this that her fright turned again to hysterical anger. "You low-down-coffee-loving-nigger-rich-son-of-a-bitch," she screamed.

"I don't drink coffee!" David yelled.

"Then what have you got them for, you goddamn heathen, to show off to your friends? You kneel down and pray to them every morning?" Suddenly her anger vanished and she was once more enervated and defeated. "It's not fair at all."

"Now just what the hell's eatin' you anyhow?" Dave asked.

"Those urns. It's those urns. They don't belong in a house like this."

Dave thought: Kelly was a friend of the late owner of the urns. "Okay. Okay," he said. "I'll see that they're returned in the morning. Who do the damn things belong to anyhow?"

"How the hell do I know?" Kelly wailed. And then she added, "I waited so long and now this."

Knowing that whatever she had intended was ended, Dave said, "Go on home, kid." His voice was gentle.

Kelly shrugged.

"Okay, Dave, I'll go." With the door wide open, she turned once more to Dave. "Those urns, Dave. You should throw them away. A coffee pot is big enough for any man. You're not Emperor Jones. Throw them away, Dave. Please."

"Oh, for God's sake," Dave exclaimed, seeing the light. He reached out and pulled her back inside the house . . .

11

————————

Dave wondered if Kelly was playing possum. Her snores were a little too light. He smiled indulgently, remembering last night. Kelly had been a continuing surprise. Although the first thing he had thought of when he first saw her was going to bed, he never dreamed that it would be fun. Kelly was fun. The little imp had kept him laughing half the night. Her brand of humor, flecked with profanity, was all new to him. He reached over and fondled her breast. She murmured appreciatively and encircled him in her arms.

"I thought you were asleep?" he said.

"When there's rape to be had, I am never asleep, lover." She yawned. "What time is it?"

"Early. About nine, I guess."

They lolled silently for a while. "Dave," Kelly said suddenly. "How much education do you have?"

"Why in hell don't you ask me what my name is? After what you and I went through last night, the very first thing you got to ask in the morning, 'Are you ignorant?'"

Kelly rolled over on her back and began to lead an imaginary band. "Fight! Fight! Fight with all your might!" she chanted.

But Dave did not think she was funny. That question had spoiled it all for him.

Kelly was still chanting. And Dave tried to tell himself that Kelly was not the girl for him anyways. She was too pretty. Too crazy. Too damn intelligent. Nothing normal, nothing real.

"Isn't there a goddam thing human about you?" he grumbled.

"Put your hands between my legs."

Dave laughed. He might as well get used to this, he told himself. He was a fool to think that he could ever give up this amazing girl.

"I got in three semester at Tennessee State before I quit," he said. But a weird kind of jealousy made him angry all over again. "What do you care?" he sneered. "You only get your kicks from an educated d—?"

BLAAP!

Kelly's reflexes were quicker than a snake's and even while his jaw still stung, Dave felt a grudging admiration. He had not seen the slap coming. He looked at her. Kelly was lying flat on her back, and Dave wondered if she had delivered the slap from that position.

"That hurt," she said quietly.

"You're damn right it hurt," Dave muttered. He was slightly demoralized, afraid to get too angry because she just might get up and walk out on him.

"Not you—me," Kelly said. "That was a little too close for comfort." Then she was atop him, kissing him. "I'm sorry, lover, but my conscience is still raw from last night," she said between kisses. "It's things like that we've got to get straight between us." A dry sob came from her lips, and for a moment she looked very sad.

Dave thought that she was sorry for her flash of temper. He tousled her hair; it revived her spirits, and he realized that she liked to be fondled like a puppy. That made him love her more. And while he thought about it, the fact that she had slapped him made him love her even more.

Kelly sat up and began to draw imaginary doodles on his chest with her index finger. "Dave," she said, "please let's get things straight. We started out like two very negroid clowns yesterday."

"You mean last night."

"Yesterday," she said firmly. "Way before that, in fact." She took a tremulous breath. "I was so scared, I can hardly remember."

"Scared, how the hell can you say that? You looked and acted like the whole world was one of your personal possessions. Damn if you didn't have *me* believing it."

109

"It was an act. All of it. Didn't you know that I was posing only for you?"

"What?"

"Honestly. It was all an act in Booker's. I was raised in a whore-house, and I was well taught."

"Damn it all, Kelly. You could drive a professional nut crazy with your damn lies."

"Sorry, lover, but I thought you should know." She smiled secretively. "Well, anyhow, a good friend of mine who is a lady of sophistication drilled that trick into my empty head. Once you catch a sucker's eye, all you have to do is stand perfectly still, and he'll hook himself."

"Well, you hooked me okay. I couldn't take my eyes off you."

Kelly put her head on his bare chest. "I had to, Dave. I had to write Kelly so deeply in your memory that every time you heard my name called you would sicken like death."

"I don't get you."

"I didn't want you. I don't think I want you now," Kelly said in confusion. "But I had to have you. Just like some men have to climb mountains, I had to have Dave Greene. I'm not very proud of it, but it is the truth. And all the time I was scared spitless, Dave."

"Even after last night and right now, I can't imagine a girl like you wanting me. But you weren't posing, Kelly. You were too natural."

"I gave you the front view," Kelly laughed. "Then the chill, still profile. Finally, the rear view. Nice legs, huh? But we were downright stupid last night," she said seriously. "Especially me. And now that I know I had no cause to be afraid, I'm mad. But I guess it was a cumulative thing the way I acted. And that's why I asked you about your education. It wasn't a meaningless question."

She was doodling again on Dave's chest and it filled him with a lascivious languor. He hardly heard her words. He listened only to the sound of her soft voice.

"Now there is absolutely no excuse for that performance I put on in the kitchen," Kelly said. "I tell you I was scared, dammit. And it was cowardly and stupid. And me the fearless thinker. Sure you could have hired an interior decorator and a maid, but where are you going to find a decorator in this town who would take on a job from two colored bachelors? Instead of appreciating your masculinity, I pitched a wingding because the place doesn't look like two pansies were shacked up here. It was an insult to you and Blueboy and I apologize. I'll never make the same mistake again."

He pulled her to him and kissed her roughly.

"Dave, if you don't stop playing with my titties I'll kill you—with all I've got."

Suddenly they were wrestling all over the bed. And Dave was wondering if he had ever been truly happy before in his life.

"Two-three-seven-three-two," Kelly shouted out of the blue.

Dave stopped wrestling. "How you know that?" he exclaimed.

"I tell you that we've got a whole lot of things to talk over, but you won't listen." She was taunting, and breathless, and beautiful. "For over a year now I have been trying to get up enough nerve to call you on the phone, but my courage would only let me go as far as looking up your number in the phone book. I was gutless, and still I had to be with you one time. So I finally conceived that crazy entrance scene yesterday."

"What's this all about, Kelly?"

"You seduced me over a year ago, lover."

"Cut it out and tell me the truth, will you?"

"But it's true, lover. That's why I am so mad with myself now."

"But we never met before."

"I saw you driving past the Campus one day and you looked so much like a man who had a definite place to go that I just wanted to go a bit of the way with you. I asked who you were, and although I don't approve of your profession, I still dropped my drawers."

Kelly speaks her body; all other girls speak their minds, Dave thought with pride. And she was actually crazier than Blueboy. And if he didn't know better, he'd really believe that she was raised in a whorehouse.

"We could have been lying here like this a year ago," Kelly said. "I'm pretty damn mad."

"But what were you so scared of?"

"I'm a minister's daughter," Kelly said. "I was afraid of you. I didn't know how you would act. They said you were a gangster. I don't want to be a gun moll. I'm a damn good student."

And it was easy for Dave to imagine all that the girl had to go through before she steeled herself to meet him in Booker's. Kelly had guts. He turned over and got atop her and kissed her for a long time.

"I guess you wouldn't expect a former college student to be in numbers," he said later, "but numbers isn't a racket. It's big business. Blueboy and I are in it for a reason."

Kelly serenely bobbed her head up and down. "I'm not afraid of you now. But even so, I'm not sure I want to go with you. You

111

think I would stand in the chem lab and let some idiot tell me that the moon is made of curdled milk? Lover, you're just as important to me as the sun and the moon, and yet I allowed the unlearned to convince me that you were a common gangster. Yesterday when I walked into Booker's, I came with the cold-blooded intent of screwing you." Her voice was cold and harsh. "I had to. You were on my mind too much. I was having daydreams. They were affecting my schoolwork. So I intended to give you so damn much and to demand so damn much from you that when it was over we would be sick of each other. Can you understand that?"

"I felt a little bit like that last night," he confessed. "I wanted you to go to bed with me, but I'll be damn if I expected it to be fun."

"Well, it didn't work out exactly as we planned. And although I'm happy right now, I'm not sure at all. But this isn't the last time, lover. I can't deny you now."

Kelly leaped out of bed and disappeared into the bathroom. Watching her naked body, Dave couldn't help thinking about a copy of the *National Geographic Magazine* he had seen as a kid in which he had come across some pictures of a Hottentot village. All of the women had funny-looking rumps; a little too narrow and more than slightly protuberant. Kelly's backside was not as bad as those women, but there was a marked similarity. Dave was delighted to find his goddess was comical underneath her fine clothes. Kelly, he thought, would probably not like being compared to a Hottentot woman, but there was no way of telling for sure. The gorgeous screwball just might look you dead in the eye and ask if you had expected all that fine floating power in an American-designed job.

Kelly was a godsend. And her imperfections were a godsend, too. If Kelly was truly as awesomely perfect as he had first thought her to be, her life would have been blighted and empty. And he had to be thankful that Kelly had taken the initiative. If she had not, he would still be a mute, if fervent, worshiper from afar. Suddenly he was struck with the possibility that Kelly might not be beautiful at all. Crazy as it seemed, it was true that when Kelly smiled she was not as good-looking as when her features were composed. So maybe she might not be pretty at all, he reflected.

He grunted with disgust. Why bother to analyze the points of a girl he *had* to marry? And why quibble about it? Dave had to keep that quick and thrashing body all to himself. No use in making up a bunch of romantic tales about the chick; he was marrying Kelly because of what she had between her legs. Sure. She had brains and plenty of them, but he would have had to marry Kelly if she had been a mongoloid idiot.

And Kelly loved him; her body had told him so.

He walked over to the open bathroom door and called her name over the noise of the running shower. Kelly stuck her lather covered head through the curtains.

"You gonna do it in the shower, too?"

"Do you realize that you and the school are no longer affiliated?"

"Nooky does things to your head, love. You sound right stupid." She closed the curtains.

"You don't think you can sleep all night with me and then go wandering back to the Campus whenever you get ready and the Dean of Women don't say anything, do you?"

Kelly's head reappeared, followed by her glistening body. "I forgive you," she said quietly as she reached for a towel, "but don't ever do it again, lover."

"Forgive me for what?"

"Demeaning me. Please don't ever do it again, because we will both suffer. I would never allow myself to sleep with you again."

"Demean? How?"

"Kelly Simms may love to do it, but she will never lose her head while doing so."

Her anger disarmed Dave completely. Her voice certainly demeaned *him,* he reflected. "Well, what can you do now?" he said querulously. "Look at your hair. It'll be hours before you can leave for the Campus."

"Balls, Mr. Greene."

She said it so carelessly and inattentively while toweling herself that Dave's temper flared for a second. Then he realized that he was more jealous than angry. Kelly's preoccupation with her toilette excluded him. He was, in fact, jealous of Kelly's attention to Kelly. And you can't get any crazier than that, he admitted to himself. "Why do you cuss so much?" he grumbled like a little boy.

"I told you I was raised in a whorehouse, Mr. Greene," she said as she buttoned up his fly.

She poured a generous amount of mineral oil on her hair and began to rub it in.

"You're a minister's daughter. You forget already?"

"Have it your own way, Mr. Greene, she said as she raised the other leg.

"You go to hell!" And he was more angry at himself than with Kelly. Any damn fool should have known that Kelly had some kind of weekend pass. Who the hell was he to think a smart college kid would get herself kicked out of school just for the privilege of screwing Dave Greene? And he should be thankful as hell that Kelly was in a lighthearted mood.

Kelly was now saturating her hair with Listerine. Dave watched as she picked up a comb and ran it through her closely cut hair. Every gleaming strand fell into its sculpted place. It was a beautiful sight.

"I'll be damned," he murmured. "A white gal can't even do that, can she?"

"Some can't." She laughed companionably. " 'Tain't like the day and 'tain't like the night," she sang. "It's Kelly's. God sure gave me a break when he passed out the grass."

Kelly looked like a well-scrubbed choirboy. Mexican or Italian, perhaps. The cowlick was now a part of a sedate pompadour, and he was convinced that Kelly had the cleanest face in the world, if not the most beautiful. "You part Jap? Oriental or something?" he asked.

"Not a chance. Daddy looks like a white man. We are Rhode Island Reds, you know." She put away the comb and assumed the air of a person reading from a tract. "Rhode Island Red: a name given one Negro group by another," she quoted. "Name may be considered derogatory. These tribal offshoots are an exotic blend due to inter-marriage between Portuguese fishermen, American Indians, and that newfangled contraption hereinafter referred to as a damn-fool nigger. The Rhode Island Red prefers the mandolin to the banjer but like his darker brethren, he is partial to knives, gaffs and sundry blood-letting instruments. He is indolent, but lovable. He could very easily pass for white, but is too lazy to get up and try. He is probably very stupid, but is too lazy to prove that either. Unquote."

"Are you kidding me?"

"From Springfield to Maine you will find them and you are welcome to them."

"I thought you came from Cleveland?"

"Daddy was called to Cleveland from Providence, as your nigra ministers would put it so deliriously."

"I swear I don't know when to believe you. All the different things you have told me about yourself just can't be true."

"Be sure and tell your friends, Mr. Greene, she said as she tucked the quarter in her boozum."

"Well, what does your mother look like?"

"She . . ." Kelly began only to stop. And once again Dave saw a fleeting look of sadness on her face. Several times last night he had seen it. Or rather he had not seen it. He had sensed it. It was like an invisible shroud that fell over her and covered her and made her separate from him. He was jealous of that shroud; it proved that they were not one.

". . . died soon after I was born," Kelly finished the sentence.

"Too bad. I'm sorry," he murmured, but he was more concerned about that pall of sorrow that had descended over her. He was sure that it signified much more than the memory of her mother's death. And there was no doubt about it. He was jealous of her sadness. She was so definitely alone with it. And it was nothing she said or did. It was not even in her eyes. But it could make her literally disappear from a conversation. Whereas other people dropped a topic, Kelly simply disappeared from a conversation, becoming an island while the world and its chatter eddied around her; never touching her. It was eerie.

He sought to bring her back to him. "So your father looks like a white man, eh?"

Kelly smiled gratefully. "He looks like Walter White," she said lightly. "It's embarrassing as hell."

"Embarrassing for who? How?"

"For Daddy, stupid. The bastard thinks he is the only true image of God, or vice versa. And it's embarrassing for people to keep coming to him and tell him he's the spitting image of some lowly mortal."

Kelly had finished drying herself but had made no move to leave the bathroom. She seemed not to care that she was nude, but Dave had one of his flashes of insight. "Kelly," he asked. "Have you ever stood naked before a man like this before?"

Her face crumbled like a monkey's. "You X-ray-eyed-bastard. How did you know?" she whispered, her voice breaking.

"I don't know why you're doing it, but ever since you walked into Booker's you've been trying to make me think that you really was raised in a whorehouse. But you weren't. And it just dawned on me that if I let your crazy talk faze me, I'll go nuts for real."

Kelly said nothing, and her shoulders sagged.

"Know what?" Dave said. "I know you well enough by now to know you won't lie deliberately. So from now on when I want to know the truth I'm gonna ask you point blank. Nobody else can tell me a damn thing about you."

Kelly stood stark still, naked and lovely. "That statement, Dave," she said, enunciating each word carefully, "dropped my drawers now and forevermore." She sobbed and stepped forward into his arms. Her tongue slid hungrily between his lips as if it sought to find some hidden strength and solace there.

And when she finally drew her lips away from his, Dave whispered: "And so all we have to do now is get married."

"Oh—God—no." It was a prayer wrenched from her guts.

And now once more Kelly was an island, alone and unaccessible. As his delayed anger rose, Dave suddenly knew why he had felt doomed the first time he glimpsed her. Only a moment ago he had exulted that Kelly would never lie to him, but he had forgotten that Kelly did not need to lie; she just disappeared from a conversation.

Perhaps Dave would have felt differently if Kelly had not seemed so guilty in her sadness. Dave was sure that sometime in her past Kelly had done something that now caused her sadness—something that wouldn't allow her even to consider marrying him. So why had she come to him at all?

Dave left her standing alone and went downstairs to the kitchen cabinet for a drink. He poured a drink and gulped it down. He poured another, and with the glass in one hand and the bottle in the other, he moved to the kitchen table and slumped in a chair.

It rankled him all the more to realize that he had suffered premonitions of this refusal of Kelly's. So why had he left himself open for it? And why the hell had Kelly come to Booker's Blue Monday in the first place? Dave's utter contempt for those who could not finish what they started made him hate Kelly.

But his second drink softened his attitude. That whimpered, "Oh —God—no," had been a plea for mercy, but it was not from him that she had begged mercy. Kelly had been talking to God. He grew bitter again as he realized that he had been ruthlessly excluded. That was the part that hurt the most. That, and Kelly's sadness. Those two things had expressed a finality akin to death.

And how can you be in love with a girl whose past haunted her? For a brief moment Dave had an urge to go back upstairs and beat the story out of Kelly, but bitter reason told him that it was impossible, and he was not sure he wanted to hear her story anyway. It was as if he preferred to be jealous of her sorrow. He began to hate himself.

Kelly walked into the kitchen. The look of utter defeat on her face shocked Dave, and he was filled with a pathetic sense of being buffeted by her and somehow for her. As he sat there and fluctuated between hate and what once was love he studied her drawn face and saw that her lips were still undaunted.

She came to the table and picked up the bottle of whiskey. With only a perfunctory glance at the label, she put it to her lips and began to drink steadily. After a few moments Dave almost reached up to take the bottle away from her, but something mean inside him

116

would not let him do it. He sat and watched, hoping that she would choke, gag, stop and beg for water. When at last she stopped drinking from the bottle, she pursed her lips and expelled a cooling stream of breath through her burning mouth.

It was sheer bravado, but Dave had to admit that the girl asked no quarter. Kelly had guts. He watched her from what seemed a great distance. The valiant shoulders suddenly squared.

"Is . . . was my body a part of yours last night?" she asked.

"What difference does it make?" He was surprised that he had been able to answer so cruelly, but he told himself that he had said the right thing.

Kelly's chin shot upward as if in delayed reaction to a blow. "Before you asked me to ma-marry you . . . just before you asked . . . do you remember what I told you? Promised you?"

"No."

"Call me a taxi."

It was an imperious command. No doubt about it, the kid had guts. And that was the crux of this whole situation. Guts is the wrong word for women. They weren't supposed to have any. Spunk? Yes. Guts? No.

But for one fleeting breath of a moment Dave had almost gone down on his knees in entreaty. Even now, if Kelly would explain, everything would be all right. But for her to suffer alone like this was to make him her pimp. And it was by Kelly's choice alone that he was in this mess. He got up from the table and went into the hall to call a cab. After phoning he punished himself by returning to the kitchen. It would have been better to stand at the front door for the short five minutes it would take the taxi to come from the stand on the Block.

They stood in the kitchen, staring uncomfortably at each other, never speaking. When the taxi beeped politely, they audibly sighed in unison.

Then Kelly took a deep breath and said, "I know I haven't been fair with you, Dave, but I happen to love you. I'm hopelessly in love. And that really isn't my fault." She paused before she said, "I know that it's wrong to offer only a part of myself; but we can't even talk about getting married—that is the way it has to be, Dave. I'm going to be at the University for a year and a half. After that I will have to disappear from your life forever. But there is one thing you can be sure of, the remaining eighteen months that I'll remain on the Campus, I'm going to spend making your life heaven or hell. You can see me again whenever you want . . . or try and forget me. It is up to you."

117

"Forget it." Dave stared at the floor. Her words were idiotic. They were an empty challenge. He wondered if she knew how she sounded. Kelly had left him standing there and he heard her heels tapping toward the front door. The tapping stopped.

"Dave?" Her voice floated back to him. "It can be a year and a half of heaven. You'll never regret it."

The door made a hollow sound as she closed it.

The sunlight made a pretty red glow in the whiskey bottle on the table. That was the day that 582 came out . . .

12

The natives of rural Arkansas are much given to committing homicide and mayhem, each upon the other, in the name of Respectability. These simple acts of violence are necessitated by a recurring need felt by the natives to reaffirm their honor and the honor of their kinfolk. It has been claimed that one Arkansan slew another during a philosophical discussion concerning the repute of one's hound dog.

This proclivity for manslaughter is not partial to race. It being malady that strikes down white and black alike. The disease would seem to appear in a more virulent form among the whites, but the same illness has struck down entire Negro families. Sometimes for generations.

Respectability must never be confused with self-respect; the two terms are antithetical in meaning.

From early childhood Professor James W. Greene suffered monstrously from this disease. And, handicapped as he was, he attempted many things that were humanly impossible in his struggle to gain respect from his fellow man. The professor's first month's salary as a teacher went toward the purchase of a pair of pince-nez to becloud his 20/20 vision in a vain attempt to gain more respect.

Without a doubt the professor's father must have suffered outrageously from the respectability disease. For there is no other explanation that would suffice as to why he did not take a pick handle and drive his elongated son out into the fields to labor as every nine- or ten-year-old lad should do in the professor's community. It was this twist of fate that made young Greene the only male member in his graduating class of five. The five graduates, having completed two years of secondary education, were granted normal school certificates and bade to go forth and teach. Professor Greene taught.

He taught in the one-room shanty of a schoolhouse near the place of his birth. He was sixteen years old at the time, but, as already noted, he immediately began to demand respect.

A tall youth, wearing pince-nez, who walks like Groucho Marx, is not the most august-looking human on earth. This is especially true if that youth happens to be a Negro and the possessor of a voice not unlike that of an indignant fishwife; but young Greene was a dedicated man and he earned respect of a sort. White merchants gave up trying to overcharge his monthly bills because he was a "contentious nigra." He was. The school board made several concessions and improvements at the schoolhouse of which he was master.

The board made these Christian gestures in the vain hope that the professor would shut up. His voice was so distracting that in one sense of the word, the man was invincible.

A year and a half of teaching convinced Professor Greene that he would be forever unsung and unrespected on his home ground. He married his prettiest pupil and journeyed to Nashville, the Athens of the South. The year was 1912.

He had come, the lad announced, to be admitted to the bar. Black Athenians were delighted and/or astounded; it depended largely upon their intelligence. The less enlightened believed, ipso facto, that the man was a lawyer and immediately granted him the title of "Lawyer Greene." Knowing it to be his due, Lawyer Greene graciously accepted the honor.

While he "read" for the bar, the sometime schoolmaster sustained himself and his child-bride by waiting on tables in the city's largest hotel. He remained in that capacity the rest of his days.

Lawyer Greene was astonished and provoked when he failed to pass the state bar examination, but in time his chagrin evolved into victorious grandiloquence. His pince-nez quivered and his eyes grew slightly mad when he informed his wife; "They'd a done the

120

same thing to Fred Douglass. And you know why? The answer is plain. White folks is scared of black legal brains. It's the law gonna set us free and equal some day and not no church preaching neither. Yessiree, m'am. They hated to do it. They just hated to fail me, but they had no choice in the matter.

"Do you think they wouldn't like to pass some ignorant black fool and then sit back and laugh when he tried to plead a case in court?

"Yessiree, I tell you that if you demands respect of folks they gotta give it to you. They might not show it in just the way you wish, but never the lest you gets it. Now just imagine that! The sovereign State of Tennessee has admitted that it is afraid to allow James Greene to practice law. Now ain't that an honor?"

For the next twenty years Lawyer Greene delivered this tirade in the church, the hotel locker room, various lodge halls, and in any other place he could corner an audience of one or more.

Lawyer Greene's speech was not illiterate, but the poor man had an ignorant-sounding voice that belied what sense he did have. As it was, some souls liked and applauded his oratory, still others were unnerved by this perennially indignant man who so much looked and sounded like a demented hen.

In all fairness, Lawyer Greene must be judged a stupid man, but in his very stupidity there was a kernel of celestial ignorance that caused him to be arrogantly unaware of his limitations.

A grotesque dynamo, he ran a rudimentary letter-writing service and gave quasi-legal advice to quasi-intelligent people. The more sagacious were steered to a white drunkard who paid him a sort of finders fee. He sold the Negro vanity books of the day. These were the autobiographies of contemporary race leaders and educators, and through the years he sold hundreds of these books to the unlettered masses at a profit. As the local agent for Mother Brown's Elixir and Rub he did much to increase poverty and disease among his people. These were only minor tasks in addition to being a regular waiter at the hotel. At night, before he went home, he proceeded to the offices of the largest law firm in town to perform char duties.

It is not remarkable that Lawyer Greene barely paused in his activities to celebrate the birth of his first-born, a son named David. The man was too busy preparing the world for the child's second coming. This being the day when the boy would graduate from Harvard Law School. The incident of birth was only a small part in the over-all master plan, and the father and son were strangers from the beginning.

121

Lawyer Greene left the boy's upbring entirely up to Mrs. Greene. To friends and neighbors alike, Mrs. Greene remained an unknown quantity. She was very young and very pretty, and she was the lawyer's legal wife; no other definitive statements could be made about Mrs. Greene.

Whether or not she was capable of mother love was a particularly moot question. The shrewder of her acquaintances often pondered the possibility that the child-mother might not have cherished the gift of a doll, or a puppy, or a bright red fire engine any less than a baby son. She was a bride and a mother before her sixteenth summer and was barren thereafter. Because of her youth, no fair-minded person could claim that her choice of a mate reflected in any way on her judgment; but, it was also evident to any fair-minded person that Mrs. Greene had been given every opportunity to escape. No one believed that the good lawyer kept her fettered while he was at work. Indeed, the only times the man came home in the daytime was due to an "appointment" with a "client." Whenever he managed a free moment from his many tasks and ventures he would loiter about the city's courtrooms. He was a courtroom buff.

Mrs. Greene was a tactical expert at evading the expression of a personal opinion. A beautifully knowing smile was her forward line of defense. When the more violent pressed an attack on the ramparts of her intellect, she would ingeniously counterattack with a phrase of lore from the mind of her husband. If, for instance, one should inquire about Mrs. Greene's health, she would invariably reply that only that morning the lawyer had said such and such about her health. Her mind was a territory she shared with no one.

Mrs. Greene was lazy as any teen-ager has a right to be, and sometimes she was lazier than that; but this fault in no ways interfered with the care of her infant. The child-mother could sit for hours looking at her son, never showing any signs of restlessness or boredom. In this respect she made an excellent mother.

In short, Mrs. Greene was probably the only person in the history of man suitable to marry the perpetually piqued lawyer. It must be remembered that Lawyer Greene's conversations were cruelly one-sided affairs. Fortunately, he never directed his indignation upon his listeners; his wrath was subjective and directed against inanimate objects such as the Negro, the white man, window panes, automobiles, newspapers, and sundry other articles that cluttered his existence. Lawyer Greene's personality as gladiator-lawyer-husband demanded a pupil-listener-wife. They were a met pair.

From birth, David had a ridiculously noble upbringing. His mother's near-morbid watchfulness precluded his gaining the empirical knowledge available to most toddlers. She never permitted him to learn that hot objects burn; that stairways can cause hurtful falls; and never was he lost. He was a totally unlearned child and was well on his way to becoming an unthinking youth by the time he reached high school. Dave simply did not have to face the problems other children had to face.

The first word the child actually understood was, "Daddy's." It was his mother's command of refusal, an admonition not to touch. Dave displayed a truly noble arrogance by immediately losing all interest in whatever it was that belonged to Daddy. Similarly, the first word he uttered was, "Daddy's?" If the mother answered affirmatively the child would show no further interest in the article, be it food, toy, or whatever. Strange behavior in a child, perhaps, but it is quite evident that little Dave's world was divided into two separate realms. One belonged to Daddy, the rest belonged to him. His mother had no possessions that he knew of, and if he had known of any, he would have probably taken them into his protective custody as a princely favor to a faithful underling.

Soon after Lawyer Greene became a steady waiter at the hotel, he very stupidly purchased a tract of abandoned pasture situated just inside the city limits, and by the time that Dave was able to walk, the silly man had built a modest home on this land. Years later, the more prosperous Negro families wisely decided to build in the suburbs, and many of them were obliged to purchase parcels of Lawyer Greene's worthless pasture.

But when Dave was a child his father's house was the only one on the land. Thereby, the princely analogy continues. Like any other medieval princeling, he had his yokefellow and mentor in the person of his young mother, who often wore overalls in the daytime. He was also friendless in a noble sort of way. Dave accepted his solitary childhood with regal stoicism and probably was never acutely aware of the fact that he had no playmates.

If Dave's home was his castle, then all who came to its gates were lowly subjects seeking favors. Hat in hand, they came bringing letters to be read, interpreted, and answered. They came to beseech his father to accompany them to the morgue, the undertaker's, the offices of irate creditors, and various other formidable places. In part payment for these services they would fawn upon the son of their benefactor. Mrs. Greene was much too young and pretty to be fawned upon by these illiterates, and so the child received much undue attention. Dave, so immeasurably unthinking, accepted this kind of behavior as his due.

It is quite evident that at no time in his youth did Dave think of

Mrs. Greene as being his mother. In infancy she had been his protectress; later, a boon companion; still later, there was the difficult period when she was an older sister; and then finally, the mother became a mild nuisance of a younger sister.

This illogical situation was due, in part, to the essential femininity of the mother. In conversation she invariably treated the child as an equal, and she shared small secrets with the boy. As time went by, she came to seek his advice in all matters, including her dress and the choice of meat for supper. Mrs. Greene asked Dave far more questions than he asked her, but asking questions was a conversational habit with the mother. She probably did not expect logical answers, but Dave never knew this.

Throughout his childhood Dave had no reason to question his father's professional status. He knew, of course, that his father was the breadwinner and an active, preoccupied man. In his early teens Dave was still an imperceptive boy, and he gave no thought to his father's career. True, he did hear scraps of legalese about the house:

"If I can get away from my other duties, I want to hear the summation."

"Tell him that I'll have the petition ready tomorrow."

"We'll simply have to take it to court."

"The parole board will listen to me."

It all sounded very boring to Dave, who judged his father to be a decidedly dull man. As he grew older, he did begin to appreciate a certain amount of social prestige due to his being Lawyer Greene's son. That is, he was welcome in all homes in Nashville, whereas, the sons of waiters in general were not invited to parties given by the children of professional and businessmen.

High school was a socially rewarding experience, as it is to most youths in an all-Negro school. Even more so if the student, like Dave, was tall, handsome, and not too poor. Dave was also a football player. The coach considered Dave to be an outstanding prospect in the backfield during his first year on the team. The coach subsequently came to qualify his enthusiasm. Dave was lazy, he said. Later the coach concluded that Dave was yellow, but he never voiced this opinion.

Prior to high school, Dave was totally unaccustomed to physical contact in sports. He simply had no playmates to come in physical contact with. As a grade school pupil he had won his share of scuffles and fist fights, but fighting was not athletics, in Dave's opinion.

When he reached high school age, Dave's mind was beginning to

124

show belated signs of being able to produce original ideas and opinions. Since he was a born conservative, he quite naturally was of the opinion that it was silly to allow other people to playfully murder you in the name of sportsmanship. He really did not like football.

Because that noble taint of the blood called respectability flowed in his veins, Dave had a curious football career. The disease manifested itself in one of its most insidious forms in Dave's case. He suffered a fear of ridicule and/or humiliation. This forced him to doggedly remain on the team long after he lost all interest in the game. As a mediocre substitute, he won his letter in high school, and all the girls thought he was wonderful.

Since his fear of ridicule made him reticent, Dave was foreordained to be very popular among a certain type of schoolgirl. This type of young lady is not a true cannibal—not outright—but she is closely related to the black widow spider. Very often she is referred to as: "popular" "the active type," "It girl" . . . and worse. Regardless of nomenclature, this predatory female considers reserved types, such as Dave, choice human tidbits. And while these girls almost never kill their males, they do anesthetize them to the extent that the male thereafter becomes exceedingly tractable. Dave was exceedingly popular with this kind of girl, who managed to seduce him several times before he graduated.

It is also a fact that these predatory females were the architects of the sexual pattern that was maintained throughout Dave's whole life. Never in his lifetime did Dave ever go with a girl who had not already made up her mind to entrap him long before he thought to bait his own snare.

Dave graduated from high school in 1929, and at his father's insistence, went to work as a busboy at the hotel. It was Dave's lifelong conviction that his father committed a gross and inexcusable impropriety that summer of 1929. It was as if a hunchback should suddenly take to parading about town clad only in swimming shorts. He was never able to understand why his father should insist upon revealing his nakedness to him.

There were no financial factors involved, and a busboy was only an apprentice waiter who worked long and hard for very little money. Moreover, the State College for Negroes had already accepted Dave as a freshman, and going to State entailed little more expense than attending high school.

Dave had always been entirely uninterested in Lawyer Greene's manner of livelihood. At this stage, it can be stated that Dave did know his father was not a lawyer, but that he was respected as

125

Lawyer Greene and it was as Lawyer Greene that he earned his living. Dave may or may not have realized that his was a rather confused approach to his father's means of a livelihood. It is very difficult to divine what went on in the minds of the three members of the Greene family.

Dave was still a bit of an unthinking individual, but he was not stupid, and after a few days at the hotel, he came to know that the headwaiter was not in need of daily counsel from Lawyer Greene; that the choice cuts of meat the good man had always brought home in his brief case were not gifts from a grateful management. These facts were mentally tabled by Dave for later consideration. More than likely, it was a subconscious sense of preserving his own respectability that prevented him from delving these matters further.

The climax came one day in the locker room when Dave overheard two irate waiters discussing his father. Several rows of intervening lockers prevented him from seeing or being seen.

". . . and so here comes this Lawyer Greene with his greedy self and all the time bowin' and scrapin' and a knowin it's my station. He a no-good banjo picker, dat man . . ."

Dave stopped dressing to listen. He knew that a "banjo-picker" was a disparaging term used by waiters to describe another waiter who "Uncle Tom'd" his way. He was a waiter who employed buffoonery and bootlicking instead of giving efficient service to enlarge his tips.

"So naturally when the man sees him pulling out chairs," the voice of the angriest waiter continued, "he turns to his friends and sez: 'Lawyer Greene heah is one of our bestest waiters. Ah know we gonna git good servuss now.' You know how dem high and mighty white folks sez things . . ."

". . . and I know exactly whut happen," the other waiter said. "That sorryass Lawyer Greene done run to the headwaiter and tell him that de man done made a special request for him to wait on him and his special guests. And before you can bat your eye he done taken the order and scooted. I know that Lawyer Greene. He do dirty all de time . . ."

"Trufe. And dat's stealin'!"

"He a lowdown niggah in a dinin' room. He a disgrace to the perfesshun. Stealin' bread outen anotha waiter's mouf like dat . . ."

"And I happen to know dat man . . . He's a good tipper and he got a party of four more wid him. It's hard 'nough to git somebody to sit on that big round table of mines and then when I finally do git lucky he go and steal de party. I oughta cut his damn throat, but then where I be?"

126

" 'Tain't fair and I'm gonna say this right here and now: that man is a disgrace and we orta get up a grievance committee. Thass whut we do . . ."

"He think he de only one know how to draw up a pettishun . . . and he ain't no lawyer no way. And dey orta make him call hisself James cause dat the name Gawd give him. Lawyer. Huh! Stealing from widders and chillun and makin' believe he doin his Christian duty."

"Trufe! Him and his countrified walkin' self and his breefcase and his nose-pincher glasses and talking about how much work he got piled up at the orfice . . ."

"Scrub work he got piled up in dem white folkes orfice he mean . . ."

"They is one thing I believe. Dese here white folks likes the idee of callin' dat black fool 'Lawyer Greene' cause it show how ignant we be . . ."

"Trufe! Den dey goes on back to de orfice and sez; 'That nigger lawyer gimme good servuss today.' "

"He disgrace us all. Makin' like niggers jes loves to serve white folks so much and even if they edicated they jes gotta take time out from they law business to come wait on white folks. Bowing and a scrapin' for de lovin' white folks . . ."

"Him and that fine house and propity jes like he a big-shot lawyer for real . . ."

"Bigshit liar. That whut he be! But I'm glad to see dat boy of hissen ain't like him atall. He right mannerly. Jes speak when spoken to."

"Trufe! That boy got mannus. He gonna make sometin outa hisself some of these days."

Soon after that the disgruntled waiters departed, and Dave crept from his place of concealment. The conversation had been no shattering revelation to him; it was a more awful process. It was as if the many pieces of a jigsaw puzzle had of themselves come together and formed a hideous whole.

Humiliation is the most terrifying symptom of the respectability disease. Lawyer Greene had been a fool to leave himself open to humiliation such as this, and Dave felt that his fool of a father had betrayed him. At this very moment there was born in Dave a loathing for the counterfeit and the makeshift that would goad him the rest of his days. The incident created a weird sense of honesty in Dave. He would have revered his father if he had been a successful bank robber or a confidence man. His father was the fell victim of ridicule and humiliation, and, to Dave, these were deadly sins. He eventually came to hate his father.

Dave's feelings toward his mother were more unreasonable. They might best be described as unfathomable. She was a co-conspirator with Lawyer Greene, in Dave's opinion. At thirty-one she looked to be only twenty-one and that, somehow, made her a counterfeit mother. She should have been fat and ugly like the mothers of his schoolmates. He relegated both of his parents to the status of idiot relatives. Neither parent had the slightest inkling as to Dave's mental attitude toward them.

That fall Dave entered college and managed to dodge football by becoming an extra banquet waiter at the hotel in the evenings. Banquet waiters received one dollar a banquet and very few if any tips, but three or four banquets a week made Dave a wealthy man on the campus. His affluence gave him status among the drinking students, toward whom he gravitated. Drinking students, by and large, tend to be thinking people the world over, and their thinking is rather communicable. Dave's career as an unthinking young man soon came to an end.

Fortunately, Dave was still malleable, and he soon became susceptible to the processes of doubt and reason. What dogma he had learned at home went the way of the doubtful respect he once had held for his parents. He was as friendless as ever; never having a confidante, yet he was a popular man on the campus. He had no enemies.

As a scholar Dave was mediocre at best. His fear of ridicule made him take the initiative in denouncing the curriculum at State. "A glorified high school" was the epithet used by Dave and his cronies to describe their alma mater. His group considered themselves too intelligent to strive for excellency in scholarship at so unworthy an institution.

Dave was guilty of another conceit: he allowed his drinking companions to believe that his pocket money came from his successful lawyer-father. This deceit never conflicted his sense of honesty or hatred for the sham.

To further maintain the masquerade of rich playboy, he worked more and more banquets at the hotel, finally reaching the point where he would cut classes in order to serve luncheon banquets.

In the middle of Dave's sophomore year, Lawyer Greene dropped dead on his job. This event could have been highly embarrassing to Dave, but he never returned to school after the funeral, thereby eliminating the necessity of having to explain what the wealthy

Lawyer Greene was doing in the hotel kitchen at the time of his death.

With cunning hypocrisy Dave managed to convince his mother that he was too ill to attend the services. He was unable to conceive of the bereaved young woman needing his aid. He was afraid that the assembled mourners would burst out into gales of wild laughter when they recalled the posturings of his father.

He was mistaken.

". . . and there may be those among us who will say that James Greene was a contentious man. The Good Lord knows what kind of man James was. He made him.

". . . but it was James Greene's fussing that made our city a better place to live in. He was after the school board, the parks committee, the charity board and he got us things we wanted.

"There are people here right now that would be behind prison bars if James had not interceded for them by going to the judge's chambers or by putting in a good word for them as he faithfully served that judge at the hotel.

"Dear family . . . loving friends. The Good Lord has seen fit to seal the lips of this good man . . . and we is poorer. But you know, and I know that James Greene was a good Christian man who has now fussed his way to Heaven.

"May God in His Infinite Mercy grant his troubled spirit the peace this world denied him.

"Let us pray."

The huge black minister raised his arms and prayed.

The dear friends forgot to remember the ludicrous gait, the briefless brief case, and the indignant voice. They remembered James Greene's battles and they wept.

And Mrs. Greene wept, even as her son wept alone.

And because Dave Greene did not know his father, he walked in fear of ridicule the rest of his days.

A thousand imaginary indignities were heaped upon Dave in those days following the funeral. People continued to come to the house, bringing their condolences, but Dave did not hear them. He only listened for the concealed mockery in their words and searched for derision in their eyes. One night, in his solitary room, he came to wish that Lawyer Greene had never existed.

Lawyer Greene's estate was another indignity; it mocked and rebuked Dave's shame. This was during the depression years, and yet the deceased had left insurance policies totaling six thousand dollars (one thousand outright for Dave). There was a modest bank account and nine pieces of income-producing, unencumbered real estate including the family residence.

The moment the news of Lawyer Greene's death reached him, Dave had held only one real desire and that was to flee. Now that Widow Greene was in comfortable circumstances, he felt free to roam.

He had only the skills of a tyro waiter, but locker-room tales of the rambunctious life of the traveling waiter enthralled him.

And so it was that Dave Greene may have been the wealthiest nineteen-year-old Negro to go forth to seek his fortune in the depressed world of February 1931.

When he kissed his mother good-by he gruffly muttered: "Be good now . . ."

The beautiful and totally feminine young woman smiled brightly and promised to obey. Those were the last words she ever spoke to him. She died two years later, cancer-ridden, broken in spirit, and alone.

13

Hot Springs, Arkansas, 1932.

Horses, craps, bingo, pokeno. During the season, you can place a bet twenty-four hours a day in this breezy little town. It's a wide-open but classy resort, with little of the degradation and violence found in other sporting towns. When the horses start to run, a flamboyant crowd descends on the city, filling it to five times its normal size. Touts, hustlers, rich men, poor men (but no beggars), hard-rock gamblers, and just plain tourists fill the gambling casinos, the baths, and the brothels. Everybody has fun except the extremely ill, and they don't count . . . they've already had it.

And to serve them comes that hard-drinking, devil-may-care-rascal, the traveling waiter. Traveling waiters seem born to their profession, a breed that just naturally can't be anywhere else but where the action is. It's the traveling waiters who fill up the cheap hotels on Malvern Avenue, the street the Negroes love and call "little Chicago."

Always, probably since the beginning of time, the morning train is met by a dark band of churchly women. Their smiles are disarming but their attack is stubborn. They latch onto the younger

131

among the arriving waiters, assaulting them with questions, cajolery, and their own brand of super-sales talk.

Once these young men are firmly in their clutches, these land-ladies begin their tales of sin, lechery, murder, and rape (yes, men get raped too) on Malvern Avenue. After they have filled the poor man with apprehension, they proudly depict the advantages to be found in their own sacred homes, where no "dirty" women are allowed.

One of these Christian souls seized Dave's arm and told him how nice and respectable he looked, while at the same time infer-ring how cloddish he looked since she said he needed someone like her to keep an eye on him.

Having once painted the portrait of vice gone mad, the women usually stand back and let the weary arrival make up his own mind. They wait in a silence full of insinuation; they have done their duty and now the poor man can decide for himself. He can thank-fully engage a room in a Christian home or he can admit to the world that he is a whiskey-drinking-poker-playing-woman-chasing-sinner who prefers to sleep in the very gates of hell.

When this particular fiend of heaven stepped back to await Dave's decision, he knew himself to be a coward. His mind shed tears; he longed to experience the horrors just described, but not a drop of courage could he summon to refuse the hag. He bowed his head in shame and waited to be led away.

A firm male hand grabbed his elbow and with terrifying strength propelled him toward a parked taxi. The landladies fell back in a kind of homage, and in the blur of confusion Dave heard a strident, take-charge voice saying: "C'mon, son, shove on through. You're too young to get bedded down amongst these gospel-hens. Avast and away!"

He entered the cab so hurriedly that he received a sharp bump on his head from the door frame.

"Sorry, friend, but one little lick on your pate is better'n having Sunday School lessons for breakfast," the man said pleasantly.

Once inside the taxi, Dave was able to inspect his savior, and he saw that the man was short, not more than five-seven, and was of that color often called mahogany, or black coffee. He reminded Dave of a tiny bull, with a round "scople" head with hair cut so closely the barber had even put a permanent part in it with his razor. The man was neat beyond description, but exuded too much masculinity to be called dapper. He appeared to be about forty-five years old. All in all, Dave was overjoyed with what he saw.

132

"Make it Kootchies on Malvern," the kind stranger told the cab driver. He turned to casually examine Dave, and then grunted rather pleasantly: "Pretty big, but just a kid."

It was an honest observation, but Dave was terribly hurt.

After the long, jolting train ride and his narrow escape from the landladies, Dave was stripped of all self-confidence. He took the stranger's statement to be some form of dismissal. He had not been in Hot Springs ten minutes and yet the entire town seemed to be showing him a marked lack of respect. He felt like crying but was afraid to.

Out of the corner of his eye he reinspected the stranger. The little man sat erectly as a child might sit when riding in an automobile. Whoever he was, he was partial to autos, Dave decided. Either that or he was too busy traveling about the world in ocean liners and trains to be bothered with owning a car. He also decided that the man could not be a waiter. He was apparently too well fixed by the look of his expensive dark blue suit.

"Those old hens meet the train every morning," the man said. "Only damn town in the world a man can't get off a train in peace. And the hell of it is that as soon's you rent a room from them, they makes you about as welcome as a six-foot rattlesnake in August."

The man's voice was without any identifying accent. He could have been a native of any part of the United States except, perhaps, the deep South.

"Well, you sure saved my life. I was scared . . . almost . . ."

"I know how you felt. Church folk are more fearsome than the devil himself. Fact is . . ." He paused to clear his throat authoritatively. "That's why they gotta keep going to church; they ain't fit company anywheres else."

Dave laughed giddily, enjoying a manly feeling of impiety. He had rarely heard church people ridiculed like that before, the irreverent daring of this man thrilled him. He wondered why the man had not introduced himself, and concluded that the man was so well known that he assumed Dave would know his name.

"I'm Dave Greene from Nashville," he offered.

"Shake, Davey-boy. I'm Blueboy Harris, the answer to all yaller gals' prayers and the best friend Table-Waiting-Sam ever had."

"Who's he?" Dave was sure that "Sam" was a fictitious character, but he wanted to keep the conversation going and he could think of nothing better to say.

Blueboy rolled his eyes heavenward. "Help us this day. You a waiter, ain't you? You ain't a cripple and you're too young and

133

clean-looking for syph. So what you come here for if you ain't a friend of Table-Waiting-Sam? You ain't dirty! This is Hot Springs. You either comes for a reason or to work the season. Now don't tell me you just stopped off to take a bath!"

Fearfully tongue-tied, Dave wondered if this eccentric expected an answer, but before he could frame a reply the little man had started to pray. ". . . and help me to keep this little lamb unshorn and succored. And don't let nobody touch a hair on his stupid little haid. Amen."

The taxi turned into Malvern and drew to a stop before a two-story building. Between two store fronts, a broad staircase led up to the second floor.

Dave did not chance an invitation; he got out first and tried to pay the cabdriver, but Blueboy brushed his money aside and paid the fare himself. Turning to the broad stairs, he let out a whoop and vaulted up the steps.

"Come and get it, Kootchie!" Blueboy bellowed as soon as he reached the second floor.

At the head of the stairs was a common room . . . it was too wide to be called a corridor. About a dozen doors faced onto it. From the one door with a glass panel came a tall, extremely pleasant-looking girl.

"Hush that fuss you clean-headed little rascal you," she cried, rushing into Blueboy's arms. Or rather, since she was a good six inches taller than Blueboy, she encircled him in her arms. After the embrace, she stepped back, and Dave was thrilled to see that Kootchie was devouring his companion with her eyes. "I do declare: the season's here cause the *reason's* here!"

Blueboy place a possessive arm about Dave's shoulders. "This here's Dave Greene from N'Yawk," he said proudly.

Kootchie politely dropped her glance "Pleasure, Mr. Greene," she said in a hushed tone of voice. Quickly she turned to Blueboy. "He's really from N'Yawk?"

"Only woman I lies to is my maw and that's only cause I'm scared to tell the truth."

Shudders of joy and doubt took turns going up and down Dave's spine. It was a compliment to have Blueboy introduce him as a friend, but that New York bit frightened him. Dave had never met a native New Yorker, much less been there. And then there was Dave's own sense of honesty to be reckoned with. Dave Greene, Harlemite, was too close for comfort to his father's imaginary title, James Greene, attorney-at-law. What would Kootchie think of him

134

when she found out the truth? It never occurred to Dave that he and Kootchie wouldn't be friends.

"Well, Mister Dave, you know you can't expect us to have things real nice like in N'Yawk, but we gonna keep clean what we got for you and . . ."

"I said he lived in N'Yawk! What in hell a man with his own apartment on Sugar Hill know about what to expect in the line of hotel rooms?" Blueboy screamed at Kootchie.

Dave wondered how any man could scream without sounding womanish but Blueboy managed it somehow. Apparently the man could manage anything with ease and aplomb.

"Blueboy, you little black spasm, if you don't stop making me look silly in front of my guests . . ."

"I ain't making you look like nothing and if what you looks like is silly, then you can give me a little piece of silly anytime you please." He gave the girl a hearty thwack across her shapely backside. Laughing, Kootchie skittered away to unlock the door of a corner room and permitted the two men to enter first.

"You gonna share?" she asked in a sudden afterthought. "Cause if you ain't I don't know what I'm gonna do."

"Makes me no difference long as you got two beds," said Blueboy.

Dave's heart palpitated like a girl's. Blueboy had not even paused to consult him! It was the first time in his life he had been accepted by a man who was not obliged to cater to him in some way or the other. From that moment on, there was nothing humanly possible for Blueboy to do that could alienate Dave's respect and affection for him.

Blueboy and Kootchie were arguing like two fishwives. They had to be good friends, Dave observed with a twinge of envy. They made each other happy. He firmly believed that true friendship was the ability of the two friends to enjoy each other, to amuse each other. Which is more than likely the major reason he had never had a close friend . . . he had always looked for too much seriousness from all his acquaintances.

While his new-found friends chattered, he inspected the room. It was large and airy and clean, with windows on two sides. A lovely room, he decided. The furniture was not too worn, and the beds looked comfortable.

"When the hell is Buddy gonna put running water in these crumby rooms?" Blueboy demanded.

Kootchie tried to look severe, but her smile would not go down. She pointed her finger in a vain attempt at reprimand. "Blueboy, you know full well that Buddy leases from Mr. Poli as is . . ."

She stopped and stared, then doubled up with laughter. "Neither one of you children shaves anyhow . . ." she gasped between outbursts.

Blueboy, middle-aged and beardless, bristled like a terrier. "How the hell you gotta know so much? I got skin all yaller gals loves to touch. You jealous cause that rough-ass nigger you got rubs an inch a skin off your silly face every time he kisses you good-by. And I wish I had me some of my women here to whup your haid cause you ain't got no sense no ways. And you don't know how to treat your guests . . . for two cents I'd go down the street to the Woodsmen's Hotel! Be gone! Git! Go and be black! You no-good Hot Springs trollop!"

Kootchie's laughter was worse than any reply. When she stopped laughing she extended her open hand.

Blueboy glared. "What in hell you want now? You ain't no bellhop! We toted our own bags. Git!"

"If you and your N'Yawk friend think Kootchie ain't gonna have a drink on you, then you're crazier than I thought, Blueboy. And I'll toss your raggedy suitcase out the window if you don't."

"Git out!" Blueboy screamed.

"I ain't."

"Git out!"

Kootchie stood her ground. "Make me," she taunted him. "I just dare you, and I'll tell Buddy!"

"Buddy'll gimme a free season's rent if I killed you for him."

"Okay, then. Since you are so cheap I'm gonna buy me and Dave a drink and your eyes may shine and your teeth may grit, but nary a drop of Kootchie's likker do you git. You hear me?"

"The ladies with whom I associate wait to be invited to have a drink."

"My name's Kootchie. I drinks when I wants, not when you wants, or Pappy wants, but when Texas Kootchie wants. You hear that?" She advanced ferociously. "Now do I get my drink or do I have to throw you outa my hotel! You're undesirable anyhow. You talk too loud. You scare my lady guests."

Dave gaped at Blueboy, who was standing perfectly still. But, by some mystery, when you looked at his face you were quite positive that he was stomping around in circles.

"Give her a dollar, Davey," Blueboy said in a hoarse voice. "I'll be damn if I take a single penny outa my pocket to buy this dizzy dame a drop."

"No you don't neither." She picked up Blueboy's suitcase and strode to the window with it.

Blueboy screamed a mighty flow of invective that only made the girl smile more triumphantly. "Okay," he grumbled at last. He threw some money on the bed. "Bring us two pints of rotgut while me and Davey washes up a little."

"Shoulda gimme it in the first place and saved all that lip for someone that's afraid of you." She was gone before Blueboy could reply.

Turning to Dave, the little man took a deep breath and launched into a lecture that never really ended until the day he died. "You got something that most young boys don't have nowadays, Davey, but don't ask me what it is cause I don't know. Maybe it's that you have sense enough to shut up when you don't know the answer. It could be just that simple."

"But you messed me up, Blueboy. Honestly. I never even been to New York. How'm I gonna make believe I'm some Harlem pimp?"

"Don't worry about it. These clowns ain't been there either. Now in the long run it's gonna make people like you. They gonna say that even if you is from the Big Apple you don't try to make out like you knows everything. The biggest thrill a yokel can have is to help a big-time city slicker. You're my boy, Davey. I'm gonna see that nobody messes over you. You're young, but I can see you ain't so young that you run away from home. You ain't got no hunted look. Now take all your duds and things outa your bag and send all your suits to the cleaners."

"But they're all clean and I got an iron and pressing cloth . . ."

"I know you ain't the type to pack dirty duds, but this is a small town. Fast but small. I want you to let these folks know that you didn't come here all raggedy-assed and broke. You got any money?"

"Not much, about seventy-five dollars, I guess."

Blueboy whistled admiringly. "Not much, eh? Boy, there's plenty waiters works the season and don't have that much in their jeans when they boards the train on getaway day. Some only got the fare to Memphis and the Peabody. Of course those are the sorry-assed ones, but sometimes a smart waiter gets weak-headed and plunges on some dog that ain't worth a damn in the Derby, but somehow you ain't weak-headed. You're weak kinda, but not in the head. Fact is, you ain't no gambler. Not for real. Neither is you selfish; but you are a money man. Now a gambler ain't no money man. They might tell you they are, but they ain't. Most of them deep down inside likes to go broke. It's like self-flagellation." Blueboy proudly waited for Dave to assimilate that word. "Now

137

don't ask me why cause I don't know, but that's the way it is. Now I can just look at you and see that you are scared to death of going broke."

The accuracy of Blueboy's observations jarred Dave from his usual reticence. "Only a fool would refuse to listen to you, Blueboy. Anybody can tell that you been somewheres and learned a whole lot." It was a vow of allegiance, not a statement.

"That I have. That I have. I ain't no wise man, but I been everywhere and done everything a black man can do in this white bastards' world. And you are welcome to any facts I mighta picked up."

"You really been all over the world?"

"Navy. Twenty years. Woulda been there yet, but it burned my ass to see them refuse our boys and beg foreigners to be messmen. I decided I'd had enough, and nobody begged me to stay."

"Somebody told me you had to be a Filipino or something to get in the Navy now. I didn't believe them."

"It's true, son. But don't worry; we got more important things to think about than who gets to shine some cracker's shoes. Now when that last nag runs at Oaklawn, you gotta have your getaway money in your jeans, like I said. Because that's all there is; there ain't no more."

Dave appeared so bewildered that Blueboy went on. "I mean that when the last horse race is over there's no more work, so most folks go straight to the railroad station. They've already sent their baggage ahead. So if you don't get it and save it while the gittings good, you are stranded here and you can starve. Maybe you ends up on the pea farm for vagrancy. If you gonna be a sad-assed waiter, you might as well find it out now and on getaway day you can start hiking back to Nashville. I'd be kinder to you that way than taking you any further away from home than you are now."

"I'm never going back to Nashville as long as I live!" Dave wondered why he had made the statement. He did not dislike his home town, and for the life of him he could not say why it had become so important that he never return.

"Play and save. Some can and some can't," Blueboy was saying as Kootchie knocked at the door.

"Here's your rotgut," she said to Blueboy. She tossed two un-labeled pint bottles on the bed, took three glasses from atop the dresser, and went to rinse them out.

Dave crossed over to the window, and while ostensibly looking

138

out, he prayed, prayed that this friendship would last. It was the first time he had prayed since his father had died.

"As I was saying about your clothes," Blueboy resumed. "You gotta do the needless sometimes. It's sorta like giving the low and the ignorant their due. Seeing is believing, they thinks, so let 'em see. Besides we got this here recession on, and some hotels might not work a full crew this season. If so, the headwaiters are gonna pick the more likely-lookin' waiters that can hustle. Not no lazy, drunk, and sloppy-dressed bums. Them kind only gets hired when help is short. And where the hell is Kootchie with those glasses?"

The magnitude of hero worship reflected on Dave's face created a doubt in Blueboy's mind. Maybe the boy was stupid after all. It never occurred to Blueboy that Dave had never had a friend or confidante before in his life. He probably would not have believed it if someone had told him so. Damn if this boy don't look just as happy as if he'd died and went to heaven last night, Blueboy reflected.

Kootchie returned with the clean glasses, and the three of them lounged and drank contentedly. Kootchie had stopped dueling with Blueboy, and they now were busy talking about old times.

While in college, Dave had not associated with the truly carefree. His drinking companions had a knack for taking themselves very seriously and drank by rote, mainly to keep up their position on campus as "drinking men." But Blueboy and Kootchie were rackety elves of people. They talked, played, and drank exactly as they pleased. They knew how to laugh at this world. Dave was sure that they would also laugh at him, as soon as they got to know him. And he would rather die than be laughed at by these two.

Without warning, a severely handsome woman strolled into the room. Laughter vanished as all three stared at the intruder. Nobody spoke, and Dave was shocked to see that Blueboy had lost all of his animation. He sat timidly on the edge of the bed and Dave thought he looked like a bad little boy unwillingly submitting to the careful inspection of a severe schoolmarm. Blueboy was not Blueboy at all now, and Dave was horrified.

The intruder's appearance was striking and she would have caused a reaction in any room she entered, but Dave was unprepared for the oppressive silence of Blueboy and Kootchie. The stranger was definitely a Negro, but Dave had seen no other colored female like this before. Her hair was exquisitely groomed, yet it was not "good hair"; it had to be straightened, but she'd had a beautiful job done on it. Her rich brown skin had undertones of deep red, and it was incomparably smooth. Everything about her was smooth and expensive-looking. She was the first colored woman Dave had ever seen who dressed exactly like a rich white woman. No different.

With careless indifference the lady exhaled a cloud of smoke into Blueboy's face. She was too lady-like to have done it on purpose; Dave was sure of that. Her mind must have been on other things, but when she calmly took the glass of corn whiskey from Blueboy's hand and turned it up to her lips, Dave gasped. He could not imagine what Blueboy would do to her now.

This woman was so cool, so unconcerned, so . . . masculine. Yes, Dave decided, that was the word for her. This epitome of womanly beauty subtly called to mind all of the masculine descriptives: suave, debonair, sophisticated, handsome (not pretty), and . . . arrogant!

The silent and statuesque beauty finished the drink and sighed contentedly. It was the first expression other than arrogant boredom she had registered since she entered the room.

Blueboy cleared his throat, "Jawja Brown," he said softly, "you ain't nekkid."

Georgia Brown ignored him.

"The only woman ever took a glass outa my hand without saying something was lying there beside me in bed and she was buck nekkid."

"Yours is such a kind invitation . . ." Georgia Brown's voice was as warm and velvet as sin. All sin! It thrilled up and down Dave's spine; it whispered all about whiskey, and soft thighs, and clean beds with the lights burning low. Everything nice and soft. In comparison to Georgia Brown Mae West was just another gal who beat the damn bass drum in the Salvation Army band. No woman had the right to have a voice like that, Dave thought. It just caused violence among men.

He nearly jumped out of his seat when the cool calm Georgia Brown took a couple of steps toward Blueboy and screamed at the top of her lungs: "Kiss me, you crazy black bastard!"

Dave had never dreamed that two people could be so happy to see each other as Blueboy and Georgia Brown. They were lost to Dave and Kootchie and were in a world of their own. Never had Dave heard such profanity. Oaths bounced off the walls like pistol shot. He reverently watched and listened. He noted the holy look of joy in the eyes of Georgia Brown. He told himself that he was too bashful to ever get a woman to look at him like that.

"Oh, Little-Boy-Blue," Georgia said in a husky whisper. "You look so good I could cry."

140

"Hard-hearted as you is, you wouldn't cry at your own funeral," said Blueboy. And his voice was gruff and choked.

Dave's head teemed with unasked questions: Was this the nearest two sophisticates could come to speaking endearments? With teen-age intuition, he detected a deep and unusual link between the two. But was it love? It could not be: No two lovers could be so profane, and yet . . .

Blueboy put his arm around Dave and drew him close. "This here's my protégé, Dave Greene, and this here's *the* Miss Georgia Brown!"

It had to be her stage name, but Dave could not recall any great show person of that name. Of course there was the song of that title, but . . .

"Jawja Gal, how much pork you toting this year?" Blueboy asked abruptly.

"Only three this year."

"Don't seem like hardly enough. Recessions here . . . prices way down. You gonna catch hell, if you ask me . . ."

Georgia chuckled. "Needless to say, I wouldn't ask, but I'm not worried. What I do have is young, strong, and pretty. Who could ask for more? One looks white; I could send her right through the front door of the Arlington . . . no questions asked. But she's got the brains of a fruit fly, and when drinking, she can get twice as fruity."

"You and your dimwit whores," Blueboy grunted.

"All whores are stupid," Georgia said equably. "That's why they need me to manage them, and that's how I make it. If they had brains they wouldn't need me. I'd go broke yesterday."

"But do you always have to tote the very dumbest baggage on earth?"

"You're talking to hear yourself talk, Blueboy. My girls are no dumber than I allow them to be, and don't you forget it. And when all is said and done, Georgia Brown's girls have a rep . . . they give good service . . . so give me credit once in a while my dark but handsome friend . . . And they are clean, and, above all else, they are ladies while they work!"

"Ladies," Blueboy mimicked and sniffed primly. "Oh well. Me and Davey got a few coppers in our pockets. We'll buy 'em a drink or two. What say, Davey? . . ."

"Wonderful," Georgia said. With feline grace she rose from her chair and went to the open door. "Hey there," she called down the corridor. "Come and get it and see Gawd's gift to naughty

141

girls at the same time!" She returned to her seat and crossed her legs—the act was a work of art.

Dave believed he *understood* most of the conversation between Blueboy and Georgia but that the conversation was a lie. Georgia Brown was too smooth and handsome to take poor girls away from their homes and make prostitutes out of them. She was rich— it was written all over her—she did not have to stoop to such things. All the same he would feel a whole lot better as soon as Blueboy got a chance to explain things to him. There had to be an answer.

"Oooooh! Men!" Three voices cooed in unison. Dave stared at the three girls who had just entered the room. Each wore a see-through negligee over a bra and very brief panties. Extremely high-heeled shoes were their only other clothing.

Georgia, every inch the lady, made the introductions. But when she sat down she said, "That damn Blueboy is the best cut-buddy I ever had and whatever he says, goes."

"Blueboy?" the girls cooed, and Dave was positive that the trio effect was practiced; it was too pat.

Blueboy glowed. "Thass me, and please be seated before you break something."

"Everybody talks about Blueboy Harris and we never see him," the one named Didi panted. "I was beginning to think you was make believe."

Dave saw that she was practically chinless. How had he believed that she was pretty? He examined the other two and saw that they were not pretty at all either. Each girl, in a way, was sexually attractive, but this was based on imperfection rather than perfection. Didi of the receding chin had enormous eyes and pretty skin which, in toto, gave her a weak-willed, kewpie-doll appeal. The girl next to her was called Becky and she had a lush, wickedly shaped body, but her lips were large and rubbery. The third was an outright freak. Her name was Honey and she had a white complexion with smooth brown hair to match, but there the similarity ended. If she had been a white girl, she would have been the most negroid-looking white person ever born—her features were African. Dave could only think: She *looks* like a nigger! She looks more like a nigger than anyone else in this room! But it was the mammoth breasts of the girl that made her a true freak. Footballs they were, and to top it off, the girl was sway-backed. Dave imagined that many a man would take her to bed simply to find out if those breasts were real.

142

All of the girls walked alike. Their hips, not their legs, propelled them.

In no time at all the room teemed with visitors. Although there were several couples dancing to the music of a radio that someone had brought in, Dave judged the occasion to be a reception rather than a party. People from all walks of life came in and immediately went up to Blueboy with a glad welcome. Georgia remained at his side like a devoted bride. Or was it matron of honor? Dave could not guess, but one thing for sure: Georgia and Blueboy were a two person receiving line. Gamblers, pimps, stablehands, touts, doctors, teachers, hotelmen, and housewives; they all came to greet Blueboy.

And Dave was not unwelcomed. News traveled faster than lightning in Little Chicago. Most of the females who came up to Dave were both flirtatious and diffident. Harlem, it seemed, was heaven to them.

The men showed more varied reactions, and Dave was astonished to see that some of them were jealous. But of what? Harlem? Or being Blueboy's sidekick?

"So you finally had to go to Harlem for a young stud to show you the way!" a waiter jibed Blueboy.

"I'm an international waiter," Blueboy yelled in return. "N'Yawk's just another port o'call to me. It's a place where some of my women live, is all!"

"Tellum, Blueboy, tellum!" Kootchie yelled from across the room. "Tellum who you really are!"

"I am the one and only Neatfingers, international thief and gambler. Answer to all poor whores' prayers," Blueboy cried.

"What about white gals?" Kootchie asked.

"Ain't no poor white gals . . . their color is their fortune. But the rich ones screams for me so loud their husbands get to hear of it . . . That's why I travels!"

"Tellum, Blueboy, tellum! Tellum all about it," Kootchie cried.

"I've left more babies across the United States than this goobereating fool's left peanut shells; and now he got the nerve to say I got to send for Davey-boy to show me the ropes. I oughta pull his arm off and beat his brains out with it!"

"Tellum about that poor whore in Natchez," Kootchie urged.

"'Twasn't Natchez, it was East St. Louis, and I was drunk and weary. And I only went in this joint for a nightcap, but this poor whore wouldn't leave the ole Blue Kid alone. She just *gonna* make me buy a trifle . . ."

"What you complaining for?"

"This poor whore looked like goddam-it-I'll-bite-you!"

The room roared with joy.

"What's that look like, Blueboy?"

"Like somethin' ugly that's been left out all night in the rain and then stomped on in the sunshine!"

Didi cornered Dave. "Let's dance, David." It was a little girl's whisper of conspiracy. "Let's have a *nice* time."

Dave wanted to hear more about the poor whore in East St. Louis, but, lamblike, he accepted, and they began to dance sedately.

Over the din, he could hear his friend saying, "So I hands her this old piece of a mat and tells her to try giving curb service."

"I never had so much fun in my life," Didi said primly. Her enormous eyes held a reproof, as though she just dared Dave to smile at Blueboy's coarse story.

"I thought 'nice times' were all you girls had," he replied.

"Shucks, David, you've got it all wrong. We work hard and it's no fun at all."

"I don't really know much about it."

"Well, do! As my friend Makepeace would say."

"Makepeace? Who's he?" Dave figured Makepeace must surely be a relative of the imaginary Table-Waiting-Sam.

"Oh. He's a good friend of mine. He's always talking about Blueboy. They're cut-buddies. If you won't meet him here you'll see him after. You're gonna French Lick aintcha?"

The query was not only unintelligible, but it sounded pretty obscene to Dave. He mumbled inaudibly, and Didi was quite satisfied with his answer. She yattered on. Dave nodded his head periodically.

"I hate to think of starting back to work," she said.

"You're not working now?" he asked carefully, praying that he had heard correctly. He wouldn't know what to do if she began to seriously solicit him.

"Certainly not. Why the ponies haven't started to run yet, David. The season ain't here yet, not for real. And Georgia hasn't even found a house for us yet. That's why we're staying here at Kootchie's. Why Georgia hasn't even paid off yet and got permission to open. So how could we possibly be working?"

"Well, you know . . ."

"Right now, all we do is take the baths . . . not that we *need* them."

"Eh?" He could not understand her emphasis not knowing that the hot baths were reputed to bolster the healing effects of Neo-salvarsan.

144

"I keep forgetting that you don't know nothing."

"I understand English."

"But people with bad blood come here," Didi cautioned. "And I want you to stay away from them. Anytime a girl tells you she came here because she's got arthritis or something like that I want you to leave them alone. You hear me now?"

Dave's pique was magnificent. The fool girl sounded like a half-witted hygiene teacher. And, after all, she was probably younger than he was.

Didi was far too engrossed in her self-appointed task to note Dave's displeasure and so she talked on without pause until she had worked herself into a wonderful state of moralistic wrath at all lustful women. These women, she was convinced, were all coming to Hot Springs for the sole purpose of debauching one innocent David Greene.

"Don't worry 'bout me," he said, struggling to regain his cosmopolitan façade as sweat beaded his forehead.

A ribald exchange between Blueboy and Kootchie filled the room with laughter, but Dave felt that some of those laughs were at his expense.

Didi's chinless chin quivered valiantly, and her Adam's apple—she had one too—quivered compatibly. "Just the same you are young and good and you need somebody to keep an eye on you."

"Don't worry about me and Blueboy . . . well in Harlem . . ."

Didi cut in; she had advice to give. "Yes, and I'm going to speak to Blueboy, David. And Georgia too. Now Blueboy's been around; he should know . . ."

"We don't need no speaking to . . ."

"I think of you just like a brother, and I'm not gonna have these Hot Springs women messing you up."

"But I don't know any, I tell you."

"Oh, you will. These Hot Springs hot boxes are not gonna pass up a chance at a N'Yawk man . . . if he's young. You know about lemon juice?"

"Yes . . . no," he whispered. Desperately he wished that some-one—anyone—would come and break this up, but it seemed people didn't cut in on dancers in Hot Springs.

"Well, you put a little on the tip of your finger when she's not looking and . . ."

He did not wish to hear it. "Okay. Okay. If I ever want, I'll come see you," he gasped, certain he had settled the issue.

"But you can't," Didi wailed. "You know Georgia never allows us to deal in coal. Everybody knows that. Why, I wouldn't be

145

respectable any more. You wouldn't want to see that happen, would you?"

Dave made a gurgling sound in his throat.

Later that night, after the guests had left and Blueboy and Dave were ready for sleep, Dave found himself wondering why Blueboy was only a waiter. It seemed to him that Blueboy was a born professional man if there ever was one. Dave could not conceive of the man failing to attain any goal he desired. This, in turn, led him to wonder about Blueboy's education. Certainly he had no less than Dave; a year or two of college at least. His speech and vocabulary seemed to prove that. But Blueboy's speech had a strange quality. Sometimes he spoke like an Amos and Andy character while at other times his speech was as clipped and precise as a college professor's. Dave's curiosity about Blueboy's education finally resolved itself when he remembered those twenty years in the Navy. As a waiter, steward, or orderly—the only positions open to a Negro in the Navy—he would have enjoyed close daily contact with Annapolis graduates for twenty years.

In later years Dave would come to insist that Blueboy had had the benefit of a "hearsay Annapolis education."

And Dave was not too surprised that night to see Blueboy shove a chair to the side of his bed and with gravity place a worn Bible and dog-eared dictionary on it. Neither was he alarmed when Blueboy crawled into bed, lit a cigarette, and launched into a discourse relative to the evils of smoking in bed.

After his little black godfather had thumbed through the dictionary for less than five minutes, he dropped off to what had to be a dreamless sleep.

Dave got up and put out the light, but sleep was impossible. He was intoxicated by this day of "firsts" and reluctant to see it end. Today Dave had taken drink in a gentlemanly fashion for the first time. It had been a far cry from the furtive gulps in parked cars, dance-hall lavatories, or the hotel locker room. Why even now at this very minute he was experiencing another exciting first: he had never slept in a hotel before.

As he lay contemplating this best of all possible worlds, a torrent of profanity broke the silence. For a brief spell he had the feeling that he was above and out of reach of the brawling riffraff beyond his locked door. But, as the curses grew louder and the sound of crashing bottles and other articles resounded, he grew uneasy. Two voices in the melee were all too familiar. Didi and Becky were fighting someone. The person they were fighting did not have a familiar voice, but that voice painted her clearly in Dave's mind. She was a mad slut, old, gray-headed, and depraved, with all the sins of the world glowing insanely in her eyes.

Even the voices of Becky and Didi contained qualities that were foreign to him. They were a blend of rage, hysteria, and something that was both savage and desperate . . . jungle abominations . . . sadistic atrocity . . . it was all there in their voices.

The romanticism of his new-found world faded, and he was filled with the fear of the stranger who must sleep among the unknown. It slithered into his belly and eeled up into his throat so he could hardly breath.

"Georgia, if you don't stop her I'm gonna take this blade and pull her goddam head off!"

The threat sent him into a frenzy of panic. What part was he supposed to play in this mad dance? He heard Georgia give a taut command and he listened as the sound of slippered feet scurrying toward his door grew more distinct. Someone was evidently flinging bottles at the girls as they fled, because now the bottles were crashing against his door.

He got up and put on the light, glancing at the peacefully sleeping babe that was Blueboy. Dave was smothered in fear, and it was not physical fear—he believed he could subdue any woman alive —it was fear of ineptitude, fear of ridicule and failure. But as the sounds grew louder, imagination went to work and, having never seen blood ooze from a razor wound, the thought of it made him grow faint. His tongue was a ball of cotton.

An insistent rapping came at the door. He had visions of his smooth young face covered over with razor scars. He trembled violently. Cowardice begot a happy thought: it was now his duty to awaken Blueboy and get help. Stifling a sob of relief, he gently shook Blueboy. The little man bolted upright and transfixed Dave with a deadly stare.

"Whuzzat? Whuzzat?" he demanded and promptly laid back down to sleep.

The crashes, the curses, and the knocking at the door reached a crescendo and Dave made another desperate try to awaken his friend. This time when Blueboy bolted upright, Dave held him so that he could not lie down.

"Whuzzat? Whuzzat?"

"Georgia's girls are fighting somebody and they want in."

"Let-tum-min!"

"Su . . . suppose they . . ."

"O-pin-nit!"

Dave felt tiny slivers of steel in the barked command. Blinded with tears of shame, he opened the door. Didi and Becky scampered past him; each chose a bed and dived into it, Didi into Dave's, while Becky scrounged down behind Blueboy's back.

Dave's only thoughts centered about where he could sleep, now that a razor-wielding prostitute had taken his bed. So befuddled was he that he forgot to lock the door. It immediately swung back open and hit him in the mouth, but the pain hardly fazed him when he saw Honey take a drunken step into the room. Her lovely hair was so tumbled about her face that only her loose and insane lips were visible. Curses like vomit dribbled from those lips and in the corners of her mouth were white patches of foam. She clutched a jagged remnant of a milk bottle in one hand, and with the other she shoved against Dave's chest.

"If you take one more step inta this room I am gonna kick your asshole through your teeth!" It was Blueboy's statement of fact.

The girl heard and believed. "Ah ain doon nuthin, Mist Blueboy," she simpered. "Them two bitches try to double back me . . ."

"Bitch! I ain't gonna tell you twice!"

"Ah wooden come in your room lessen you invituss me, Mist Blueboy. You know that . . ."

"Yass! I do know that!"

The whiskey-maddened girl wavered uncertainly in the doorway. She opened her mouth as if she would voice a threat or challenge at Didi and Becky, whose heads were completely under the bedcovers. Like Dave, she must have sensed the deathly quiet of Blueboy. "G'night," she mumbled, and went away.

"Lock that door and get inta bed!"

Dully, like a robot, Dave obeyed, wondering all the time as to just what manner Blueboy would use to abandon him in the morning. Would he do it colorfully? Or would he quietly say in the morning that he could not associated with a dumb young coward?

And because he read the grieving lad's mind, Blueboy said, "Never let a drunk bitch think that she is crazier than you are." His words became a whisper of intensity. "Because if you do, a drunken bitch will do anything! You hear me? *Anything!*" And then in a voice that was as casual as a "good morning" to the postman he said, "Look in my suitcase."

It was the first of the countless times to follow when the two friends communicated without coherent speech. Involuntary reflex sent Dave to the suitcase to hastily find a bottle of prescription whiskey that he did not know was there, and it was not until he

148

had finished pouring four drinks that he realized that he and Blueboy were still together.

Becky and Didi popped up from under the covers.

"We need one bad," Didi said firmly. "That Honey's got too much Indian blood in her. She ought not to try and drink with me and Becky."

Becky's head bobbed in agreement. "I wouldn't want to hurt nobody for the world, but business is business and it's hard enough for a colored girl to make a living as it is, without her face being all scarred up. Men look at them scars and figger you're tough. They don't stop to think that it's the one that ain't tough that gets the scars. I'da killed her if she'da slashed me with that bottle."

Didi had been slowly sipping her drink, but now she began to giggle softly. "It was the damnedest thing," she snickered.

"What was?" Blueboy wanted to know.

"Honey," Didi replied, still giggling, "she goes to the bathroom and she musta dropped her panties in the can because she comes back and accuses us of stealing 'em . . ."

"That is not funny," Becky reproved her. Her accents were as righteous as any other member of the DAR. "I'm supposed to get my face all messed up because some simple-assed whore loses her panties in the can? You are silly, Didi; it ain't funny at all. I woulda killed her. I'm telling you."

After they had finished their drinks and the room once more was dark and still, Didi snuggled close to Dave and whispered, "Let's talk ourselves to sleep."

Another new experience.

On this night Dave learned that it was the anticipation of sex and the imminent refusal of sex that caused him to be so tongue-tied in the presence of girls. Knowing that intercourse with Didi was out of the question, or at least not mandatory, he was fluent and confiding. In a matter of minutes, they were close friends, sharing intimacies. Dave was often to recall that night and say that they talked of everything under the sun.

He was shocked to find that his bedmate was another Lawyer Greene: Didi was a hairdresser, she said. But as the night wore on and the conversation gently flowed, he either forgot or forgave. He never could remember which.

Naïveté plus a sound Christian upbringing had given Dave to know that a prostitute lived a sad, cruel life. And like most people, Dave considered the life of an alcoholic, the nymphomaniac, and the otherwise utterly depraved as being one and the same thing. This "same thing" was also the life of a prostitute. Didi kindly rid him of his ignorance on all these matters. Dave was reluctant to relinquish some of his more cherished misconceptions. He felt cheated when he was told that the professional leads an uncommonly prosaic life and he was extremely unhappy to hear that a whore with a heart of gold is a contradiction in terminology.

And it was in bed with this little whore that the seeds of his future livelihood were sown. With unerring logic, Didi revealed that only those who catered to man's misfortunes were ever likely to become rich. This, she said, held especially true for Negroes. Shylocks, undertakers, pawnbrokers, doctors, lawyers, preachers and spiritualists were among the chosen few who catered only to man's frailties, Didi asserted. She further insisted that bookies and the proprietors of gambling houses were doomed to everlasting riches because the desire to get rich quick was the most prevalent and incurable of all man's unfortunate diseases. Dave accepted her words as gospel.

They philosophized and consoled, they bragged, and they whispered their fears in the early morning light. And before they went to sleep Dave knew that he had finally attained true manhood. He knew how to treat a whore, and that was the root of all knowledge.

The girls awoke shortly after noon and politely thanked their hosts and protectors. They left only to return in a few minutes with breakfasts prepared in the community kitchen of the hotel. They continued to do so until the season opened and everybody went to work.

"Well, at least we get a free breakfast this morning," Blueboy observed between yawns. There was a gentle rapping at the door, and Blueboy shouted a "Come on in." Honey hurriedly entered and seated herself close to Blueboy's side. Placing her head in his lap, she broke into shattered sobs. Several times she raised her head and tried to speak, but sorrow would not permit her.

Blueboy stroked her long brown hair, so like any white girl's. "Don't cry, baby. You ain't hurt nobody. Whiskey made you sick, but it didn't take your courage so that you couldn't come in here now. Since you know whiskey makes you sick, you is lucky. You don't hafta drink it any more. Just tell folks it makes you sick. You are too young to get sick like that again, baby . . ."

"I—I'm so ashamed . . ."

"If you wasn't ashamed, I'd be forced to feel sorry for you, but since you man enuff to apologize, you man enuff not to drink it. That makes me feel right good, little girl."

"I tole Georgia I wuz leaving," she moaned. "I can't face

Kootchie and folks . . . everything . . . all that broken glass Georgia hadda sweep up . . ."

"Better stay here with you friends, little girl," Blueboy said with amazing softness. "They won't let you get drunk any more."

She raised her head and tried to smile. "Blueboy, please be my friend."

Honey, too, Dave thought; he was not alone.

"Didn't Georgia tell you that already?"

"She . . . she said . . ." But Honey could say no more.

Blueboy began to speak softly with a wisdom that healed.

Where, Dave wondered, had the rocky fellow learned so much more than anybody else?

Blueboy's accents were careless, unconcerned . . . almost happy-go-lucky, and in some way the girl began to forget. The ghastly night receded to its proper place, like any other bad dream.

Honey put her arms about Blueboy's waist and held him tightly, as if in this way she could bring some of his strength into her own weak form.

Dave gazed at this portrait of a fatherly little wise man and the weeping white child. Where was the iron-voiced menace that kicked women's behinds? What had become of the drunken whore? The magic of Blueboy was for real.

French Lick, Lake Delavan, Saratoga, Fort Myers, Myrtle Beach. In Sault Saint Marie, Dave had a dream the night his mother died. In the dream, as it so often happened in real life, he was split into two selves. As a grown man he watched a little boy, about four years old romping in a field with a beautiful and delicate teen-age girl. He recognized the boy as himself. The girl constantly asked the little boy question upon question, and it all seemed very silly to Dave because the young girl already knew all the answers. One look at her high and intelligent forehead told him that. Just before he woke, it dawned upon him that the lovely girl was teaching the boy to think and to make his own decisions.

Dave awoke in a cold sweat. The lovely teen-age girl had been his mother. Now he knew the answers to all her questions. Twenty years to learn that his mother was not a stupid girl.

All at once, a tremendous love for her and a longing to see her again came over him. A natural-born procrastinator, Dave took over a week before he finally called his mother. It was then that he learned that his mother was dead and buried.

Blueboy took the shattered boy to Nashville. And it was Blueboy who arranged for a real estate agent to manage the property.

151

"Maw's dead. Paw's dead. This ain't your home no more, Davey-boy, but don't worry. Someday you'll hit a town and you'll say to yourself: 'This is where I belong!' So until then we might just as well travel."

And so they traveled the length and breadth of America.

14

Shortly before Easter Monday, 1937, Dave Greene's numbers bank reached its condor years. It was now the Ward's merciless and impersonal god. It gave and it took away without rhyme or reason.

It was only nineteen months after Eggy Manone wrote his first numbers slips when a bored coroner's assistant scribbled "acute acoholism" upon Eggy's death certificate. The hotel employees collected moncy for a wreath and generally agreed, "Too much money."

By his own hand, but equally as dead, was Deacon Arthur Preston of the First Baptist Church. Prior to the advent of numbers playing in the Ward, the deacon had been a prosperous shoemaker and a pillar in his church. But overnight his credo changed from Christianity to numerology and his bible became those murky pamphlets so dear to the numbers player's heart: *Policy Pete, The Rajah, Lucky Day Workout, The H. P. Dreambook,* and similar reading matter.

The numbers-crazed man needed only to hear strangers, conversing in the street, mention a three-digit number and he would beg, borrow, or steal the money to play on that overheard number.

He wrote in answer to the countless ads in Negro newspapers and hired their "lucky services" and he "bought" numbers by mail from frauds who gave out numbers in the very same way that race-track hangers-on touted horses.

Preston's business faltered and failed. He had spent too much time roaming the Block, discussing the perfidy of numbers with anyone who would talk to him. And Preston would journey to distant parts of the city to find a new numbers writer, hoping that this man would bring him luck. When he was a deacon Preston would take a drink or two on Saturday nights, but once the gambling mania struck him he foreswore strong drink so as to keep his mind clear at all times for life's most important task: playing numbers.

The city marshal was enroute to padlock the bankrupt shoe-repair shop when the former Baptist deacon slit his throat. The coroner's report should have read "acute numbers addiction." But it didn't.

Morton Jones, treasurer of the Seventh A. M. E. Church, was also an addict. The number 888 obsessed him, and he played more than five dollars a day on it for six months. It never came out, but this fact only served to convince Morton that 888 had to come out soon. To support his conviction, he used church funds entrusted to his care. One despondent night he wrote a suicide note to his wife and secretly boarded a bus for Baltimore.

Lila Brown, housemaid, won over two thousand dollars on 931. For one whole day she and her friends celebrated. That night her husband poisoned a drink of the corn liquor she loved so well. The coroner fumed: "As long as you police allow rotgut whiskey to be sold in the Ward you're going to have deaths like these. It's murder, pure and simple! These bootleggers are murderers!" He deigned to order an autopsy in this open-and-shut case.

Widower Brown promptly remarried and soon thereafter became the proud father of twins. He now owns the prosperous restaurant once owned by the late Jim Penney; 722 came out the day that the twins were born and the good man hit it handsomely.

The Liberian Knights' Burial Society is now defunct. Too many of its members began to play numbers with the small change they once used to pay their weekly dues. The day the society's officers suspended operations everybody played 000, but it never came out.

Randy Jones, bartender and numbers writer, hit 144 for twenty-four hundred dollars. Every cent of that money is in the colored savings bank, and Randy vows that it will stay there until his only child, a girl, is ready to enter college.

The most senseless slaughter in the city's annals occurred when a near-delirious drunk boasted that he, Dave, and Blueboy had all been members of a Southside gangland mob in Chicago. A mentally retarded cabdriver became incensed when the drunkard further boasted that Dave and Blueboy had been drummed out of the mob because they were homosexuals. The cabbie refuted him, saying that Dave and he were cousins from Valdosta, Georgia. There on the street corner the two complete strangers engaged in a murderous knife fight. Both men were buried in the city's potter's field, which is behind the poorhouse.

Neither Dave or Blueboy heard of the incident, but 021 played the day the two men knifed each other to death. Nobody hit it.

By 1937 the pickup men had become fair game for the city's police. Through pure chance the officers had stumbled across a good thing. They had found that they had only to stop a pickup's car and lean in the window. If they stared long enough and silently enough the numbers man would eventually fumble in his pocket and produce a five-dollar bill.

Curiously enough this tactic worked with quite a few young Negro men and women who were not connected with the numbers racket. Whether these people were lawbreakers or just plain rattle-brained is a moot question, and the greedy police did not care so long as they were "tipped" by these motorists. This dodge became so good that some of the greedier cops took to stopping all colored people driving new Fords. If they were not tipped, the cops merely shrugged and mumbled something about having received a lookout signal for a car such as the stopped person was driving.

John Brown, Gordon Penn, Tony Bailey, and Arthur Gardin, numbers writers, were all feloniously assaulted by violently in-toxicated numbers players who mistakenly believed that they had hit the number. The number was 244 the day that Blueboy sent for Makepeace Johnson.

In view of the fact that Dave both hated and shunned politics it is ironic that his stature in the Ward so nearly approximated that of a big-city political boss. And the pickups were his ward heelers. Slightly less ironic was the circumstance that as Dave's name became more and more a byword he personally became an enigma. He was virtually unknown by the general public. Only numbers men and people on the Block knew him personally. With the exception of the flower shop and the countinghouse, the only places Dave frequented were Booker's and the Lil Savoy, and it was seldom

155

before midnight when he entered these places. The good and solid citizens of the Ward were long since asleep when Dave roamed the Block. And he no longer drove his car about the Ward for obvious reasons.

Characteristically, Dave did nothing to forestall the growing tendency of the Ward to make him both an unknown quantity and a celebrity. If the truth were known, Dave wanted both. His desire to keep the bank secure from policemen made him wish to shun notoriety, while at the same time that old fetish of respectability motivated him to seek it. And so, while he was still taciturn among strangers, socially lazy, and never gregarious, he wished to create a public image; although he was not at all sure just what form that image should take. Probably a demure Blueboy.

Dave had no close friends. Cokey, Pigmeat, and Blueboy were too close to be described as such. These three comprised Dave's immediate family. Yet this in no way describes Dave's true position in the Ward. Daily he sat like a Solomon and dispensed justice. Writers and pickups alike were constantly squabbling over territorial rights. It became necessary for Dave to divide the entire city into recognized areas for the pickups, and in some cases to subdivide it for the more aggressive writers in order to prevent bloodshed. Operators of kiffs, pads, and gambling dens came to Dave with past due bills and, in essence, asked Dave to garnishee his employees. In this respect Dave ruled over a court of thieves, and in all these matters the Ward accepted Dave's judgments as law. He also had to hold a daily court of arbitration for complaining numbers players who came with their problems of off-slips, lost slips, and those rackety cases of mistaken identity when a numbers writer payed off the wrong person, or said he had. Dave was even called upon to settle domestic squabbles of some of the less worldly of his writers. Because Dave stood for the bank and its untold wealth, he was considered infallible.

Whereas his role as the Ward's chief dispenser of justice was pleasing to him, Dave was not at all pleased with his status among the Ward's Four Hundred. The Ward's social elite had not invited him to their homes or social affairs. Dave never doubted that he was to the manor born, and he wished the Ward to show it.

The Ward's social slights rankled; and the fact that he and Blueboy were often hosts at Booker's Square Table to male members of the city's black elite served to further goad Dave's anger. Anybody with good sense was welcome as far as Blueboy was concerned and he was the benevolent autocrat of the table. Many times local men would come singly to Booker's for a late snack and many

156

of them preferred to take a seat at the Square Table rather than eat alone. If these men wished, they paid for their tab and left soon after eating. But if they were disposed to stick around for a few drinks and the inevitable debates, they automatically became the guests of either Dave or Blueboy, since the nightly liquor tab was almost always borne by one or the other.

It must be remembered that the Square Table was at all times divorced from the numbers racket. Only a few of the pickup men came to it. In the main, the Knights of the Square Table came from respectable walks of life.

If Dave had been a true social climber his secret aspirations would not have been so peculiar and insidious, but Dave did not have the slightest desire to hobnob with the Ward's upper crust. He only wished the invitations to prove that he was respected—Arkansas style.

Dave's frustrations—which he kept secret even from Blueboy—began to bother him more and more. He gradually became obsessed with a desire to avenge his honor (respect) by seducing a pretty girl who came from the Ward's elite. Only his shyness, his morbid fear of failure or rebuff, deterred him from trying to do so. His morals had nothing to do with it.

In the heat of that hectic evening with Kelly, Dave had momentarily been free from his wish, but the finality of Kelly's refusal to marry him served to return him to his rather lecherous desire.

It was the morning after 088 came out, and Dave sat at the kitchen table as he tried to forget Kelly and tried to convince himself that this invitation from Dr. Parks was two years too late. He hoped that Blueboy would concur.

"Everything I got I got from ordinary people and now that I got it I'm supposed to run out and spend it on some black-assed Four Hundreds," he mumbled aloud.

Blueboy was unabetting. He poured another cup of coffee and pretended that an answer was not expected.

"They wait until they think I got more than they got and then they start sending invitations." Dave waved the envelope in a vague gesture of irritation.

Blueboy noisily sipped his coffee. Blueboy insisted that he drank his coffee heartily; Dave said he slurped it. Blueboy dearly wished to ask about the plurality of one invitation, but the little man believed that absolute silence would be much more cruel at the moment. He kept silent and slurped.

"I'm a lawyer's son. If they was so socially knowledgeable they would have extended invitations time I got here."

"What the hell do you know about being socially knowledgeable?"

Dave shifted in his chair and looked distastefully at the glass of whiskey before him. "Since they claims to be the cream of society it was their duty to welcome the cream of society from another city."

"Cream? You was a black-ass floating waiter when you hit this town."

"That's one lie you could have saved."

"If somebody hadda wrote to Nashville for your social credentials or whatever you call them, what would they have found out?"

"Plenty. And okay, too."

"Plenty is right. They'd of found out that you up and quit college in your sophomore year to go helling and drinking all over the U.S.A." Blueboy cleared his throat and shifted into his verbal high-gear. "Further investigation would disclose the fact that you had to live in a fleabag hotel when you got here. You didn't have a friend, respectable or otherwise, to bunk in with. They would also find that you came here with a nefarious harebrained scheme to conduct a lottery amongst the underprivileged Negroes in this fair city. When you come to the Ward you claimed you was a professional gambler."

"You sure like to twist hell out of everything, don't you?"

"You think I'm the only person in the Ward knows how to twist? A goddam Georgia cotton-picker wouldn't of wanted you to keep company with his pregnant daughter, much less see you marry her, when you got here. And you is socially knowledgeable?"

"I had damn near two thousand bucks in my pocket when I hit this town."

"Mebbe you stole it." And Blueboy noisily slurped.

"Are you trying to say I should go?"

"I ain't trying to say nothing. But since you asked, I will say that them folks showed good sense in waiting to see if you was crazy or not. And that they are showing good judgment now in inviting you out . . . once't!"

"Nigger society. And I gotta beg in."

Blueboy glanced up sharply. "All depends," he said quietly. "Anybody in Negro society is in it because they earned a position in it. White folks gets borned into it whether they really belongs in it or not. Whichever is the phoniest is a matter of opinion."

"I heard of this Dr. Parks guy, but who is he? What's his story? I never seen him around to know of."

"There's four Dr. Parks."

"Four brothers? All docs?"

"Two brothers. One's an M.D., the other's a dentist. Each has a son, an M.D. That makes four."

"Regular medical dynasty," Dave said.

"Like Booker's, only different," Blueboy said, with a touch of malice.

"Go to hell," Dave said mildly. "They all practice in the Ward here?"

"No, I don't think so. The two brothers do, but the young'uns is in nearby towns. Like Jonesville and Kingsport. Now them sons might practice a coupla nights in their dads' offices. I dunno. I do know that they run the colored hospital."

Dave scoffed. "Open door to death."

"Mebbe. You can call it what you want to. Nursing home, charnel house. It makes no difference. On paper it says that all four Dr. Parks is on the board of directors or something. That sounds real important when you read it real fast."

"I get it," Dave said. "So who is this invite from?"

"Howinell I know? I ain't even read it and if I did I don't know nonc of thems first names anyhow. All I know is that all of them lives side by side on Kings Mountain."

"Rockpile."

"It's theirs that live there," Blueboy retorted. "And I never heard of nobody getting their throat cut at a pigfoot supper out there."

"Restricted real estate development for restricted niggers. How very lovely. Just what Abraham Lincoln had in mind probably."

"Wasn't you raised in the suburbs?"

"Anybody that had the price of a piece of land could move out there, too. They didn't have to be voted on and sign a piece of paper saying they're gonna spend such and such on the house they're gonna build. They could've lived in a tent if they wanted."

"You can live in Kings Mountain in a tent so long as you signs papers promising to pay at least eight grand for it."

"Why the hell don't you go get a job with Butterbeans and Suzie or Silas Fields, you blackface comedian?"

"It would probably be more edifying than working for a two-minded fool that can't make up either one of them. You, yourself, useta sit around and cry over the Ward here. Talking about folks building mansions in slum districts. Now when a few decent people decide to build a few decent homes in a pleasant neighborhood you start acting up like they had petitioned Congress to revoke the Emancipation Proclamation."

"So what do I wear?"

"Clothes mebbe."

"How in hell you managed to live this long without getting yourself lynched is a mystery to me."

"I got good white friends. Females. Besides. I never been in a respectable home in my life lessen it was my maw's."

"What? All over the world you been and now you're gonna try and tell me that?"

"When? Where? Me and you ain't never been in a respectable house when we was traveling. Lessen you wants to call some pads and whorehouses more respectable than others. Them years in the Navy was worse than it is now, and ain't no sailors being invited nowheres now except mebbe to cathouses. Everybody said us sailors were drunks and cunt hounds."

"I thought that only went for white boys," Dave said slowly. "Looks to me that any Negro with a steady income would be welcome by some sorta respectable colored people."

"Educated colored hated us for joining. We was only galley slaves if you know what I mean. And the cracker officers hated us only a little less than the colored people. I didn't know what the word democracy meant when I joined up; I was that dumb. But you can bet I knew what it meant when I left the Navy. Me and it is on mutual terms now. We owes each other nothing!" Blueboy paused and then exclaimed, "Cracker naval officers, cops, and foreigners. They all come out of the same pile of horseshit."

Three nights later Dave went to the party at Dr. Parks's with some slight misgivings which were confirmed as soon as he got there. The host looked like a little stinker. The very same one who raised so much hell on his first day in school that the teacher gave up and sent the urine-soaked crybaby home in the care of an older pupil. Dr. Parks's pants were dry now and the stench of urine did not hover about him, but he was the same little stinker, and Dave hated him.

Once rid of his host, Dave moved among the guests, and for the first time in his life he was conscious of age groupings as a social factor. Traveling waiters, he realized, never considered age when they socialized. Vocation, money, and the right attitude were the equalizing factors, and the girls had always been young with the accompanying attractions of youth. Tonight Dave was among grandparents, and he began to wonder if he and Dr. Parks were the only young people in the house. There evidently was no Mrs. Parks to go with this particular Dr. Parks.

Dave had never thought about it before, but now he was face to face with the fact that respectable Negroes are the most boring

160

people on earth. This party was a parody of some cruel thing that should never have happened in the first place. These guests all acted like the inmates of a madhouse, docilely performing their roles in a parlor farce at the insistence of the institution's therapist. They stood around in dull, lifeless groups, almost mouthing their lines correctly, but it was evident that these maniacs did not have the slightest idea of what they were saying or doing.

Every topic of conversation was fitfully worried to death; no subject died naturally among these dullards. The only activity in the entire house was confined to the next room where three tables of whist players sat in stolid concentration. And it was among these whist players that Dave glimpsed the incongruity that must forever be present in anything negroid. Kid Flick, his top pickup man, was playing at one of the tables and seemed to be perfectly at ease. In fact, the Kid was the most relaxed guest at the party as well as being the best-dressed.

"You won't mind if I introduce myself? I'm Helen Deas."

The nice-looking girl in her matronly twenties had ended her words on a note of inquiry as if she was asking Dave if her name really was Helen Deas. Dave gulped with distaste. This girl knew damn well what her name was and if that question mark at the end of her sentence meant she wanted to know his name, she was still dotty. She knew damn well he was Dave Greene. Helen Deas was a fairly regular diner in Booker's, and although they had never met, Dave believed her to be as genuine as a three-dollar bill. Whenever she entered Booker's she was invariably wearing a riding habit. Crop included. The nearest riding academy that catered to Negroes was four hundred miles away from the Ward. Dave always wondered if Helen Deas knew that fact.

Suddenly Dave decided to play along with the girl. He smiled graciously. "I'm Dave Greene, and I've looked forward to this pleasure for a long time." Dave could be smooth when he wanted to be. Dining-room-captain suave.

Helen Deas, Dave knew, was the niece of Ed Deas, the National Grand Commander of one of the largest Negro fraternal organizations in the world. Ed Deas's detractors called him the Iron Duke because of the grasping, iron-fisted manner in which he ruled over his semiliterate brethren. His salary was in the five-figure category, and he doubled it by making personal appearances all over the country for ten months out of every twelve. It was like a royal progression through the land and all the serfs gave gifts of gold.

Helen Deas was the velvet glove of the Iron Duke and was a national officer in the women's auxiliary of her uncle's lodge. Of

161

late, she had become engaged in the manufacturing of hair pomades and similar beauty products. So although Dave thought her a phony she was at the same time the Ward's only female of national prominence. Negro newspapers referred to her as "Cosmetics Queen," "National manufacturer," and "Sepia socialite and business figure."

Because of some muscular inadequacy Miss Deas was not able to smile; she could only grimace. Sometimes it was not a grimace at all. It was that fleeting expression one might glimpse of the face of a child just as it swallows a piece of ice.

When Dave said that he had always wanted to meet Miss Deas, she had grimaced and batted her eyes. "But why in the world would anyone look forward to meetin' poor little me?"

This was definitely a question, but Dave was convinced that she had somehow told an untruth. And this made things all wrong because topmost in Dave's mind was a desire to invest in Miss Deas's pomade business. It would be unlike his other pie-in-the-sky ventures; this was a going concern that produced tangible products. Dave was not interested in profits as such. His only desire was to see his money at work in an intelligent venture that was operated by Negroes. Miss Deas's flirtatious attitude was not conducive to preliminary financial negotiations.

"You are a prominent woman of affairs," Dave said. "From now on I will be proud to say that I know you personally. I've waited a long time for this honor."

She grimaced fondly. "You should have come over and introduced yourself in Booker's. All you had to do was say that you were a brother. My. You certainly must be bashful."

It was all wrong and getting worse. If Helen Deas thought that Dave Greene was one of her uncle's ignorant lodge brothers she would never make a fit business associate. He decided to end the conversation as quickly as possible.

"How's the hair-grease business?"

"Cosmetics," she murmured. "But business is really wonderful. Of course we're only small potatoes at present, but we will grow . . ." She suddenly darted a look of suspicion at him. "I did not know you were interested in beauty products, Mr. Greene."

Her sudden change of attitude puzzled Dave. "I am and I'm not interested," he confessed. "You see, I like to see my money at work in anything smart the Negro is doing. It's hard to find really worthwhile colored businesses to invest in."

"And I'm so sorry for you, too," she said. Dave thought that this

162

time the girl was being honest, but what the hell was she being sorry for him about?

"And I suppose everybody turns you down," she said.

"Eh?"

"Now take my little concern," Helen said. "We work hand in hand with the churches." She giggled. "Uncle Ed can preach a sermon at the drop of a hat, and he hates gambling. I guess that's why the entire lodge worships him."

The light of truth finally dawned on Dave: This gal wanted no numbers money backing her business. He breathed a sigh of release when Helen wandered off to mingle with the other guests. It suddenly came to him that Helen Deas was the unofficial hostess of this sorry soiree.

A black and ugly man accosted him. It was obvious to Dave that this man had been created for the sole purpose of reassuring all other Negroes that they were not the most horrid sight on earth. "I'm Hyams of the University," the man wheezed in an asthmatic falsetto.

Dave felt ashamed for the man. Not sorry, but ashamed. The three hundred pounds of burnt blubber that composed this man's body was only one of the many indignities he presented to the human eye. Hyams's piggish eyes were wet and hungry. His face and body also seemed to be wet. Not sweaty, but wet with some offensive moisture that was a part of him. Dave's shame was multiplied when he saw that Hyams of the University was very proud of Hyams of the University. And even the man's fingernails were not like other people's. They were an opaque mother-of-pearl. Having never heard Cokey or anybody else from the Campus mention any Hyams, Dave wondered if the man was attempting some sorry kind of joke.

"I hear that you are a banker, Greene."

Dave wished for the venomous wit of Blueboy . . . or Kelly. "No," he said slowly. "I operate the flower shop on Vessey near Macon."

"Now why should I have thought you were a banker?"

"I haven't the slightest idea."

"But you're in the Ward?"

"I live in the Ward. Yes."

"Well, I heard you were a gambler."

"If you're looking to start a little crap game," Dave said, "you will have to count me out." He wondered what kind of grade Kelly would give him for that. "I never gamble," he continued. "Once in a blue moon I used to try my hand at stud, but I just don't have the time any more."

163

"Er . . . what?"

"You're quite a pleasant surprise, Dr. Hyams. I thought that bankers and college administrators were two groups of men who simply could not afford to be known as gamblers. Do you start a game everywhere you go? At parties, I mean?"

Hyams went away, and Dave stood and wondered how he could have been so silly as to want invitations from people such as these. He also made a mental note to ask Kelly who Hyams was. But he would not be seeing her again! And Kelly had spoken the truth. His life had been lonely as hell these last thirteen days. He spied Flick standing alone and walked over to him.

"Hi, Boss. You having a good time?" The Kid's eyes were all solicitude.

"Fine, but it's kinda dry, isn't it?"

"We got punch in the kitchen," Flick said, and Dave mentally gasped at the "we." "But I wouldn't try it if I were you," Flick added.

"Why not? What the hell could be wrong with it?"

"Well . . . it's got real cheap whiskey in it. And pineapple juice too."

"Well, I'll be a sonofabitch," Dave said.

"Doc Parks got a flask in his pocket," Flick said. "Good bourbon. C'mon."

That his host was ambling about the premises with a flask of whiskey in his pocket was no more confounding than the fact that the teetotaling Kid Flick was privy to it. Dave shrugged helplessly and followed the Kid.

"Sure thing, old man. I always keep a drop of private stock for special guests," the little doctor said manfully. He produced a silver flask and poured a drink in the tiny cap of the thing and offered it to Dave.

Dave felt like a fool, but gingerly downed it. It was good bourbon. Flick had left them, and they were standing in the dimmest corner of the front porch. Dave resolved to let the doctor go back into the house first and he would simply walk off the porch and leave the party.

"You know, Dave, it's about time you and I got together." The doctor's heartiness rubbed Dave the wrong way. He definitely wanted no familiarity from this squirt, but he remained grittily silent. "And all those cars. We need them. Every single one!"

"What cars?" Dave asked. "Cars for what?"

"Yours! Motorcade. Political Action," the man yattered. "We're going to take those cars and go all up in the mountains. Nobody

164

can stop us. I knew you would have the right attitude. When I first heard about all those cars of yours I didn't believe it, but everybody says it's true and so you've simply got to let us have those cars for a week. Right?"

"I don't think I get you, Doc," Dave said slowly. "There's got to be a mistake somewheres. Now if you're under the impression that I own every car that people in the numbers business use, you're wrong. In the first place it's pretty hard to say who is an employee of mine. Numbers is largely a commission business. I don't have a large payroll."

"But we know you've got the cars," Dr. Parks said excitedly. "And we want 'em. Every one."

"You talk like I'm some kind of rich playboy," Dave said. "I'm a businessman. No matter how many cars I got, don't you think I need 'em? Would you go to the owner of a taxi company in the Ward and ask him for all his taxis? No. You wouldn't think of talking to him the way you're talking to me." Then curiosity overcame his pique. "What the hell is the motorcade for anyhow?"

"A political motorcade," Dr. Parks said rapidly. "We've got to put on a real show. We'll have speakers and workers going through all those mountain counties, telling the people how to vote. Who to vote for. We've got to give FDR a real team. He can't do it all by himself. And you, a numbers banker, should be right there in the forefront."

"Me?" Dave squeaked in surprise. "Me? What the hell business have I got in politics? You just said I was a numbers banker."

"Who cares where your money comes from? We need all the support we can get. Roosevelt needs men like you and you need him."

"I don't need Roosevelt and he don't need me," Dave said flatly. "I don't need any damn cracker in my business."

"FDR's no cracker."

"There's more crackers get invited to the White House than boogies, see what I mean?"

"Why, that's awful."

"Damn right it's awful," Dave snapped, "but it's true. And the bastard lives in Georgia more than he goes to New York. Me? I hate politics. I hate everything that's phony; I'm freakish that way. But just out of curiosity, would you please tell me why a numbers banker in his right mind should go driving around the state minding other people's business? Makin' enemies he don't need? And while we're at it, don't you think you're kinda dumb? What the hell have you to gain? And can't the governor or one of his buddies

165

mess with you? Mess with your license for malpractice or whatever they want to put against you? Why you want to make an enemy of the governor?"

"Make an enemy? What are you talking about?"

"Sure," Dave said patiently. "The governor got elected by running against somebody, didn't he? Now suppose you had backed the guy he ran against, where would you be now? I'll tell you: up shit creek. You remember that colored druggist in Tennessee who got into politics and the white bosses put cops out in front of his store and wouldn't let nobody go in to buy anything?"

"This is nineteen thirty-seven! No white man would dare to do that now."

"That's what you think. Crackers is still crackers!"

"I see," the doctor muttered. "You're one of those niggers who would be satisfied with a jar of corn and a watermelon patch!"

Those words, coming from the meek-looking little doctor, so surprised Dave that he forgot to resent them. Dr. Parks sighed a farewell and turned to go back in the house.

"So long," Dave said weakly. "And thanks for the nice time." He descended the steps and went to his car. He paused. Someone was calling his name. There was a female figure on the porch and that figure was gesturing frantically. Dave mentally shrugged. More tickets. Every respectable dame in the Ward had tickets to sell for the damnedest worthy causes. And Dave Greene was not expected to buy only one. He had to buy them by the dozen. Involuntarily he ran his hand in his pocket for a ten-dollar bill; he would give her that and go without listening to her sales pitch. He opened the door, got in the car and waited.

The lady was Helen Deas, and she was furious. "You . . . you numbers bankers." And it was a remarkably unlady-like snarl. "You could have had the common decency to wait a little longer. What do you think I am anyway?"

"What's the matter?" he asked.

Helen got in the car. "Well, hurry up. You aren't going to stand here all night, are you?" she said harshly. "You want everybody to notice?"

It was a hell of a way to sell tickets, but Dave was resigned to all forms of madness by now. "Hurry up where?" he said testily.

"Straight ahead, and stop trying to be cute."

Kings Mountain is not a mountain. It is not even a hill. It's a rock-strewn plain. The entire development contains but sixteen scattered houses. A forked road comprises its two streets which in reality are asphalt-paved lanes. Both lanes end abruptly in a continuation of the rocky field. When Dave could go no further he braked the car to a stop and automatically switched off the lights.

The quiet blackness of the moonless night immersed them. And then Helen Deas was writhing and moaning in Dave's arms.

"You didn't have to make believe it was my business you wanted. And don't bother to lie. I know your type. And don't mess my skirt up either. No . . . wait. Let me get it up around my waist . . ."

15

As Dave sped from Kings Mountain to Booker's, he wondered if he had been raped. If he had been, then Helen Deas was the most unwilling rapist known to man. Helen had made no bones of the fact that she disliked him even as she violently made love to him.

Entering Booker's he was sorry to see the Square Table was crowded. He had been looking forward to a private session with Blueboy and maybe Cokey. He took a seat at the table next to Blueboy and was made more unhappy to find that Topic A, as it was every evening, was the Race Problem. And as usual, the white-looking Professor Blake was leading the discussion. In the past two years the teacher had gone through quite a metamorphosis. He was now the most vocal and rattlebrained member of the Square Table.

"No black boy ever committed treason," Blueboy was yelling down the table at Professor Blake.

But Dr. White answered for him. "That's because the Negro never wanted anything very badly," he said. "And the reason we are downtrodden is because the white man takes our allegiance for

168

granted. We should cultivate the art of the doublecross and then someday we would get what we want."

"What the hell does the Negro want?" Blueboy asked.

"Who the hell knows what a damn fool nigger wants?" Dave grumbled.

"You can say that again," Joe Kelso said to him.

"The Negro wants all that he has been missing which is everything," someone at the end of the table said.

"Then he wants a goddam brain," Dave said.

After that the table was in a hubbub, each man voicing his opinion of what the Negro needed and wanted. And it came to Dave that these men gathered around this table didn't have great needs or wants.

Over the babble came Professor Blake's voice. "I just want to see the Negro family re-established," he cried querulously.

"Damn right," Dave said in a voice half choked with emotion. "I'd rather be a starving Chinaman with ancestors to worship than the richest nigger in the U.S.A." No one seemed to have heard him. He settled back in his chair in an angry silence.

Meanwhile Blip was loudly calling for higher wages and more recreational spots. Nobody was listening to him either. In fact, Dave was the only one listening to anybody as all the men at the table tried to voice their opinions. As far as Dave could make out, Dr. White wanted a separate but equal Negro government inside the United States. Although Blueboy was silent now, Dave knew that his friend wished total commercial integration with absolutely no intercourse with the white man after business hours.

Suddenly Blueboy cleared his throat with such a loud harrumph that the table grew silent. His voice when he began to speak softly caressed each syllable just as a lover might caress his beloved. "What I ask for the Negro is not benevolence, not pity, not sympathy, but simple justice," Blueboy said. "The white American people have always been anxious to know what to do with us, the Negro. I have had but one answer from the beginning.

"Do nothing with us. Your doing with us has already played the mischief with us. If the Negro cannot stand on his own legs . . . let him fall. All I ask is the chance to stand alone.

"Let him alone.

"If you see him going to school, let him alone. Your interference is doing him a positive injury.

"If the Negro cannot live by the code of eternal justice the fault will not be yours; it will be His who created the Negro and established that code for his government.

"Let him live or die by that.

"If you will only untie his hands and grant him a chance, I think that he will live."

The last words had been delivered in a whisper of intensity, but it was a few moments before the table realized that Blueboy had finished speaking. First there was a concerted kind of grunt and then everyone was asking Blueboy questions.

"You write that, Blueboy?"

"When?"

Blueboy smiled. "Those are Fred Douglass' words," he said. "He told the white people that over seventy years ago, but they didn't listen. Neither did the darkies."

"It seems as if everytime we gather I learn to respect you more and more, Blueboy," Dr. White said.

"Same thing a gal tole me in St. Joe when I kicked her butt," Blueboy replied graciously.

"Well, according to that speech, Frederick Douglass was not a Race man," Professor Blake said.

"He damn near led the Emancipation Movement singlehanded," Dave exclaimed. "What the hell more do you want?"

"That speech is as silly as a blind mute demanding to be left alone," Blake said. "And the Civil War didn't help things anyhow. It made things worse. Before the war white Southerners treated their colored children like their own. Educated them and . . ."

"Nerts!" Dave said. "What you are trying to say is that the white man would have eventually screwed his way to a solution of the race problem."

"That's right," Cokey said. "But the white man went and created a monster when he started fathering Negroes."

"And he shall pay for it with his own blood," Dr. White said. "The white man's blood will flow in rivers down every street in America one of these days. And it will be his own bastard children that do the bloodletting."

Dave looked at Professor Blake, who was so obviously half white.

Dr. White sighed and added, "Well, at least the Negro people have no deadheads to carry. We owe Uncle Tom and his lady nothing."

"Now what the hell does all that mean?" Dave said.

Dr. White, looking as ugly and pedantic as ever said, "Men should be willing to die for their freedom. Old Negroes had their chance and refused to kill or be killed for their freedom. Therefore, we have no sages, no heroes, no elders to befog our minds and our

170

acts. Only black youth is important; and I hope that they have more guts than their forebears. The black ones at least. I suppose our white ancestors were rather brave."

"Shame. Honor your maw and your paw. Shame upon you," Blueboy bawled.

"Oh, my God," Dave muttered.

"I agree with what you say, but you shouldn't call your parents a coupla bastards just to prove your point," Blueboy said sternly.

"Do you honor your father and mother, Blueboy?" Cokey asked.

"I ain't got no father," Blueboy said, and Dave was no less confounded than the others by this revelation. "My maw said my pop was no gentleman. She refused to marry him. I tell you that black women cause confusion," Blueboy added.

"Do you know who your father was?" asked Dave.

"He was a world's champeen boxer, Maw said. That's why she wouldn't marry him."

"He was colored?" Dr. White asked.

"Miscegenation's a sin. My Maw was a church lady."

"How can you say miscegenation is a sin?" Professor Blake asked.

Someone else said, "Yeah. That sounds awfully ignorant to me."

"Do you understand what Anglo-Saxon means?" Professor Blake asked.

"It means two white people had a baby a long time ago," Blueboy said. "But the miscegenation I mean is that between white and black. And any Negro bitch who commits miscegenation is guilty of perpetrating every damn one of the seven deadly sins!"

Dave knew that no man at the table, including himself, could enumerate the seven deadly sins. They all smiled insipidly at each other, afraid to challenge Blueboy.

"A black woman and a white man are the only two people able to commit miscegenation today," Blueboy said.

"You mean that they are the only ones who can do so without fear?" Cokey asked.

Blueboy nodded emphatically, but someone else said, "Anybody who claims a white woman ain't free is nuts. White women own the U.S.A."

"The richest white woman in Georgia is free only to associate with white men," Blueboy shouted. "There is no white woman in the world who is as free as the crumbiest black whore alive. A colored gal can sleep with the head of the KKK in Georgia and nobody . . . including the President of the United States and J. Edgar Hoover . . . can do a damn thing about it. That is being free." He turned to Dave. "How was the party?"

171

"Lousy," Dave said and turned to Dr. White. "Who's Hyams?"

"Nobody."

"Hyams of the University, he says to me, like I'm supposed to fall flat on my face or something."

"Hyams is a minister with a couple of country churches," Dr. White said. "And I think he might substitute for some of the divinity men now and then, but he is not a bona fide member of the faculty."

Dave snorted. Now the University has Lawyer Greenes, he was thinking.

"But I think Hyams is," Professor Blake said. "I think that he has been granted some title of office. It might not be official yet, but I think he has it. I notice that he is the one who conducts chapel everyday now. I have an idea that he is now Dean of the Chapel, University Chaplain, or something like that."

"What's it pay?" Dave said sharply.

Dr. White spread his hands. "Salary? In nineteen thirty-seven you quibble over salary? It's the title that counts; the money will be sure to come later."

"You teach this to your students?" asked Dave. "In economics you teach this?"

"Dave, the positions we teachers hold are secured in the main by filling out applications. 'Dean of the Chapel' looks pretty good on an application blank," Dr. White said.

"He can't eat it," Dave said.

"He will eat before the applicant who is forced to insert 'unemployed' or 'just graduated.'"

"He'd be lying."

"Who?" Dr. White did not follow Dave's trend of thought.

"If a job don't pay, it ain't no job," Dave said.

"You refuse to face facts, Dave. This man, we are presuming, has a title. It is his. He earned it or is in the process of earning it; and so he has a perfect right to use that title as he wishes. Especially if he wants to get a better job."

"Okay," Dave begrudged that point, "but why does he come, tell me? I wouldn't hire him to sweep out the flower shop. Furthermore he calls me 'Greene' . . . no handle, no nothing to it. So he sure in hell wasn't looking for a job from me. So why does he tell me that he's Hyams of the University." Dave almost choked in his anger. "The bastard was lying to me."

"You are a pathological perfectionist," Cokey said to Dave.

"Halleluiah," Blueboy screamed.

"You go to hell," Dave said mildly. He had not paid too much attention to Cokey's words, and he thought Blueboy was drunk.

172

"You want everything in its final stage of perfection before anyone dares to invent it," Cokey said and there was an apology in his voice.

"Give him hell, Texas Boy," Blueboy yelled gleefully.

Dave turned to Blueboy. "Nobody's that crazy," Dave told him. "Everything has got to have a beginning . . ."

"If this here boy came to kick your butt without lying, let him kick it," Blueboy said with carefree malice. He turned to Cokey. "I've been trying to tell this predated bastard the very same thing for years, but he won't believe me."

Cokey smiled gently. "Honestly, Dave, you simply refuse to accept halfway measures even in an emergency. It's not a healthy mental attitude."

"You mean half-assed measures," Dave grumbled.

"Personally," Cokey said, "I hate Hyams's guts, but I refuse to hate his ambitions. This is in the middle of a depression, and he's trying to gain stature, to make himself eligible for a better paying job. Call him what you may, but it's inhuman to take a man's dreams and tear them up and then throw them in his face."

"What are you driving at?" Dave said roughly because one of his many minds was asking another if Lawyer Greene had possessed a dream.

"I tole Orville and I tole Wilbur the damn thing would never fly," Blueboy yelled.

Dave thought to change the topic of conversation. "Is Helen Deas an intelligent woman?" he asked Cokey.

"Hell, yes. Why'd you ask?"

"Well, why should an intelligent woman come in here, wearing jodphurs and things when there's not a riding stable within four hundred miles of this place? Leastways, none that caters to colored."

"Same reason these Vessey Street chicks wear them motorcycle clothes," Blip said.

"Furthermore, Ed Deas might own a farm around here somewheres. You ever think of that?" Blueboy said.

"Well, does a man have a right to dress according to his dreams?" Professor Blake asked unexpectedly.

"Now what the hell does that mean?" Blueboy wanted to know.

"Well," the teacher said uncertainly, "I think Herbert Hoover's collars are uncomfortable. Why does he wear them? And a riding habit is not the most comfortable or inexpensive attire a girl could choose to wear. I think psychologists should take a closer look at a person's attire."

Dave laughed. "Little Boy Blue and his blue suits."

"Jimmy Walker's the same way about gray," Blueboy said.

"Study clothes and every damn nigger in the U.S. would end up in the booby hatch," the insurance man named Joe Kelso grumbled.

"Why would a waiter wear a brief case to work?" Dave said it so bitterly that the Table was momentarily silenced. He looked across the Table at Blip-Blip and said, "I never knew Kid Flick was in society. He always hangs out with that Kings Mountain crowd?"

"His pop was the first to build out there," Blip said. "Thought everybody knew it."

"Heck no. I thought he said his old man was a janitor in a bank

"It's like this, Dave," Blip said. "Mr. Johnson is a respectable man. He is respected in this town by white folks, and that can mean more than money in the bank."

"White-folks-nigger," somebody grumbled.

"Mebbe," Blip said, "but a janitor don't necessarily have to Uncle Tom. He works for white folks is true. And they think a whole lot of him is all I know. Now mebbe them white folks use Mr. Johnson like a Judas goat to make fools outen rich niggers. I dunno. Mebbe they wants to show their appreciation, and so they builds a home out there and gives it to him. Who knows that either? All anybody knows is that they subdivided that land out there; it ain't fit for nothing much anyhow. And then they sets up these restrictions and calls it Kings Mountain and sells the lots to the high and mighty Negroes. Mr. Johnson builds out there first. They give it to him? They loan him the money? Mr. Johnson born with money? Who knows? Them half white families is like icebergs anyhow."

"You mean, for instance, that Mr. Johnson might be a blood relative of one of the bank's officials?" Dr. White asked.

Blip nodded. "Could be. Some of these light-skin families seem awfully lucky at times. Looks like their daughters don't never have no trouble getting jobs teaching school in town here. The black gals gotta go out in the country. It's like hidden power they got, but you can't ever really see nothing. Can't prove nothing. Old Man Johnson is a janitor what lives in Kings Mountain; that's all you see."

The conversation drifted on. Dave caught Cokey's eye and mouthed the words: "Let's get out of here." He rose from the Table and beckoned for Delilah.

"Yassuh, Mist Greene?"

Her words served to renew Dave's latent suspicion that Delilah

174

deliberately tried to provoke him with her strange accents. He could not help but think that she talked differently to other guests in Booker's. And he felt a mild pang of regret: he had no way of knowing. Since the first time the beautiful little girl had waited on him two years ago she had never engaged in any conversation with him or any of his guests. Sometimes Cokey would talk to her before he sat down to the Square Table, but he had never heard the two converse at the Table. So in all the two years Delilah had said little more than "No, sir," "Yes, sir," and "Thank you." Dave could not recall her ever having said as much as "Good evening," and yet he really was provoked by the way she said those few words.

Dave was also sure that Delilah hated him, and it always angered him when he thought so. "Where's my check?" He could not help but to make his voice spiteful.

"Leffum ova sideboad. Ah gettum."

"Never mind," he said reproachfully, and handed her a ten-dollar bill. Then he abruptly turned away from her as if he was afraid that she would not say thank you.

Cokey grinned at the poker-faced Delilah and then followed Dave out into the street. "You got a weakness for Delilah?" he asked.

"No. Why?"

"Kinda big tip you gave her, wasn't it?"

"How do I know? She didn't show me her check. She can keep the change, and if it's not enough Blueboy can pay the rest. I just didn't feel like hearing her say another word in that ignorant way of hers."

"Wish you'd get mad at my accent," Cokey said. "Blueboy paid a good-sized tab just before you walked in. Of course I am glad to see the ebon angel make it. I was just interested in why you did it. Thass all."

"I can't help it," Dave said. "I can't stand to have her around me since she's gotta talk that way. That Geechie accent bugs me, and besides, I think she does it to me on purpose."

"Well, she's too pretty to make me mad even if she cussed me and my cat."

"It's not her looks. I think she's pretty, too, but her way of talking is so ugly I don't want her around me."

They had reached Macon Avenue and stopped. "You know," Cokey said, "I'll never understand how a bigtime operator like you can find time to let a million little things bug him. You're going to end up with a nervous broke-up."

"Between you and Blueboy I'm already broke-up."

"Which do you hate the most—Lila or the Square Table and its darkest knights?"

"Both," Dave exploded. "All three, in fact. Each is worse than the other. But most of all I hate that damn table. I hate the wood it's made out of; the shape it's got." He started walking on Macon and Cokey followed slightly behind him for a few steps. "That goddam table looks like a nigger," Dave yelled.

"The Square Table looks like a nigger? How?"

Dave glanced suspiciously at Cokey. "You know damn well it looks like some kind of freak that ain't got no business being nowhere and especially where it is. And those damn crows that sit around it every night look and talk just like that damn table."

"Have you mentioned this odd impression to Blueboy?"

"You ain't stupid. Or are you? He thinks more of that freakish table than he does of me or anything else. Where would you find white college professors · sitting around in a public joint—and a bootleg one at that—and talking such crap to their students? And don't try to tell me that Booker's is the same as a students' beer hall. Niggers don't even lead an imitation of life. Just like that lousy-assed party I went to tonight. When it's black it stinks!"

"You really think our lives are a farce, don't you?"

"Hell, yes. And what the hell do those crows talk about at that table? And won't they ever learn that you can't make a cracker change his mind by talking behind his back? All the breath they waste could put the Negro race in the dirigible business. You ever hear them talking about how to cheat the Internal Revenue people? Or how to invent something? Corner the market for something? You ever hear them talk about how to make and save a dollar?"

"Like the Black Dollar?"

"What in hell are you talking about now?"

"You think we could talk about just any old dollar?" Cokey asked. "We, the Knights assembled, must have color in our topics! Like *The Black Investor, White Capital and Black Labor, Brown America and Its Dollar, The Black American's Fight for the White Man's Dollar*. We gotta have color in our talks, Mr. Greene of the Black Lottery."

"You and Blueboy must stay up nights thinking new ways to bug me."

"Could be, but what's on your mind? Or did you think I needed airing?"

"Damn if I know," Dave said, morosely hunching his shoulders. "I'm so damn restless I could go climb a mountain right this minute. I can't go to bed and I can't stand any more of that table tonight.

176

Let's go by some pad we haven't been in lately. Mebbe something will happen. Even if it's just a strange piece of tail."

"Okay by me. By the way, I hear you operate the Nigger Pool."

"Yeah, I heard. A lousy cracker can't say numbers; he's gotta use two words instead of one."

"I like that."

"You really crazy?"

"It means that the white boy is playing numbers to his own shame and regret. It means that he has come to you, a black boy, for what he wants. A wishful dollar. The white boy has shown his financial feet of clay. Very satisfying to me."

"You've been drinking too much of Blueboy's likker."

"Gee, thanks. I'll only drink yours from now on."

"White boys are smarter than niggers. I don't like it."

"Who does?"

"What I mean is that some white boy is gonna get the idea of banking numbers soon. Now if white boys had started banking numbers in the Ward, not a single darkie would have dreamed of banking them too. But, like I say, white boys are smarter with a dollar. You wait and see what happens. Might even be trouble."

"Do you know that a lot of people here in the Ward would welcome the opportunity to play their numbers with a white banker?"

"Why the hell you think I hate that damn Square Table so much?"

"What the devil has the Square Table got to do with it?"

"It's just like what Dr. White said tonight. Negroes are unable to take a realistic view of a Negro. Every nigger claims he don't, but niggers think like niggers. You're damn right they would like to lose their money to a cracker. Just like they prefer to have their heads whipped by a cracker cop. It's like Blueboy says. A white foot in a black ass is the acme of racial intercourse."

Cokey laughed.

"Look here," Dave said tightly. "I've got a little candy store and smoke shop with another fellow. It's losing money, but do you think the guy that runs it thinks anything of carting home five dollars' worth of cigarettes with him? And the hell of it is that I don't think the fool knows he is being dishonest."

"Borrowing?"

"Hell, no. He never intends to replace them. It's just another one of his goddam civil rights, I guess. He can't even realize that he is stealing from himself. And what the hell is a man gonna do with five bucks' worth of cigarettes at fifteen cents a pack?"

"Sell them of course."

"The black sonofabitch can't sell them over the counter," Dave said. "He gonna sell them for less than he paid for them? And they're half his. I tell you, Cokey, those guys at that table talk about some mythical Negro. They don't know the facts."

"So how do you explain your pickup men and the guys who count your daily receipts?"

"They're probably the most intelligent Negroes in the Ward, and that includes all teachers, doctors, and lawyers. I got two girl pickups now. Sweet workers. And every single one of my seventeen pickups is capable of holding down any money job in this damn city. But they don't have a college degree or a white ass, and so in a way, I offer them the only chance they got to work with their brains. Why a goddam Negro insurance company wouldn't give them a break at a job. And then too there is glamour of a sort in numbers and those free cars gives them prestige kinda. Makes them professionals in a way. My people are too damn smart to be crooked with me."

"You realize you're talking out of both sides of your mouth?"

"But those guys at the table talk like every damn Negro in the Ward is like my people, and it just is not so. And they say it's just an opportunity that the black boy needs. But, it's something else too. And you gotta be born with it, or maybe learn it in early childhood, but whatever it is the average Negro ain't got it."

"According to you the average Negro is inferior to the average white man."

"I don't really know, Cokey." Dave sounded tired and lost. "I know that whites steal too, but they steal intelligently. A damn nigger that can't read or write will steal a Greek dictionary. See what I mean? And it all gets on my nerves. I got plenty of money. I can afford to lose some, but it's having to face the fact that a nigger ain't shit every time I invest that gets me down. And so I have invested my last dollar in Negro business until the Negro is ready. He ain't ready now. The Negro has no loyalty other than to himself personally. The only thing that holds the Negroes together to a certain extent is the white man's hatred of him. The black man's got no family, no history, no cause to hang together except being hated. You ever hear of the Black Hand Italians? They are like blood kin. It's like royalty. The King is dead? Long live the king! But when a nigger dies everything he ever stood for dies too."

"Dave?" And Cokey's voice broke with the magnitude of his thought. "Suppose. Just suppose you sent your seventeen brilliant pickups to seventeen different towns to start a numbers bank?"

"I ain't got the guts," Dave said softly.

"Yeah, I know. If they screwed you, you would be a screaming maniac the rest of your life and it wouldn't be on account of the money either."

"Yeah," Dave said, "and there are other excuses I could give you like there ain't seventeen or even one town open for a Negro to go to and start a numbers bank. This was the last good-sized town left in America. Unless you want to count the ones with less than five thousand Negroes in them. But I gave it to you straight. I just don't have the guts."

16

The telephone screamed, penetrating into the alcoholic depths of Dave's slumber. Searing flashes of a magnificent hangover blinded him; very slowly he picked up the receiver. He feared he would retch if he moved too rapidly.

"Hallo, theah. Greene's Farm?" the caller asked in the clipped accents that Dave knew so well and had come to despise. The accent conjured up a ready image of the person: young, white, female, rich, and horsy. A girl who thought a damn sight more of a horse than a nigger waiter. He had served meals to this voice all over America. The Homestead, The Greenbrier, The United States, Mackinac, French Lick, Fisher's Island. Everywhere the money went, this damn voice went too. It was a money voice. He replaced the receiver with a vicious swipe and turned over on his suffering stomach.

The phone rang again.

"I say theah . . . I want stud service . . . I rally must have youah stud service."

Joy burst through the tight drum of his headache. "Kelly?" he squeaked. "Kelly?"

180

Cool and pure as the heavens her voice came to him. "And who else calls for stud service at this time of the morning? I only wish to remind you: it's either heaven or hell. I take a stroll along Tinton Road at four P.M." She said no more, but Dave heard the notes of a starry giggle before she hung up.

Thinking of how little good it did him now, Dave recalled one of Blueboy's lectures on women: Keep your women off balance! If you ever let her get set, she'll knock your dick-string loose. She thinks you're taking her to a movie? Take her to church. She puckers her lips? Light a cigarette. She turn her cheek for a good night buss? Kiss her titty. You can do any damn thing you wants with a woman as long as it ain't what she expected. And if you don't do it that way, she's gonna get bored, and tell you to haul your tail elsewhere. Keep 'em twisted. Never give a bitch time to think.

Dave smiled ruefully. Blueboy would pitch a bitch if he knew, but the devil in hell couldn't keep Dave Greene off Tinton Road at four o'clock this afternoon. He lit a cigarette and considered the spunk of the girl. Crazy, mebbe, but she had not deigned to wait for an answer. He loathed the way he had spent the night loving her—only to turn his back on her in the morning. But now everything was all right. Kelly cared. She had challenged him to stay away from Tinton Road if he could. She had already won, hands down.

He jumped out of bed and began a day of endless toil. He refused to relax; take a drink; or even look at the clock. He was afraid to even indulge in thoughts of their rendezvous. If he allowed himself to worry about Kelly's not being there, he would take a drink, and then he would worry some more and take another drink, and by four o'clock he would be roaring drunk.

This was the morning that Makepeace assumed complete control of the countinghouse. Then there was the long-drawn-out talk with Colonel Eldrege. The Colonel was a man who dearly loved to split hairs; he called it being "business-like." If Kelly had not called him, Dave would have backed out of the deal with the old man. He did not dislike the old codger, but he didn't want to become too close to a man who was said to be so close to the police and the powers that be. However, on this particular day, he was glad to immerse his mind in negotiations for leasing an abandoned fraternal hall and converting it into a roller-skating rink.

Dave had several moments of regret. He was breaking his vow not to invest any more money in the Ward's bankruptcy-prone ventures. With a grin, he convinced himself that Kelly was totally responsible for this one. On the spur of the moment, he instructed

181

the Colonel's lawyer to put his share of the venture in the name of Kelly Simms. It gave him a sensuous feeling of partnership with the girl. He had never considered Kelly's monetary status before, but, as of today, she could boast of a twelve-hundred-dollar interest in a roller-skating rink.

It was after three-thirty when he wound up the day's work and headed the Cord toward Tinton Road. In one of his many minds he cursed the fate that made him fall in love with a Barn chick. He imagined that a Barn chick just might get kicked out of school for associating with him. He was not sure, because he did not know what the school authorities thought of him, but he doubted if what they thought was very good.

What the hell. He only had two choices: go crazy with Kelly, or go crazy without her; and he was not too stupid to make the best of all possible decisions. He grinned and bore down on the accelerator.

His loins froze when he spied Kelly. She was walking in the same direction as he was headed. Her glossily sculpted head was bent as if in meditation, her hands thrust deep into the pockets of her skirt. That rhythmic, toed-in stride flowed effortlessly. All this he saw and loved.

Dave believed that Kelly's manner of walking was the only negroid trait in her outward appearance. Her stride was negroid only in the sense that Dave had never seen a white girl walk as gracefully as that. Very few Negroes, and no whites, he reflected.

He slowed the car to enjoy that miraculous gait. Almost, but not quite, she looked as if she were skating. She either sensed his presence or recognized the powerful rumble of the motor for she stopped, turned, and came quickly to him. Her smile was torture for Dave. Behind her cockiness was gratitude, and something else that only he and Kelly could name. He realized that she had not been sure that he would meet her, and he sought to reassure her. "You knew I was coming," he said.

"Good boy, lover," she murmured as she settled in the seat beside him. She raised her hand and absently swept the cowlick from her brow. The gesture was a sensuous excitant, and Dave saw it to be the most aesthetic motion any female could perform.

"Where to?"

She moved her shoulders with a feline indifference. "Anywhere . . . No, I don't mean that. I . . . take me home, your home. I feel matronly today."

"Matronly. Hows that?"

"Being sociable . . . sitting and talking . . . I don't really know," she confessed.

182

"What line did you feed the Dean this time?" Dave asked confidentially.

"Why, lover? What difference does it make?"

"Cokey told me about your problems with the Dean."

"I'm not having any trouble with the Dean," she said. "Although I might admit that the Dean is having her share of troubles with me. I refuse to let the Dean of Women besmirch my reputation. Anyone who willingly kneels to the rules of ignorance as set forth by the Dean of Women is no better than an animal. I behave like a person—the Dean's got trouble."

Dave did not have the slightest idea of what Kelly was seeking to prove. In fact he believed that she just felt like arguing and so he argued to please her. "Your honor tells you to break every rule and regulation governing the conduct of the girls in the Barn, right?"

She turned and leaned over so she could face him directly. "Some ecclesiastical perverts have taken one hundred and more, perfectly healthy, sex-conscious girls and penned them up in a barn—dormitory to you—and these perverts expect the girls to not only to suffer it, but to like it. The bastards."

"White schools do the same thing."

"Damn white schools," Kelly snapped. "I've read about Smith and Vassar girls having fun and games with Ivy League men in New York. The New York *Times* reports these gala affairs. Do you mean to tell me that the *Times* scrupulously reports the activities of girls that have sneaked off the campus?"

"Negro schools can't afford to let a whole dormitory get knocked up. Don't you realize it would look like hell?"

"You animalistic sonofabitch. It's time for you and your black brethren to learn to keep your pants buttoned until you get invited to the picnic. What the hell are you anyhow? A man or a stud? Slavery ended several years ago. Forced breeding is no longer feasible. If I understand you correctly, it would seem that your only reason for existing is to propagate more propagating black bastards."

"Now don't fly off the handle, Kelly."

"Who's excited? I'm simply speaking to you in your native tongue so you'll be able to grasp the fact that I, for one, am tired of being called a damn whore."

"Nobody's calling you a whore, but you gotta admit that the faculty of a Negro school has its problems." And Dave felt that he had covered the situation very well.

"The faculty of a Negro school has only one problem that I can readily think of: it needs to be educated. If the Dean of Women thinks that I can't be let out of that damn Barn for five minutes without demanding to be screwed by the first man I meet, she is a damn fool to try to educate me. A sheep-skin is not a chastity belt. If I'm a screw-happy undergraduate now, I'll surely become a screw-happy graduate. I'd like the opportunity to leave the Campus occasionally and prove for myself I'm not a nymphomaniac. You have to watch out, you know, or you start thinking like the Dean. A lot of the girls on Campus are like that. They may very well be virgins, but seduction and sexual intercourse are all they think about. Their lives are dedicated to the proposition that every man alive has but one fiendish desire and that is to bed them, and in their imaginations they love to put up the good mental fight to preserve their doubted virginity. If a man should ask one of them to accompany him to a funeral, they are immediately convinced that the man is mad. Now how in the hell does he expect to screw her at a funeral?"

With a sigh of relief, Dave brought the car to a stop in front of the house. He was proud to note that Kelly looked admiringly at the handsomely built brick home. This was followed by an attack of uncertainty. Did Kelly still expect an apology or was he already forgiven? Although the conversation had been peppery he somehow thought of it as being on an impersonal plane. Had that been Kelly's intention?"

"I hope Blueboy is home," Kelly exclaimed. Her look of happy expectancy intimidated Dave. She really didn't know Blueboy, other than having met him at the Blue Monday.

"Why?" he asked cautiously.

"I think he'd be fun to know."

"He's always at home this time of day. He listens to the news. Then he goes to the Booker's for dinner."

"Please, Dave, please let me cook dinner?"

"Go on in." He smiled. "I'll get some groceries."

Her smile of thanks whispered a promise.

Blueboy answered the doorbell. "Astarte," he cried.

Kelly's carefree grin matched Blueboy's. "Astarte was no lady, and I think you know it."

His eyes sparkled appreciatively. "But she ruled all beauty and mebbe she was the only unique gal in all the world," Blueboy declared.

"I shall take your assertion under consideration and pass my decision later. You have either nailed me to a cross or sent me to heaven postpaid. But for openers, I think you called me a dirty name. So cut it out and let me in."

184

"Well, I'll be damned. Your face bewitched me. I thought you was already in and sittin' down."

"I love to hear the liquid notes that drip from a serpent's lips."

"You ain't Eve, and don't ask me for no fig leaves. Or no apples, neither. Where's Davey-boy?"

"He acted as if there was no food in the house."

"Food? Guess mebbe there isn't. We ain't in competition with Booker's. What's up? You mad at Booker's?"

"I have a yen to cook for my menfolk."

"Menfolk? Seems like you're including me in." He grew suspicious. "What's the matter? Don't you know how to cook?

"Don't be silly. That's all I learned in high school."

He still eyed her narrowly. "I wants no burnt offerings."

"You will rue this day and that remark."

"You got more nerve than a brass monkey." But he could not hide the admiration he felt. Then he looked crafty. "Is you intending to poison Dave?"

"I wouldn't harm a hair on his poor head."

"Damn right. You never harmed a hair on his head. You just went and took the whole stupid thing! He's been a brainless wonder around here ever since."

They were sitting in the jumbled parlor, and Kelly smiled, remembering. With stupid impudence she said, "This is a remarkable room, isn't it?"

"Davey-boy don't think so no more. You gave him a bad case of inferiority with complications. Why you take so long to return to the scene of your triumph?"

The light smile held a wisp of regret. "Lovers' quarrel."

"Lovers, now, eh?"

"Why don't you ask Dave, you big-eared relative of a mule?"

"I'm big-eared enough to whup you, gal. And don't you ever forget to remember that."

Kelly leaned forward.

"I love you, intrepid gentleman," she whispered huskily. "Why the hell don't you give Dave a transfusion?"

"He ain't bashful and you know it. He's reticent."

"He should see a doctor. Is it contagious?"

"You ain't no lady."

"You said that before, and I told you I adore you. So why didn't the reticent patient have the guts to call me?"

Blueboy was unaware of exactly what had gone on between Dave and Kelly, and so he said, "Wal . . . you know Dave."

"I thought you were his mentor. You could have picked up the phone and placed it in his trembling hands."

"I tole you that he ain't got no head any more."

"And you have no spine." She laughed. "The spineless leading the headless. Why that is really wonderful. How do you do it?"

"Gal, I got more nerve in one fingernail than you and Davey both got. I can outdo you in any game life's got to offer. I can even be dumber than you is if necessary!"

With exaggerated slowness Kelly asked, "Can you play poker?"

With equally exaggerated understatement Blueboy replied, "I think so."

"After dinner you can loan me three dollars and I'll take all your money," Kelly stated factually.

"You are the maddest woman that crazy boy ever brought in here," Blueboy shouted. "No! Why should I loan you money to gamble against me for?"

"Against you and Dave, I won't be gambling."

Blueboy screamed with joy. "I been to the four corners of the known world, and I have always held my own in every port o' call. Blueboy Harris is a worthy man in any man's poker game."

"Then loan me three dollars."

"No," Blueboy snapped, "but what you wanna play, stud?"

As if she had time and money to burn, Kelly lazily lit a cigarette. "I've got two dollars and some change. Your three makes it six. I'll play you anything you want to play . . . head to head. When I get up to ten bucks, we start to play stud. Dave, too. Okay?"

The doorbell rang, and Blueboy went to answer it. He returned in a moment, followed by Cokey, who grinned his surprise. "Where'd you come from?" he asked Kelly.

"Hi, Cokey. I came to bedevil Dave and his mad Keeper. Where you coming from?"

"I served a wedding reception at the Hotel Lee."

"Good boy. Loan me two dollars for an hour."

"I only made two and I spent a quarter already." He handed her all he had. Kelly rose and headed for the kitchen. "Come, Blueboy chile," she said over her shoulder. "I take it that an international gambler such as you has a deck of cards in the house."

Blueboy grunted, but got up and followed her. He took a deck of cards from the drawer of the kitchen table and then eyed Cokey with scathing contempt. "You is lower than a pimp," he charged. "If you got money, why can't you play yourself? Big as you are, you gotta go and hide behind the skirts of this poor crazy lass."

"I did it in the name of research," Cokey drawled, unabashed.

186

"Kelly got a rep on the Campus at penny ante. I want to see what she can do with a so-called professional."

"I'll so-call you in a minute, schoolboy. I ain't to be played with."

"Kelly challenged you. I didn't. Why pick on me?"

"Because you is crazy! That's why."

When Dave returned, he was treated to the unbelievable spectacle of a girl driving a middle-aged man insane with a deck of fifty-two cards. Kelly's smile was fixed as she won pot after pot with boring regularity from Blueboy. Dave immediately took a hand thinking to cool off Kelly's luck, and he was convinced it had to be luck.

Kelly continued to win. Blueboy and Dave knew exactly how the girl was outwitting them but were impotent to prevent the slaughter. Kelly's game was at the same time capricious and coldly logical. She never called when Dave or Blueboy held the best hand, but she bet wildly when she held the better cards. And she was not averse to stealing a pot now and then. Her playing was as unpredictable as her conversation.

Later, when she left the game to go upstairs, Blueboy fumed, "I think she was born in a Chinese gambling den."

Dave was sheepish. "She's always saying she was raised in a whorehouse, and damn if she don't act it sometimes."

"You can say that again," Blueboy growled.

Cokey gently poured salt in their wounds. "She was raised in a hardshell Baptist parsonage. Her father graduated from divinity school right here."

"No preacher's daughter's gonna know how to nit and plunge like she does," Blueboy said. "She handle this game like we wuz her country cousins."

"I was thinking the same thing," Cokey agreed with apparently innocent candor.

"I tole you not to loan her that money," Blueboy said.

"And I said I was doing it in the name of research. Seems like I found the answer."

"You ain't welcome here no more."

"You mean I can't come in or ain't welcome?"

"Both! And I'm gonna see that you is suspended from the Square Table for this," Blueboy yelled.

Cokey's eyes widened in amazed disbelief. "You mean you gonna tell everybody what she done to you?"

"It's that damn smile she got," Blueboy alibied. "She looks like a kid with jam on his face, and so your common sense tells you

187

she is stealing the pot and so you calls. And then what does she show you?"

"Everything," Cokey said.

"Thanks for the compliment," Kelly said graciously as she strolled back into the kitchen. "That is what I call a rare compliment—almost raw."

"That warn't no compliment," Blueboy thundered. "You plays so close to your chest, nobody can get a decent bet outa you. People is suppose to call my bets. I ain't suppose to be calling some chump's bets. I give you my money, I did."

"I don't think we should discuss a lady's chest in public." But Kelly's demure smile was all-forgiving.

Blueboy didn't want any forgiving. "I wish you was a man," he grumbled.

"I'm sorry, Blueboy. I never dreamed you could not afford to lose. Here. Take every penny of your money back."

Cokey roared.

All at once Kelly turned into a hardworking harlot, madly in love with her pimp. Her voice was hoarse and warm as she approached Dave. "I won it all for you, lover," she pleaded forgiveness.

A snort of bafflement escaped him. "One of these days, I'm gonna brain you," he promised with love.

"You are angry. I didn't win enough for you. I'm so sorry, lover," she moaned in shameful guilt.

Dave reached out and pulled her into his lap. Ruffling her glistening locks, he said, "Okay, you nut. I forgive you for everything except for what you did to Blueboy. He'll never be the same again."

"Don't you go playing me cheap," Blueboy yelled. "Anybody can have a freakish run of bad cards. She couldn't do it again if she lived a million years. Why, Georgia Brown never done me no dirt like this." He looked at Kelly with malice. "You ever heard of her?"

Kelly was suddenly a gun moll. "She's out of Chi," she said conversationally. "Know Big Kid and St. Looey?"

Dave gawked and Blueboy choked. Then, remembering that Kelly was from the Midwest, Dave was able to see how any colored youngster could rattle off the names of Big Kid and St. Louis Kelly. But Georgia Brown was another matter; she wasn't notorious like the two nationally known colored gangsters. "You really know Georgia Brown?" he asked, confounded by the realization that Kelly Simms and Georgia Brown had a hell of a lot in common.

Kelly admitted nothing. "Her sister's a swell guy," she said.

"That is a lie, Miss Smartypants," Blueboy kindly asserted. "Georgia Brown ain't got no relatives. She's an orphan. She tole me so."

Kelly feigned boredom. "Savannah Brown claims to be Georgia Brown's sister. Now if Georgia Brown claimed kinship to Savannah Brown, Ph.D., one might look askance, but when a nationally famous educator says that she and a shady lady are siblings, I am inclined to believe the doctor."

"Well you is inclined in the wrong direction," Blueboy insisted.

Kelly remained silent, but it was the silence of one who rests on superior knowledge. She absently riffled the cards.

"Dr. Savannah Brown teaches English on the Campus," Cokey said.

"They still can't be kin," Blueboy insisted. "And I know Georgia better than most."

Kelly became curious. "What makes it so unbelievable, Blueboy?"

"Why should Georgia Brown go to such great pains to make her best friend think she was entirely without a family?" Blueboy asked in return. "Like you say: there's no reason for a whorelady to deny her kin. Especially if her kin don't deny her. One of our brethren is in the woodpile."

"All I know is that there is a thousand-dollar scholarship available once every four years to a friendless girl—no one in their right mind would try to tell you what that means, or how it is decided. I was never interested in it myself, because the scholarships I do have automatically disqualify me. But every four years Dr. Savannah Brown's sister renews the thousand dollars. In other words, the girl who is granted the scholarship is given two-fifty a year for four years. Then it's given to another friendless girl. It's called The Helping Hand Award or some such drool."

Blueboy was unimpressed. "'Tain't no kin of Georgia Brown's," he said.

"You really know her, Blueboy? Tell me what she's like."

"Seems like you should know, you bein' raised in a whorehouse and all."

"Stop teasing," Kelly pleaded, while Blueboy basked in his triumph. "And you know I really wasn't raised in a whorehouse."

"Not from the way you play stud I don't."

"If I tell you how I learned to play stud, will you tell me?"

"Nope. I ain't interested in how you learned. What I wants to know is why you bother to go to college since you already got a money-making profession."

189

"The same reason I bothered to learn poker, I guess," Kelly said.

Cokey set up Blueboy for the *coup de grâce*. "To her it's only an interesting game that requires a definite mental skill if you are going to win."

"That's a lie and you know it," said Blueboy. "I give her them pots. I just wanted to see if she was greedy enough to take 'em."

"Dave?" said Kelly. "I was awful, wasn't I? I had no right to take Blueboy's money. Look how hurt he feels. I really wasn't a nice girl at all, was I?"

"And *you* shaddap, too." Blueboy could hardly contain himself. "I am going to send an anonymous telegram to the Dean of Women and tell her what you done."

"See? Now Blueboy says I cheated him," said Kelly in her sweetest voice. "We should have played something Blueboy knew how to play," she lamented.

"Git her out of here," Blueboy screamed at Dave and Cokey. "And never bring another schoolgirl under this roof as long as you lives or after you're dead either!" He stomped out of the kitchen, and a few moments later the three young people heard him go up the stairs, whistling a happy tune.

The number that day had been 054. More than twenty people hit it.

17

Dr. Leon White had been feeling like a crazy man all day, blue as hell. Just like right now he wanted to throw himself at Blueboy's feet and beg the man to take him to his bosom.

Unconsciously Leon White shook his head like a befuddled bull, as they say he did before he rushed a line in football. When Dr. White realized he had done this, his mind went back to those days in school. Jubilant friends had borne him on their shoulders and nobody had thought of color then. But that was wrong, he remembered, because always in every game there had been the drunk who yelled from the stands, "Go, nigger, go," or had it been Black Boy? He could not remember. He only remembered the look of apology on the colorless faces of his teammates. And he had felt guilty. It was his face and his skin that had brought the anguish to them.

He wondered how Blueboy would have felt.

Blueboy was addressing him and he tried to shed his crazy revelry to listen, but he couldn't. This table was Blueboy's toy, he reflected without rancor. He moved the minds of these men here like so many chessmen. All pawns.

Dr. White stared at Dave. Something prodded him to debunk the numbers banker. And just who the hell was Dave Greene? he reflected. Dave, like every other man at the table, was hopelessly flawed. And Dave was only a fringe Negro at best. His cool reticence was born of an inability to be assimilated by the black man. He was a freak, a brown-skinned white man. Dave even had the deceptive intelligence of an Irishman who, be he a known success, would always be referred to as a Dumb Irishman.

Dr. White's eye found Joe Kelso, a not too bright egomaniac who believed he was possessed of a gift for business administration. The man was only an insurance agent, making less than twenty-five dollars a week. But Joe would never be able to encompass the fact that he was born to debt and failure. The seedy little man would never be more than a respectable Vessey Street hustler.

Dr. White's thoughts turned to Cokey, a charming oaf who laughed at his own inadequacies. And the doctor was sure that it was cowardice that kept Cokey off the football team. And why didn't the boy stay on the Campus where he belonged? A college student would not let himself be used as a mascot for racketeers.

". . . Call them house niggers if you please, but . . ." he heard Pollyanna Blake saying. Dr. White tried to shut out his own thoughts to listen to this gutless spittlelicker of the entire Negro race. He tried to pay heed but his own thoughts kept intruding.

Why should a man constantly be apologizing for being born good-looking? It was all too apparent that Blake was deathly afraid of Negroes and sought to contain the savage beasts by heaping praise upon them with every breath he took. Dr. White wondered if Blake was really sane. This time he resolved to listen to what the fool was saying.

"Once we have a civil rights law on the books all our problems will be solved," Professor Blake was saying. "The white man is civilized. You forget that. And there are millions of white Southerners who want to give the Negro all that is due him, but are afraid of the public opinion of a few ignorant and backward whites. But once they are able to say, 'This is the law; we must obey it,' then we ourselves will be free."

"Not a chance," Cokey said sharply. "This is no law-abiding country, and furthermore, how are you gonna make stupidity illegal? And that is what race prejudice is: Stupidity!"

"You are very cynical," Professor Blake said to him.

"Well, all I know is what I read in the papers," Cokey said.

192

"Incidentally, I see where a colored numbers banker loaned a candidate for governor seventy-five cars for a political motorcade."

"That's a goddam lie," Blueboy yelled.

"That's what the governor of Tennessee says," Cokey replied cheerfully. "And what are you screaming about? You mad about the seventy-five cars or you mad because a numbers banker votes?"

"Me and Davey never votes," Blueboy said primly. "We are smart citizens and don't have to vote."

Dr. White's thoughts returned to the table with a crash. Here was a part of what had been making him feel down all day. "You will weep bitter tears for that idiocy," he said to Blueboy.

"White is white," Dave said "and never votes black. What have we got to lose?"

Dr. White glared at Dave. "And it is because your public servants are white that you should do all in your power to control them. And public officials know only one god, and that is political power."

"Yes," Professor Blake chirruped. "Power. Power at the polls has got to be felt."

"You two teachers are a disgrace to the colored race," Dave growled. "You ain't even smart enough to believe in smoke-filled rooms, and they are just fables for the ignorant. Real political power ain't got nothing to do with votes. And it's wielded in well-ventilated hotel rooms and usually at resorts. I know; I've waited on those meetings all over the country."

"Cynicism," Professor Blake said with a sniff. "The Negro public will be heard."

"You are damn right the public will be heard from," said Dave. "The Negroes in this town are heard from every day but Sunday, and they personally tells me that they likes to gamble. So who makes the anti-gambling laws? God? The People? You? Me?"

The two professors exchanged knowing smiles.

"Come, come, Dave." Dr. White knew that he sounded superior as hell, but he couldn't help that. Dave was dumb. "Who plays numbers? A handful of dolts."

"We see over ten thousand numbers slips a day," Blueboy bellowed. "That's over ten thousand votes from dolts, ain't it? Sometimes two, three people got their numbers on one slip. There's plenty of elections in this town ain't decided by ten thousand votes."

Dr. White was shocked out of his depression. "You're not serious," he managed to say.

"What about?" said Blueboy.

"Ten thousand slips," Dr. White said.

"A slip averages a quarter's worth of bets. We take in well over two thousand dollars a day. Now you figger it out."

"But . . . but . . . some people play dollars, I heard."

"So what? We got housewives play ten numbers for a penny each. We got nickel slips and two-bit slips, but they all averages out to a quarter a slip."

"You and Dave are the head of a corporation that handles ten thouand transactions a day. It's unbelievable."

"What's so phony about it?" Dave wanted to know.

"Not phony," Dr. White murmured. "I'm just astounded to learn that a Negro is involved in a commercial venture that has a round daily figure of ten thousand connected with it."

Cokey chuckled. "So was I when Blueboy first told me," he said. "Don't that many Negroes get arrested a day in the United States. I don't think a colored garbage man collects ten thousand pieces of garbage a day."

But Dr. White was engrossed with the other side of the coin. "Ten thousand of us can play numbers a day, but not a single one of them will pay their poll taxes once a year," he muttered.

He stared down the table in rage, feeling once more that he was surrounded by idiots full of sound, but minus the fury to live like men. From the depths of his soul he said, "Without the shedding of blood you and your children must wither and die." Then even in his rage his curiosity got the better of him and he turned to Dave. "Are you the biggest numbers banker in the United States?" he asked.

"We're just small potatoes," Blueboy answered for him with utterly false humility. "The only thing that gives us recognition is that we are the only bankers in this town and we don't have a damn cent of white money backing us. Harlem got a numbers banker on every other street corner they tells me. But take a town like Richmond. They got five white bankers and two Jewish ones. Not one single nigger. The Jones brothers of Chicago are the biggest and the blackest, I guess."

The talk drifted on and Leon White returned to his melancholia. Seven years wasted in lonely classrooms. And for what? To sit here and be an outsider among these barren men?

The blues that would not leave him increased. He was not only an outsider among these men, he was a stranger to their women. They all had spurned his blackness.

All except Kelly.

Only Kelly.

And as he thought of the brilliant girl he was no longer blue,

194

until he remembered that he was an outsider to her too. But Kelly was the only woman who had accepted him fully as he was. But when he had asked her to accept his love she had smiled ever so softly and told him about Dave.

But the only thing worthwhile that he had to remember about this goddam University was Kelly. He tried to stop feeling blue by thinking about Kelly. But why was the finest jewel the black man had produced madly in love with a criminal? And criminal was what Dave Greene was.

And maybe that was what was the matter with him today. Maybe the Ward had become too small for both him and Dave. But that couldn't be true. Dave was nobody. Dave was only the moon to Blueboy's sun.

But when all was said and done, the fact remained: Blueboy possessed that gift of never being alone. And that was all that mattered to Leon White today. When you came down to it he was not much darker than Blueboy, but Blueboy could rise above his blackness. Leon White could not.

His mind reeled on. Not for one more damn minute could he stand to be alone. But no one would let him join them. Not even Dave. Not Blueboy. And not Kelly.

He was even too damn black for the Black Nazis who were dominated by the evidently mongrelized like Dave.

If only he could become a bosom friend of Blueboy he knew he could withstand any and all ostracism. Once more he wanted to throw himself at Blueboy's feet and beg the man for friendship, but he feared Blueboy's contempt more than he wanted his friendship.

A cool, calming thought came to him: God had made him Black so that he would be sure to participate in the destruction of the white man's whitest towers.

He, Leon White, would make that long-debated decision. Membership in the Communist Party.

He began to feel warm and good, as if he already belonged. He would be a living man who had friends he could talk to and touch. No longer would he have to live beneath contempt; he would be the worthy foe of worthy foes. With sensual imagery he felt the pleasant relief of white billy clubs on his head, and he could feel the pleasant joy of smashing his fist into an Irish cop's red face.

And now that he had come to decide to cast his lot among those whose cause he doubted, he felt braver and stronger than he ever felt in his life. Robert E. Lee had fought a losing battle for a cause which he did not believe in, but his name would live forever in history.

Dr. White casually got up from the table. Professor Blake looked at him with inquiry in his eyes, but the young economist shook his head. He didn't want Blake to accompany him home tonight. He went around to the head of the table and touched Blueboy lightly on the shoulder. He held his breath. If Blueboy turned to him with a friendly smile in his eyes he might ask for a job in Blueboy's racket, but then he reminded himself that the die had been cast. He turned away from the table and quickly left the restaurant.

"The Negro has been granted every opportunity to use his brains as a white boy has, but the black boy has been too interested in God and respectability to seize his chances," Blueboy was yelling at someone. Dr. White thought it a fitting if enigmatic good night.

Fifteen minutes after Dr. White walked out of Booker's the dining room suddenly became silent. Panic was in the air, but no one knew what was the matter. The women at the various tables began to give little shrieks of either excitement or fear. Once the silence was broken a controlled buzz of whispering filled the room. The men at the Square Table glanced angrily at each other, daring the other to show panic.

"Goddam," Blueboy said softly.

Dave looked around and saw Old Man Booker crawling about on his hands and knees. Dave stared at the old man until he saw that Mr. Booker was going from booth to booth, gathering up the whiskey bottles that his ostensibly beer drinking guests kept hidden under the tables.

Then a babble broke out, and everyone in Booker's knew at the same time that the police were in the Block.

"Put the whiskey in your pockets," Dave ordered and got up from the Table.

The Lil Savoy was now on the lips of everyone. And it was the same controlled excitement as if there had been a fire in the neighborhood. The Knights of the Square Table rose and left the restaurant in a body. The Lil Savoy was located above the colored taxi office, directly across the street from Booker's.

It was a real speakeasy in comparison to the kiffs and pads in the Ward. It had a bar, a tiny space for dancing and several tables. There was a jukebox, but a faggot played the piano and sang most nights. On Sundays and holidays there might be an added attraction of a female shake dancer and a male tap dancer who told smutty jokes. And always, but always, there was the crap game in the back room.

The speakeasy was, in a sense, a front for the crap game, but it showed an excellent profit and was just as illegal as the gambling operation. The Ward was hypocritical in its own peculiar way. There was no social stigma attached to drinking in an illegal bar, but the more respectable element in the Ward frowned upon crapshooters.

All in all, the Lil Savoy was a pretty sleazy setup, but it was the Ward's only apology for a night club. It was owned by Colonel Eldrege, the venerable "boss" of the Ward.

A throng of gawkers stood in the middle of Vessey Street, blocking all traffic. The occasional shrill of a police whistle heightened the excitement, and the crowd gradually began to take on a holiday air.

Blueboy was standing beside Dave. "Colonel's supposed to have the Ward sewed up downtown," Blueboy murmured.

"You think I ain't worried," Dave said.

A bystander yelled, "Kuhnel ain't paid off de cops dis week."

The crowd tittered. Dave could not control a shiver that went through his body. The raid on the Colonel was unprecedented in the Ward and it made things look bad for everybody, especially Dave Greene. Dave was sure that the police were searching the Lil Savoy for numbers slips, because, although the street was lined with police cars, the police had brought no one out of the club. No sooner had Dave decided this than a police van pulled up to the front door of the club and the police began to herd their prisoners downstairs and into it.

They brought out no women. That meant that the police were only after the gamblers. Suddenly the crowd gasped. Dave, who was already rattled, jumped at the sound of the crowd's gasp of horror, and angrily wondered what was wrong now.

"Lookee her."

"Stop her."

"She drunk."

"She crazee."

It was several moments before Dave saw the woman. She was creeping along the ledge of the second floor of the building. It was evident that she had crawled out of a window, but nobody came to any window to call her back.

A big bear of a policeman was stationed on the sidewalk. He beamed his flashlight on her. "Git back in thar, gal," he called. "Git back now, ah say."

The crowd began to chant: "Git back. Git back."

197

Someone yelled, "Jump, fool."

Some in the crowd tittered nervously, deliciously. Dave felt sickened by it all; the girl and the crowd were a part of one abominable whole, but he could not take his eyes from the girl on the ledge. Her face was a fright mask. Her lips convulsively formed soundless words like some weird and grisly fish just landed from the sea.

"'Taint nothin'," someone called out. "Ain't no women getting took."

The rabble picked it up. "No women," they chanted in hysterical repetition.

The woman's eyes were two white balls of fear and they told Dave that she did not hear. Then she leaped.

Her body made a dull sound as it hit the pavement. Most of the women cried out in the night and Dave was keenly aware of all the sexuality in those cries over this sudden death. The burly policeman did a slow eccentric shuffle around the lifeless body. Then he stopped and stared first at the body and then at the throng.

"Now see what you done?" he demanded, of everyone, of no one.

Blueboy cleared his throat with a kind of grunt that said he needed a drink. Dave wordlessly followed him back into Booker's. One by one the men returned to the table. "Who's got the whiskey?" Dave demanded.

"I handed both bottles to Joe Kelso," Cokey said, gazing around the dining room. "He must not have come back in."

Through the mind of each of the ten men at the Table went one thought of guilt. No one spoke, each man feeling that he alone bore the blame and that the others were ashamed of him. That Joe Kelso, local Negro business leader, had stolen two half-filled bottles of whiskey from his fellow club members, each man had to acknowledge to himself. Of course it really wasn't a club, and Joe wasn't a business leader for real, but the facts would not down. What facts? They all knew and they all sat silent and guilty.

"Bring me two bottles of whiskey," Blueboy roared. The command started a chain reaction. Delilah heard it and leaped to Blueboy's bidding. Mr. Booker heard it and reached down under the showcase of sweet potato pies. He stood holding the bottles, waiting for Delilah to come to him. No one thought of the street full of police just outside the front door.

"Jesus! How could she have been so dumb?" Blip said.

Blueboy grunted in sober reflection. "I've seen fear," he said. "I seen more than my share mebbe, but nothing like that. In battle, at least you knows what everybody is scared of, but this was dumb fear. What the hell could she have been scared of?"

"I don't think . . ." Cokey had begun, but he stopped as though he had changed his mind in midsentence. "No, that was panic on her face, but even so . . . maybe she committed suicide."

"She went to a night club to do it?" said Dave.

"Damn! That's right," Cokey said. "She sure in hell didn't go to a night club to commit suicide. Death comes fast on this damn street. She looked like a slut; it's a wonder they let her in there."

"She ain't dead yet," Blueboy said carelessly. Every man stared at him. "You guys never hopped bells in a hotel. Below the fifth floor you can run out and try to give help. If it's above the fifth, pick up the phone and call the coroner. Of course that ain't for the ones that dives head first."

Dave looked up and saw Colonel Eldrege enter the restaurant. With cane in hand the old man was slowly making his way back to the Square Table. Dave watched the old man's progress and reflected upon many things. The Colonel was a sort of honorary Knight of the Square Table. He was a teetotaler, but he would drop by the table several times a night to chat. It was as if he came to the table for a breathing spell from his duties as operator-owner of the Lil Savoy, but right now Dave was bewildered. This man's gaming room had been raided, but here he was, unarrested and presumably uninterested. And nothing about the raid made sense anyway, Dave was thinking. The Colonel was Bob Stricker's voice in the Ward; there was no doubt about that. And Bob Stricker was the absolute Boss of the city and co-Boss of the state.

The Ward had always whispered that Boss Stricker and the Colonel had the same white father. Nobody seemed to know for sure, but there was not the slightest doubt as to the Colonel's power. He could limp into court and say, "Jedge, that's a good boy. He jest went and got too much of that devilish likker in him." And most times the judge would hand down a suspended sentence. This, of course, was when the accused was guilty of a crime perpetrated against a Negro. Colonel Eldrege did not speak for those colored gentlemen who were so stupid as to commit crimes against their white brethren.

Although Dave and the Colonel were friends and business partners, they were not intimates, and Dave had never asked the old man to intervene for any of his writers and pickup who happened to be arrested. None of Dave's men had ever been arrested for numbers playing, but quite a few had been arrested for loitering, breach of the peace, and other minor charges.

Dave had always felt that to pay the fines was the wisest course. He was rapidly acquiring a morbid distaste for publicity and he'd rather pay the fines than create talk, even if it was friendly talk.

As soon as the Colonel reached the table, Dave said, "What's up, Colonel?"

"De raid?" Whether the man's voice was trembling from anger or exertion Dave did not know, but the Colonel sounded as if he had been running. "Dey looking for that no-count-murdering-niggah, that's what."

The table was stunned. They had all witnessed the woman's plunge and yet they all connected her act with the Colonel's mention of murder. They forgot that the raid preceded her leap.

"How they figger she's murdered?" Cokey asked.

"Ain't thet fool," the old man wheezed. "This here Jim Penney went and got hisself murdered."

"Jim Penney," the group cried in concert.

"He was here last night," Professor Blake said. "I remember him. He was a student of mine."

"It wasn't last night," Blueboy said. "It was over a week ago."

That Jim Penney had been such a modest little guy made his violent death all the more shocking to Dave. Jim Penney, a mousy little chap, had sold bootleg corn whiskey in his prosperous fish-fry restaurant located on the west side of town. Jim had been a schoolmate of most of Dave's pickups and had stopped by the Square Table to chat occasionally.

"Word jes come," the Colonel said.

"Come?" Blueboy said irritably. "Come from where? He got killed in his joint, didn't he?"

Makepeace joined the group, wedging in a chair beside Dave, who noted that his huge comtroller seemed very contented. "Where you been?" Dave said.

Makepeace smiled complacently. "Found me a little hairdresser that loves big men, Davey."

"Wasn't no fight and it was a hunnert miles from here, up in de mountings," the Colonel was saying.

"What the devil was Jim doing in the mountains?" Cokey exclaimed. "Jim was always kidding about he was a real city slickster and had no use for the country. I remember him saying that nearest he ever got to the sticks was when he went up on the Campus for a semester."

"He was murdered and robbed," Colonel said.

"How?" Blueboy said.

"Jim jes didn't think. He let his own greed kill him." The Colonel

200

paused and then asked, "Remember that joory story robbery awhile back?"

"Sure," Blueboy said. "Somebody got five thousand bucks' worth of rings out of the joint in broad daylight and nobody knows how it was done. But Jim didn't do it. Or any other nigger either, I don't think. But Jim didn't have the moxie or the brains."

"Trufe. But this heah lowdown-crap-shooting-niggah comes to him with this tale about he did it and Jim can have all dem jools for three hunnert cash dollars."

"And Jim went for it?" Blueboy asked. "But what's murder got to do with it and what they doing in the mountains?"

"Thass where dis murderer say he got 'em buried at. And he wants Jim to go with him to dig 'em up. Den Jim s'pose to give him the money and den the niggah s'pose to git on a bus for Harlem and neveh came back. And Jim that dumb and greedy to fall for it."

"So what happened?" Blueboy said.

"Dat de way it s'pose to be, but de niggah ain't got no jools. Nevah did."

"So what Jim do?" Blueboy asked. "Get mad and start fighting?"

"No. Dey gets in de mountings and starts de diggin' and someways or t'other, de niggah sneaks up behinds Jim and beats his brains out wid de shovel in de mountings."

"How come the cops know so much already?" asked Blueboy.

"Wal, Jim's wife starts a worryin after he gone a whole night and day, and she jes know somethin's wrong. Mebbe she doan like it from de git go, but she his woman, what she gonna say?"

Dave watched the entire group nod their heads in agreement. They seemed notably stupid to him. What possible use is a wife if you can't sit down and talk over problems with her? Once more Dave thought that his mind simply did not work like the minds of other men. He definitely had to be a freak.

"Wal, she call de p'lice jes about de time de body found in de mountings; it ain't nowhere off de road, but it unidentified. Den de p'lice finds Jim's car right heah in de Ward. 'Bandon like wid de bloody shovel still in it."

"They know who the guy is that did it?" Dave asked.

"Eveybuddy know," Colonel said. "He owe me three dollahs right dis minute. De no-good-crap-shooting-murderer. Dem cops know he's somewheres right now in a crap game wid his bloody money. Dat's what de cops raidin' for."

"Kills a man to get in a crap game," Cokey said to Dave. "And why would he pick up the shovel and put it back in the car?" Cokey asked brokenly.

"See?" Dave whispered. "I keep telling you niggers is always playing games. Jim? He wants to make believe that he's a big-time fence like in the movies. What's he gonna do with fifty engagement rings? Niggers don't buy fifty engagement rings a year. The other guy? He just gotta be a big-time crook and gambler. I tell you these damn nigers will kill you just to be playing their games."

Cokey nodded, biting his lip and Dave realized just how upset the youth was. "C'mon, let's go," he said. "You might as well stay with us tonight."

The next day everybody played Jim Penney's address, which was 890 Westend Avenue, but the number was 171, and Pigmeat hit it for seventy-five cents.

18

It was a lazy spring day just made for lolling in bed. Kelly grinned voluptuously and murmured, "You know, when two or more girls are gathered together in your presence you're hopelessly tongue-tied. It's not the least bit fair to you, but who am I to complain?"

"We've got the pick of the Ward, if you know what I mean," Dave said. "There's hardly a dame around who wouldn't sell her soul to go with a numbers guy."

"You!"

"Me what?"

"I am trying to tell you that this romance must end graduation night, June 1939. I'm trying to tell you that you shouldn't let me be the only flower in your life. That's the proof of my love for you."

"June 1939 and we'll probably be married," Dave said and then watched the sadness descend over Kelly. He inwardly cursed his clumsiness, but how the hell do you lie in bed with a beautiful chick and never mention marriage? "Okay," he said. "So we won't be married. Mebbe we just won't be speaking to each other. Okay?"

Kelly smiled gratefully. "Yes, lover. It's very easy to imagine our not being on speaking terms. It seems as if all I do is argue with you."

He kissed her nipple. "I like to argue with you."

"You sure?"

"I'm sure."

"But you cherish your ignorance so. I just have to argue you out of some of your ideas. You sure you don't mind?"

"If I did, you'd know it. You've got me where you want me now."

"Stop it." But she did not move his hand. "Resourceful is what I was. I engineered this whole thing beautifully. And I think of it as a purely mental feat, even if I did have to fall back upon a mattress to complete the deed."

"Neither sex or brains had anything to do with it," said Dave. "We both got a weakness for lying in bed and chewing the fat. That's how it was. Compatibility. Seems like I can't think straight when I'm with you unless I'm lying on my back. Mebbe I'm a bedroom freak. You want a drink?"

"I'd love a drink, lover. Do you want me to go get us one?"

"You're a professional when it comes to needling somebody."

"I wasn't needling you. I really wanted to know if you wanted me to get the drinks. I don't mind. I like to wait on you."

Dave went to the dresser and poured two drinks and brought them back to the bed. "What'd you tell the Dean to get off the Campus this afternoon?" he asked.

"I told her that I had to go shopping."

"You mean that you can get off the Campus every time you want to go shopping?"

Kelly smiled crookedly. "No, lover. It won't work. If that's what you're thinking of."

"How do you know what I was thinking of?"

"You're a numbers king. Right?"

"Every man has a right to buy what he wants if he has the money."

"And every girl has got the right to refuse."

"I know you've got this feud on with the Dean, so why won't you let me help you?"

"I'm managing to slip off the Campus twice a week as it is. More than that would be straining it quite a bit."

Dave came over and kissed her. "Okay. Okay. But sometimes I get the feeling that you exclude me. Don't want my help. It's a funny feeling."

"Please don't feel like that, lover. It's just that I don't need your help."

204

"Do you realize that you and that damn Square Table are my only relaxations?"

"Please don't mention me and your Square Table arguments in the same breath."

"Okay, but answer this one question before we quit. Why won't you admit that there is a race problem?"

"I really don't think there is one," Kelly said.

"The Bible says so. You talk like you never read the Bible."

"No, I don't, lover. I prefer the sports pages, but what has Bible reading got to do with the race problem as you see it?"

"Where it says that all men are created of one blood. I guess that's a laugh, too, eh?"

"Chickens have been telling that to eagles since time began, but I doubt if very many eagles read your Bible."

"That ain't funny. The Bible is no jokebook and neither is the Negro and his problem."

"Well, why blame me? Indeed, I agree with you. The Nigra is a problem. But then I suppose Jews, Italians, Mongolians, and poor white trash are also problems. All males are idiots, and all idiots are problems."

"Are you, by any chance, trying to create an ethnic group out of the Negro again?"

This high sounding sarcasm piqued Kelly although her face did not show it. "If your Nigra is not a race, he better damn well hurry up and make himself a race because Black and White never the twain shall meet save on a mattress and that doesn't count."

"That means that the Negro is different from the white man. What makes him so different?"

"This is no longer the question. What makes us different is that our enemies treat us that way. Hitler has succeeded in making the world Race Conscious. And racists are here to stay."

"Nerts," Dave said. "How come you read the sports pages?"

"To reaffirm my conviction that man is a born imbecile. Have you ever noticed little girls playing hopscotch?"

"Of course. Why?"

"Well, have you ever seen grown women playing it? And all the while a large crowd of women stand around and cheer? And have you ever seen these same grown women dash madly to their typewriters when the game is over to dash off a few hundred words on the technique, character, and redblooded Americanism of the Women's National Hopscotch Champion? Whenever I feel discouraged I pick up the sports page and read man's idiocy to man."

"Words of pure genius."

"The sportswriter is one of our national disgraces."

"They make damn good money. And who was it that defended that dame that swims? In the Olympics, I mean."

"And only on the sports page must a grown woman have to be defended for putting away childish things."

"And just for a chance to get off those cracks you gotta go and make fun of the Bible?"

"I've always considered the Bible too terrifying to be laughed at."

"Say that again?"

"I said that I don't read the Bible because there is nothing in it that gives me solace, aid or understanding."

"Every human alive can find help in the Bible."

"For instance?"

"What are you trying to argue about now?" Dave yelled. "You just said that you never read the Bible so how the hell are you gonna discuss it now?"

"I said that I don't read the Bible now, but I have tried to read it and to study it. I failed and I admit it. My attitude is more intelligent than yours; you never read it, but you're always ready to throw around your Biblical misconceptions at random."

"Can you prove it?"

"Prove that you never read it? You and all your equally ignorant brethren prove it everytime you open your pigfoot-eating mouths."

"So now the whole Negro race don't have religion, according to you. Don't you know that the Bible is the one book that all Negroes read? They even read it in secret during slavery. Why the Bible belongs to the Negro race. Kelly, to be intelligent is one thing, but to make fun of your own people, *and* the Bible is just being sophomoric. 'A little learning is a dangerous thing.'"

Dave was amazed by the change his words brought about in Kelly. Before his very eyes she nearly broke out in tears of contrition. "Please forgive me, lover," she pleaded. "I know I was wrong and I'm glad you brought me up short like you did. When one strolls through any Negro neighborhood in the world they are bound to see all the fine churches we built, which prove that we are a Bible-reading people." Kelly's voice took on the timbre of a sister testifying in a camp-meeting. "Only a fool would deny that the Negro is a Bible-reading man. I can watch the Negro as he goes about his daily tasks and tell that here is a worthy laborer in God's vineyard. And when I listen with profound respect to the quotations that fall from the Negro's lips like so many black pearls of wisdom, I am certain in my heart that the Negro is a Bible-reading man beyond compare. The Negro is the world's foremost biblical scholar.

206

Each and every one of us has read the Bible from cover to cover many times, and it is a staff that helps us through every trying day. Every Negro alive could teach the white man about the Bible and how to read it to get the most out of it. And the most wonderfully excruciatingly miraculous thing about it all is that the GODDAM NIGGER CAN'T READ," she screamed.

Dave howled louder than any Blueboy. "You are a dirty atheist. You got a mind that is lower than a white slaver. You got no more business in college than I got."

"Save it, lover."

"Do you realize that you are no credit to the race even if you are a brilliant student?"

"You and your double-tongued buddies like to prattle about your race, but each and every one of you would sell your souls to the devil in hell in exchange for a white skin. I would not. I love my bastard race. But I hate to see it err. I only seek to cure the Negro's love for the meaningless and ignorant. And if this is the race problem then count me as a Race Leader, but don't ever come to me whining and expecting me to let you suck titty just because some damn fool cracker won't let you eat a ham sandwich in his crumby luncheonette."

"Your dirty mouth is the biggest problem the Negro has. Your mouth is so filthy that I'd be ashamed to take you to a dogfight much less a white restaurant."

"Good. Call me a taxi."

"You ain't dressed even. You leaving naked?"

"It's no longer your property, so don't faze yourself over who looks or doesn't look. I'm through. Period."

"Oh no you're not. You don't walk out on me like this."

"Like what? Naked? You should be proud. No other man in this damn Ward ever got Kelly Simms to strip for him, I'm sorry to admit."

"Where you going? What you wanta do?"

"Do?" Kelly screamed. "I want to go back to the Campus where I belong. In this chem lab I don't have to be bored with listening to a savage racketeer." Kelly was now hollering more wildly than any Vessey Street slut and Dave sensed that she was acting. "I'd rather experiment on inorganic mysteries than lay in your ignorant bed. Let me up. They aren't yours any longer—lover."

And so went Dave and Kelly's stolen afternoons and Friday nights.

The afternoon that 483 came out, Dave and Kelly were talking in the kitchen.

"Dave?"

"Yeah?"

"Do you ever feel lonely? Way out of place?" Dave could not recall Kelly ever having been so intense before. She reminded him of one of those unwashed and uncombed white girls who lived in a content state of intensity. He did not like it. Intensity did not become his sex goddess. "Don't you ever feel as though you really weren't a damn nigger?" Kelly insisted.

Dave was suddenly wary. Kelly's questions came too close to where he often dwelled within himself. "Being a Negro is not a concrete sort of thing; it is a condition of stupidity."

"Very well put, lover. But where do we go from here?"

"Here? *We* go? What do you mean?"

"Do you ever feel like a white sheep among a flock of black ones?"

"Are you calling me a freak? What the hell. You're the one who is damn near white. Why ask me?"

"I'm sorry, lover. Forget I ever asked. It was silly."

"Like hell I will. What makes me so damn freakish?"

Kelly cleared her throat and seemed to wrap a cloak of impersonality about her. When she spoke her voice was rather chill. "At nineteen years of age you had one thousand cash dollars and three semesters in college to your credit. You could have continued your studies at any college of your choice. Waiting on tables, scholarships, and you could have been an Ivy Leaguer if you chose."

"How come you know so much about what I had when I was nineteen?" Dave was quite outraged. Like some girl would be if a total stranger had abruptly told her the exact time and place of her deflowering.

Kelly knew just how angry Dave was, but she had to talk this thing out to the end. "The bankbook is lying upstairs in a drawer like an old dance program. You never touched that money. Where did you get it from anyhow?"

Dave had nearly forgotten that pass book. "Insurance from my father, but since I didn't throw the money away, what's your beef?"

"I honestly don't know," Kelly said. "Only sometimes I get a kind of niggerish feeling about you and me." She paused and went to the sink and rinsed out the cocktail shaker before she continued. "I am going to ask you a question, lover. And it might sound completely insane, but think it over and give me your answer. And I want you to tell me if I, or anyone else has the right to ask this question."

"Okay. Okay. You don't have to be so damn dramatic, do you?"

"I am a college student of exceptionally high IQ, and yet I think I have a right to ask this question. This idiotic question."

"Get the hell on with it."

"I am asking a young Negro male, a member of an under-privileged minority, a man twenty-six years of age who is well on his way to becoming a millionaire before his thirtieth birthday, I am asking that enterprising young man if *he has any ambitions at all?*"

"I am sick and tired of this crap," Dave said tightly. "Every bastard and his brother thinks me, my brain, and my money is something that belongs to him personal like. And I am goddam sick and tired of it. You hear me? As of this minute, my only ambition is for niggers to leave my private affairs alone. You hear me? Left-goddam-alone."

"Lover, this is not a quarrel," Kelly said like a wail.

"I don't want to hear any more about it."

Taking a deep breath, Kelly unconsciously extended her hand in entreaty. "I'm in love with you, Dave. And I feel so possessive about you that all your wealth, all your pain . . . all that you are belongs to me. Please correct me now if I'm wrong. As for me, I can deny you nothing. Nothing at all." She stopped and sobbed before she went on. "Whatever I have refused you was for your own good. It was a refusal to stifle your life. You must believe that. You've been generous and kind. And yet I often get a feeling of nothingness when I think of you as having one million dollars. *One million dollars.* It's so strange," she murmured. "It's as if your goddam money has betrayed me.

"I don't want a mink coat or a flashy car or any of the other odds and ends that go with being the common-law wife of a budding millionaire. Why is that, lover? I feel that your goddam money has outwitted me, made a fool of me—of us. To have wealth and then lack the brains to spend it wisely is awful."

"You and Cokey," Dave sneered. "Every time one of you starts talking about something serious you end up saying 'I'm scared.' So don't worry about my dough. You better start worrying about whether or not a damn nigger can stand an education or not. There is a numbers banker in every eastern city of the U.S.A. that's got more than five thousand boogies in it. And I've never heard of a single one of them running around yelling they're scared."

Then for the first time Dave saw the broken look on Kelly's face. His voice softened, became almost a plea. "Kelly, spending money wisely is only three silly words; they don't mean a damn thing. Nobody can spend money wisely. Invest it wisely mebbe, but you can't spend money wisely no more than you can pee wisely. You gotta do both to live. So you buy what you want and need if the goddam white bastards will sell it to you. And there is your answer: the goddam peckerwood is not gonna let a nigger spend money wisely in the first place.

"I can't buy a franchise to sell a damn thing in this Ward. You think I can sit down and write a check and be the owner of an automobile agency? You think the manufacturer of electrical appliances will give me a franchise? You think I can rent movies from a local distributor? You think I can get a Coke concession?" Dave's voice was rapidly growing hoarse like a jackleg preacher's at the end of a revival-meeting sermon. "You are so goddam right you don't even know it! We *are* niggers. And it takes real money like I got to find it out. But do you think that's gonna make me stop banking numbers?

"And neither am I gonna cry and suck titty. I make and I save. And one day the NAACP might wake up and find out that it would be real smart for them to fight for the right for niggers to sell things to niggers.

"When the day comes that I can open a retail store selling gas ranges, or radios and stuff, or anything else a darky really needs in his home I'll be ready to invest every penny I got. But right now you niggers ain't ready. I am, but you're not. And me and my bank is gonna stay ready. Now what more do you want to know?"

"But that's not true, is it?" Kelly asked.

"Kelly, I couldn't even get a license to open a pawnshop in Harlem. And I never will!"

"Good God. I never dreamt we were so low." Then a roguish grin stole across Kelly's face. "But we, you and I and Blueboy, are like jackasses. We're a hell of a lot smarter than the other white man's beasts of burden."

"And what the hell am I supposed to say to that?"

Kelly slumped wearily, putting her head on her arms at the kitchen table. "Nothing, lover. I guess I want you to say something big and fine, but jackasses can't do that, can they? Come on, lover. Take me to bed."

Suddenly they were both afraid. And, because they were afraid, they made love violently there on the kitchen floor. Over and over again.

210

19

The white man's moment of truth is a pale and ignorant vanity that amuses all black men. It is a conceit, a game of mirror-mirror-on-the-wall, a childish fantasy. No American Negro has ever felt the need to climb a mountain or fight a bull; why should he yell at the waves in the ocean of fate?

Each and every Negro knows that he was born to be castrated. And there is no need for him to seek out his moment under the knife. It comes faster than death and is the ultimate. There is no afterlife.

In this dread moment, death and courage are fatuous words. Mere whispers of hope. To each black man it is a time when all gods are but empty idols. And the nigger's only objective is to keep his sanity.

Some black fools have sought to do the job themselves through alcohol, Christianity, narcotics, Communism, and other, more bizarre means in the hope that they would be considered already unmanned. But on the day of the keening knife it is they who suffer the most and cry the loudest. The knife knows that they are black fakers and that all blacks must be taught by the cut.

This is the moment when the nigger must stand, naked and alone, and survey the ancient truth of it all. The time of the knife is a teaching. That, now and forevermore, he is a NIGGER. It is a time when he must accept the fact that he is fatally black, and the liquid of a thousand excuses cannot wash away the ink in his veins. And the nigger finally comes to know that his life is beneath pity, tears, or justice. From that moment on, until he reaches his grave, he is barren. Sick unto death, the nigger always wonders why his woman bothers to sob for him and to insist upon calling him a man.

No nigger knows the hour of his emasculation. The moment and the place is chosen with abandon. Anywhere and everywhere it may come. The knife has descended in crowded courtrooms, in churches, at work, riding in the public bus, or in the nigger's own castle of a cabin while he watches his woman moan in terror and shame.

There is no truth or nobility in the moment.

It was the day after 518 came out straight and so that made it the middle of April, 1939. Dave stood in the hallway and stared at the silent telephone. A cold oil oozed from the pores of his forehead. He wiped it off and stared at the slime on the palm of his hand.

Only minutes ago he had answered the phone. It had been Blueboy, sounding clipped and metallic. "Don't bother to come by, baby. I'm on my way to jail." That was all.

According to their prearranged plans, the phone should be ringing now with call upon call. Its silence meant only one thing: nobody could call. But how could every single man he had be arrested at one time?

And already he could hear Kelly pronouncing her verdict. "Lover, you are in the exquisitely negroid dilemma of not knowing the first damn thing to do now that your five-hundred-thousand-dollar-a-year numbers bank has been raided by the mean old white people. It is my firm conviction that even an amoeba is able to consider its pregnability and prepare for emergencies!"

And her voice would seethe with contempt, but Kelly's tirade would not be fair because Dave and Blueboy had considered the problem a thousand times. But this thing that seemed to be happening today was beyond their wildest nightmares.

They had planned that whenever any important operator was arrested all other top men were to call Dave for instructions. And by the same token, it had been decided that Dave would not make any out-going calls. Makepeace had not called, or Blip, or Flick.

212

Nobody was calling. That meant that every topflight man was in jail. Or had they fled like children?

Dave was ashamed of that thought as soon as he had it. No. His men were all in jail and he had to do something to get them out. Get them out and save his bank. But how?

Every avenue of action seemed to lead to disaster. The bank was founded on and existed through secrecy and the white man's unawareness. But how do you get twenty men out of jail secretly?

He headed for the kitchen and a drink. He lit a cigarette after he had gulped the drink and mused upon the possibility of being run out of town. If the bank was lost it wouldn't matter and now that the secrecy was off anything could happen. Dave recalled that the brother-in-law of the chief of police in a nearby town had taken over the operation of the numbers after the colored bankers had been run out of town. His crotch froze with fear for his bank. Then suddenly, from out of nowhere, he had a savage hunger for Kelly's body. For one frantic moment he toyed with the idea of getting Kelly to come down from the Campus and go to the station house with him to see what had to be done.

He sat down at the kitchen table and told himself that he was panicking. He tried to be calm and constructive in his thoughts, but all of his mental processes were sexual desires and aberrations. He thought of Pigmeat and, of all people, Delilah. What he wanted was their naked bodies near him to tell him what to do.

With a curse, he threw his glass in the sink. His whole world was being shot to hell and all he could think of was pussy. He picked up the bottle and drank from it. This time the whiskey brought his brain back from near hysteria. The whiskey became a heady potion just as if it were Kelly's blood and energy he was drinking in.

The action was on Vessey Street, so why was he standing around the house? He didn't even bother to take another drink before he left the house and headed for the Block.

Once in the street he found that life could be very simple. Walk easy! Jaunty as Blueboy, shoulders squared like Kelly, and know all men to be children. His knees were numb, but he forced his legs to step lithely, arrogantly assured. He was his own man now, and his mind was as analytical as a general's. For the first time in his life he did not care what the crowd thought. And there was a crowd.

Every front porch and stoop held gossipers who silently stood and stared as he passed. His pulse throbbed; just by allowing them to see him strolling toward the Block made him feel as though he had thrown a handful of pennies for them to catch. These gawkers

213

were nothing but poor black trash. One thing, Dave Greene was not poor. Money would solve this thing. Money always talked and in everyman's language. He felt high and lordly; he was Dave Greene, King of the Numbers.

"Suzy calls up and sez she wuz arnin' when she hear all dese sirens jes a goin'."

". . . and it looked like they weren't never gonna stop bringing them outa that countinghouse."

"Dem pickups so cute in dere Wolmuth suits. Bet they is a sorry crowd now."

"Here tell they busted into the flower shop and the countinghouse at the same time."

"Sakkrin-nization they call it."

". . . and Blip got a hole busted in his haid this big."

"Yeah. Them cops mean. And po Blueboy daid, dey say."

"Dat's pure murder."

"Folkes oughta git toggedder and tell off dis man's law."

"Efen the bank close the Ward starves, didja think of that?"

"Trufe. Now my man, Jacko, meks hisself twenny, thirdy dollah a week writing them digits. And he ain't strong. Where else he gonna make that kind of money?"

"Cain't mek ovah twenny-seben fifty in the tobacco factory and the white gals got all the easy jobs that ain't killing."

"Booker gonna suffer . . ."

"Colored gonna suffer. And all our best young men."

"Wonder what's gonna happen to all dem cahs?"

"Dem pickups volunteer dem cars in anybody's funeral."

"Dave Greene done paid many an unfortunate's funeral bill."

Dave knew what was being said and it didn't upset him in the least. It was strange. Now that his bank was in the clutches of his enemies and he was entering into battle, he had peace of mind for the first time since he was a child.

Turning the corner of Vessey and Macon he soon passed the flower shop. He glanced in and saw a solitary policeman standing behind the counter. Dave grinned, the damn fool thought some more numbers men might straggle in. Just as if the Ward's telegraphy was not swifter than tom-toms and silent. But Dave did concede that a few idiots in the Ward might call the shop to ask if Dave was going to pay off the day's winners. That brought on a troublesome thought. Should he pay off? And then he knew he would. He had to.

Old Man Booker rushed up to him time he entered the restaurant. "Hello, Dave. Guess you already heard the news?" Mr. Booker paused anxiously, and Dave thought, distractedly.

214

Dave grinned a wry reply.

Suddenly Old Man Booker changed a la Kelly Simms. The man simply stopped being an old fuss-budget. "Well, now then," he said. "The Colonel took it on hisself to go down and get the boys out. Since he's a professional bondsman, it looks better that way, we thought." Again he anxiously paused. "You don't mind, do you?"

Mind?

Dave inclined his head. He was so touched that he did not trust himself to speak.

And he was not alone.

These two silly old men, these two whom the table sometimes scorned, had jumped, unbidden, to defend their young.

Dave sighed heavily; he had reached home.

"We didn't think you would mind, but it's always best to ask," Mr. Booker went on. "And it's best that us old faces be showing before these white police folks, son.

"So this way you ain't even in it. You know your boys ain't gonna breathe your name. So you just go on back to the Square Table and relax until the Colonel brings 'em back." The old man patted Dave on the shoulder and walked away.

Dave went back to the table. Momentarily he was exhilarated, giddy, and carefree. He caressed the top of the Square Table and murmured aloud: "You ugly old bastard."

Then he sat down and laughed out loud. And who the hell said that Dave Greene didn't belong? There must be over twenty men in the police lockup, but without a single thought the Colonel had rushed out to furnish bail.

Mr. Booker and Colonel Eldrege had transcended friendship: This was *race*. This was the real Negro that nobody knows. Asses together, heads out in a common defense. Where had he heard that before? Blueboy? Never mind, it hit the target. The Ward took care of its own and that's all that mattered.

Delilah, more startlingly black and beautiful than he had ever seen her, came to the table. Her normally impassive gaze was tear-dewed, and Dave almost gasped at her beauty.

"Mist Dabe," she said awkwardly, "ah be sorry for dis trubblus ting . . ."

"Thanks, Lila," he replied, blinking. This was the first time she had voluntarily spoken to him since the very first time he and Blueboy had entered the restaurant. And surprise came with the afterthought that her Gullah accents were wonderfully soothing today. "Bring me a pint of whiskey if you can find one, "he said.

"Trute mout. Ah mek a pace."

Joe Kelso came to the table. "Sorry as all get out, Dave," he murmured. Dave was certain that the sneaky little insurance man meant what he said. And maybe Joe really forgot that he had the whiskey in his pockets that night when the woman jumped from the Lil Savoy. After all, watching a woman jump to her apparent death could make anyone forget what they were carrying in their pockets.

"Thanks for your sympathy, Joe," Dave said. "Sit down. Colonel Eldrege has gone downtown and should be back soon with all my boys. How's business?"

"Can't complain. From now on I'm a broker. When you want insurance tailored to your individual needs, come see me."

"You got any raid insurance?"

The two men laughed indulgently and relaxed in their new-found palship.

"What the hell. A raid is no big thing," Joe mused. "What's a few fines? Look at all the free publicity."

"But I got a weak spot, Joe. I operate outside the law it's true, but I don't know a damn thing about courts and how they work. I don't even know what's happened today or is gonna happen later. For too long I've kidded myself that I'm a businessman. I forgot to learn the angles."

"Well, whatever you do, don't hire a colored lawyer. Now I'm a race man all the way, but you can't afford to gamble with your freedom when you go before a white judge in this man's town."

The knife loomed again and Dave was pulled down from his high and carefree state to wonder just what the white men wanted from him. If the white-trash cops wanted to take his bank, what good would a lawyer of any color be? And when you came down to it, the nigger was beneath gang warfare. White folks had cops to do their dirty work, even murder.

"I wish the hell I could get in touch with Kelly," he said.

"This is no time for women," Joe said. "Wait until after everything is settled and then celebrate."

"You don't understand, Joe. Kelly has brains. She'd know what to do."

"No she wouldn't. Women never know what to do in an emergency. Say, Dave. If you should retire tomorrow, how much dough would a guy have to have to take over your bank?" Joe asked.

Dave took his time to answer. "I guess you already know I couldn't sell the bank. No colored man I know has that kind of dough. It's an illegal operation and so it would have to be strictly a cash deal. I'd only be asking for trouble if I went for a time-payment deal. Now if I just up and quit and somebody just stepped

216

in and started to bank numbers on their own the answer would still be too much money for any colored man. The bets are too heavy now. There is no way of telling how much money you would need. After all, banking numbers is gambling."

"But you can name a round figure, can't you?"

"No. Let's make believe that Joe Louis comes to town tomorrow morning. When the Ward lamps his license plate numbers they are gonna jump on it with both feet. Say it starts with oh-seven-two. Now if oh-seven-two plays that afternoon or any day this week, I would have to pay out so many thousands of dollars that I break out in a cold sweat just to think about it. I don't know what the dream books give for the name Joe, but whatever it is there would be a heavy play on that too."

"Seven-oh-four plays for my name," Joe said.

"Okay. If seven-oh-four comes out the day after oh-seven-two hits, it would cost me hundreds of thousands of dollars, and I might go broke. Now how is a guy gonna take over an operation like that?" Dave knew that it was almost impossible for him to go broke now, but there was no sense sitting here in Booker's, claiming untold wealth immediately after the raid.

"Why would you have to pay out so much more on seven-oh-four?"

"The first day we are paying off nickel, dime, and quarter bets mostly, but after they hits oh-seven-two everybody will have got a taste of blood. We would have a gang of nigger-rich gamblers who are suddenly betting fifty centses and dollars on seven-oh-four. And don't think it can't happen that way."

"Why some fools would be bettin' five and ten dollars on seven-oh-four after they'd hit oh-seven-two for a quarter."

"Like I say, when you bank 'em you're still gambling. And I mean *gambling*. Now on the other hand a real lucky guy could take over the bank without one red cent, and if he manages to last two or three weeks with nothing but penny and nickel hits on his books, he'd be on top of the heap and ready to stand the big hits when they came and the big hits are sure in hell coming sooner or later."

"And everybody thinks that banking numbers is a sure thing," Joe said. "Why a guy could start out with a hundred-thousand-dollar bankroll and end up stone broke in a matter of days."

"It is possible, but not probable. After all, the odds say that he can't go broke. A man would have to have a really freakish run of hits to go through a hundred-thousand-dollar bankroll."

Joe nodded. "Thousand to one chances to hit and you only pay

217

six hundred to one odds. By rights you should put four out of every ten bet in your pocket."

"We got operating expenses," Dave said. "Salaries, cars—everything."

"Dave, why don't you buy off the cops? It's insurance really."

The futility of it all showed in Dave's face. "Everybody likes to forget that I'm as black as they are," he said. "The Law is white. Do you realize that I don't know a damn white man in this town? So who do I go to with a bribe? Just walk down Main Street, waving hundred-dollar bills until some cracker is kind enough to accept them from me? I'm a respectable businessman. I don't know anything about crooked police.

"You and me are in the selfsame business," Dave continued. "I say that a man can't guess what the number is gonna be today and give him odds he can't. You and your company bet that I won't die today and offer to pay my beneficiary a thousand bucks I won't. It's just that simple. I'm no gangster. Mebbe I should try to be. Until today, my color and the Ward were my insurance. I only dealt with Negroes and told my men to do likewise. Now look what's happened. As long as the white man knew from nothing we were safe. Now the bastards are gonna know all our business."

"Well, there's one consolation," Joe said. "Every man has his price."

"Baloney. Even the lowest white trash on earth ain't gonna let himself be bought by a nigger," Dave hooted. "And you say buy the chief of police?"

Dave wondered why he had been so vehement in stating what he knew to be untrue. As a matter of fact, he and Blueboy had "bought" innumerable white people of both sexes. Sometimes they had worked as bellhops and had pandered with the "bought" assistance of the clerks and house detectives. And in poorly managed restaurants they had bribed cashiers, food checkers, and chefs— all white—to look the other way. So why had he said that white men can't be bought?

"I doubt if any accepter of a bribe ever stopped to consider the color of its source," Joe said.

And then Dave told the bitter truth. "Whatever I gave a white man would not be enough. Sooner or later that damn peck is gonna figure out for himself that the simplest and the easiest thing in the world to do is to pay some cop to run me out of town. To pay off is to admit you've got a gold mine."

"F'chrissakes, Dave."

"For chrissakes what?"

"You dumb enough to think the mayor or the chief of police is gonna resign his job to take over the operation of your nigger pool?'

"That's a damn good question. And the answer is that all respectable white people have poor-trash relatives and in-laws that would come in right handy as fronts in any illegal racket they wanta enter."

Pigmeat came to the table. "Hiya, fellas. Who'da thought the city had so many cops? And they arresting people like going to court's gonna go outa style tomorra. Lawd have mercy, Dave, whatcha gonna do?"

"I'm gonna send you to the station house, and by the time you gets through talking to that desk sergeant he'll be so mucked up he'll end up paying you to get outa there and take my people with you."

"I'm not playing, honey. What do you want me to do?"

The concrete simplicity of Pigmeat's question tied Dave's tongue. Blood and sinew, Pigmeat stood ready to serve him; she only asked his command. It was such a beautiful gesture that he was sorry that he had nothing for her to do. And as he looked at her he realized that she was prettier than ever today. Pig and Lila were both saturated with beauty. Imminent peril must be the most powerful aphrodisiac going, he thought. He had not the slightest doubt that he could go to bed with Kelly, Pig, and Lila at the same time and satisfy them all.

And it was not only him, Dave believed. The smell of sex was all over Booker's, all over the Block.

Lila brought the whiskey, and the three of them sat and drank silently. Dave ran his hand in his pocket and brought out his huge and comforting bankroll. He peeled off a five-dollar bill and handed it to Pigmeat. "Change that into quarters and put 'em in the piccolo. And while you're up tell all the waitresses to see what their guests will have to drink on Dave Greene. And if anybody asks, tell them that the bank is paying off all hits today. We might be late, but we'll pay."

"God, this place is crowded," Pigmeat exclaimed when she got back to the table. "It looks like Friday night after a big basketball game."

"Mostly Vessey Street chicks and hustlers who heard that Dave was in here," Joe said. He looked at Dave. "Why the dickens did you tell Pig to tell the waitresses that you were gonna pay off? The cops loaded a truck with numbers slips. How in hell you gonna pay off and you don't even know who to pay off? It seems kind of dumb to me for you to give people false hopes."

Dave smiled grimly. "We got a way to pay off even if the cops grabbed today's work, which I doubt."

"Well, I don't see how you can," Joe said.

"You seen a numbers pad, haven't you? It's got three pages of different colors all the way through for writing in triplicate. Well, the white tissue slip remains in the writer's book. It is his receipt. I'm gonna let each writer bring in his pads of today's work, and if the tissue is clean-looking, not tampered with or erased, looks on the level, we'll pay him. And the pickups should still have their ribbons, I hope."

"Somebody's gonna slip you a limber dick."

"So what?" Dave exclaimed. "I gotta protect the rep of my bank. Money don't mean a damn thing right now. I'm only worried about them white bastards putting their fingers in my pie. And what those damn cops are gonna do."

"Dave," Joe said, "the cops can't stop numbers playing no more than they can stop sex."

"You can say that again," Pigmeat said.

"Goddamit," said Dave. "They can take the bank. Call me and Blueboy undesirable characters and run us outa town. Sell the bank to some white rich bootlegger. The cops can do *anything*. Can't you two understand that?"

Just then a hush fell over the restaurant. Then a happy murmuring swelled, mingled with scattered handclaps. And then all hell broke loose.

Blueboy led the procession. His hat was cocked like an old-time cakewalker's. He did not walk, he pranced into the restaurant, leading the way to the Square Table. All the time he was bowing and shaking hands like a newly crowned heavyweight king. Behind Blueboy came Makepeace, all two hundred and fifty pounds of him, doing a graceful version of the latest dance craze called Trucking. He was an elephantine wisp of joy. After Makepeace came the dapper band of pickups and ribbon men, followed by lesser dignitaries in the profession. It was a glorious spectacle that turned into a drinking bout in three minutes flat.

"You missed it," Blueboy bawled in Dave's ear. "You shoulda been there by all means."

And the crazy black fool meant it, Dave decided.

"It was twice as good as a piece of white pussy to see them po' white trash cops' eyes bug out when they sees all that money."

Blueboy naturally took it upon himself to get up on the Table and tell everybody exactly how it was. "Davey-boy, these cops see all this money. And just to show you that white trash and a damn nigger is the same chickenshit thing, they starts loading their pockets with the silver. Damn if they wasn't scared to touch the folding money. You'da thought it was fulla leprosy germs or some such."

"That's right," someone else shouted. "And then the brass comes in and steals the paper money."

"Them cops got so much silver in their pockets they's listing to port side like a drunk," Blueboy rhapsodized.

"I jes naturally loves a damn fool cracker," Makepeace said. "They comes in the countinghouse and they look at all that equipment there and the first thing they say is: 'Whut you boys steal these machines for?' He thinks we crazy as hell cause he *knows* damn well that niggers don't know how to use adding machines."

"And in the precinct when they is booking us," Blip said, "one of the cops pockets sprung a leak and silver started rolling all over the floor."

"Yeah," Flick said. "And then Blueboy took and yelled: 'Lawd have mercy. White folks so lucky they done started pissing money.'"

"Them cops coulda killed Blueboy the way they looked at him."

"You mean they wanted to kill that fool cop whose pockets had holes in 'em."

Dave sighed complacently. "Well, I'm glad to hear they stole all the money. That's the only evidence they really got. What'd they charge you all with anyhow?"

"Everything except rape and murder," Blip said.

Blueboy put his arm around Dave and said, "Colonel says he wants to talk with you over the Lil Savoy as soon's you get a chance. He says he's gonna explain it to you."

The number that day was 505, and Dave and Blueboy had to pay out over two thousand dollars in hits.

20

After the raid, everyone in the Ward played 000. Just why this number was preferred was a mystery, but Dave guessed that three zeros were picked because the Ward felt that his bank was doomed. Dave accepted all bets on 000. Blueboy noted the heavy play on the number and advised Dave to cut the odds to 300 to 1, but Dave got stubborn for the first time in his life, and the day that 009 came out he died a thousand deaths.

For over a year Dave had been using the racing results to determine the daily number. The three digits came in by telegraph one at a time. The bank received the wires after the first, third, and seventh races had been run. On this particular day the first wire gave a zero, and an hour later the second wire came in saying that the second digit was a zero. It was then that Dave and Blueboy began to sweat. A total of eight hundred people had placed bets on 000, and 00 was already confirmed. If the final wire listed another zero as the last digit Dave would have faced bankruptcy. Eight hundred bets to honor, and they ranged from penny wagers to dollars!

When the final coded telegram arrived, stating that the third digit was a 9, Dave relaxed in a trembling heap, knowing that he had proved his courage to the Ward.

Later that afternoon he managed to get Kelly to slip off the Campus and join him in Booker's. Cokey and Blueboy were also there and somehow the conversation got around to passing for white.

"Suppose DuPont offered you a hell of a job, thinking you were white, would you take it?" Dave asked Kelly.

"Certainly. But I'm a black scientist. And just as soon as I got on the payroll I would issue a news story to one of your Nigra papers, stating that I was the first Nigra to be employed in such and such a capacity. If I'm really any good I won't have to hide my race."

"Youth must be served its black eyes and kicks in the butt," Blueboy mumbled.

"That's life," Kelly said lightly.

"But Kelly's complexion is not as embarrassing as yours," Cokey said to Blueboy. "They just might let her keep the job if she promised to shut up about her color."

"Whatever I got belongs to us niggers," Kelly said. "I'm not passing for anybody. I hate black bitches who provide mare service for white studs even if it is for gain. Need I say more?"

Blueboy smiled at her. "You might be talking about your grand-maw, gal."

Kelly shrugged. "She probably had no choice in the matter."

"Can't you all talk about anything except the nigger and sex?" Dave asked.

"Don't ask me," Kelly said. "I'm a stranger here myself."

"Well, I want to talk about this trial that comes up day after tomorrow," Dave said.

"What is a Negro problem," Kelly said.

"Cut it out, Kelly. You ain't funny," Dave said.

"I am serious. Very serious. I consider it to be the first race problem I have ever encountered in my short life. You chaps sit around yon Square Table with your squareheaded eyes brimming with square tears over the refusal of some poor white trash to break bread with you and over the great misfortune that you and your children are not condemned to attend school along with the spawn of Gerald Chapman, Frankie Yale, and the assorted members of the KKK instead of facing up to man's only immediate problem, which is survival."

"Stop it. You got me dying from laughter," Dave snarled.

"You are dying, but damn if it's my fault. Why can't you stand still and solve your problem? Niggers is niggers. And you might as well learn to live with that truth. Now numbers are nigger business. The white man has begun to molest *our* business, *what do you intend to do about it?*"

"But . . ." Dave began.

"No buts, lover. Nigras do not consider numbers to be a mortal sin. Numbers are outside the white man's province. Outside his law, too. It's now your black-assed duty to either ignore the white man's law or circumvent it. Do I make myself clear?"

"Sure," said Dave. "I'm supposed to let these white bastards beat my brains out because it's my duty to die insisting that a damn fool nigger has a God-given civil right to play numbers."

"Don't make me any madder, lover."

"But you don't make any sense at all, Kelly," Dave said. "Why don't you say that I own the Negro Reserve Bank and that it is just as legal as the white folks' Federal Reserve Bank?"

"I am waiting for an answer," Kelly insisted.

"What damn answer? I don't know what these white bastards are gonna do. How can I make plans?"

"And I hate your guts."

"Wait a minute, Kelly," Blueboy said. "You and Dave both are trying to make that raid a hell of a lot more important than it really is. Any colored person can get arrested for gambling. And no crapshooter with money in his pocket ever went to jail." He eyed her sharply. "What are you really excited about?"

"I'm excited about my lover saying that he has to wait and see what his white lords and masters are going to do before he can reach a decision of his own . . ."

"Isn't that the intelligent way to do?" Blueboy asked.

"But millions of dollars are potentially involved here. I think that this is much more of a serious threat to our race than jim crow and even lynching. It's the Negro's economy that is involved here. Dave has unwittingly created a synthetic economy here in the Ward, and elsewhere in the city, that is predicted on numbers. And so it now becomes his duty to fight to preserve it. Dave has first got to decide whether he is going to operate his bank regardless of the white man's opposition, or just be another titty-pimp and silently steal away."

The three men were uneasily quiet until Dave spoke. "You talked a great game. Congratulations."

"Do you want me to sleep with the chief of police?" The girl's voice was deathly cold. Beyond all insolence; beyond all doubt.

"What the hell do you take me for?" Dave said.

224

Kelly did not raise her voice. "Generals have sacrificed whole battalions. Couldn't you forget one short and passing moment in my life?"

"You go to hell," Dave said softly.

Kelly stared around the restaurant as though she was seeking someone. When her gaze returned to the booth she looked hard at Dave. "Dave," she said softly. "I have loved you from the very first time I saw you. But I don't think that you and I know the same kind of love." She took a deep breath as if in preparation of making a last statement, but all she finally said was, "Good-by. I'll take a taxi." She stood up and shoved against Dave until he got up and let her out of the booth. Kelly nodded to Cokey and Blueboy and then turned and walked rapidly toward the front entrance.

"Do you know why she's mad?" Blueboy asked Dave.

Dave tossed a set of keys to Cokey. "Catch her and take her to the Barn. Those are for the Zephyr. It's parked in front of the flower shop." Cokey picked up the keys and departed. Then Dave turned to answer Blueboy. "Sure. She's mad because I don't grab a machine gun and take over police headquarters."

"Kelly's a smart gal. She wouldn't expect you to do something that wasn't smart."

"Sleeping with the chief of police is smart?"

"She only stated that the welfare of her man and the Negro in general is of more value than her mortal flesh."

"So what am I supposed to do now?"

"Kelly didn't mention any plans much. She said you had a decision to make."

"Do you think I'm yellow?"

"I dunno. I doubt it. Courage is only the ability to stand still and make a decision. That's all. Courage don't necessarily mean fighting. Like in the Navy, we didn't have to have courage; we were down in the magazine passing ammunition. We just passed it until the battle was over. We messmen didn't need courage, but them white boys on deck did."

"If the magazine got hit you wouldn't of had a chance. So how you figger you didn't need courage?"

"We couldn't hide."

When Cokey reached the parked car he found Kelly sitting in the front seat. "You want me to tell Dave you're waiting?"

"He told you to catch up with me and take me to the Barn, didn't he?"

225

Cokey grinned. "Don't take it out on me."

"Oh, pipe down and let's get a move on. I feel like getting drunk."

Cokey and Kelly drove to a pad three blocks away and bought a pint of whiskey. "We got over an hour, do you think we can kill two pints?" Kelly was quite serious.

"It's up to you, keed," Cokey said. "I gotta drive."

"So get high, leave the car parked and take a taxi. I would love to call Mister Greene and tell him where to go to find his car."

"Just why are you so mad?"

Kelly grinned. "Damn if I know, but it galls me to see Dave sitting around moping about that damn trial instead of doing something intelligent."

"Exactly what do you have in mind for him to do?"

"This old man who got everybody out on bond, what's his name?"

"Colonel Eldrege."

"He owns the Lil Savoy, doesn't he?"

"Among other things, yes."

"Well, he, Mr. Booker—and there may be others—have been doing illegal things here in the Ward for years and evidently with a kind of impunity. So why doesn't Dave go to them? Even if it is true that they are handkerchief-headed-Uncle-Toms, they do possess certain diplomatic skills. They have remained out of jail. And they are common lawbreakers as far as I can see, but they carry weight downtown. Am I right?"

"They've bootlegged for years, and run gambling games. And, in the long ago, I'm positive that Mr. Booker or his dad ran a sporting house. But until this minute I presumed they were just lucky. Kelly, you might be right. I think those men do know how to handle the police."

Kelly nodded. "You and I are students, Cokey. Just big children. And we're not studying with the intent to enter a life of racketeering, but that's no reason why we shouldn't expect Dave and Blueboy to know every single dodge of the criminal."

"Yeah . . ."

"We Negroes need criminals just as badly as we need doctors and lawyers."

"Now wait a minute, Kelly."

"Come off it, Cokey. The day a Negro successfully robs a bank instead of a chicken coop we can honestly claim to be emancipated. If Dave allows the bank to get out of his hands, it means that the white racketeers will pocket forty cents out of the Negro's gambling dollar. Can't you see what that means? This is a race problem."

Cokey smiled wistfully. "I wish the battle lines were a little clearer."

"The lines are very clear. What you really wish is that we had a more respectable business to fight for. But you forget that Negroes like and condone numbers playing. The white man denies us the vote in this state and so it can be said that the Negro is denied the chance to make lotteries legal. And so we have every legal and moral right to disobey the law."

"Well, don't take that theory up on the Campus with you. I think I'm going to punch Professor Jones course in Psych 303 because I said in class that the largest commercial enterprise the Negro owns is numbers. He had a fit and ended up by saying that I had no right to attend a church-supported school. So if that don't mean he intends to flunk me, I'll be mighty surprised."

"Even if the Bible is a fable, the black man re-enacts the cruci-fixion every day," Kelly whispered.

"What do you mean?"

"The Negro in his ignorance crucifies someone every day."

"What did the Negro do to you, Kelly?"

Kelly's grin was twisted and good natured. "If I told you, would you promise to forget it and never bring it up again?"

"Sure."

"I didn't attend public high school. I went to a Negro boarding school. I happened to arrive there with a douche bag. It was given to me by some . . ." Her lips curled impishly, ". . . prostitutes . . . white friends of mine. Well, the first time I took a shower, I went skipping down the hall with it. You know, carefree and lighthearted, swinging that bag. Honestly, Cokey, I didn't know any better; my mother died where I was born.

"And that's not all. After I took the douche and shower, I combed my hair and went to class. I think that was the greater of my crimes. I didn't know Negroes then, Cokey."

"So what happened? What could have happened? Sure. I can see the nappy-headed chicks in the dorm being jealous of you taking a shower and just having to comb your hair in order to go to class, but what could they do or say?"

Kelly stood up and took a restless step or two. "All Negroes it would seem, are compelled to explain the unknown. A Negro can explain anything he doesn't know a damn thing about. Since ninety-nine and nine-tenths per cent of the girls in the dorm had never seen a douche bag before, they quite naturally felt called upon to explain it. Most of them claimed that I was treating myself for a venereal disease; others thought that it was an instrument used to give myself an abortion, and still others claimed that I used it for masturbating. I was fifteen, Cokey, and those little bitches hurt."

Cokey stared helplessly at Kelly, wanting to get up and take her in his arms. And Kelly looked so tiny now, and so purely pretty.

Kelly spoke into his thoughts with hard even accents. "Never ask me to condone the Negro's ignorance, Cokey. I will do all in my power to eradicate it, but please do not ask me to forgive it. And besides, ignorance needs no champions. It's a powerful thing that can crush truth to the ground with a whisper."

The padlady peeped in the room to see if they wanted anything. Cokey and Kelly started guiltily; neither one had hardly touched their drink.

"Do you think it possible that Dave is only a lucky dumbbell?" Kelly said.

"You ask me that?" Cokey exclaimed. "If you don't know, who does?"

Kelly smiled ruefully. "Sometimes I hate his stupid guts, but the dizzy bastard is mine, for the time being anyway. You know," she said. "It's bad enough to have your man quote the Bible, but my boy quotes things that aren't even in the book." Her eyes widened in astonishment. "And he believes them, too."

"Personally, I think Dave's a genius."

Kelly scowled. "Dave's strange. He can't even see that he and I would be an impossible marriage."

Cokey laughed. "Well, I guess you may have made your point when you offered to do a job on the chief of police. Were you serious?"

"About sleeping with the chief of police? Damn right. It would be a pleasure."

"I thought you were kidding."

"I am not kidding, Cokey. I'd be proud to do it. As the prostitutes say: I'd be turning a million-dollar trick."

"How come you know so much about whores?"

"I was raised in a whorehouse, Mr. Louis. But getting back to screwing the chief of police. I think it would be my duty to do so if I could. It would be just my luck to find that he's devoted to his wife."

"You think it would do any good?"

"I don't know anything about white men," Kelly confessed. "But if what we say about them is true then I guess anybody could make the chief of police leave Dave alone."

Cokey picked up the half-filled bottle of whiskey and looked at it. "Come on. It's time for me to be getting you back to the Campus."

228

"I was so mad at Dave when I came in here I thought I could drink a gallon by herself," Kelly said.

"You're not mad at Dave any more?"

"Oh, what's the use? Besides, it suddenly occurred to me that Blueboy isn't worried. I have great faith in Blueboy's perception."

"Come to think of it, he's *not* too worried, is he?"

"No. Are you going to put this whiskey in your pocket or leave it here?"

"I guess I'll take it. I'm not that rich."

A little later they left the pad and headed for the Campus. This, of course, was the day that 009 played. Nobody hit it.

21

Blueboy's face was a pudding of self-satisfaction. "And we shall have a cornpone and chitlin supper," he finished saying. He and Dave were in the kitchen, having their usual morning conference.

"Are you so scared of this trial that you've gone crazy?" said Dave. "Everybody I got working for me is about as much use as a faggot at a whores' convention. But I still got a brain left if nobody else has, and I'm gonna hire me some lawyers."

Blueboy casually slurped his coffee. He felt sorry for Dave, but it was best to let him suffer. Blueboy's paternal love for Dave did not make him unaware of Dave's weaknesses and blind spots. Yes. It was much better this way. Dave had this mental block about "Respectability" and so Blueboy was leery of divulging the facts of life involved in this particular instance before the trial was held.

Dave was crazy enough to insist upon going to jail if it suited his preposterous ideas concerning the Ward's respect for him, and Blueboy had no intention of letting that happen. And so he hardly listened as Dave let off steam.

But when Dave had worked himself up into a state where he

was becoming incoherent, Blueboy sighed and said, "I tole you and I tole you. There ain't a goddam thing to worry about. So why don't you get drunk and relax or something intelligent like that? This is a cracker town, is true, but this time it's gonna be in your favor. It's the best kind of break that a man in your position could ever have hoped for. Now since this is a cracker setup and you is a blackboy, you might as well sit back and enjoy yourself. There is no need for a battery of lawyers. Whenever one of these hoogie towns decides that a nigger is guilty, the town gives him a bunch of lawyers gratis. Which means, for free. So they can convict him all legal like, and give him the chair like he's supposed to get, but since you ain't even on trial it don't make sense for you to go hire a bunch of lawyers. Who the hell they gonna defend anyhow?"

"It's my bank that's on trial. I know that you guys can't get much more than a ten-dollar fine for gambling or ten days' sentence, but it's the life of the bank that's really at stake. So I want all of you men proved innocent in court."

"Neither you or Kelly is cognizant of the situation. Why, goddamit, you two are trying to write a Greek tragedy out of a blackface minstrel. This trial, as you insist upon miscalling it, is no more serious than going to court for a back-alley crap game."

"You're dead wrong, Blueboy."

"I loves that little Kelly-gal for making that offer to intercede for you with the chief of police, but it just ain't necessary."

"You want me to diddle while they take away my bank?"

"As far as someone destroying the bank is concerned, you talk like a drunken actress. The bank is no damn building. What they gonna destroy? Your brains? Mine? Makepeace's? The pickups? The man's gonna take all our brains away?"

"All over the world you been, Blueboy, and you ain't even learned that the goddam white man don't ever want us niggers to have nothing."

Blueboy expelled his pent-up breath in exasperation. "Here you is, ain't even been arrested and you're running around yelling for lawyers. The crackers don't have to take nothing from *you*. Your big mouth is gonna tell them just where to go to pick up the goose that lays our gold and eggs. You is a poor-assed blackboy as far as the white folks is concerned, so where you gonna get money to go running inta court with every lawyer that is greedy enough to take your money? And next time we is gonna have a 'banker' to take the fall. Remember Billy Bowlegs? We gonna have the same thing. A hired fall guy. So shut up and get the hell over to the club and give it a

231

last minute going over. Don't forget. We opens Wednesday night. Rain or shine."

Blueboy was referring to Dave's most recent venture in the Ward, the Club Babylon. It was to be a respectable Lil Savoy minus the crap table in the rear. It was situated a few doors from Booker's, over the cleaning and pressing shop. The primary purpose of the club was to get rid of some surplus cash and to raise the social level of the Block.

Of late, money had become an everyday nuisance. Dave, in his procrastinating way, had been intending to open a dozen or more accounts in out-of-town banks, but he and Blueboy seemed unable to tear themselves away from the Ward during legal banking hours. The house was overflowing with cash; there were caches all over the place. And the irony of it all was that the Club Babylon had every prospect of becoming a big moneymaker.

The club was tastefully decorated with an imitation walnut interior. All of the equipment and furnishings were brand new. Dave was very proud of this fact and had boasted to Kelly that he would personally see to it that on opening night the money in the cash register was brand new.

Dave and Mr. Booker had exchanged assurances that the interests of the club and those of the restaurant would not conflict. Mr. Booker felt that the club would increase his late-hour food business, and now that his restaurant was doing so well, he secretly wished to wean his customers from drinking whiskey on his premises. The Knights of the Square Table were another matter, of course. They had risen to the eminence of being a tradition in the Ward, and Mr. Booker wanted their trade, while Dave, on the other hand, had seen to it that no table in the Babylon would comfortably hold the nightly quota of Knights.

Ostensibly heeding Blueboy's advice, Dave left the house for the club, but it was not to give it a last-minute inspection; he had an appointment to meet a lawyer there.

Dave let himself in and went directly behind the bar and opened a quart of bourbon. He poured a generous drink and drank it. A few moments later the lawyer walked in. "Good morning, Mr. Greene."

Dave looked up and didn't like what he saw, or what he had heard. As his wealth had increased, so had Dave's suspicion of all the social amenities. People who added a "mister" to his name usually had to be watched. Kelly had persuaded him into making this appointment and he was already regretting having listened to her.

232

The lawyer was one of nature's more malicious mistakes. He was what Blueboy would promptly describe as a "polka dot nigger." The man's rhiney-yellow skin was covered with a mass of brownish mauve freckles that sometimes looked like tiny warts. The dun-colored hair was pasted to his head with an adhesive pomade.

"You gotta be Lawyer Jones," Dave said for no other reason than he felt it necessary to waste a few words before sending this man away.

"I don't make a habit of this." The young lawyer waved his hand to include the interior of the club. "However, in view of the fact that you are a busy man, I assumed that you wanted me to take a firsthand look at some damages."

"Naw. I thought that we could meet here and nobody would be the wiser," Dave said, nettled by the tacit apology the man had evoked from him. "My girl friend advised me to hire a lawyer. A legal adviser on a permanent basis. I haven't made my mind up as yet, but I thought that this was as good a time as any to kick the idea around and . . ."

From the heights of stupidity and hunger the lawyer brusquely interrupted Dave. "Legal services run high, Mr. Greene. I doubt that any race man in town could afford the kind of retainer you are evidently suggesting, but suppose you tell me what your immediate problem is."

"I gotta be in court tomorrow morning," Dave said.

"Which court, sir?"

"How many damn different courts do niggers go to?"

Attorney Jones smiled. "You have had some trouble with the police? Here?"

"Naw, this ain't even open yet. But mebbe later I might need you for this too. Right now, though, it's my bank."

"You went to the bank and had some difference with a teller? There was some error and you got in an argument?"

"Naw, damn it. *My* bank. I'm a numbers banker, you know that."

"I've heard rumors to that effect, but a lawyer cannot afford to deal in hearsay. And naturally I am not going to be involved in gambling of any kind. I am a much bigger man than that."

This clown was proper meat for either Blueboy or Kelly, but Dave was too disgusted to parry with the fool. Here, in the midst of his trials and tribulations, he was again face to face with the fact that the average nigger was about as useful as an ice cube in hell. If a Negro lawyer was not interested in defending gamblers, knew nothing of the numbers racket, was entirely ignorant of the only business

233

in America that was open to every enterprising Negro, then what the hell was he good for? Civil rights? "You are a lawyer here in the Ward, aren't you?" Dave was being sarcastic.

Hunger pangs made Lawyer Jones both irritable and defeatist. *"You* people have A. C. Keane, why do you come to me? I am a respectable member of the bar. I can't help you."

"A. C. Keane? Who's he?"

"For a man whose main source of income is without the law, you astonish me."

"Come again? Skip it. Let's talk about you for a minute."

The lawyer went on at length and Dave was frozen into open-mouthed disbelief. Here was a licensed and practicing Lawyer Greene! Before the man had finished, he had dug up and refurbished all of the lamentations bewailed by Dave's father. They were couched in better English, but they were the same excuses. Lawyer Jones' speech ended with an assertion that Dave was a felon, and as a member of the Ward's underworld, should know that Negro lawyers do not practice criminal law.

Dave was strangely touched by it all, and although alcohol was the father of the impulse, he wanted to help this frustrated man. He made a tentative offer. The Chinese, he had heard, only pay their doctor when they are well; Dave suggested that he and Lawyer Jones might well work out some similar deal.

Lawyer Jones, twenty-seven years of age and three years after being admitted to the state bar, had exactly one five-cent piece to his name. In all fairness, it must be stated that he was too hungry to think. It is only for the gods to know what legal and financial heights he might have reached had he cynically hitched his fortunes to Dave Greene's rising star.

"I didn't work my way through law school for that," Lawyer Jones flung over his shoulder as he took his hunger elsewhere.

He left Dave in a depressed mood. This had been a very negroid and somehow prophetic interview. Dave felt that he had just witnessed a great defeat. Only he was not sure just who had been defeated. He downed several more drinks and finally he began to feel a carefree highness. He suddenly had a desire to apologize to Blueboy for something or the other. He put the bourbon away and left the club.

Blueboy was screaming at someone over the telephone when Dave walked into the rear of the flower shop. When Blueboy finished talking he turned and beamed his approval. "Damn if you don't look half drunk," he said. "It's about time you started to act like some-

234

body that's got good sense. Or is it just because you and the Kelly-gal made up?"

"I am drunk, and I'll get drunker so that I'll have the same amount of intelligence that everybody else around here's got."

"At your age you ain't supposed to have a reason for getting drunk except, mebbe, you is young and healthy and ain't got no better sense. If you got any other reason for drinking in the ante meridian, you shouldn't! It's begging for trouble."

"Who the hell is A. C. Keane, Blueboy?"

"There is an A. C. Keane in every cracker town in America; he comes with the system. He is a legal pimp, he panders to injustice." He paused to note if Dave appreciated that happy phrase. Dave didn't. "As long as you ain't committed murder you can hire him to plead your case. Provided you got fifty bucks, of course, or mebbe a hot-tailed woman. In either case he goes up and whispers to the judge the equivalent of: 'This nigger's got fifty bucks. Let's me and you split it and let the boy go free this time.' That's all there is to it. The town don't get that particular fine. A.C. and the judge splits it."

"Crackers ain't that smart or that crooked," Dave said.

"Nobody in their right mind ever accused a cracker of being crooked. White trash just thinks different from honest people. That's all. Besides, it ain't none of your business. Your business is banking numbers."

"Oh yeah? Well, I've made up my mind. You nuts are not gonna go into that court barefooted. I'm hiring the best criminal lawyer the white trash got to offer."

"We ain't criminals."

"What the hell, if you want to be technical about it, A.C. ain't no criminal lawyer. He's just a goddam messenger boy, that's all. And I'm gonna send that judge a thousand-dollar message."

"Davey-boy, you ain't on trial and you ain't gonna be. Now you is a nigger and you ain't even supposed to have a grand to your black ass. And just because you never been to court for gambling don't mean that you got some special right to be stupid. There's some things that you is supposed to be born knowing, and one of them is that you don't offer no cracker judge no thousand-dollar bribe."

"I'm not so sure about that."

"Hell. Kelly sees the kernel of the matter better than you do. Seems though a kid that young ain't got no right to be so cynical about what life's all about, but at least she was on the right track. You don't even know where the switch's at. And so now for the last time, I'm telling you that we is gonna have a prayer meeting and chitlin supper. And Colonel Eldrege is gonna lead the prayers."

"I'm getting outa here before I go crazy too."

"Prayer is good for the white folks' soul," Blueboy shouted after Dave. "And so we is gonna do the right thing for them in prayer."

Flick was just coming in as Dave went out the door. Dave took him by the arm and led him down the street. "I know who A. C. Keane is," Dave said, "but what's his real story?"

Flick smiled. "You take and give him fifty dollars, or if you ain't got it, you sends your woman, and then she takes him five bucks a week for twelve weeks." He looked at Dave. "What trouble you in, boss?"

"Trouble?" Dave said. His voice was a controlled scream. "You mean to stand there and ask me what trouble I'm in?"

Flick shrugged. His luminous eyes were as commiserating as any girl's could be. "A.C. can't do no more for you than Colonel Eldrege can," he said painstakingly as if he was helping a child learn a very difficult lesson.

And it was this manner of Flick's that made Dave want to shriek at the top of his lungs and punch anybody and everybody in the jaw. And this was not the first time that someone had insinuated that Colonel Eldrege could help him. But this numbers trial was way over the Colonel's head, Dave was sure of that. At best, Dave considered the old man to be a white folks' nigger who was also a bail-bondsman with a touch of Lawyer Greene added for good measure. Furthermore, Dave distrusted Colonel Eldrege. At least he distrusted the man's ability to get him out of this trouble without letting the white people know all of Dave's business.

"C'mon and walk home with me," he said to Flick. "I need a drink." As they walked, Dave said, "I've talked to the Colonel. I thanked him for getting you guys out on bail, and Blueboy paid his fee. But Colonel ain't offered to help me. He ain't said a word about court, and I don't even know if I want him to help me in this particular case."

Dave was unprepared for Flick's reaction. The Kid was visibly upset. Dave could only surmise that Flick wished to attribute magical powers to the Colonel. Come to think of it, the entire Ward wished to do likewise, Blueboy included.

"Boss," Flick said shyly, "Colonel took and tole us how it is. He say the judge gonta throw the whole thing outa court." Dave swelled with rage, but Flick did not notice. "That's if we act humble in court. Colonel say we ain't guilty of anything he knows of. There ain't no city laws against numbers playing, and it's gonna be hard to take and prove that numbers is gambling because white folks don't

236

know what numbers is to begin with. Colonel say if you would only come to him he would tell you how it is."

"What the hell is this anyhow?" Dave demanded. "If Colonel knows so much, why the hell he go bragging about being able to help and don't say a mumbling word to *me?* Everybody in the Ward he tells but me. The feeble-headed bastard is lying to make folks believe that he's got a pull which he don't have."

"Colonel proud. He's not gonna take and give advice unless you takes and asks for it. Colonel say you are a credit to the race. He say he gonna do everything he can to protect you."

"Protect me? How the hell can he protect me? I bet he can't protect himself!"

"Anything the Colonel tell the white people they believe, boss."

"That's just it. I don't want him telling the white folks anything about me." And just as suddenly as his temper had flared Dave was drained of all energy. All he wanted was to be alone. "Okay, Flick," he said absently. "I won't hold you up any longer. You might as well start on your rounds."

Dave continued to sit at the kitchen table after Flick had left. The Kid just did not make sense. "The Colonel could . . ." "But the Colonel gotta be begged . . ."

So there it was. And Kelly was absolutely right: the goddam nigger is a stupid son of a bitch. And how in hell was a bunch of dumb black bastards, going into court without a lawyer, going to be able to prove that numbers was not a form of gambling?

Dave sat at the table and got drunk. And he stayed drunk. The next morning he had to take several stiff drinks to attain a semblance of sobriety. Blueboy, chipper as ever, had rushed out of the house at eight o'clock like a carefree child on his way to a Sunday school picnic.

The jam-packed court revived Dave's jitters. Why the hell had all these peanut-eating-nosy-half-drunk-idiots come here? Was it impossible for these adult black children to see that they were giving added importance to this case? Dave knew that these were the very same people that had turned Jim Penney's funeral into a circus. Now they were here to turn this trial into a funeral.

Dave was too upset to remember that these people would rush from their dinners to look at a dog just struck by a passing automobile. And Dave erred in his opinion concerning the effect this motley crowd would have on the officers of the court. The city attorney observed the grinning black horde and began to doubt the veracity of the police department. They had flatly stated that foreign New York gamblers were running a crooked gambling ring in the

Ward. If there was anything sinister connected with this case, these peanut-eating-Nigras would have been too wily to set foot in court. The city attorney knew his Nigras and there was something definitely wrong with this nigger pool case. He should have sent for Colonel Eldrege and found out exactly what *was* going on in the Ward. Only a fool would take a police officer's word for anything. He felt as though he had been gulled, but time was gone; the clerk was calling the court to session.

The court's first business of the day was always the same, the disposition of the Ward's drunks. Evidently the city had no white drunkards. And Dave saw that the judge had some strange system of his own to determine the amount of the fines. And his honor's personal appearance was no comforting spectacle to Dave. He was a round-faced man of stern stupidity, a born service-club member attempting to impersonate a judge.

The next batch of culprits were the wife beaters, and, in attitude, the judge was as impartial to race as were the wife beaters themselves. There were just as many whites as Negroes, and they were all berated alike by the bench. Dave was impressed by the judge's sincerity as he castigated these lawbreakers, and the fines and sentences, although severe, were more uniform.

Next came the bootleggers (pad and kiff owners). All Negroes. They each received a choice of sixty dollars or sixty days in jail. They all paid their fines and fled the courtroom. It occurred to Dave that even if it were true, as the white man asserted, that Negroes did not carry their share of the tax load, they did make healthy contributions to the city's coffers every day but Sunday. He had no sooner conceived this idea than he began to chide himself for bringing Square Table inanities into court with him. He had enough troubles of his own without worrying over those of other people who were probably guilty anyhow.

The judge peered at his docket and dryly exclaimed, "Well, I must say that this looks like a monstrous crap game."

The judge leaned back in his chair and smirked. Every white man in the courtroom died with laughter. Dave realized that these white men *had* to laugh at this silly man's joke. Like marionettes, each lawyer and court attaché produced a handkerchief to dry his eyes. And Dave knew that any lawyer who dared not to laugh would never see another client go free in this particular court.

And the bank was at the mercy of this silly old fart.

The clerk droned out the names of Dave's men: "Llewellyn Harris, Edgar Johnson, Roger Bailey, Makepeace Johnson, Gordon Brown . . ." The clerk called out over twenty names.

Blueboy appeared first, creeping along like a terrorized maniac, followed by his co-defendants. Blueboy's face was buried in the whitest handkerchief that ever held black tears. Upon reaching the space in front of the bench, Blueboy suddenly bucked like a mule in unholy terror, and Dave was certain that his crazy little friend intended to bolt the courtroom. Over the excited murmurs of the crowd he could hear Blueboy's wail: "Oh, Jesus! Sweet Jesus!"

The whole thing was too bizarre for Dave to take in at one time. His eyes would blink as he took glimpses at his men. He died a little when he saw the spectacle of Colonel Eldrege escorting Kid Flick. Flick was apparently afflicted from head to toe with a horrible St. Vitus dance. And Dave wondered what the hell was Colonel Eldrege doing up there.

Then Dave saw Blip-Blip. He was shuffling about in a tight little circle with his hands clasped before him in oriental fashion. Big, black Gordon Brown fanned himself with a Sunday school supplement. Edgar Johnson kept wiping his head, and Dave fervently prayed that he would rub all the skin off his scalp before the judge noted the fraternal ring on his head-wiping hand.

It was left for Makepeace to conclude the horrid parade to the bar. The huge comptroller had resurrected an old frock coat from the gaudiest of his headwaiter days, and now he hobbled to the bench with the aid of a cane. In his other hand he carried a battered tin washtub. When at last he reached his place in line, he wearily deposited the tub on the floor and sat down on it.

Dave did not bother to be shocked any more.

The judge banged away with his gavel, but even his dulled eyes seemed unable to tear themselves away from the apparition that was Makepeace. The courtroom became quiet.

"Nevah again, oh Jesus," Blueboy shrieked into the stillness.

"What's this?" the judge shouted. "And whar's them international gamblers?"

Mr. Adams, the city attorney, was nobody's fool. He promptly changed mules in the middle of the stream. "Your honor," he said, cautiously feeling his way, "there's been a plot on down in the Ward. N'Yawk gamblers have come here and swindled these here boys inta playing Policy Pete, which some folks calls the Nigger Pool. And these here furrin' gangsters come here and just about took over the Ward."

"Yassuh, Jesus," Blueboy bleated.

An awful curse spewed from Dave's lips and he cared not who heard him. He was a man broken in two. One half of him fought to remain seated and quiet, the other half of him was now in a foaming rage. He wanted to run up to the bench and shout the truth at this silly old judge. He also wanted to knock the hell out of Blueboy while he was up there. And he wanted to tell the whole courtroom that these were the most intelligent men in the Ward. He wanted to scream to the world that Dave Greene's men could count money faster, better, and just as honestly as any white bank teller in the whole damn city. And that they could operate adding machines faster than the eye could see. And with a mighty shriek he wanted to toss thousand-dollar bills in the judge's face and to tell him to keep the change after all the fines had been paid.

In his rage Dave forgot all about the preservation of his bank. He stood up, ready to charge to the front of the court but some slimey blob of sanity in the depths of his rage told him to walk to the rear of the court. And suddenly he knew why he could not rush forward with the truth. No one would hear him. No one *could* hear him because he was no longer a man. He had been cut by his own friends, but it had been the white man who had handed them the knife to do the job. He stood in the back of the court, and his breath came in sobs. He longed for Kelly's body and wondered why, because he no longer felt like a man.

The judge looked as ferocious as any lady bear. "Whar's these N'Yawk gangsters?" he roared.

The prosecutor cleared his throat. "We nipped it right in the bud, your honor. We never gave them a chance, but I'm sorry to say that they left these boys holding the bag, and they are guilty of a whole slew of offenses, tending to corrupt . . ."

"I'se corrupted, Lawd," Blueboy bellowed.

The judge had received a call from the powers that be to "handle" this case. He did not know why, but now he had reached the conclusion that this whole thing was something the police had cooked up in order to make his Nigra boys look silly. And wasn't Colonel Eldrege standing right up here with them?

Judge Bascomb did not like any of this worth a damn and said so. He launched into a speech he had been saving for the Fourth of July. He orated vehemently and incoherently for nearly ten minutes and finally sputtered to an end with the fuzzy proposition, ". . . and if I ever catch any white man, local or furrin', messing with this here nigger pool thing I am personally going to see to it that they is run outa town *after* they does time!"

The city attorney pondered long upon the judge's opinions.

The dignity of the court dissolved in a controlled babble with a few scattered handclaps which the judge assumed were for his little oration. His estimation of *his* Nigra's intelligence rose a few notches.

240

And now Dave saw it all. He knew why Blueboy had never been worried, but the very thought of having to congratulate his men nauseated him, and so he fled the courthouse. Above all else he had to be alone except perhaps for Kelly, but seeing her right now was out of the question. She had to be in class.

Homeward bound in a taxi, Dave knew that Blueboy and the men had used a most logical plan to outwit an illogically conceited foe, but try as he might, he could find no elation in the victory.

Once at home he poured a drink and for the first time in his life he wished that there was some way to get drunk without having to drink whiskey. Drink in hand, he walked from room to room. He felt dirty and wanted to go upstairs and take a bath, but could not find the energy to do it. In fact, what he wanted to do was to go to bed, but the very idea of having to go to bed without Kelly made him rush to the kitchen for a fresh drink. In the kitchen he told himself that none of this was Kelly's fault, but at the same time he was positive that he was incapable of ever making love to Kelly again. At least, not the way she liked to make love.

The doorbell rang and Dave ignored it; just to be by himself was too much company right now. Whoever was at the door was insistent, and Dave fervently hoped he would not have to go to the door and kick somebody's ass. When he heard a key being put in the lock he assumed it was Blueboy.

But it was Kelly who walked into the kitchen. In his arms her body was warm and soothing. Some place near his neck her face was hidden.

"Don't feel hurt, lover," she breathed. "Don't let them make you want to cry."

Dave gulped back angry tears. But at least Kelly knew he had a right to cry with rage.

"I know that you want to be left alone, lover, but if you don't need me now, you never will. And so I had to use my key. Please don't tell me to go away. I need you, too, lover," she whispered. "I was there and it was a low-down rotten dirty shame." Her voice broke completely and she cried out in anger: "It's a goddam shame to make a real man sit and suffer the bites of gnats. I'll hate all white men until the day I die." She drew back from him and now her face wore a smile of supreme arrogance. "I was afraid to come to you, but I watched. When you stood up I almost died. You were going up to that judge, weren't you? I could read your every thought. You must not murder Blueboy in his sleep, lover."

Her arrogant smile dissolved Dave's feeling of utter frustration. Together they burst out laughing. Once more Dave pressed her

241

clamoring body to his. And Kelly's mouth breathed in his ear, "I feel just like the whole damn world has been destroyed and only you and I are left, lover. Please take me upstairs, lover. Please."

It was almost midnight when they pushed their way into the bedlam of Club Babylon's first night. Everybody was there, yelling at somebody else. It was a bright and brittle sort of gaiety in the atmosphere of the club, and everybody took careful pains to ignore it. Like two children caught in a storm, Dave and Kelly clasped hands.

"Hiya, Dave." It was Pigmeat and by the depths of her dimples Dave could tell that she had something on her mind.

He smiled jovially and said, "Okay, so what do you want now?"

"Nothing, really. Only now that you mentioned it . . . I just remembered that Lila said she wanted to work for you."

"That's a damn lie, Pig," Dave said and his voice was almost absentminded. "That kid never said anything like that and you know it."

"Honey, why can't you be nice to my little angel? It isn't fair. You know it isn't."

"She's too young. Only a kid."

"She's nineteen now, Dave. She's a woman and carries herself like one, and you should know that."

Now what the devil did Pig mean by that statement, Dave wondered in amazement. "Whadya mean? How come I should know it so much?"

Pigmeat retreated behind her gentility. "Is that all you want me to tell her?" she asked.

"Yes," he shouted over the hubbub.

The bar was too noisy for Kelly to hear the conversation, and Blip had been yelling some nonsense in her ear, but she was very much aware of the fact that Dave was arguing with Pigmeat.

A little later she asked, "What are you feuding with Pigmeat for? I like her. Leave her alone."

"Well, she don't like you," Dave retorted.

"Nix, lover. All pretty women like each other."

"Have it your way; I'm drinking, not fussing."

"Lover, if I say fuss, then we fuss. What did Pigmeat want?"

"Nothing. A job for her girl friend."

"Well, why deny a most reasonable request?"

"This kid, Delilah, is too young. And she don't know how to meet the public anyhow."

"You running a whorehouse or something?"

242

"Why don't you go wash your mouth out with soap? Lila's just a dumb country girl, and this joint will be full of hardrock hustlers."

"Everybody loves that little black beauty but you. And if she wants a job, she gets it."

"And just who the hell do you think you are to be telling me how to run my business?"

"You know damn well who I think I am. And when you want me to stop being that, just let me know."

Dave gulped his drink and wondered how best to change the conversation. "You ready to leave now?" he said.

"Yes, lover. Take me from this madding crowd."

When they reached the street Kelly paused to inhale the fresh night air. To Dave, the rise and fall of her diaphragm was a spectacle of sexual delight. And he wondered if there was anything on earth that the girl could not do provocatively.

"Do you think of sex much?" he asked.

"What the hell kind of proposal was that, lover?"

He returned her grin. "Damn if I know, but so help me, it seems like your simplest move is a calculated gesture of seduction."

"Why, Dave," and her voice was a husky purr, "you can be quite lingual at times. But the answer is no. It is imperative that I keep sex in its proper place, and I do pride myself on that score. Actually, I don't think I give it a thought when I'm away from you. Since we reached our little understanding, I know it will come and darn near when. So that leaves my mind free to rassle with life's lesser problems like calculus, analytic, and stuff like that there. As they say, sex is really mental—if you got a mind. Want to get a sandwich in Booker's?"

Dave put his arm around her waist and led her into the restaurant.

Mr. Booker rushed up with royal greetings. "Hear tell that that jedge sez that numbers is Negro propity and for white folks to keep hands off. Ain't that right, Dave?"

"I don't know, Mr. Booker," Dave said, smiling dryly. "That judge talked so fast and so crazy like that I don't think he knows himself for sure what he said."

"Well, that's what the Colonel sez."

"Then mebbe that's the way it is. He understands these court people better than I do."

Mr. Booker had led them to a booth and, without asking their permission, sat down facing them. This was something Dave had never seen the old man do before.

Mr. Booker cleared his throat several times. "Dave, you been amongst us over three years now . . ." He paused, carefully weighing each word just as he had done the day of the raid. "Now white folks be funny. Seems like you gotta spend half your time just awondering what's on they mind, and then sometimes you guesses them wrong." He fixed Dave with a rheumy stare. "You ain't gettin mad?"

The uncalled-for question embarrassed Dave and at any other time he would have been peeved. Did Mr. Booker think he was a hot-tempered fool? And what had he ever done to make the old man think that?

At the same time Dave was filled with pride by the cool finesse of Kelly. She was engrossed in putting a new flint in her cigarette lighter. She had literally vanished from the table and its conversation.

"Dave, I wants to see you pay out a little money. Do you mind?" Mr. Booker asked in a voice filled with apology. "It's this way. If the Colonel places a little money in a certain quarter every week, you are gonna be allowed to operate here in the Ward as long as you wants without too much botheration from the police."

Dave squeezed the unbelievably soft inner side of Kelly's thigh. Her hand moved to cover his and hold it there. "I like what you say," Dave told Mr. Booker.

He beamed. "And Dave, I wants you to always remember that them white folks ain't no fools. If they was we wouldn't be under they foot like we is, and we ain't fools, but in lots of ways they is smarter than most of us."

Dave caught himself just in time to prevent his giving Kelly a quizzical look. He said to Mr. Booker, "I'm not so sure I know what you mean."

The old man was plainly embarrassed. "Well, it's like this: them boys had to do what they did in court." To soften the thing for Dave he added, "You ain't no poorer, son."

Kelly lost her ability to stay out of the conversation. "Do you mean that the white people in court knew that our boys were not as ignorant as they made out to be?"

Mr. Booker nodded assent. "Those in the know did. But it seems like they won't trust us lest we act in a certain way. They ain't gonna trust no colored boy what ain't got good sense and don't know how to act." After that, Mr. Booker stood up, smiled genially, and left the booth.

Kelly and Dave looked at each other with confused grins. Kelly giggled. "You couldn't possibly be thinking the same thing I am, lover."

"I dunno. What are you thinking?"

244

"Well, first of all, I shall never use the expression dumb cracker again," she said. "Why, do you realize that they have calmly reduced us to savages without half trying?"

"You mean in court? That minstrel act?"

"That was only the warm-up," Kelly said. "Lover, you're now a savage that worships some tree god. Every week you must leave some offering under a tree for this unseen god. You'll never know the god's identity, or even if it's the god or the jackal who gets your offering. But you have no choice."

"So?" Dave said testily.

"Nothing. I merely stated that you have no alternative. It won't break you. And I, for one, believe that the tree god exists. It's your beloved race problem actually at work. The crooked politicians wanted to know if you people could be trusted, whether or not you were good niggers."

"And mebbe I should believe none of this. That stupid-assed judge was on the level; he didn't act like he had any orders to set anybody free." Dave's voice was choked in a rage of indecision. Only one thing was certain: white people today had shown a singular lack of respect for Dave Greene. "And mebbe I should have told Old Man Booker to go to hell."

"Yassum Mist Greene, Miz Kelly." It was Delilah to take their order. "Behave yourself," said Kelly.

"Ma'am?"

"Call me Kelly like I told you. And if the world isn't going to hell fast enough for you I guess the next best thing for you to do is to take a job in this man's bootleg joint down the street. But I'm warning you that you're too damn expensive-looking to blend with the cheap and tawdry scenery up there, which in this instance means the guests. However, you may work for Dave anytime you want, but I hope to God you won't."

"Dat whut Mist Booky sez."

"He did?"

"Ee say it ain't so much de badniss, it de fastiniss ob de ceebin' and de soon mans I be waiting on in de club."

"The man is right," Kelly said. "There are plenty of deceiving men here in Booker's, but in here, Mr. Booker hopes and prays that they will keep a modicum of sobriety. Club Babylon operates on an entirely different principle."

Lila seemed to watch Kelly's lips like a deaf mute.

Kelly's voice became softly pleading. "Promise me that you won't take a job in the Club Babylon unless you really need the money?"

"Posit me wud, Kelly," Lila said.

"Thanks, Lila."

Dave rose to let Kelly out of the booth. Lila watched as Kelly walked to the ladies room.

"Trus me Gawd dat uh mussiful purty ledy," Lila murmured.

"Do you really like Kelly?" Dave asked.

"Ee badmouf dat girl, but Lawd know ee uh lie," she said darkly.

"But what the dickens can they say about her?" Dave said irritably, knowing full well that there was a lot that was being said and being left unsaid about Kelly.

"Trus me Gawd, ah neber repeat it. You want two ham sangwidges?"

"Yes, Lila."

The look of lonely brooding on Dave's face made Lila hesitate and then say, "Mist Dabbid?" She waited his permission to speak.

"Yeah?"

"Doan beleeve no she-she talk." Then, with a defiant air curiously like Kelly's, Lila walked away.

Dave sighed and told himself that it was time to ask Kelly about her pall of sadness, a sadness he feared might be one of guilt. He mentally steeled his nerves for the coming ordeal, but when he saw her lithely striding toward him all his resolve melted. Kelly Simms was above slander. And what right did he have to disturb her by repeating vicious innuendoes?

After they had finished their sandwiches Kelly said, "Take me back up to the club so that I can say good night to Blueboy, and then let's go home."

And that's exactly what they did do. Later, in the early morning hours, they talked some more about the trial. It was Dave who finally asked the question that had been on each of their minds for hours. "Do you think the Colonel and Old Man Booker are on the level or you think they're playing some kind of game?"

"No such luck, lover."

"Whose side are you on anyway?" he demanded.

"Yours, of course. But wouldn't it be lovely if those two old codgers turned out to be con men? After all, the money is already committed. Spent. And I would like that much better than their just being ignorant bribe collectors for some smart white politicians. Wouldn't you?"

"Well, yeah. But you don't have to hope so fervently that I'm gonna get swindled."

"But, lover. Look at all the racial progress it would signify. All of the races of mankind are judged by the caliber of the thieves they produce. We call it civilization."

246

Dave replied with a hoot of derision.

"Never you mind, lover, but the man who steals a railroad and the man who steals a watermelon are not brothers under the skin."

"Kelly, do you realize that nobody was scared, but me and you? I swear, Blueboy and the rest of them weren't even worried. Don't it look like mebbe we were cowards?" He held his breath, waiting for her answer.

"Cowards? No. You and I always have our eye on the big things in life. It's our weakness, our strength, and our own private little hell. We dream of more perfect things. Most people can't. They see no majestic triumphs, and no utter defeats."

The number that day was 981. Over twenty people hit it.

22

Althea Goins was a mature four-teen years of age when she left her rural home to invade Harlem. A serious shortage of funds made it necessary for her to make a brief stop in the Ward. She temporarily accepted employment as a waitress in order to get enough money to complete her journey to the promised land, but somehow her stopover never ended, and in no time at all she became the reigning beauty of all the Vessey Street chicks.

"Pigmeat" is a catchall term in the Ward. Sometimes it means easy pickings, but it is used more often to describe and compliment the beauty of very young girls. Miss Goins was the deification of pigmeat in human form: she being young, tender, and of a vaguely pinkish hue. She was also smoothly larded. Pigmeat gladly accepted her nickname as any country girl would do.

Even though a born conspirator, she remained ever popular among both sexes. Pigmeat loved to plan things . . . any things. The more complicated the merrier. The mere whisper of a surprise party or shower was sufficient to send her into a frenzy of prearrangements.

Like most young people, she was socially conservative; she never

248

deviated from the established norms of the Block. With regularity she changed boy friends every six months, but never was she accused of infidelity to a single one of them. The feminine elite of Vessey Street had a vague sort of theorem that the periodic changing of boy friends was a practical and handy birth-control measure. It might have been.

In all ways did Pigmeat comply with the proscribed mores of the Block. She was neat, manually efficient, and probably not very bright. However, it is very difficult to properly assess the true intelligence of friendly and complaisant young girls who happen to be pigmeat. Pigmeat's boy friends were all respected members of the Block's socially accepted class, known as the idle rich. They were pool sharks, gamblers, or hustlers from all walks of unindustrious life.

The height of Pig's career was reached when she snared Dave Greene, the rising young numbers baron of the Ward. When she became Dave's woman-emeritus, she was promptly given a new, unique status on the Block. She was at one and the same time social arbiter, hostess extraordinare, and elder states-lady—with the dashing overtones of a gay divorcee. That Dave insisted upon paying her rent after they had formally parted was the supreme accolade.

Once settled in her regal semi-retirement, Pigmeat cast about for a protégée and to everyone's surprise she chose Delilah Mazique. The lovely Delilah was totally unaware of the purple mantle which Pigmeat wished to place upon her. Delilah was oblivious of Vessey Street life. It is true that she worked as a waitress in the Block, but it could never be said that she was of the Block. For, in Lila's own words, "De Block wickety."

When work was done, Lila took herself home to her worn Bible and equally tattered schoolbooks. She loved to read and this quirk in her personality amused, confused and at times, disgusted Pigmeat who believed in all things vocal.

Delilah's Geechie accents were so esoteric that often students from the Campus would drop by the restaurant just to make her talk. They never tired of mentioning the weather, because they knew that Lila's beautifully unintelligible reply would sound something like: "Ee cold, but ee ain't so cold, but, but ee cold dough."

When they attempted to correct her speech she casually replied that they: "Use dem mout so funny." And when they joked with her, she said they were: "cutin de clabash." And when they became too familiar she told them to: "tie up de mout."

Strangely enough, Pigmeat and Delilah were both born in or near Jonesville, hence, relatives, and this hint of kinship may have decided Pigmeat's choice of her heir apparent. If it was true that Pigmeat, among others, thought that Delilah was lonely, they most certainly could not claim the child to be friendless. Mr. Booker himself loved her like a grandchild and liked to boast that he was unable to spoil her. She was his most dependable employee. Her co-workers liked her uncomplaining and unflirtatious ways and never had any guest complained of her manners or service. Everybody was Lila's friend except Dave Greene, who hated her, and to prove it, tipped her many times over what he normally tipped the other girls.

Subtlety not being her strong suit, Pigmeat began her campaign to have all her former titles bestowed upon Delilah with a direct assault.

"Lila, honey, when you gonna come and live with me?"

"Shush, Pig. Yo doan whan me. Yo got no useta fo no mudstick lukkuh me."

"Honey, I've got a lovely place and you know it's your duty to come live with me cause we're kin and you need an older relative to keep an eye on you."

"Ah be nineteen, one mont."

"Well, that just goes to prove what I just said. Everybody around here thinks you're only sixteen and here you are nineteen almost. And you know that's not right!"

"Oh, Pig, ah skayd."

"Scared of what, honey? That's why I want you with me so I can keep an eye on you."

"Yo got friend-boys. Ah doan whan no juntlemon yet awhile."

"Friend-boy. Juntlemon." Pigmeat scolded. "You and I are cousins and born in the same place and you talk like a foreigner. And besides that, you're too pretty to talk like you do. Sometimes you sound right Geechie and you know that ain't no way to sound."

"Round yoah juntlemons ah be skayd tuh crack ee teet."

"There you go again. You do it on purpose. I just tole you to try and talk proper like and here you are spouting Geechie talk at me just as if I knew what you was talking about. And I bet Dave Greene would love you to pieces if you'd only to stop making yourself say things like that, so why won't you behave yourself?"

"Ee ceebin man. Enty wuth," Lila mumbled in a strange sort of defiance.

"Delilah, you make me mad. You know very well that Dave is not a deceiving man, or even an ordinary hustler, much less being worthless. I guess that's what you called him. You know I don't know Geechie talk. And even if you are part Geechie, you ain't got that much Geechie in you. And for that reason alone you should live with me. Then you'd get to know how to talk like a lady."

"Ah skayd. Trute mout, ah skayd."

But fate seemed to be on Pigmeat's side. Lila's room was burgled and all of her good clothes were gone. Like all honest people, Delilah held a great respect for the efficacy of the police; she never doubted that in a few days the kind police officers would return all of her stolen garments to her, clean and undamaged. She thoughtfully refrained from buying a new overcoat and temporarily wore a heavy sweater that the thieves had left behind. Nature took its turn at the wheel, and in the twinkling of a few coughs, Delilah became the prisoner-patient of a joyful Pigmeat. As it later turned out, the girl never left Pig's house because the rooming house in which Lila lived burned to the ground one night. And so it was that Delilah became Pigmeat's permanent roomer.

Informed that Delilah was a patient in Pigmeat's home, Dave straightway called Cokey.

After a few minutes of noncommittal comments about nothing at all, Cokey finally drawled, "So what's up, Dave?"

"Nothing much. I just was wondering if you were doing anything tonight. That's all."

"It'll be the same old story: sit around and beat up my gums with the rest of the Square Table's darkest knights."

"Okay. See you around." And Dave hung up.

Cokey had long since learned to interpret the blurry content of the numbers king's telephone conversations. It was apparent that Dave had something on his mind. Of that Cokey was sure.

Booker's was babbling with its usual Friday night quota as Cokey made his way back to the Square Table. There were Professor Blake, Dr. White, the Colonel, Joe Kelso, Blueboy, Makepeace, Dave, and one or two others.

Cokey wedged a chair in beside Dave. "What's up?" he whispered by way of greeting.

"Nothing," Dave growled, "but these sorry-ass arguments."

"Then let's get some air," said Cokey.

Dave shrugged his shoulders and followed Cokey out the door. The table babbled on:

"You can't deny it. Colored dames are all latent dikes."

"No they ain't. It's like Doc sez: nappy-headed women can't afford romance!"

". . . but they stink more than white ones."

"None of you sonofabitches been close enough to a white gal to tell what they smells like."

251

"All women stink. It's in the Bible."

"Is you a fool?"

"Don't it say all women is unclean?"

"Did they have soap and water in biblical times?"

"They washed Christ's feet, didn't they?"

"I hear Delilah is sick," Cokey said once they were on the street.

"She is?" Dave feigned surprise.

"I wondered if you knew it," Cokey said with exquisite deceit.

"Well, then, let's take a walk by Pig's," Dave solemnly suggested.

"Pig's? For what?" Cokey tried to keep a straight face.

"Well, I heard she was visiting Pigmeat."

"And got took sick?" Cokey asked, marveling at his cruelty.

"Goddamit. I can't believe everything I hear in the Ward. Somebody said she was at Pigmeat's. Now you want to go or don't you?" Dave yelled.

"Sure. I ain't scared."

Dave glared balefully. "Who said anything about being scared? I ain't scared. Why should I be scared?"

"I know you're not. I just said that I wasn't scared either."

"Okay. Okay. So I don't like Lila, but us Vessey Street folks gotta stick together."

"Lila ain't no Vessey Street people and neither am I. So what does that make you?"

"So why make a big issue out of it? Don't you appreciate her waiting on us? She's sick and might need our help."

"And just what sort of help do you think we should offer?"

"Are you trying to bug me?"

"I don't recall having said a bugging word all night," Cokey said indignantly. "What's the matter with you?"

"C'mon," Dave said. "I know what you're trying to say, but you're wrong. You know I don't dislike Lila. I just don't think any human being has a right to talk like that."

"You de one use dem mout so funny."

Together they crossed the street and strolled the block and a half to Pigmeat's. They went up on the porch and rang the bell.

"Oh goody, it's Dave and Cokey. Hiya fellas? C'mon in," Pigmeat said.

"Tell the beloved sick and lovely that Sampson and company have arrived," Cokey drawled.

"Oh, you crazy Cokey! Just what Lila needs to cheer her up." With that, Pigmeat bustled out of the room to prepare her charge for

252

the eyes of visitors. Cokey looked at Dave rather steadily and said, "You got a secret passion for Lila, haven't you?"

"Why you keep asking that?" Dave exploded. "You really are nuts. The kid hates my guts, and I couldn't go with her even if I wanted to. That Geechie talk would drive me stark raving mad in no time at all."

"Yeah," Cokey murmured. "And you a soon-man anyhow."

"Now what the hell does that mean?"

"I dunno. Ask Delilah. A con man probably."

"You think Lila talks that way on purpose?"

"She was born talking that way wasn't she?"

"Hell no," Dave exclaimed. "She and Pig was both born in the same place, Jonesville. They're related even. You don't know nothing. Lila wasn't born no Geechie. She's a self-made Geechie, if you ask me."

"I won't call you a liar. Let us say you're in possession of some erroneous information. Lila is a Geechie woman. And that would make a lovely topic for the Square Table: Why and/or how, did the Geechies manage to stay pure black in this land of the great white father? Even you should enjoy that one."

Pigmeat came in cutting their conversation short. Without a word she led them to Delilah's bedroom.

Delilah was beautiful. There was no doubt about it, and it was mirrored in the smug smile of possession and accomplishment that covered Pigmeat's face.

"Hiya, sis," Cokey exclaimed, and plumped himself down on the bed beside Delilah.

Dave was mildly confounded to see the impassive girl hug Cokey and all but kiss him.

"Cokey. You so good duh come see me," she said.

Happiness made her unbearably beautiful to Dave, and in some strange way he felt acutely guilty in her presence. Like an intruder he stood caught between the patter of Cokey and Lila, all the time wondering why he had been so anxious to come. Now that he was here, he knew that he had no business being here. He should have sent for Pig to come to him for whatever was needed.

Dave was not even sure if Delilah had spoken to him, and even if she had, she had eyes only for Cokey. It was ever like this, Dave consoled himself. He must have been born to play second fiddle whenever it came to being the life of the party. He felt no bitterness, but he did long for one smile from Delilah.

"Dave here drugged me in," Cokey was telling Lila.

"Tanky, Mist Greene," she said formally, dutifully.

". . . but I was coming tomorrow anyhow," Cokey added.

"You come anyhow tomorra and read with me." And her voice lilted with the sweet notes of friendship and possession. Dave gathered that he had summarily been dismissed, but he knew not how to make his exit. And he was determined to make it graceful.

"You want me to go for some ice cream?" he fumbled, knowing that he sounded like a country bumpkin.

"No, tanky. You sabe yoah monee," Lila instructed him.

He was positive that he had been dismissed. Like a drowning man reaching for a straw, he pulled out his vulgar bankroll. He peeled off several bills of large denominations and handed them to Pigmeat. "Give her what she wants," he said brusquely.

Before she opened the front door, Pigmeat hugged and kissed Dave impetuously. "You always make me proud that I useta be your girl friend, Dave honey."

He chuckled indulgently and asked who was Lila's doctor.

"No you don't, honey." Pigmeat anticipated him. "Lila would have a fit." She giggled. "Dat she-she business, with her. No males allowed. Now don't you go doing nothing to upset her, cause I'm working on her for you."

"C'mon, cut it out," Dave pleaded. "Ain't you ever heard of Kelly Simms?"

"She is low, Dave, so very low that you wouldn't even believe it. You gonna be sorry, Dave, and hurt." She quickly shut the door in his outraged face, but Dave managed to temper his rage by telling himself that Pig's accusations were a natural result of the jealousy of the Vessey Street chick for the Campus girl. He also knew that he and Kelly were foredoomed to have a long and painful talk some day.

Pigmeat returned to Lila's room and stood glaring at her with what she hoped would be taken for unbridled wrath. "I am ashamed of you, Delilah. Ashamed," she said. "You practically ran Mr. Greene outa here."

"Ah didunt."

"You did. You know you did. Didn't she, Cokey?"

Delilah rebelled inwardly and suddenly. "Enty wuth. Ee stan sukkah sto. Eebody howmuchum," she muttered.

"You know good and well we don't know what in the wide world you are talking about," Pigmeat screeched. "Do we, Cokey? Honey, puhleeze try to talk like a lady."

Lila retreated behind her mask of impassivity.

Cokey gently intervened. "Didn't you say that Dave looks like a man standing in a store?" Delilah nodded vigorously. "That last part; what did it mean, Lila?"

"Him always look like he reading the prices on people. How much eveybuddy cost him. He buy his frens and it wickety. He doan hab tuh do dat wid me. Ah be his fren foah nuthin."

23

The same afternoon that 222 came out, Kelly unexpectedly dropped by. She found only Blueboy at home.

"It's been a long, long time since you and I had a session of gab together," she said to Blueboy.

With a grunting sigh of contentment, Blueboy sank into a chair facing Kelly. "That we haven't, Kelly-gal, that we haven't."

"Three more weeks to graduation, Blueboy, and then it's all over. I'm going to miss you."

"That goes double, Kelly-gal." Blueboy's words were little more than a whisper.

At first Kelly had thought Blueboy to be tired, but now she was aware that her friend had aged rapidly. They drink too much, she thought, while she studied Blueboy's face. It came as a shock to Kelly to see how this aging process had gone on unnoticed until now. Moreover, she sensed that it was not age alone that marked her friend; nor was dissipation completely to blame. This was a spiritual thing.

He looks as if he has retired, she sorrowed. That Blueboy should voluntarily retreat from life was unthinkable—at least it had been until now.

"You don't act too pert today," said Blueboy. "Something wrong?"

"No . . ." Abruptly she brightened with no conscious effort, but her grin could only be described as rugged. "I was just thinking about how much I'm going to miss you and . . . Dave. I don't know which one of you I truly love the most. Not really. Did you know that you two are all I have?"

"You know I do. You, Dave, and me is an immediate family to each other and I, for one, am proud of it. Seems like God didn't see fit to gimme children of my own flesh and blood, but no father on earth could be prouder of his'n than I am of you and Dave. Kelly?"

"Yes, Blueboy?"

"Why did you do it?"

She looked up, startled. "Do what, Blueboy?"

"Start this thing, you and Dave? You are said to be something of a genius on the Campus. You got years more of college already planned up North. You got a brilliant future in front of you. And mind you, I'm all for it. It's you youngbloods that's got to liberate the colored man, not us old ones. It's gonna take young brains to settle this thing."

"Oh no, Blueboy," Kelly said. "You can't believe that I went into chemistry just to settle your crumby old race problems."

Blueboy was undeterred. "Mebbe you are bashful to say it outright, but one of these days one of you kids is gonna invent a synthetic gasoline that sells for ten cents a gallon. Or something just as worthwhile. And that is gonna be the day when we can tell the white boys that we is now free and equal."

"Hush, Blueboy," Kelly gently admonished him. "Let's not feed on those kind of dreams. We would surely starve if we did, or else go mad. If I end up in a laboratory at DuPont, I'll consider myself as having written history. I have never dreamed of being another Carver or Curie . . . or perhaps I have, but I refuse to live by daydreams."

"I don't care, Kelly-gal. You reach for the moon if you want!" He was gruff, all-protective. "I got me a goodly sum stashed away and I'm intending to plow it all into the first sensible thing a young Negro boy or girl invents. I don't figger I got any other duty in the whole wide world but that one."

Kelly was dismayed: the worldly Blueboy was ignorant of the existence of cartels, over and covert, and of their power. "Please don't dream too big for me, Blueboy . . ."

"Well, something's just gotta give, Kelly and you're just as smart as the next. And don't worry. When the day comes, me and Dave's gonna be ready!"

"So many panaceas!" Her laugh has a strangely forgiving sound as it floated across the room. "Well, eat your opium and be happy . . . I suppose."

"But you never answered my real question, Kelly."

"What question?"

"Since your life and future was already dedicated, why did you stop to pick daisies?"

"I fell in love with Dave," she said simply. "I was pretty helpless once it started."

"Mind you, I'm not criticizing; I'm just curious." His smile was a wistful thing that ripped at Kelly's reservoir of strength. "Seems mighty silly," he fretted, "for you two to kindle such a big fire just to get your fingers burnt trying to put it out."

"Is that why you once asked me about people having good sense?"

"Well, yes and no, but since you asked, are you and Dave acting very bright?"

Kelly's soft sad voice was firm. "I really don't know. Nuff sed?"

"Mebbe."

"You know, Dave is a rich man. If I get all hot in the ass, I'm sure I could get plane fare from him to return."

"Sounds real logical, but you wouldn't have put that cuss word in there if you really thought you was being logical."

"Go to hell. And I was raised in a whorehouse, remember?"

"Dave drinks a lot now."

"Don't you all?"

"Supposin' he won't get sober after you leave? Would you come back and make him?"

She stretched out her lovely legs and carefully inspected the toe of one shoe. "No," she whispered. Her eyes caught fire with the light of pure rage. "When I go, I'm gone, you sonofabitch, you. I'm not iron. Kelly Simms is a flesh and bone human being. And I am going." Her voice broke and she lapsed into a sultry silence.

"I don't know as I can say that I understand what you're saying, but your voice tells me how you feel about it," Blueboy said. "Deep down inside you don't think Dave is a man, do you?"

Kelly could find no reply.

The following three weeks sped by in a flash, and neither Dave nor Kelly could account for the time that passed. All of the plans they had made never materialized.

258

Tonight, each looked with guilt upon the other. Each, to himself, felt that they had betrayed their love. For each had promised himself to make these last weeks so hectic that parting would be a welcomed respite.

This was the eve of Kelly's graduation, the end of it all. The two lovers sat facing each other in the front room and wondered if they were not strangers.

Where had they been?

And they had always been together.

How could each have failed the other so completely?

Kelly broke the circle of puzzlement and disbelief.

"Pretty rough, eh, lover?"

"A guy, knowing that he is gonna die in the morning has naturally got to feel worse, but, damn." His shoulders drooped in frustration and of despair.

". . . and so to bed?"

His answer was a puzzlement to both of them. "Let's wait awhile," he muttered. He tried desperately to be careless, offhand, but his words betrayed him. "It's gonna be a long time before we walk into Booker's together again, and every bastard in the joint stares at you like . . . well, hell, you know." He tried to smile his love for her.

And so they went to Booker's, to say farewell to the Block.

Kelly walked before him as they entered the crowded restaurant and something happened in his throat as he watched her effortless stride. And as usual, a hush fell over the big room.

The King and His Woman.

And what a woman. Her hips were a promise of heaven. The jaunty shoulders informed the world that here was a noble friend or foe. Take your choice. She was wearing a man-tailored white silk shirt, open at the throat, with that studied carelessness that was Kelly's trademark.

As soon as they were seated, Dave once again began to feel the depth of his despair. It seemed like only a few weeks ago that she had led him like a dumb animal to this very booth and started the whole thing. And after tonight that thing would be dead. Stone cold dead, and who was to blame? And that had to be Kelly, and Kelly alone. And who was the loser? And Dave knew that Kelly would still be Kelly wherever she might be. But Dave Greene was to be left behind, the only loser.

He sat still and silent. Only a fool would have ever become involved with Kelly. No normal girl could have made all the violent love over this past year and a half and then selfishly cast the object of that love aside like a used rubber.

And all for a crazy thing called a "career," he taunted himself. Kelly was smart; she knew that "black" and "career" could never go together. The desire to run her down was strong. Was Kelly fleeing the black race?

He looked up and saw Mr. Booker beaming down at them.

"Miss Kelly," the old man said, "they tells me that you are gonta walk away with every honor that they got up there on that Campus tomorrow, and I'm right proud to see you do it. Now you take an ugly gal . . . well, she ain't got nothing to do but study and get good marks, but you is a gorjuss and fun-loving young lady. And I like it because you is like white folks. You rules the books, de books doan rule you. And the same thing goes for lady-like manners, Miss Kelly. I ain't never seen no good-times rule you neither. You is always above reproach. And I wants you to promise to always come by and say hello to the old man whenever the Lawd see fit for you to travel this way. Now Gawd bless you and keep you safe, Miss Kelly."

After Mr. Booker departed, Kelly grinned hugely and said, "Was that there a left-handed compliment or not, lover?"

"What? I dunno."

"Well, reading between the sheets, I would say that the old dear was congratulating me for not getting pregnant."

"I wish the hell you was pregnant!"

"Coward."

"Like hell I am."

"Go shoot Bilbo and your death will be short, sweet, and meaningful. I assure you that marriage is a slow and tortuous thing."

"You gotta make a joke of every damn thing? Me and you is just one big joke to you, ain't it? Kelly," he said, "do you really have to go now?"

"It's best," she said gently.

And with the hearing of those words he was struck by the reality, the finality, of it all. He was glad. Only the beginning of the end is agony. The end is absolute release.

And let her go, God bless her. He had fought against this moment since the day they met. This was a time of Kelly's own making. Tomorrow, after the commencement exercises, she was leaving; hell bound for Rhode Island to visit some obscure relatives. They both knew that the trip was unnecessary. After she had received her diploma she would have been free to live openly with him until it was time to leave for Chicago and her graduate studies. And she could have returned every holiday and summer vacation, he reflected in cold anger. But Kelly refused to have it that way.

And his best had not been good enough.

They ate a terrible meal in a wary silence that even Kelly did not seek to break. After dinner they went across to the Lil Savoy, and Colonel Eldrege said the exact same things to Kelly that Mr. Booker had said earlier. Kelly quipped that the two old codgers must have rehearsed the damn thing together.

Still later they pushed their way into the crowded barroom of the Club Babylon. Dave's night spot held a motley crowd—tomorrow's graduates with their proud parents and girl griends, a few high school graduates who had come for their first glimpse of the Block after dark, a goodly number of Vessey Street hustlers and their chicks, plus quite a few rural schoolteachers.

Over the hubbub, Kelly's voice begged Dave, "Lover, promise me that I won't be reading about you."

"Hell, Kelly, I'm in the Life. I'm a numbers banker. You might pick up a colored paper and read most anything about me anytime. You know that."

"But nothing to make me ashamed, lover, please. Not for nigger things. Not for income tax; not for fighting; not for being unwise. I couldn't bear it, to pick up a paper and read that you had betrayed me."

He grinned harshly, then shouted in her ear over the noise, "Since I'll probably be sleeping alone from now on, what dif does it make? I won't be no lonelier in jail than I will in the street."

She whimpered like a wounded puppy and seemed about to have reached the breaking point, but then she renewed her spirits. "When we met, I threatened you. I even went so far to say that I was probably being unfair to you by starting this little romance. But now, I think that I was both fair and honest. I denied you nothing. I'm proud of that fact. We've been infinitely kind, one to the other. I'm proud of that, too." She, too, was shouting now over the noise. "There is no way in hell that either of us can say that we are not richer because we shared our lives with each other. I shall never marry—will not—but this you may be sure of until I die: whenever you come to me my drawers will always be dropped." And then she really cried.

"Hush, Kelly, hush," he murmured like a lullaby and held her tightly in his arms. "I don't understand you, but you've proved that there ain't a phony bone in your body. Mebbe you're wrong this time, and if you are, you'll admit it pretty soon."

When she had recovered a little, she tried to smile, and her heart still seemed to be filled with tears, but she leaned toward him to intensify her words. "All those things I talked about. Please, lover, like in remembrance of me. Please think big, and don't repeat ignorance. That's all I ask of you. For if you don't, I don't know what will become of you and Blueboy."

"Hush. Don't be silly," he reassured her.

"But I mean every word, lover. You two have a lion by the tail. Too much money can spoil a child . . ."

"I ain't no child," he laughed.

"Oh yes you are. You're walking where few colored men ever dared to walk before. You're as inexperienced as a child. That's why I want you to seek for the truth in everything." She looked at him with fear and quickly asked, "No regrets?"

He picked up his glass and saluted her. "No regrets."

Blip and Cokey joined them and it soon became a valedictory drinking bout. It was early morning when Dave and Kelly returned to the house on Gay Street. And, then, they came to their final hours. And it was good and it was theirs. And for a long while they forgot about tomorrow.

Dave slept soundly while Kelly, knowing that sleep could not come, got up and took a shower. After that she dressed quickly and carefully as if she had a rendezvous with a lover. Fully dressed, she took a seat before the dressing table that Dave had bought expressly for her. She peered at the mirror and tried to grin. She failed.

Everyone said she was pretty, but what did that matter? She stared hard at the mirror and then suddenly closed her eyes. Her shoulders drooped with all hope gone. Certainly she must be pleasing to the eye, but why? Had the same God who had given her beauty also been the same God who had given Dave his wealth? She turned to look at Dave through tear-blinded eyes and was terrified to see that his face was to the wall.

Suddenly her mind was full of thoughts of her family and her brother, Ted. Ted did not know that this was her graduation day.

But where, O God, was Ted? Ill? Dead? In a sanatorium?

Numbed, cold, frightened, she sat fixed before the looking glass and was overcome by the odorless, dull sterility of the parsonage that had been her childhood home.

Kelly's father, Reverend Simms, had religiously fed the two children three times a day, but never could she recall ever having smelled food or any other odor of human life.

Kelly's father loved Sin. He believed it to be his life's mission here on earth to seek out and denounce sin. He searched high and low for sin, and he never failed to find it. Old Maid was the very first lesson in gambling. The devil invented checkers for idle hands. And a cigarette was tobacco rolled up in paper with fire on one end and a dirty sinner on the other end. The man was unquenchable and unbeatable, as he tracked down sin through every walk of life. Whenever he found it, his light-colored eyes would become aglow with the light of climax.

The Reverend Simms was more than amply equipped to become a successful Negro Baptist minister. He possessed all the charms that are so necessary to titillate the souls of Baptist sisters. Included in his repertoire were two motherless children, Ted, a boy of six and Kelly, a girl three years younger than her brother. The youthful minister also had a white skin, a handsome face, a college education, and perfect diction, which he purposely slurred to generate togetherness with his southern-bred flock when he came from Rhode Island to Cleveland.

Reverend Simms was a Negro, but you had to take his word for it, for in every way imaginable he was a Caucasian-looking man. To the indifferent observer, Reverend Simms was just another dapper little white guy who more than likely was a fair-to-middlin' song and dance man.

The front pew of Reverend Simms's church was designated as the "repenter's bench" and the man of God was never happier than when it was filled with self-confessed backsliders. He would feverishly urge them to give voice to their errors until the hysterical backsliders would shout out all sorts of sins they had committed. After the repenters had begged for both mundane and heavenly forgiveness, the little cleric would pray long over the transgressors. It was a hellishly good performance, and his flock loved it.

The Catholics, cried Reverend Simms, were wrong from here to hell, but the most flagrant of their sins was their confessional, which had been inaugurated by Old Satan himself.

"You cannot hide sin," he preached. "You got to drag it out into God's own purifying sunshine. You can read this Book"—he pounded on the Bible—"until your eyes wear out, but never will you find one word in it that says it is all right for you to creep up to a little black box with a foreigner hiding on the inside of it, and you whisper your sins to him instead of God. You are only compounding your sins when you do that unto God. It ain't right, and you know it ain't right. You have to confess your sins one among the other to gain salvation. And that is the rock that our church is built upon. This True Rock of God."

The good women of the congregation had tried from the very first to take Teddy and Kelly to their collective heart, but Reverend Simms aborted them. The man was a would-be mother himself. The parishioners often brought gifts of toys to the parsonage, which the man destroyed immediately. When storybooks were brought the man hid them in unaccessible places until he should find time to censor them, but he never did find the time. Until this day, those storybooks must still lay hidden somewhere in that bleak home in Cleveland.

Kelly blinked into the mirror and wept softly. The insistent memories wracked her and she was powerless to stop them.

She never learned, but simply knew, that she and Teddy were different. From the very beginning the world had decreed that there should be a closer bond between this brother and sister than is usual or necessary. In school the other children had known immediately that the two Simms children were strangers abroad in this world. The pair of them were too handsome, too well-dressed, too polite, and too lonely. And the girl child was the more damnably different of the two, for she was one of mankind's eternally cursed: she was a compassionate being. The little girl even loved her father dearly and utterly, and because she loved him so, she did not know that he was a cruel man.

One hot, stormy night of the summer Teddy was to graduate from high school, she had heard Ted step swiftly into her bedroom. "Teddy?" she whispered into the dark.

"You still awake?"

She did not answer, knowing that his question was only a prelude to something terrible.

And after a pause the boy whispered, "I'm running away."

"No." It was her first real plea to God.

"We don't live right. I don't think God meant it this . . ."

The light went on and in its glare Kelly stared at her father.

"I wouldn't let you go out of the house to sin and so you took to fouling your own nest. Your own sister."

With a scream of outrage, Ted struck his father to the floor.

Frozen in terror, Kelly watched the fleeing form of Teddy as he left the room. Left the parsonage. Left her.

Through the looking glass Kelly surveyed Dave's bedroom. Perhaps she had not come to Dave with clean hands, after all. In her misconceptions and romanticism of the Negro underworld, had she thought that Dave had access to some mysterious pipeline into every town in the U.S.A.? Had she sold her body to Dave for the price of finding her brother? And why had she not collected her price? Dave was a rich man. Why had she not asked him for the money to find Ted? Private detectives can find colored people, too, can't they?

Like a true Christian soldier, Reverend Simms did not languish over the loss of his son to the devil. But he did resolve that he would never lose Kelly to the devil, even if it killed the child. Her life became a nightmare of prayer. To the horror of his church members, he forced the child to sit on the repenter's bench. It was rumored that Kelly's appearance on the repenter's bench was the direct result of Reverend Simms having to find it necessary to drive his son from the parsonage in the still of night. At the age of twelve, Kelly was the center of a scandal that rocked a church of nine hundred souls.

Grace before meals became an obscenity of religion. Reverend Simms dramatically placed his pocket watch beside his plate and prayed aloud for fifteen minutes by the watch. He castigated Kelly in the third person and begged for her deliverance from evil.

Some months later it was discovered that Kelly had tuberculosis and she was sent to a state sanatorium.

Although she was only thirteen at the time, Kelly's age was listed as "uncertain." She was obviously too intelligent to be a colored child of less than sixteen and her menses had already begun which is unusual in a tubercular child of any color. They placed the child in an adult ward which contained twenty beds.

Kelly found the ward divided into two distinct groups. There were ten devout Catholics in one group and nine irreligious renegades in the other. Kelly was never fully convinced whether or not she was a full-fledged member of the renegade one or not. But she definitely knew that she did not belong among the orthodox ten.

The group of nine came from the wrong side of the tracks—morally speaking, at least. They had gone out into the world and contracted TB. (It had been *brought* to the ten devout.) Extroverted, profane, materialistic, and possessing vast capacities for both rage and compassion, this unholy group seized upon the innocent Kelly and proclaimed her to be their own personal property. Four of the nine were professional prostitutes, and they immediately went about the business of simultaneously charming and intimidating the head nurse into putting Kelly in a bed between them. They succeeded and Kelly lay in a bed for twenty-four hours a day for twenty months flanked on each side by two outspoken women of the street. There is no doubt that Kelly Simms was raised in a whorehouse.

"Never beg! Even if he's raping you. Relax and enjoy it. And he might not kill you."

"All men are swell lovers . . . if you tell them so."

"Always get yours before he gets his, or you won't."

"And don't worry about your good name. Half my tricks begs me to marry them. If old maids took to walking the streets for a coupla nights, there wouldn't be any."

"Fer Gawd's sake, stop fidgeting, Kelly. If you gotta pee, go pee, but stop jiggling around. You make a man think you got crabs or something. And men is scared enough already without you driving them battier."

"If whores make such good wives, why don't they?"

"Stay on good terms with one doctor and one lawyer and you won't need no friends."

"Kelly! Stop talking with your hands. Half my trade came from the husbands of bitches with expressive hands."

"The easiest way to catch a man's eye is to stand perfectly still and make believe you don't even see him. The dumb bastard can't stand that . . . he gonna say right away that you're *Different*."

"All habits cost money. Dope, whiskey, men, even chewing gum or going to church. It's a hell of a lot cheaper to lead a clean life."

"Always dress like you intends to undress in front of a man. A bitch with a safety pin in her drawers can give a guy blood poison."

Kelly soon came to be the favorite of almost everyone on the staff. The librarian loved her and always brought new books to Kelly: "Read this, dear, so I'll be able to tell the other patients what it's all about . . ."

A rugged little lesbian who looked like Mickey Walker taught Kelly how to play a mercilessly close-chested game of stud poker. The professional hijacker and jailbreaker had hard-rock rules. "Less than ten jack, turn down. Let the suckers complain, but they won't quit until they go broke anyhow."

After she had had twenty long months of bed rest, the doctors pronounced Kelly's case arrested, and she was free to go home. The kind sisters of her father's church stepped forward with money and sent the child to St. Paul's School in rustic Lawrenceville, Virginia.

The doctors at the sanatorium had told Kelly her case was arrested, but could never be called cured. They had also warned her about sex, the belief at the time being that a tubercular person used the same amount of energy in sexual intercourse that a normal person used on a fifteen-mile hike.

So while still a maiden, Kelly renounced marriage. She knew that she could refuse nothing to the man she loved. Dave had been Kelly's calculated fling at life. To Kelly, marriage would be tantamount to suicide. She would have died for Dave Greene if dying

266

was all there was to it, but Kelly could foresee the cough-racked bed and a worried Dave waiting for her to die.

She looked into the mirror and was surprised to see that her lips were twisted into a taut grin. Her grin broadened as she remembered Celeste returning to the sanatorium after a Christmastime home visit. "Hell, I walked forty-five miles before we ever got around to decorating the goddam tree." For one fleeting moment Kelly wondered how much she had shortened her life by going with Dave, but she was not sorry.

As she sat and thought it seemed to her that she was doing a cowardly thing. And finally she knew she was. But God in heaven knew that she would surely go mad if Dave turned his back, no matter how gently, upon her because of the TB. This then was the final hour.

She picked up a comb and looked at it. She was numb now. Satiated. And she wanly hoped that she might remain in this state of sexual limbo for the rest of her life. After all, having once loved Dave was enough to last her a lifetime. It had not been a sham romance. She scowled; having loved Dave, there was room for no other man.

She tried to smile wryly, but the mirror only showed an ugly twisting of the lips.

Suddenly she snapped out of it and quickly redid her make-up. She would leave now.

In a few moments she arose from her seat before the looking glass and turned to look once more at her sleeping lover. She still could not glimpse his face, and she knew that this was best, for Dave was now consigned like her mother, her brother, like her wish to love and be loved, to the over-all scheme of her life's tragedies.

She knew that she was being melodramatic, but she indulged herself to whisper aloud: "Good-by, lover."

"Good-by, Kelly."

His voice came like a clap of thunder and she was shaken, afraid.

"I—I'm leaving now . . . I'll write." And she knew that she must not. "That money you put in my purse . . . I found it. Thanks, lover . . . I'm rich now."

He refused to turn over and face her. He did not even move. In times of crisis he always fumbled for a cigarette.

Wondering if he was crying, she took a step toward the door.

"Kelly?"

"Yes, lover?"

"Did . . . you ever . . . screw . . . your . . . brother?"

267

From Cleveland, to Lawrenceville, to the Campus, to the Ward! Where next? How had she ever dreamed of ever marrying anyone?

"No, Dave, the last time I saw my brother I was less than twelve years old."

"That's what I thought."

He remained motionless and Kelly wept for him. Wept that it had been necessary for him to ask. But it was still her bloody defeat.

"You heard that?" she murmured in an amazed voice. She knew that it was not her voice and wondered who had been kind enough to ask the question for her. Whoever it was, their voice had been muffled with tears.

"Yes."

"When? I mean, how long ago?"

"Long time . . . long ago."

"You heard and still loved me? You never believed . . ."

"Yes."

She broke completely, but managed to say, "Thanks, lover . . . forever."

Dave closed his eyes to better hear her high heels clicking out of his life. He held his breath as he heard the sound of the front door being opened, but he did not hear the sound of her footsteps, nor the sound of the door being closed.

And then he knew that Kelly Simms was pausing to take a deep breath, to square her shoulders, before she stepped out into the morning sunlight.

24

Cokey Louis was a member of the class of '39, but he was too drunk to attend the commencement exercises. He was nearly, but not quite, as drunk as Dave, atop whose head was perched the mortarboard that Cokey should have been wearing on the Campus at this very moment. The two of them had been sitting in the same booth at Booker's when the restaurant had overflowed with breakfasting commencement visitors, and they had remained while those same visitors had returned for lunch. Now it was late in the afternoon and Booker's was almost deserted.

"I'm gonna miss that goddam screwball," Dave confided to Cokey for what must have been the fiftieth time at least. "S'funny how I went for that chick . . ."

Cokey was of a like mind. "Wouldn't be so bad if you had loved and lost through some thought of your own, but you ain't done a damn thing. Not a single goddam thing. Still and all, that don't make the titty taste no sweeter." He looked as if he had suffered a great personal defeat. "Kelly was too damn smart for us," he declared.

269

Dave listened with only half of his attention. ". . . that little bitch could make more love in five minutes than the average dame knows how to make in a lifetime. Kelly was a love-machine." He stared dreamily at nothing in particular. Then, as if in delayed reaction, he snarled at Cokey, "Whaddya mean, too smart? And where do you get the 'we' stuff?"

"I loved her for you just as much as you did," Cokey said. "But she was too far above us. We're too low to dream her kind of dreams. Life slipped us a limber dick and all we got left to do is drink." He raised his glass and drank deeply. "Now if Kelly had been a stupid broad, she would have married you before you even had a chance to say no. But leave it to you to go find the brainiest girl in America. And do you know what that makes you? Here you are, one of the few guys in the world that don't need a dame with brains, but who do you fall for? Answer me that."

"And why not?"

"You got brains and luck enough for any two people. It don't need brains to marry a millionaire."

"You mean it don't take brains to make that last statement you just made. You sound like every damn dumb dame got a perfect right to marry me. Which they ain't."

"They got a perfectly legitimate right to try," Cokey retorted. "Black millionaires don't grow in trees no more. At least not very often. And now that I'm thinking about it, Kelly ain't too bright either. Just who the hell does she think she is? Anyhow? What right has she got to refuse your hand just because the dough of a nigger pool is in it? Neither of you two had a right to meet and fall in love anyhow. A pox on both your houses."

"Thass the honest truth." Dave agreed in all sincerity until it dawned upon him that he had not the slightest notion of what Cokey was talking about. "What damn houses?" he asked in the strictest confidence.

"*Both* your houses," Cokey repeated.

"Neither one of you got any excuse for not getting married if you really wanted to. Career? You could have bought her a whole damn laboratory for a wedding present. Which is exactly the point in this case. You and Kelly are unmet. You two don't have a single thing in common and you both know it. I regret my former tears; neither damn one of you deserved them. You looked at life from opposite poles. Kelly is a cynic; you're a true believer . . . in any damn thing. She's an iconoclast; and you worship the same white elephants as every damn conservative Republican banker. You look at God and tremble; Kelly made friends with The Guy long ago,

270

they're on the best of speaking terms. You two are natural-born enemies and don't even know it. And I'm not going to bother to state who thinks like a white boy and who don't."

"Blueboy sure schooled you, but Blueboy can be just as loud and wrong as the next guy at times. To hear you tell it, I was too goddam dumb to get married to Kelly."

"Republican bankers are never dumb and they're always right as hell."

"I still think you're trying to call me a stupid bastard."

"Whazzat a question? You sure you want an answer?"

"Jes becuz we're drunk is no reason why we can't respect me," Dave replied grandly.

"Very well spoken, my friend. Very well put, I must admit, but as of today, I'm free to insult you as much as I damn well please. Soon I'll be leavin'. My days of free lodging are over, but thank you kindly, Mr. Anthony."

"Sonofabitch," Dave whispered softly. "You and Kelly both . . ."

Cokey was touched. "You're nice people, fella," he said with simple sincerity.

"Same to you."

Pigmeat squeezed into the booth, and her presence dispelled the gloom. "Hiya, fellas." She reached for a glass. "What're you all using for chasers? Don't you know that plain whiskey will eat the lining offen your stomicks? And liver? You should always dilute it, and have you two eaten anyhow?"

"Yass, Pig," Cokey drawled, "we both ate some anyhow."

Cokey's revelation seemed to mollify Pig. "Oh, there's Lila. Hiya, Lila? C'mere!"

"Yes, Pig?" And then she smiled. "Don't tell me. I know. Chasers." She went away.

"That is the sweetest chile I ever laid eyes on," Pigmeat happily declared. She cut her eyes at Dave. "I thought you and her'd be on real good time by now, and she's speaking real good now, too. You notice? I betcha'd be surprised to know that I taught her how. You see, everytime she slips inta that old Geechie talk I corrects her. Real nice like, and she's gonna be talking like a real lady real soon now."

"Why teach a monkey to talk?"

Pigmeat was agitated with an emotion that was the nearest she possessed to anger. It was an unique blending of dismay and reproof. "Do you mean that?" she asked Dave. "Or is that supposed to be a joke? I don't think that was a very nice thing to say to a lady about another lady."

"I was only kidding," Dave said. The three sat together in an uncomfortable silence.

"Dave? . . ." Pigmeat finally said, ". . . remember one night long ago? And I told you something I heard?"

"Yeah."

"I never repeated it again. I don't know why I repeated it then. I'm sorry," she said. "It wasn't like me at all. I never said dirt of nobody before. I guess . . . maybe . . . it's because I think I kinda own you or something."

"Yeah . . . I understand," Dave replied. "It's not true about her, though," he added.

"I know it, too. Now."

He was surprised. "How?"

"Why you can just look at her and tell," Pig exclaimed. "When I told you, I had never seen her real good, but since I got a chance to, I know. You can see that whatever God made Kelly, He didn't make her low-down."

"You're damn right."

"But, Dave, I still know that I am right about her not being for you," Pigmeat said insistently.

"What difference does it make?" he demanded sharply. "She's gone, ain't she?"

"But I hate to see you all moody like this, Dave, honey. I don't care if you drank the ocean dry as long as you was laughing, but you ain't, and it hurts." She stopped in dismay as he punctuated her statement by moodily pouring another drink. "Honest, honey, she wasn't for you. Kelly wasn't a woman." Pigmeat was possessed of a strange evangelism. "I don't mean she was queer or nothing, but Kelly is not for any man, and I think she knows it. It's something I know in my bones and it ain't superstition neither. Kelly is a lovely girl, but it's just as if somebody went and squeezed all the real woman outen her once. Can you imagine Kelly holding a baby? She'd be scared. Or being six months pregnant?"

"Damn." Cokey laughed softly.

"You see what I mean, don't you, Cokey?"

Cokey and Pig continued to worry the subject until Dave snapped, "Goddamit. Whose woman was she? You fools act like you gotta introduce her to me."

"Yes. And that's just the reason I want you to be nice to Delilah," Pig said kindly to the drunken man.

With alcoholic stoicism Dave decided not to scream. "Please stop shoving that kid down my throat," he said. "I admit she's cute and all, but when I pick me another steady chick she ain't gonna be one that talks straight outa Amos 'n' Andy." He paused to reconsider. "Hell. Don't nobody on 'Amos 'n' Andy' talk like her."

As Pig and Cokey talked on and on, Dave concentrated on his social future. He was convinced that it was time for him to start playing around. He had been playing a dangerous game for the past two years, being virtually married to Kelly. He had made no passes at a girl in over eighteen months. He had been thinking of his interlude with Kelly as being a time of sowing wild oats. Now it was his duty to settle down and play every pretty chick in the Ward. And with Blueboy so enamored of the Square Table, Dave saw he wouldn't have an honest-to-goodness drinking buddy left with the coming departure of Cokey. He was gonna be one lonely sonofabitch.

He was gonna be lonely as hell if he didn't watch out. Delilah materialized before him in her irritating way, as if from nowhere. He wondered if he had summoned her.

"Lila," Pigmeat said sweetly, "Dave here has invited us to his house for dinner. Ain't we lucky?"

Delilah's face seemingly showed nothing but indifference, but for the first time Dave saw the inner turmoil behind the mask. She was like some tiny beast that, sensing impending danger, still did not know from where the attack might come. Maybe his drinking was at fault, but he had a strong urge to shield her from all harm.

"Ah . . . I . . . gotta wuk late," she finally said.

"You're off now, honey," Pigmeat said, "remember? This is graduation day. You came in early and worked lunch."

"Oh, Pig, you knows ah jes spile do fun," Lila protested.

"It's fun to just sit here and look at you," Cokey countered.

"Tie up de sweetmout. I mean, hush." She gave it up with the tiniest of giggles and a shrug. Her startlingly white teeth flashed into a glorious smile. She touched Pig's hand for moral support.

Dave spoke up out of nowhere. "See here, Delilah."

Three pairs of eyes were glued upon him. No one remembered Dave ever speaking directly to her before.

"Yassuh, Mist Greene?"

"Do you love me?"

"Ah doan rightly know, yet, Mist Greene," she replied as coolly as if he had asked her if Booker's had any ham left for sandwiches, and walked away from the booth.

Dave immediately returned to apparent sleep, but Pig and Cokey were agog.

"Now," Pigmeat panted. "Will wonders never cease?" Starstruck and happy for Lila, she gazed at Dave with devotion. But it was not long before she forgot to marvel and began to scold him. "Four

273

years you had, and you gotta wait until you wuz practically drunk to do it."

"She knew I wuz only kidding . . ."

"But her answer," Cokey exclaimed. "That kid wasn't kidding!" He laughed appreciatively. "I only wish that I could stick around and watch this. Lila didn't even bother to play it all shy and crap. When you opened up on her she stood her ground, squinted down the barrel and fired right back."

Dave was slumped in the booth and wasn't even listening.

"C'mon, fellas," Pigmeat said, getting up from the booth. Cokey looked from Pigmeat to Dave, and wondered if she intended carrying Dave wherever she was going. He knew that he was in no condition to tote his friend, who was every bit as large as he was.

It was Dave's day for doing the unexpected; he wordlessly began to struggle out of the booth. Prolonged drinking had robbed his memory of the art of extricating oneself from the clutches of Mr. Booker's booths. He was trying to stand erect before sidling out.

"What you gonna do about Lila?" Cokey asked Pig. "She won't come if we don't wait."

"Don't worry, I'll show you," Pigmeat said over her shoulder; she was trying to help Dave in his struggle for freedom. When they passed Delilah on their way to the exit, Pig stopped and frowned severely. "Mind now, Lila, don't you dare keep us waiting all night."

Plainly distressed, she nevertheless nodded obediently.

"You see?" Pigmeat said to Cokey once they had reached the street. She gaily took Dave and Cokey by the arm and marched them down the Block.

"See what?" Cokey wanted to know.

"How sweet and good that chile is." Pig's voice showed complete surprise at Cokey's obtuseness. "Poor thing . . . she's scared to death, but now that I made her promise to hurry, she'll come. Lila never breaks her word to anybody."

Cokey had to laugh at this twenty-one-year-old mother of a nineteen-year-old child. "You mean you buffaloed the kid into a position where she couldn't say no."

"She wants to come," Pigmeat said defensively. They fell silent as they walked on to Dave's house.

"What we gonna eat?" Pigmeat demanded, as soon as they had entered.

Dave walked straight to the couch and flopped down on it. In another moment he was snoring.

Pigmeat went over to Dave and untied his shoe laces. After that

274

she flounced into a chair and began to admire the room. "Kelly sure wrote her name on this house," she observed. "Everything is just as clean-cut and pretty as she was. None of that fancy junk and stuff to catch dust."

"I didn't think you would like it or her," Cokey said.

"Why, Cokey, I always liked Kelly. In fact, if I didn't, I don't think I woulda been against her and Dave being so tight."

Cokey shrugged helplessly before the logic of Pigmeat. "If you was half a woman yourself, you'd be in the kitchen peeling potatoes by now."

Pig smiled and stretched. "Do I look like a tater peelin' woman to you?"

"Damn if I know what you look like exactly," he confessed. "Don't you know how to cook?"

"That's why I ran away from home. I hate housework."

"I don't believe it."

"Honest. It makes me sick even. Ask Lila when she comes."

"So that's why you bullied the poor kid to move in with you."

"I'd want Lila to live with me if she had both hands cut off," Pig declared. "I admit she does everything around the house, mostly, but when I brought her home, I thought she was helpless."

The telephone rang and Cokey went to answer it. "Room service," he barked into the receiver.

"Cokey, you fool. Where's Dave? Drunk?" It was Kelly, and it hurt Cokey to hear her frightened and lonely.

"Out like a light," he replied, "but hold on. Maybe I can wake him for you."

"No. Don't do that. It's best this way." There was a brief pause and then she said, "Cokey?"

"Yep?"

"Aren't you going to wish me luck?"

"Kelly, my heart is with you always. You know that. Why should I bother to say it?"

"We three had lots of fun. Now I want to cry. That's selfish, huh?"

"There may be more."

She let that pass. "I'm kinda glad that Dave can't answer," she said tentatively. "We had our fond farewells this morning. No need for an encore. I shouldn't have called at all." In the silence Cokey knew she was crying. "It's like cutting the umbilical cord; I really don't want to, I guess." Her voice grew harsh and fierce. "Tell him that, Cokey. Tell him that I *have* to cut it. Tell him I said so. Tell him that I had no choice to make. Tell him that where he is concerned I have never had but one choice and that was to love him until I die. He won't understand, but he will know I feel a damn sight worse than he does. That's the hell of it, Cokey. We love each other, but we don't need each other like other people. G'luck," she sobbed.

The receiver clicked in his ear and Cokey knew that he would never hear Kelly's voice again. He knew not why, but he was as certain of it as he was of eventual death. He felt cold and sober.

"I bet that was Kelly," Pigmeat said, and Cokey realized that she was getting tight.

"Yep, from the railroad station."

"Well, I'm glad she's gone."

"You got your wish. Why gloat so much?"

"You know I liked Kelly," she said reproachfully. "And she was good for Dave in a way. Just take this room here. But not for keeps, not for marrying. She was as regular as an old shoe and she didn't take neither."

"How you know?" It was a hostile query. Cokey tried to insinuate that Pig was a stranger in the affairs of Kelly.

"One night it was real slow in Booker's and I sat in the back booth to kinda hide from the customers we did have. Dave and Kelly came in and took the next booth and they was already arguing when they sat down. They never saw me and after I had heard them I was kinda ashamed to let them see that I was there, so I just stayed there and hid like." Pigmeat spoke slowly as if it was very important to her that she relate the incident exactly as it happened.

"Anyhow, Dave wanted to give Kelly something, like an allowance maybe, but Kelly cussed him coming and going. She said that she was poor enough already without . . . Aw, Cokey . . . you know I can't talk like Kelly, but she told Dave that money would never coarsen their something or other. Half the words she used I can't pronounce. But Dave Greene knows that Kelly Simms ain't for sale, and so do I. And that's another reason she was bad for Dave."

"Now just a minute, Pig."

"Oh, I know what you're going to say, Cokey, but Dave's life is making money. That's his profession, and if a girl isn't interested or concerned about her man's profession she should find a man with another profession. But that ain't the only reason that Kelly and Dave would have ended up being unhappy. I know Dave. He's got like an empty hole in him, but a girl like Kelly will never be able to fill it up for him, make it go away. And to make it worser, Kelly got a bigger hole in her than Dave got."

276

"How you sound," Cokey murmured.

"Like a hole. And they can love each other and try and try to fill up that hole for each other till doomsday, but they never will. They loves each other, but they don't need each other, and that ain't human."

"Pig, if you had a college education you would be the lousiest psychologist in the whole U.S.A."

She laughed. "And I don't care what you say, but Dave and Kelly ain't ordinary people anyways. They're dangerous to each other. Just suppose Kelly decided to be the head of the local NAACP?"

Cokey shuddered at the thought.

Pig, however, kept right on talking. "You ever realize that they drink too much? And hardly ever show it? And they're too smart to be happy. I hear fellas in Booker's saying about how dumb and lucky Dave is, but the truth is that Dave Greene owns that bank, and he runs it so smooth that you don't think that he got anything to do with it, but it takes brains to handle all those Vessey Street hustlers. And Dave's done it without killing nobody either. And Kelly. Look at all the prizes and scholarships she won today, but I bet you won't have any trouble finding a few folks on that Campus that'll tell you that Kelly spent more time in Dave's bed than she did in class. Dave and Kelly ain't normal, but they still don't fit each other. Understand?"

"I understand what you're saying, but I'm not too sure you're being logical."

"Humph," Pig sniffed. "I bet Lila could make Dave stop getting as drunk as he does. At least she would keep him home at night."

"You're really sold on pairing them up, aren't you? But do you realize Lila's been on Vessey Street for years now and never bothered to take a tumble for anybody? And it's no use to say that she hasn't had the opportunity to meet a nice guy, that nothing but tramps and married men come into Booker's. The joint is nationally known; the better-class Negroes from all over America eat in there sooner or later. Maybe Lila ain't too normal herself."

"The darker a girl is the slower she matures," Pig asserted. "Now you take these chicks with a whole lot of white blood in them, and they're born ready."

"Like you?" Cokey asked.

"I'm Indian," Pigmeat said solemnly.

"A pink redskin?" Cokey murmured with suitable awe. "Well, I still think you're standing outside your own house, throwing rocks at it."

"And Lila's pure," Pig asserted.

"Pure what?"

"She's got all that belongs to her," Pig informed him. "No man's ever took nothing from *her*. She got everything she was born with."

Cokey didn't believe her and wondered why she bothered to insist that such a silly thing was true. "Lila's scared of fire, to say the least," he said. "She must have got a hell of a deal from some man sometime somewhere."

"Nobody's given Lila nothing. Or took nothing either. I know." So saying, Pigmeat sat back in her chair with an air of outraged conviction, indicating that the matter was now closed.

Cokey wandered back to the kitchen to inspect the icebox.

"And you really think Lila will show?" he called back to Pigmeat.

"Any minute, Cokey. You just wait and see."

"I think this is your day for being wrong."

"Lila's got plenty of reason to come. Poor thing."

The doorbell's ring corroborated her remark.

"Honey, why'd you take so long?" she asked as she opened the door.

Lila's answer was a noncommittal: "Lo . . ." She followed Pigmeat into the front room and took a chair directly facing the snoring Dave. "He look right tayhd," she observed.

"He'll wake up soon as Cokey finishes cooking."

"Oh . . . Cokey. Ah almos' fogit 'im." She stood up and started to walk toward the rear of the house. Following the light, she finally came upon Cokey at work frying bacon. "Lo, Cokey. How you doin? Kin ah hep?"

"And spoil that pretty pose? Heck no, you just stand there and make me happy."

"Cokey, you so crazy." She smiled contentedly.

The youth glanced at her with a sly look. "You come to give Dave his answer?"

"Nossah. Ah mean, no," she said vaguely.

"Then why'd you come?"

"Pig tole me."

"Now there's a good reason."

Lila playfully struck at him. "Stoppit now, Cokey. Yo muh fren."

"Well, Dave ain't got no fren-ledy now," he jibed.

"Ee wickety," Lila said with a tiny sniff of dismissal. "Ee kin always git de kine blonx wid him."

"What kind of girl was Kelly? She the kind that blonx wid him?"

278

Delilah had a great smile when she was really happy. "She froward, ah guess, but she ain't so froward fo a collitch gull, but she froward dough. She so nice dat it don't count dough. Ee a kind ledy; dat why ah come heah."

Cokey crawled out of his daze and tried to unravel the mystery of her words. He gave up and grunted, "But you here dough?"

Lila nodded her agreement. "Kelly so purty, ah know Dabe sad. Pig said that it muh duty to cheer him up, but ah doan see how. Ah jes spile fun."

"You can't blame all your sins on Pig," Cokey said.

Lila flashed her astounding smile and Cokey was amused to see that she fully appreciated his insinuation. He, too, was given to wonder if the little girl was not a much more complex creature than the Block gave her credit for being.

"Lila, do you really like the way you talk? Wouldn't you like to speak properly?"

"Nossuh . . . yassuh, ah guess . . ." She stopped in confusion. "I guess I mean that I didn't useta, but now, mebbe, ah guess I should talk more slower and pernounce my words better."

"I'm leaving town tomorrow, but will you promise me that you'll try to go back to school in the fall? You're still a kid; you won't feel out of place. Try, even if it's only for one or two classes a day?"

"Dat's what I come to the Ward for."

"What?" Cokey exclaimed, convinced that Lila was an unknown quantity.

Dave came into the kitchen and groggily went to the kitchen cabinet for a bottle of bourbon. Pouring a drink, he shuddered as he gulped it down.

"Pig tell you that Kelly called?" Cokey asked him.

"No. Why'dn't you wake me up?"

"She said not to and you was out like a light anyhow."

"Say anything? Want anything?"

"Nope. Just killing time until the train came."

"Well," Dave said quietly, "that's that."

Cokey stared at him, and then agreed: "That's that." He would have said more, but Pigmeat came in.

"What kinda convention you all holding back here? Dave, honey, gimme a drink please."

"No convention," Cokey drawled. "Me and Lila were having a most edifying conversation until you two drunks wandered in."

"Drunk is right," Dave groaned. "Damn if this rotgut don't act like it can't do without me. I'm dead and don't know it."

279

"At least you can afford it better than anybody else I know," Pigmeat consoled him.

"Nobuddy can 'ford rotgut," Delilah said quietly.

"The hell you say," Dave muttered.

"Please stop cussin so much, Mist Dabe," Lila pleaded. "It sound right wickety."

"You stop calling me mister and I might," Dave grunted.

She drenched him with her smile and as if to seal the bargain, she stood on tiptoe, placed her hands on his shoulders and kissed him lightly on the mouth. Dave, Pig and Cokey gaped as Lila swept out of the room.

"And now the angels start plunking their damn banjos," Cokey muttered, but Pigmeat was supremely triumphant.

"I tole you fellas that she got this secret obsession. Now it's blossomed after four long years," she rhapsodized. "I'm so happy I could cry."

"I still wouldn't believe it if I hadn't seen it," Cokey mumbled. "Maybe I didn't see it," he exclaimed hopefully.

"I tole you that my little blackberry was growing ripe," Pig exulted. "Like I say: the blacker the berry the sweeter the juice, and now that proves it."

In an aimlessly hungover state Dave wandered into the front room behind Lila. He thought she sat like a proper little doll in the huge overstuffed chair. She was wearing a flaming orange sweater that somehow went perfectly with a powder blue skirt.

"Why'd you kiss me?"

"You needed it."

"What makes you think so?"

"If I wuz a man and that purty Kelly tole me good-by, I know I'd feel lonesome and dead. I'm sorry you sad."

Her accent was far different from that which she had always used when she addressed him in Booker's, and it seemed like a form of dishonesty to him. "How about a drink that's already paid for? You don't have to worry about having to afford it."

"Ah nevah drink nothin."

"No time like now."

"Ah ignunt enuff awready wiffout no rotgut in me."

Very cute, he thought, but it did not raise Lila in his esteem. She evidently had overheard it in Booker's. It might even have been Kelly. And that thought nettled Dave. But since Delilah had presented herself here tonight, it was self-evident that she had come with only one purpose in mind. She came to serve as an antidote for Kelly's departure.

So let her.

He had a mild regret that she was not a larger girl. Undressed she would more than likely be smaller than Kelly, and he needed a big dumb lummox to drown himself in.

It's one of Life's caprices that often two people join forces in a common cause without either giving serious thought to the other. If, for instance, someone had told Dave that Delilah was a far more purposeful and complete individual than Kelly, Dave would have scoffed. He was incontrovertibly prejudiced; he had always refused to think of Lila as being adult, and even when he was sober he considered the beauty as being a very intelligent moron at best. Assuredly, he would never deny her beauty . . . if you liked black girls. And he told himself that he wasn't sure he did. But since Lila was here he would try her.

Having decided to allow the child to spend the night with him, he grew restless and morose. He thought he should be rewarded with a few laughs before he went upstairs to a night of boredom. He wandered back to the kitchen to bask in the sun of Pig and Cokey's conviviality. The pair were eating bacon and eggs when Dave entered the kitchen.

"How come you don't feed Lila?" he asked.

"She works in a restaurant," Pig told him. "Besides she'll be feeding offa love from now on."

"Nerts."

"Dave, what the devil have you got?" Cokey demanded.

"Me? I ain't got nothing," Dave replied, puzzled.

"You got something that other people just ain't got. You must have been born with it. And I sure in hell can't see it. I don't see a damn bit of difference between you and the next guy on the Block, but you got more than just luck," Cokey said wonderingly. "You're not ugly, but nobody's gonna claim that you're God's gift to women either. You either can't or won't carry on a conversation worth a damn unless you know the guy you are talking to better than a brother or sister or you're drunk as hell. And even money as money isn't involved in it too much."

"I know what Cokey means," Pigmeat chimed in, "but it's true and I'm not gonna tell you what it is."

"You two ain't been drinking outa the same bottle I been nipping from," Dave said.

Cokey was still filled with wonder. "Kelly Simms is one man's share of beauty in a lifetime, and to have a beautiful girl like Lila throw herself into your arms before Kelly's train pulls out of the station is just a little too much luck. You haven't even had time to get lonely yet. And neither Kelly or Lila really gives a damn abou your dough. Your luck is just a little bit too rich for my blood. Kelly! Lila! The Bank! You ought to be scared."

"What the hell. You gonna begrudge your best friend a little luck?"

"Hell no. It's damn nice living just to be a friend of yours. You make the living easy. Real easy. You got everything and everybody working in your corner, including Blueboy. And I'm not kidding. Why you have never been sick in your life!"

"Someday I'm gonna meet a black boy that don't use magnifying glasses to talk with and I'm gonna drop stone cold dead from the shock," said Dave. "What we gonna do after you finish stuffing yourselves?" he asked.

"Get high all over again and go in the front room and dance," Pigmeat said. "C'mon, Cokey, much as I hate it, I'm gonna help with the dishes."

"Leave them for the cleaning woman. She ain't got nothing to do as it is but smoke my cigarettes," Dave said. "And what the hell you think this is anyhow? This is Cokey's going-away party ain't it? And you wants him to stay in the kitchen and pearl-dive?"

He sounded the very note to send Pigmeat into ecstasy. "Oooh, Cokey, honey, and I never gave it a thought," she cooed in loving dismay. "My love is all graduated and packed, and I haven't even tried to kiss him at all." She embraced Cokey with a fondness and passion that would have been ridiculous if done by anyone other than Pigmeat Goins.

The three of them trooped into the front room to join Lila, and a little later were all dancing to slow romancing records. Just before they all started to dance the most cataclysmic event in Dave's life took place, and none of the four were conscious of it at the time.

Lila's calm statement that she did not know how to dance astonished Dave, who had always taken it for granted that all Negroes darker than himself were born dancing. His astonishment was compounded when Lila also simply stated that although she had never tried to dance, she would now try if Dave so wished her to try.

That statement and that statement alone was the tenuous thread upon which Dave's love for Lila was spun. No loud protestations and giggles, and no flirtatious making a big deal of things. She would try if he wished and that was all. Later, much later, came respect.

They danced a step called the Slow Drag. It was exactly what its name implied: slow, dragging steps in time to the music. Lila had a good sense of rhythm and it was very nice dancing with her.

282

Her waist was excitingly tiny, and although there was not an ounce of surplus flesh on her body she was not without a softly yielding feel, not without sensuality.

"Lila, what do you do with your money?"

"Spend some, sabe some, ah guess." She looked up at Dave with honest curiosity written on her pretty face. "Wuffo?" she asked.

"I dunno. I just was wondering. You go to church?"

"Eveybuddy go to church."

He had a feeling of coming complications that he should have somehow avoided. If, as Pigmeat contended, Delilah had a secret passion for him he had best watch himself. Had this little black fool come here to get him to join a church or something? He had an urge to punch Lila in the mouth and Pigmeat too. Dave's mind was really reeling like a drunkard's now, and a momentary memory of Kelly's healthy curses in bed nauseated him with a desolate longing for her return.

He glanced down with distaste at the would-be substitute for Kelly Simms, but somehow his feelings of contempt dissolved in the realization that Lila was very small although she stood as straight as a ramrod. He could only see her face when she leaned back in his arms and looked up at him. As he admired her beautiful hair, he noted that hers was exactly the same fine quality as Pigmeat's. He had always liked the sheer vitality in the way that Delilah's hair seemed to spring up from her forehead, but because Pigmeat was light-complected he naturally assumed that she had the finer head of hair. While he was mulling over his latest discovery, it came to him that the two girls had a perfect right to have identical grades of hair because they were blood relatives.

"You and Pig ever figger out how close you're related?"

"Pig say she remembah her momma say that her first cousin married James Mazique."

"That your last name?" Dave said in surprise.

"Delilah Mazique," she replied gravely.

"Damn."

Delilah looked up, hurt for some reason.

Dave saw her expression and tried to explain. "It's just that you can't figger the Negro race at all," he apologized. "Since you and Pig are cousins it would seem like you were supposed to have American-sounding names at least. But, damn, what kind of name you got? French? And since you got it, seems like you should be from N'Awlins or somewheres like that."

"Guess it don't mek much sense to try and s'plain folkes no-ways," Lila said. "Effum yuh doan likem: leffum alone."

In a flash of alcoholic clarity Dave knew who Delilah was. All the way back through the years his memory crashed until he was once more in Hot Springs with Blueboy, and remembered how in his innocence he had sat and listened to Kootchie, Georgia Brown, and Blueboy. It was that first impression he had formed of them. They had been people born knowing all the rules, he recalled. Unable to lose or be lost.

But how could this shy and artless child be of that rambunctious breed, he wanted to know. It was evident that she refused to allow life to baffle her, but she certainly couldn't be of that mettle, of that unbeatable and happy breed. Or was she?

Delilah was a stranger.

But not unwelcome.

"Soothed and sustained by an unaltering trust," he murmured.

"You an Elk?" Lila asked. When Dave smirked, she asked, "Why mek laff?" Her tiny voice was gently reproving.

"Nothing personal. Don't get mad, but those words are not the private property of the colored Elks, even if the Block thinks so. That line comes from a poem called, *Thanatopsis*."

"Thana-whutsis?"

"*Thanatopsis*. It's a poem," he tried to explain. "It's a Greek word that means thoughts of death."

"You read Greek? You a collitch man? You tinking 'bout dying?"

And all at once Dave laughed. Lila's animated questioning was more than amusing to him. She really wanted to know, and it was her genuine desire to know that made him happy, her indulgent friend.

"Dabe. You laffin."

"What's wrong now?"

"You laffin," she repeated. "I never seed you laugh happy before."

"I'm in Booker's almost every night," he reminded her.

"But this different. Mebbe you smile or chuckle like, but now you laff wid me, and happy wid it."

"Come to think of it," he replied, "I've never seen you laugh either."

She broke into a peal of airy laughter. The beauty of her shocked the breath out of Dave and he could feel himself becoming aroused. They were still doing their slow, dragging dance, and he held her very tight. After that they did not talk very much; they had told each

284

other all there was to tell. It was only a matter of waiting for the time of the doing. In their hearts they were both agreed.

When he took her hand and led her into the hallway, Delilah was willingly his, he knew. Still hand in hand, they climbed the stairs.

"This is my bedroom," he said formally, stiffly, wondering why he should be so self-conscious.

Curious as a child her eyes adoringly took in everything about the room. "Hit bootiful, Dabe," he breathed.

He opened his arms and she came to him like a magnet. There was an odd clumsiness to her kisses that added an unexpected tang. And he did not mind the least that she was shorter than Kelly. She had to stand on her toes to kiss him and that made her mound seem to cling against his for support.

In the splitting of a second her body became a thing beyond control. In the heat of it he could hardly breath, and he was afraid to change from his standing position for fear that he might throw up. He regretted every single drop of whiskey he had gulped so hoggishly throughout the day.

Lila did not seem to mind their standing. Their kisses burned with promises until she muttered in a voice so husky with passion that Dave hardly believed that it was hers: "Out de light, Dabe."

He reluctantly released her and went over to the wall switch, and then made his way to the bed in the dark. The room was silent and he wondered where she was and what she was doing. Then there was a soft rustle, and Lila was sitting beside him on the bed. She was trembling fearfully when he reached for her, but she seemed to gladly enter his embrace. When a low moan escaped her lips the ecstatic agony of the sound reverberated through Dave's entire nervous system. Anticipation turned to white hot torture and he felt her tiny hands pressing his back, rubbing him. The touch of her hands was hot and sensuous on his flesh. He worked his hand beneath her sweater. She wore no bra; she needed none.

He squeezed those mounds of love and her whole body quivered in the heavenly agony of it and he knew that she was now on a wave of frantic surrender. It was a raw passion that knew no bounds, and she frantically arched her body, as he toyed with her erect nipples. When his hand went between her legs her body was wracked with imminent climax.

But as he pulled on her panties she gave a quick animal start and tore herself out of his arms. The next instant he heard her footsteps speeding down the steps. Mad as a rutting boar he dashed after her; his brain spewing oaths faster than his lips could utter them.

It was only because she had trouble with the lock on the front door that he was able to catch up with her. Neither made a sound for fear of attracting Cokey and Pigmeat, although Dave's rage was murderous. Delilah looked into his eyes and read the hated epithet that the Block reserves for women like her: "Cock-teaser." Even in her fright she would have willingly died to erase that name from Dave's eyes, but she was powerless in her fear of a higher power than Dave Greene. For it was God who demanded that Delilah flee the joys of Dave's embrace. Of that she had not the slightest doubt. And so she struggled to unlock the door.

It was a bizarre tug of war, and Dave was further enraged to find that she was apparently as strong as he. It was impossible to break her grasp on the knob of the door latch. At last he resorted to lifting her up off her feet and turning with her body in his arms so that she had to release her grip. Once he had done that he felt that he had only to kiss her to rekindle the fires within her body. When he had lifted her from the floor her back had been to him and now he turned her body while he was still holding her in his arms. Then grabbing the nape of her neck, he brutally forced her face to his to be kissed. She moaned in fright, but never thought of surrender. And then it was her turn to make a last desperate maneuver; she firmly pressed the palms of her hands over his mouth and held him at bay.

Lila was a worthy foe, and no woman fought like this without good reason. He grudgingly admired her even while his rage went unabated. Silent minutes passed as they stood in that queer impasse with Lila's palms still holding the margin of victory.

He suddenly relaxed and tried to regain his composure. Masculine pride told him that all that was needed was a few explanations. Having glimpsed the depths of Lila's passion, his vanity informed him that he was her master. All he had to do was to hold her in his arms until she ceased to struggle. So he sought to soothe her.

He knew that he had only to calm her before he could return to the real business at hand, and he fretted because she was taking so long to calm down. He was holding her loosely now waiting for the moment.

"Blease, Dabe, opin de doah?" It was a wretched child's moan; its very piteousness was a stern command to any humane being. Dave sighed emptily and capitulated. Drained of anger, he dully did her bidding. Without a word she sped into the night.

He gasped with fear. Where was she going? And why? To Old

Man Booker? Before he knew it, he dashed out into the night after her, trotting just fast enough to keep her within sight. Half a block ahead he spied her bright sweater flash beneath a street light. She was still running.

Was she going to accuse him of rape? The Black loved Lila; she was its mascot. All hell might break loose if she accused him.

The bank could be ruined because he lost his head over a black piece of tail, he told himself. Kelly gone. And he would not have been in this mess if she had not insisted on some dog-assed trip to Rhode Island. Cokey going. And a goddam scandal to face all by himself. A trial was sure; if the little fool wanted money she would have asked for it. In his anger he cursed Pigmeat. She was the cause of it all.

His eyes continued to follow the form of Delilah; she had stopped running now and he breathed a little easier. His eyes smarted with release and thanksgiving when she reached the corner of Macon and Vessey and did not turn. She was going home. He crossed over to the other side of the street so she could not see him and be alarmed if she should happen to look back. When he saw her go up on her front porch and enter the house he snorted in relief and new-found anger.

"The-goddam-blackassed-little-phony," he cursed aloud into the night.

Having seen the counterfeit woman safely to her door, Dave retraced his steps toward Vessey Street. It was impossible for him to go home now. Pig would ask too many damn questions. Neither could he bear the yappings of the Square Table, if it was assembled. He decided to try the Lil Savoy. Maybe the Colonel felt like talking. He had had quite enough of young people for one day.

The number had been 030 the day Kelly graduated.

The Lil Savoy was crammed with college kids and the thunder of the jukebox. Students and graduates alike were supposed to be homeward bound by this time but, although Campus officialdom frowned on such high jinx, there was little that could be done or said about it. The Dean's book of rules was out the window tonight.

The graduates, especially, were in a hell for leather, we-who-are-about-to-die mood. Nineteen thirty-nine was still a depression year in the black man's book, and these graduates knew it very well. The baccalaureates had been presented; the bags were at the station; the fated-to-be-forgotten faces had been kissed; and now all they had to do was get the hell out into the world and find a job.

And they knew by word of mouth that the Negro college graduate was now acceptable to a world of washing dishes, waiting on tables, housemaid's chores, or teaching in a rural school.

College had meant three square meals a day and a lovely moratorium from going to work. Tomorrow promised nothing. This was the final act of a black comedy of manners that had lasted for four happy years. Now they had to face the truth, and they knew that they had wasted four years. Each and every one knew it, but they did not know that the other knew it, and so they all drank and made merry.

Although almost all of them were poor, they were yet the children of the Negro upper middle class. And like the offspring of mediocrity the world over, they were unaccustomed to whiskey and freedom. Free in a world they knew did not give a damn about them, they drank ruttishly, their voices thick and incoherent. They danced like copulating monkeys.

The crazy scene had a calming effect upon Dave. It filled him with a soothing nostalgia for what he thought had been. His three brief semesters at A&I became a whole lifetime of joy. Those were the days, he deluded himself. Plenty of money . . . you didn't need much then anyway. Millions of pretty chicks . . . and the loving was free and easy.

"Somebody tole me they saw you trying to sneak in here."

With a happy start he turned to greet Blueboy. "What say, man?" He was overjoyed to see his friend away from the Square Table, and he hoped that Blueboy was in a heavy drinking mood tonight. "Who's the moderator of the illiterati tonight?"

"I let the Old Man have it for a private party tonight," Blueboy said. "What the hell, I need a change of drinking scenery every now and then anyway." He eyed the students for a while and then observed, "Young people don't know how to enjoy themselves nowadays. We'da been out in the bushes by this time. And women as drunk as these?" He sighed with a contented delusion that matched Dave's nostalgia of a moment ago.

"That's a lie you could have saved," Dave cordially replied.

"Like hell it is."

"Women drunk in public when you was a kid?" Dave taunted him. "And if you got them in the bushes it would take two hours just to get them outa them corsets they wore. I don't think Lillian Russell could make it today with a Georgia cotton picker. Sex just ain't packaged the same."

"Cleopatra," Blueboy howled. "She was nekkid practically! The Roaring Twenties! Queen Elizabeth had a ball in sixteen-hundred!"

288

"You was out of high school before any Roaring Twenties," Dave said carelessly. "And Negroes still don't do a hell of a lot of drinking between the sexes."

"You got maggots of the brain, boy," Blueboy conscientiously informed Dave. "You should soak your head in something nice like lye mebbe."

For a while Dave and Blueboy drank slowly without speaking, simply enjoying each other's company. "What the heck," Blueboy murmured at last, "I guess you was right, Davey-boy. S'funny how we keep on repeating the old folks tales until we start to thinking that them ideas and stuff is the God's honest truth."

"And I'm tired of being asked to believe all this age-old crap," Dave said.

Blueboy's glass was poised midway to his lips. "What's eating you?" he asked quietly.

"Nothing. It just occurred to me, is all. Something somebody said, I guess."

Blueboy was casually inspecting Dave. "Yeah, you're okay," he said. "In fact, you look pretty cool calm and collective, considering that the Kelly-gal ain't among us no more."

"Yeah, I'm okay. Guess I feel like them old-time travelin' waiters said their wives felt whenever they left to work a resort or something."

"Glad to see them come and glad to see them go, eh?"

"Something like that," he admitted.

"You think you mean it?"

"Right now anyway. Mebbe later it'll hurt, but right now, this minute, it don't."

"You mean that the parting's over? Or the whole thing is done and did?"

Dave's inner self tightened and his voice showed it when he said, "I ain't ever gonna stop loving Kelly. I'm gonna love her to the day I die. And all I got, or ever will get, belongs to Kelly if she asks. I don't care what she asks for; she gets it. It don't make a damn if she's married, in or outa jail, pregnant, sniffing coke, in a whorehouse, anywhere. If she needs me I'm gonna be there, but . . ."

"But?"

"If I gotta go through another good-by like this one, then mebbe I hope she never comes back."

Blueboy picked up his glass and saluted him. "Wal, we come this far like men . . . Guess we can kiss a few more good-by without cracking up."

289

They became silent again, drinking and thinking in unison.

"Queer as hell how there is fads in men," Blueboy said.

"Will you please tell me what the hell you're talking about?"

"When I was coming along as a kid, all of the women wanted piano players," Blueboy explained. "You know, ragtime. With a big diamond ring and all. Why a hotshot piano player could screw the entire female population in a town at one time." He grew silent, remembering. "Nowadays a piano player ain't nothing but another damn woman hisself."

Dave laughed.

"No kidding, Davey-boy. And then, later, it was roadsters. Why, dammit, you didn't have to give 'em a ride in it. All you hadda do was own one, and if it was yaller or red, you had a damn good chance of dying from TB because the dames would rape you into bad health. Then there was soldier boys. And then roadsters again. And then guys that owned electric Victrolas and so on, until now it's racketeers."

"And what the hell is a racketeer?"

"You, me. And I guess mebbe we are, but there's plenty of others. Now you want me to give you a scientific explanation? Guess mebbe I can't, but I could tell you the standards as set by these Vessey Street chicks." He pensively rubbed his chin. "Wal, if I wuz gonna explain it, I guess I'd hafta say this: any Negro man who makes his living without sweat; and without the white boy's permission; and entirely through his own skill and brains . . ." He looked questioningly at Dave.

"Mebbe you should have added: any Negro who can stay in bed until he feels like getting up. But what interests me the most is that you haven't mentioned the law."

"That's just it, Davey. It don't much matter if you breaks the law or not. Some doctors and lawyers is welcome and mebbe a few teachers and preachers. It ain't what you do, it's the manner in which you does it."

"Might as well cut the crap and come right out and say it. Nigger women like outlaws."

"Nigger women love the nigger that can get hold of the white man's dollar without sweat," Blueboy retorted. "And that is a mighty tough assignment for a group of heavenly bastards. It's like colored women have declared war on all but a handful of Negro men."

"War?"

"Yass, but don't ask me what it means or how it's gonna end."

290

"Pardon me, gentlemen, but do you mind if I join you for just one minute?" It was a very drunken college boy, handsomely disheveled. Dave had noticed him earlier; he apparently was a popular man on the Campus.

Dave smiled companionably, and Blueboy said, "Step right up, son. I see that you are feeling no pain, which is fitting and proper at a time like this. Glad to see you young fellas enjoying life as you should. Have a drink?"

The boy was grave, almost sanctimonious in his drunkenness, and Dave sensed that he did not wish to be treated jocularly.

The weaving boy pointed an unsteady finger at them and said, "I ain't . . . it's not because I'm drunk that I come to say this, but because I got me a piece of sheepskin that ain't no sheepskin." He was visibly groping for the right words, and, maybe, the exact train of his thoughts. He fumbled on the bar at an empty glass. Dave picked it up and filled it for him.

"Thanks, Dave," the boy said between gulps, "I jus hadda come over and tell you this. You are the greatest Negro the Ward ever produced. The day will come when people will give you the respect you deserve and the honor you have already earned."

"Have another drink, boy," Blueboy said heartily.

"No need for sarcasm," the boy said to Blueboy. "What I say goes for you, too. Now when I came to this gospel-shouting University I thought I was the richest and cutest little high-society bastard that ever graced the Campus. But let me tell you something. The only rich niggers and the only niggers worthy of respect are our numbers niggers.

"Do you realize that my *rich* old man caught hell trying to pay my bills on time? And yet he is a bigshit M.D. In fact, he is so big that I'm not even supposed to speak to crude-assed niggers like you. And don't get mad either, it ain't no use. I made up my mind a coupla years ago that whenever I got my sheepskin, I was gonna come and shake your hand and buy you a drink. But unfortunately I got broke before you came in. Because I respect you more than any damn prof on that damn Campus."

The boy disconcerted Dave by suddenly yelling: "Vanderbilt, Gould, Rockefella, Astor, Delano, Carnegie, Rosenwald. You think they was preachers and teachers? Why the hell niggers gotta believe that a minister can lead them anywheres except Hell? My Pop won't like it, but what I'm telling you is the only goddam information I received with my degree. Baby, you are the savior I been telling them about." So saying, the boy slumped to the floor. Dave and Blueboy picked him up and tenderly deposited him in a chair.

"Now wasn't that a lovely doxology?" Blueboy cooed. "Doxology. We are all leaving now." He tipped his hat at a rakish angle and started for the door. "Now doxology is a beautifully sonorous word, ain't it?"

They went across the street and stared uncertainly at Booker's. "Well what we gonna do?" Dave asked. "Go in here or go up Babylon and drink for free?"

"I ain't hungry and I don't think that Old Man Booker is too set upon serving booze in front of his commencement guests, so let's go up the club."

Club Babylon was just as noisy as the Lil Savoy, but the guests were older. It was if the elders had told the children to go across the street and play.

Kelly and I were here last night. And that thought kicked Dave squarely in the testicles, but somehow, in remembrance of her, he squared his shoulders and strode through the crowd of guests to the bar.

The first familiar faces he spied at the bar were those of Professor Blake and Dr. White, drinking by themselves. He stared at them with contempt. In the very next instant, he regretted his disdainful thoughts as it struck him that these teachers led very lonely lives.

They were the only teachers he knew, but they surely must be as typical as the next, he thought. And, now, in the midst of all these graduation festivities they were still outsiders. Teaching niggers must be the lousiest racket on earth, he decided.

"Drinks are on the house tonight," he greeted them, and it seemed that both of the professors were unduly grateful. "When are you leaving?" Dave asked during the small talk.

"We're not," Professor Blake said. "We're going to teach the summer sessions. Work, work, work; that's us."

"You guys must love that Campus," he ventured as an apology.

"Home is where the heart is," the white-skinned teacher enthused.

"That mean work, women, or both?" Dave asked genially.

Professor Blake smiled service-cluby. "Work, work," he babbled. "Why we have the largest summer enrollment in the history of the University."

Blueboy joined them and started yelling something about having a quorum of Knights.

"Cut it out," Dave pleaded. "Club Babylon means exactly what the name says: drinking, no thinking."

Five minutes later they were locked in a bloody verbal combat that lasted until daybreak.

292

When Dave and Delilah left the house so suddenly, Pigmeat and Cokey smugly assumed that they were sneaking off for a moonlit ride.

Whenever Cokey tried to recall the night of his graduation, it always assumed an aspect of some mystic interlude of time out of context. Too near to God, somehow. They danced and drank sociably in the front room.

"Gee, Cokey, you're all graduated now," Pig said with a wistful sigh of regret. "Remember when you first came to school, and I waited on you in Booker's? And how I liked you?"

"Sure. And I thought that you and I were gonna make the biggest blaze since Adam and Eve discovered fire, but in two or three days there wasn't any smoke left even."

"I was ashamed of you, I guess. Don't that seem silly now?"

"If I had been a Vessey Street hustler and acceptable to your friends, you might never have met Dave. Don't you think that your life is much nicer since you met Dave?"

"Just about, Cokey," she readily admitted, as if to get that part of the conversation over and done. "But us." She pointedly hung onto the last word. "Suppose I hadn't been so silly, Cokey? What would have happened, then?"

They were sitting side by side on the couch; Cokey reached over and pulled her closer to him. "Dunno, Pig." Then he looked at her curiously. "What would you like to think?"

She stretched out and put her head in his lap, and lay looking up at him. "Maybe it's because you're leavin' and I'm high and mellow, but it seems like it would have been sooo nice."

"And so now that we didn't and I'm leaving, you're going to weep and wail?" Then as a sort of afterthought he asked, "You talking about marriage for real?"

"I could have worked. I did . . . I do. As long as your folks took care of the tuition we could have made it. It would have been easy." Her laugh was dry; coming from any other person it would have sounded harsh. "Easy," she repeated, and she seemed to be tasting the meaning of her words as Blueboy so often seemed to do. Then her eyes widened as if she had suddenly stumbled across some personal truth. "You ever realize that the four of us are easy people? We even walk easy. I know, lots of fellas have told me so. And you and Dave and Lila walk real easy like too. I'm not kidding. We're easy-livin' people, Cokey. We all have it easy. We were born that way, I think. And it's not just because all the fellas say I'm good-looking. Pretty girls get in more trouble than most. And I guess, maybe I ain't too smart, but just the same I walked away from

293

home when I was fourteen, and I never looked back. Most girls would be dead or ruined by now, but look at me.

"And look at Lila," Pigmeat exclaimed, warming to her somewhat hazy point of view. "Why they begged her to come to work in Booker's even before she got her bags unpacked when she first come to town. I bet she got more money in the bank than any single woman in the Ward, schoolteachers even. She saves it because she really ain't got nothing else to do with it.

"And you, Cokey, when you smile that lazy smile and talk that ole dry talk . . . you'll never go hungry for long. You're easy-livin', too.

"And as for Dave; well, there ain't no use even discussin' him. We're all alike." And Cokey sensed that Pigmeat was pleading, but he knew not why or what. "Easy-livers. And that's why I feel so bad now. I shouldna' been ashamed of you because you were a schoolboy. What would we be like if things wasn't so easy, Cokey?"

Cokey rolled her over and whacked her on her rump. "Philosophers in pink panties we don't need."

Pig giggled with a sigh. "Cokey, I'm gonna miss you so."

"You better."

"You were a bad boy and didn't go to your own graduation, but I'm gonna give you a graduation present tonight."

That she could look so virginal when she said it amused Cokey no end.

"I hope you like it," she said softly, dreamily. "S'funny, Cokey, but now that you're going away it seems real important. I feel like I'm gonna need you. One of these days I'm gonna need you real bad and all because I was ashamed of you once."

"Don't be silly," Cokey said, unaccountably irritated. "Dave and Blueboy and I will always keep in touch, and if you need me so bad, I'll be here."

"Sure you will. I know you will. C'mon, show me the room that Dave and Blueboy say is yours."

He picked her up in his arms and headed for the hallway and the stairs. His strong arms were like a lullaby to Pig's troubled thoughts.

"How come you never went with anyone after Dave?"

"Oh, Cokey, you know I've had lots of fellas since Dave."

He carried her into the bedroom and set her gently down on her feet. "I mean steady . . . shack-up like?"

"Well, I don't know," Pig said seriously and dimpled. "Dave still pays my rent. In fact I think he owns the house. I guess I just didn't find anyone that I wanted to get real tight with after Dave, but I always make do."

Casually, like some long-married couple, they began to undress. They hung their clothes neatly on hangers, negligently taking their time. Cokey finished undressing first and went to the bed and laid down.

Finally Pigmeat snapped off the light and padded softly over to him. She sighed voluptuously as she stretched her body atop his. Her warm sweet tongue glided between his lips, while her soft hands fingered his craggy face as if they sought every homely crevice to love. Her creamy thighs quivered in gentle recognition, and then seemed to flow down over him.

"Cokey, honey," she breathed in his ear, "let's make it good. Real good. Just for old times' sake."

The next morning when Cokey awoke, Pigmeat was gone. Putting on his trousers only, he went downstairs to see what time it was. He found Dave in the kitchen morosely nursing a bottle of his favorite bourbon. He went to the sink and rinsed out a glass, and then took a chair facing Dave at the table.

"Last night was something else again."

"Yeah," Dave grunted, exhaling a thick blue cloud of cigarette smoke. "Well, I see you scored; that's more than *I* can say for myself."

"You really expected to?"

"Whadya think? At least I did after she went up to the bedroom. Go ahead; tell me she's dumb, but what the hell, she ain't too dumb to know what a bedroom is for." He tried to mimic Lila's strange accents. "Ooht de laght, Dabe."

"How much you been drinking this morning?"

"Anybody that gets himself all hemmed up with Lila needs a drink for breakfast."

"Think maybe she was sorta feeling her way?" Cokey asked.

"You gotta have brains to feel."

"Couldn't she have been curious," Cokey asked thoughtfully. "After all, if our little black beauty has held onto that cherry for nineteen long years, she's got a right to inspect the premises where she expects to lose it, hasn't she?"

"Ahh . . . the hell with it," Dave said. "Let's get dressed and hit the Block."

Dave was still immersed in a blue funk as they strolled toward the Block. Cokey tried to cheer him up by asking about business.

"Okay," Dave mumbled. "Only . . ."

"Only what?"

"Well for one thing, the honeymoon is over. We get in a nice little taste every day, but the titty ain't gonna get any sweeter. That's for sure."

"The odds are the same; more people are playing every day; I don't get you."

"Just like everything else in the world, I guess," Dave said with resignation. "Everybody wants to get inta the act. The cops. The . . ."

"Cops? Banking numbers?"

"No, but they're gettin' greedier by the minute. And I hear that one that got kicked off the force is trying to bank numbers in some of the white neighborhoods, which is all right with me, but, he's offering my pickups three hundred bucks cash bonus if they'll leave me and start turning their daily work into him." Dave shrugged carelessly. "Mebbe the pickups made it up in order to scare me inta paying them more. I dunno."

Cokey's evident awe made him stand still on the sidewalk. "Dave, do you realize just how great you are?" he exclaimed.

"Whadya mean?"

"You may well be the only Negro in the world who has out-guessed the white man. People called you nigger-rich when you started buying all those cars for your pickups. But now, any white man that wants to compete with you has to buy a fleet of auto-mobiles just for openers. Did you figure that this would happen one day?"

"Damn if I know, Cokey," Dave admitted. "Sometimes I got like a sixth sense—especially when I'm gambling—but I swear I don't know why I bought them cars. I guess I just did it because I wanted to. But, just the same, white boys are smart."

They came to the flower shop and entered.

"You chaps don't look too dog eared after a day and a night of rotgut swilling," Blueboy greeted them.

"Youth sprang internal, man. Youth," Cokey informed him.

"So it is. So it is," Blueboy agreed, and picked up a jangling telephone. After he had barked a hearty "Hello" into the instrument, he handed the phone to Dave. "Mastah Greene," he said mockingly.

Dave took the phone. "Hello?"

"Dabe, it me, Delilah."

His heart thudded, and he was suddenly ashamed and bashful.

"Ah sorry, Dabe." It was such a little voice, and it sounded very brave in its ordeal. It also sounded lost and desperate, but enigmati-

296

cally direct. "Ah know you spect bettuh ob me, but ah git skayd, and all of a suddint ah hayd tuh run. Ah sorry. Dabe?"

"I'll be right there."

Dave hung up the phone, waved a vague farewell to Cokey and Blueboy, and left them standing there.

Cokey and Blueboy exchanged glances. "Who the hell was that, Blueboy?"

"Damn if I know. It sure was nobody that ever called up here before. That's for sure. But now mebbe I talk to that little girl every night. I dunno, but that 'Mastah Greene' sounded like that little gal Delilah, but I dunno."

Then they grinned at each other.

25

When, on one occasion, Miss
Delilah Mazique said: "When de strain leffum Whinny Ilum him
haftuh tek him foot and gone spang town" she was speaking in that
delicious oddity of the American idiom called "Gullah." An ac-
curate translation might be: "When she missed the train at Wingate
Island, she had to walk all the way to town."

Gullah is the patois or dialectic spoken by those Negroes who
inhabit the Rice Islands that dot the South Carolina-Georgia coast
line.

Folklore and fact have become so intertwined that no single
explanation would seem to explain the origin of the Gullah-speaking Negroes and their language. Gullah is an unwritten language. It
lacks logical construction and is essentially no more than baby talk.
But it is the prattle of a seventeenth-century English peasant's baby.
It is made stranger by the addition of Africanisms and time. It
defies further description.

The true history of the Gullah dialect probably lies hidden in
the seldom-realized fact that the American slave had no common
language; Africa being a continent of many tongues and nations.

Only slaves coming from the same general area were conversant. Communication between slaves from different areas was possible only through the use of the common language of the plantation, the master's pidgin-English.

At this point in any explanation, the Rice Islands' own history steps in to add to the general confusion. Prior to the Civil War, these islands were vast plantations, but unlike the rest of the Confederacy, they were never reconstructed. The plantation owners had fled never to return. So it was that their pidgin-English slaves remained in utter isolation from the mainland of the United States for years. It is the direct descendants of these slaves who inhabit these islands today.

Professor Blake, the eternal booster of the Negro, once informed the Square Table that the Gullah Negro is the only remainder of pure African blood in the U.S.A. today.

"You men ridicule him and call him a Geechie; but his is the only racial grouping in America today which has not only fought for, but has succeeded in maintaining his racial purity against all odds. No other American can say that but your Geechie. Now that is black history that we all can be proud of. It is the story of a tribe's determination to remain black. Those islands were discovered by runaway slaves. And don't forget, they have kept those islands black! And theirs is the only pure form of Anglo-Saxon extant today. Their speech is perfect seventeenth-century English."

The pedant was wrong on many scores. Any language that uses the pronoun "him" to cover all forms of "he," "she," and "it" cannot be either pure or perfect English. And while it is true that for some mysterious reason the Gullah Negroes have never mixed with the white race, there is a decided strain of American Indian blood in almost all of them.

Neither will the fable of the runaway slaves stand up; the islands were white-owned, slave-manned plantations before the Civil War, and it is the descendants of these slaves who inhabit the islands to-day. To further confute and confuse the teacher is the fact that the local government of each island is firmly in the control of a handful of whites. Indeed, a few of these isles have been purchased in toto by northern millionaires for hunting and fishing preserves, and they were not purchased from Negroes.

However, the white-man-hating Gullah Negro does exist, at least in part, but he has been shoved back into the most inaccessible reaches of each island, places that no white man has any desire or reason to go. Then too, some race-hating Negroes might have migrated to these predominantly black islands during, or just before

Reconstruction days in order to escape daily contact with the hated white man. Isolation alone seems inadequate to explain the fact that there are no mulattoes on these islands even to this day.

Probably the most remote of all the Rice Islands is tiny Wingate Island, which Delilah pronounces, "Whinny Ilum." Wingate Island Negroes tend to be totally black, tall, and strong.

Blueboy once snarled at Professor Blake, "A Geechie is just like any other goddam nigger, only more so." He was absolutely correct.

James Mazique came from Wingate Island. He was a rangy black man the color of tar, who left the island while still a boy to work on the estates of the wealthy near Charleston. He grew up at his trade, which was gardening, and subsequently traveled all over America working always as a landscape gardener for the very rich. One such position took him to Westbury, Long Island where he worked for three years. James was so enamored of Long Island that he vowed never to leave, but when his employer's health began to fail and he was advised to move South, James reluctantly accompanied him to Jonesville.

In all of his travels in America, James had never been ostracized within his own race because of the color of his skin until he reached the southern town of Jonesville.

James worked on the outskirts of the village, but on his first Sunday there he went to church in Jonesville. He arrived before the services had begun, but the agitated usher bowed him to a seat in the very last pew. Sitting alone, and watching the parishioners file in, James was struck by the astounding coincidence that each new arrival was lighter-skinned than the last. By the time the services got under way, James was amazed to behold more than fifty yaller niggers all in one bunch.

He was at a complete loss to explain this holy phenomenon.

Why would people so obviously mixed up associate with one another, he wanted to know. In his opinion, these folks should sort of try to hide amongst their darker brethren so as not to be conspicuous.

A more thorough look revealed that these people were lighter than he had first imagined, ranging in complexion from the blue-eyed blonds down to a rather weatherbeaten beige. But it was not until the services were over that James discovered that his presence was entirely unwelcome. What he had mistaken for yokel looks of curiosity during the services were, in fact, looks of disdain.

The minister pointedly overlooked the outstretched black hand of James Mazique when the services were over. That which had

300

in the beginning amused him, and then mildly appalled him, now became the object of his loathing.

James even came to hate the few brown-skinned natives of Jonesville. He reckoned that they should be ashamed to live amongst these obvious bastards, and so something must be the matter with them, too. He never set foot in the town again. For all of his personal wants he drove five miles farther on to Jonesboro, where the Negro was naturally a multi-hued thing.

But this coal-black man left his mark upon Jonesville. He married its prettiest belle. No one ever knew how they met, or how they courted. No one knew when or where they were married. Folks only knew that Doris Dennis left a note for her parents, saying that she was wed, and that she had gone to live with her husband, James Mazique, who had a cabin on the estate of his employer.

Jonesville's yellow motley did not approve of a rank black stranger eloping with one of their own, but, being an intelligent group of people, they caused Jim Mazique no discomfort. Jim, lithe and strong, commanded respect; Jonesville granted it from afar.

The first and only fruit of this mysterious union was a girl who from the day of her birth gave signs of being a glorious mixture of many racial strains. Her African darkness was blended over with Mongolian hints of golden red. Black, shiny ringlets fell all about her classic, almost Nordic, features. As she grew she showed a marked tendency to inherit her father's lithe carriage and taciturnity.

A Gullah child is often named in contradistinction to its parents' hopes for it. Many Geechie boys have been christened Hungry. To insure the virtue of his daughter, James named her Delilah.

Delilah's memory of Jonesville was more a miscellany of impressions and sensations than of actual events. One of these snatches of recall was that of the beautiful, fairy-white lady who was her laughing mother. Lila was always able to summon the warm sensation of that laugh and the gentle caress. Her mother died at home before Lila was four years old, and in this respect, the girl tended to equate man, woman, and bedroom with death and disaster in a vague superstitious sort of way. This fact probably caused Lila to retain her virginity as long as he did just as much as the word of gawd.

Of course her most vivid impression was that of her departure from Jonesville, and the long, long train ride "with the body up in front." Jim Mazique took his daughter and the body of his wife to his native Wingate Island. After the burial of his wife, Jim left the child in the care of his mother and returned to his place of employment outside Jonesville.

Granny Mazique was a gaunt, fierce-looking woman of inde-

301

terminate age who was constantly preoccupied with the "sperits" and "debils" which forever haunt the lives of all Gullah Negroes. On Sundays the natives of Wingate Island pay homage to the stern God of Abraham, but on weekdays they have a host of minor devils and spirits with which to contend. These cause milk to sour, make one late, sick, or sad; they precipitate all those minor calamities that clutter human existence. Granny Mazique was reputed to have talked to and have rassled with every sperit and debil on Whinny Ilum; she had to look gaunt and fierce, and Lila loved her.

During her years on Wingate Island Delilah ran as free as the ocean air that hovered about her head. Her only serious problems being to carefully avoid those bushes and trees where "hants" had taken a liking to lurk in wait for innocent little girls who did not know how to talk back or rassle with them. And her only task was to keep her mother's grave beautiful like the graves of all other Gullah decedents. Granny saved every piece of bright ribbon, fancy-colored jars, tinsel, and other trinkets for the conscientious child to use in decorating her mother's grave. Doris Mazique's plot was always the prettiest on the island.

School was not unheard of, but nobody ever thought about it, and so at the time of Granny Mazique's death Lila was ten years old but unable to read and write.

After his mother's funeral, Jim abandoned the Wingate Island homestead for good and took Delilah to Westbury, Long Island, where he was again employed. Thus it came about that the illiterate little girl was exposed to some of the best grade schooling that America has to offer.

Jim boarded the child with an upstanding colored couple in Westbury, and it seemed assured that Lila would stay with them until she went away to college. Several quirks of fate changed Jim's plan for her life, but before Lila left Long Island she had become an excellent pupil and a tireless reader, who was given to reading over and over again the books that she liked.

The oddest link in Lila's personality was forged in Westbury. It was here that the child developed the horrid speech that offended Dave's ears in Booker's Restaurant. It is generally said that Geechies have three variations of their strange patois. One is the unintelligible gibberish that they will affect to repulse an unwelcome stranger. Another is the beautifully fluid, albeit, still unintelligible one in which they themselves converse, and the third is the sometimes understandable one they will use to communicate with an outlander friend or welcome stranger.

Lila was a loner in school by choice, and because of this she was mocked by the other children for her odd accent. And she was treated far more cruelly than if she had a been a friendly child. In retaliation Lila retreated behind the wall of the first, or "No spika da English" version of her quasi-native tongue. It was a natural outgrowth of rebellion and protection. It must be assumed, then, that Lila's weird accents were, in part, psychological in origin, but regardless of cause, they were the perfect foil to repulse the boors who crossed her path all through her future life and saved her from many of what she considered unnecessary friendships as well.

A whim of Jim's employer took Delilah to a huge ranch-estate in the Mississippi Gulf area, and so her next four years of education were gleaned in rural Mississippi. It was here that her school progress was prodigious, and by the time of her father's accidental death underneath the wheels of a tractor she was a high school junior. Delilah was fifteen years old.

Delilah happened to come to the city and the Ward because she was painfully taciturn and factual. After her father's funeral, her father's employer asked Delilah where her next of kin resided. Lila told him that her only living relatives lived in Jonesville, and when she offered no further information, the good man bought her train and bus tickets to Jonesville; gave her fifty dollars; and bade her godspeed.

Lila was well aware of her father's hatred for Jonesville and did not have the slightest intention of going there, but she was more than willing to come to the city and the Ward. She had vague ideas of finishing high school and going on to the University. Lila never doubted that she could win a generous scholarship, and so she intended to work as a part-time maid for a nice colored professional man and his wife until she finished high school. Her strategy was simple: find a room; join a church; ask the minister to find her a job! It was that simple to the levelheaded child.

On her person was the fifty dollars that her father's former employer had given her plus three hundred dollars which had been Jim Mazique's life savings. She asked several questions at the depot, checked her baggage, and walked to the Ward. It was not until she had reached the Block that Lila became truly hungry for the first time since her father's fatal accident, and in a haphazard sort of way she chanced to wander into Booker's.

Whimsy and the child's peculiar personality again played the leading roles in choosing her destiny. Booker's many tables and booths gave her pause. She did not know where to sit, and it never dawned upon her to retreat. Seeing the impassive girl standing uncertainly just inside his door, Mr. Booker was quite sure that the child had not come to enjoy his food. He came forward and told Delilah that she was a pretty little thing and neat as a pin, but she simply was too young. Lila absently thanked the kindly old man and went to a booth and waited to be served.

This time fate donned the pretty face and figure of Pigmeat Goins as it continued to play its game. Pigmeat loved the beautiful black child at first sight, and feeling sorry for the stubborn little thing, she went to the booth and told Delilah that there really was no use in hanging around because Mr. Booker never changed his mind. Lila was too young to be a waitress.

Delilah announced that she didn't want a job; she only wanted a ham sandwich and a glass of milk. This one simple food order upset the equilibrium of Booker's more than any other order before or since. Suddenly everyone connected with the establishment felt cheated. In some mysterious way, all concerned were filled with remorse because this girl did not wish to work at Booker's, even if she was too young and Mr. Booker had already told her that she could not be hired. It really was a shame and everybody said so.

On second thought, Mr. Booker decided that he needed a busgirl about Lila's age, and so it happened that before she had finished her meal, or found lodgings in the Ward, Lila had acquired not only a job, but a lifelong friend and relative in the person of Miss Pigmeat Goins. The oddest part of it all was that Delilah sincerely did not want the job. She did not like the idea of being so constantly in contact with the public, and she was not sure if Booker's was a wickety place or not, especially for a young girl who intended to go to high school.

Last night had been a madding welter of new experiences that all seemed pleasant in retrospect. Even the struggle at the door of Dave's house seemed now to have been no more than a friendly tussle. But even if last night had been fun, Lila was now suffering a hangover from overexperience. She had never danced before; never necked before; been in the company of an intoxicated man before; and never had she courted the wrath of God before.

Blessed to be unafraid, Lila was bewildered by her total demoralization last night. She had never so much as dreamed that she could be so afflicted. She was reluctant to call it terror, but she rather thought she had been terrorized when she fled Dave's embrace and bed.

Lila's unusual fright stemmed from the fact that she was a member in good standing of a unique species within the Negro race. Since she was a female, she was not so morbidly accursed as the males of her species. For the males, at times, approach downright masochism, with overtones of self-flagellation.

This is the man whose food must be saltier than the ocean. He puts salt on ham sandwiches. His cornbread must be grittier than beach sand. If he is a football player he will complain that headgear gives him a headache and will insist upon playing without a helmet. He will loudly berate any physician foolish enough to prescribe a pleasant-tasting medication for him. His liniments must be compounded of muriatic acid or they won't "sink in." In the acute stage, he will walk to a hospital with a broken leg rather than wait on a "slow-assed taxi."

The female of the tribe is not quite so bad, although she firmly believes that any woman who will suffer a doctor to inject pain relievers during childbirth is surely going to hell. She will also pull her own teeth at times, and proudly display the dirty pliers she used, while all the time bragging that she cannot stand the sight of a needle. She prefers to be the wife of a wife-beater, and on the coldest day of the year, she will open all the windows to air out the house. She will close every window on the hottest day to keep out the heat. She believes in castor oil. She insists that burnt toast will make you pretty, and that hard work never killed anybody.

One has a sneaking suspicion that these Negroes have a mortal fear and hate for all that is pleasant. It must certainly be a pathological hangover from slavery. They worship a God of pain and sorrow, and their Church is founded upon the Book of Revelation in its entirety. As stated, Delilah was a member of this band, albeit junior grade.

Delilah constantly marveled that her life was so endlessly free of pain and sorrow. She often felt guilty about this lack of travail in her life, but she was ever too fatalistic to feel guilt for long periods of time. And Delilah was simply unable to envision any God of any man that would countenance such pleasure as she had experienced last night in Dave's embrace. Supreme pleasure, and that pleasure alone, had caused her fright. Lila shied away from outright happiness. If seduction had been an unpleasant affair, she would willingly have allowed Dave to deflower her last night.

Man in the form of Dave Greene was more than Lila had bargained for, but she was no coward.

That is why she had called him personally today.

It never occurred to Delilah that she might be in love with Dave. Her mind did not work that way. She simply accepted the fact that she must spend the rest of her days entangled in the fortunes of one David Greene.

305

Gullah-speaking Negroes refuse to war with fate. Seldom if ever do they commit suicide, and Delilah was one with them. She considered it stupidity to woe the fact that she was now the personal property of Dave Greene; but she still did not know that it was love.

Nor did Delilah consider herself to be unlearned in the matters of sex. It had been somewhat distasteful, but she had persevered through several long sessions on this subject with Pig. And Pig, like all Vessey Street chicks, firmly believed that insanity was the fate of all girls who maintained their chastity after their late teens. So it was a fact that she had to shed her virginity, but Dave's hands were so wickety.

And to complete the problem was Delilah's certain knowledge that Dave was not the marrying kind. Therefore, it had been ordained that she forever be a wickety woman. She was almost unafraid of that, but she needed time to get used to the idea. Not only her soul, but her body cried out: "But just a little more time."

So even now as she answered the doorbell's ring she steeled herself for the coming ordeal that she knew she had been born to sustain.

"But just a little more time," the voice within her begged.

She bowed gravely and opened the door wider to admit him. *But just a little more time.*

"Hi, Lila, I came right over."

"Mawn, Dabe," she said, and was dismayed to feel her pulse quicken and a warm molasses-like feeling well up around her legs to encircle her thighs and converge between her legs. "Ah doan know whut mek ah botherin' you so."

He waved his hand in impatient dismissal. "That's okay." And then he anxiously asked, "You still mad?"

"Whuffo?"

"Well, you ran last night. I made you run."

"Lak ah say, ah skayd, but ah won't do it again."

"Don't worry, I won't do it again either. I rushed you."

"Dat not h'it, Dabe," Lila said. "You doan understand."

"Well, look here. I'm gonna give Cokey a going-away party. Wanna come?"

A party meant little or no privacy; Lila had a little more time. "Shoah, Dabe. I'll be there."

"I'll be by about nine."

"You be too busy. Pig and me come togedder."

"Okay then, if you want."

Then he took her in his arms. Lila closed her eyes, but held her lips tightly together, hoping against hope that she would not suc-

306

cumb to that warm delicious feeling, but she did. And she knew her God was mad at her again.

Dave released her. "What kind of a kiss do you call that?" he said gently.

Delilah said nothing, but her mind was in a turmoil. She simply had to learn how to keep from getting like this everytime Dave touched her.

"Well, look," Dave said. "I gotta run to make, but don't forget tonight. Nine o'clock."

Back at the flower shop he announced that he was throwing Cokey a party to end all parties.

"Thought you gave me my party last night," Cokey said. "You sure this isn't an engagement party? Better yet, a coming-out party for the young Miss Mazique?"

"She been on the Block for years. Whadya mean, coming-out?"

"No she ain't," Blueboy said gently.

"Okay," Cokey said, "so I'm having another going away party."

"Don't I live in that house any more?" Blueboy asked genially.

It was a perfectly normal and reasonable question, and Blueboy's face showed that he thought so too, and so Dave winced before the coming storm. "Huh?" He tried to look innocent and perplexed.

"When this damn fool boy leaves town, I got as much to say about it as the next man," Blueboy said sweetly.

"That's what I know," Dave agreed. "So let's all go over to Booker's and lay our plans."

"The money'll start coming in in a minute now," Blueboy screamed. "I ain't no playboy sonofabitch that can wander to hell and gone whenever I takes the notion. Howinell I gonna leave now? You guys are a bunch of drunks that can stagger inta Booker's anytime you gets a thirst on—but me? I gotta work! But whadya think I am anyhow?"

"Brilliant question," Cokey drawled. "Delves to the pith of the matter."

Blueboy scowled. "Boy," he said darkly. "I ain't gonna call that party off, but one more crack outa you, and I ain't gonna let you in the door!" He turned and stomped off to a ringing telephone.

"C'mon, fella," Dave said to Cokey. "I better take you to the warehouse before Blueboy has a baby in the middle of the floor."

"Warehouse?"

"Yeah. C'mon. Do you good."

Cokey stood by the front door of the flower shop while Dave gave some quiet instructions to the girl behind the counter. Then the two left the shop, hailed a cab, and were soon speeding toward the west side of town.

"Since you're graduated, it's okay for you to go any place you want with me," Dave explained, "but while you were still in school I wasn't too particular about you being around any of the places that was likely to be raided. You can praise numbers all you want, but we're still outside this man's law."

"Yeah. And I guess you were right. No use taking needless chances," Cokey agreed. Then he fell to musing aloud. "I really earned that damn piece of sheepskin that ain't sheepskin. Now I'm gonna put some molasses on it and eat it."

And Dave wished with all his heart that Cokey would ask him for a job. But he was wise enough to know that youth wants to believe in the oyster regardless of the youth's color. Cokey only wished to excel, and Dave refused to begrudge the lad his ambition. Neither would Dave rue the fact that Cokey, like every other college graduate in America, did not wish to go from the classroom into the dishonorable world of numbers banking. Dave only thanked his fates that he, too, had been granted a little college learning; without it he might be Cokey's jealous enemy. An ignorant man would have angrily accused Cokey of thinking himself as being too good for the numbers racket and destroyed a wonderful friendship.

"Want a drink?" he asked Cokey.

"Too well raised to refuse."

"Stop at the next pad you know about," Dave instructed the cabdriver.

"Don't too many know about this one," the driver said to Dave, as he pulled up in front of a nice-looking house.

"Guess I know them all," Dave said heavily, getting out.

The pad was just like all the others, but since Dave was a celebrity, they were invited to sit in the kitchen. The lady of the house was about fifty years old, and not more than five feet tall. Her shoulders and body were hideously deformed, but she had the most strikingly intelligent eyes Dave thought he had ever seen.

"Weren't that a turble thing that happened this morning?" the pad lady asked Dave.

"We just got up," he apologized.

"James Madison and his uncle cut each other to death," the little woman said sorrowfully. "You know James Madison? He used to be in the Lil Savoy daytimes, cleaning up."

Dave vaguely recalled the boy. James was just another quiet boy

308

who did his job and stayed out of trouble. Nothing remarkable about him one way or the other. "Yeah. Young boy? Kinda quiet?"

She nodded. "He had this powerful dream that he was in the movies and the picture machine got stuck and all that was on the screen was this great big 350."

"Well, he sure dreamed the right figger," Dave replied.

"Well, first he goes to this uncle to borrow a dollar to play it with. Naturally the uncle hems and haws, but finally he agrees to put two dollars on three-five-oh."

"I remember Blueboy saying that he had a two-dollar hit to pay off." Dave grinned at the lady. "James told all his two-bit-playing friends about it, too, didn't he?"

"Guess he did. He was in here telling everybody about his dream. It cost you much?"

"Oh, we'll live. So why the killing?"

"Well, the agreement was: if the number should come out, they both have a dollar hit apiece, but if it don't, well, James owes his uncle two dollars."

"That's a fair and square gamble anyways you look at it," Cokey said.

"The uncle welched?" Dave asked the lady.

She bowed her head sorrowfully. "They fought something turble. They justa cut, and cut, and cut."

All four were silent, each with his own thoughts. Dave stared at his glass and wondered if the gaze of the others was upon him, and, if so, why the hell were they staring at him? Was it his fault that niggers were niggers?

"Wal, since money is the root of all evil, guess I better get rid of mine," Cokey drawled into the silence of the kitchen.

"No. The next one's on me," the cabdriver said quickly. He gave Dave a shy smile. "Never had the pleasure before," he murmured.

"Damn," Dave exclaimed a little later, "I almost forgot. We're supposed to be working. Let's drink up and make it."

In the cab Cokey asked Dave: "Two more funerals?"

"The dumb bastards killed themselves over ten hundred and forty bucks. They got money now. Why should anyone come to me?"

"A really negroid ending for that little black tale of death would be for the uncle to have hidden the money, never to be found. No one profits; not even the family."

"Cut it out," Dave said. "That's Kelly's part; you just say your lines. I'm supposed to be trying to forget that dame."

"Just the same, I certainly would like to hear Miss Simms's views on this latest episode in the black man's struggle for equality."

"Shut up," Dave barked, but was helpless to suppress a grin.

The taxi had now reached the very outskirts of town and was still going. Finally it stopped before a new one-storied cinderblock building. In spite of its newness, Cokey thought it to be an insignificant-looking structure, and he decided that it was because the building looked to be absolutely useless.

After Dave had paid and dismissed the cabbie, he took out a key and unlocked the front door of the place. As they entered, Cokey noticed that just inside the door was a glassed-in office area much like that found in many auto repair shops. All the rest of the interior was piled high with case upon case. All of these packing cases were of a size, and all bore a large serial code number.

"We store our slips here," Dave explained as he entered the office. He took off his coat and told Cokey to do the same. "I need a muscleman for a few minutes," he added.

Then he opened a battered safe and took out two huge ledgers.

"This is a feeble attempt to foil counterfeiters." He smiled wryly. "Blueboy's sworn enemies." Then he grinned hugely and said, "Even if Blueboy thinks you're stupid, I guess you know that each numbers slip has a serial number on it. Now all these cartons got a number on them to show what series the slips in it are. I want you to pull down and stack some cases for delivery. Read me off the series number as you go. Got me okay?" Cokey nodded, and so Dave said, "Now the first three cases is gonna be delivered to the Southside."

An hour passed before they finished stacking the boxes and recording the numbers on them. After that they sat down and relaxed.

"The florist truck will be here in a little while and he'll bring a cab with him," Dave told Cokey. He went to a filing cabinet and brought forth a quart of bourbon.

"You never get far from the stuff, do you?" Cokey said.

"And the hell of being your own boss is that nobody can fire you for drinking it. Some days I wake up and wish I had a regular job to go to so I wouldn't be able to take a snort."

"One thing, it don't affect your thinking."

"You got as many things on your mind as I got on mine and you ain't got no room left for alcohol to get loose in." Dave sighed heavily. "Take today now, I gotta go check with the Colonel. I gotta go check with the manager of Babylon, plus the countinghouse and a couple of other things. Getting drunk with you yesterday threw me off some."

The remainder of the day proved to be an enlightening, although

310

mildly harrowing experience for Cokey. At firsthand he learned that it is a nerve-wracking thing for one Negro to do business with another Negro. Colonel Eldrege was politeness itself, but the old man was both ignorant and finicky. Cokey was amazed to find that the Colonel's insistence upon a ritualistic hair splitting was predicated upon the Negro fun-word, "Business-like."

The old man really did not understand half of the things Dave explained to him, but once convinced that something was "business-like" he would immediately come to agreement.

And Cokey believed that he had unearthed the key to Dave's success in life. It was the revelation that the often brusque and restless Dave was also a man of infinite patience. Patience in the sense of being able to wait out the windy verbiage of the fools of this world. Very few people are able to do this, Cokey reflected. He also decided that Dave only argued with people whom he considered smarter than he was. Like Kelly and Blueboy. Who else? This revelation answered the question of why Dave thought time spent at the Square Table to be well wasted.

And Cokey was sure that kindness played a part in Dave's life. The skating rink was of little or no financial gain to Dave, and yet the numbers banker showed an interest in the venture that could only have been a form of kindness to the old man. Cokey believed himself to be a happy-go-lucky and generous person, and yet he wondered if he had the kindly patience to play the Colonel's game of doing-things-business-like.

Cokey also found out that one Negro (or a white man either, he presumed) cannot give another Negro a bald command, suggestion, or hint and expect obedience. The Negro has first got to be convinced that your suggestion or command is "business-like." It saddened Cokey to see that this term was the Negro's subconscious equivalent of "whitelike." This business of being business-like went for all Dave's dealings throughout the day. It even went for Makepeace, and Makepeace was a graduate of Tuskegee.

With a shudder of apprehension Cokey wondered what had he learned in college that would have helped him to carry out all of the business that Dave had done this day. He felt defeated.

It was late in the afternoon when they returned to the flower shop. The number had been 169.

"Wal, I got things all lined up," Blueboy cheerfully informed them as soon as they walked in. "That was while you titty pimps was out carousing."

"Lined up? Whadya mean, lined up?" Dave demanded. "The goddam house is sitting there, ain't it? All we gotta do is take a cab

311

to the whiskey store, go home and unlock the door. Whadya mean, lined up?"

The kind and patient Blueboy gently informed him: "Your guests might get hungry and so I took the liberty of ordering a few hams and things from Booker's. You don't mind, do you?" The rocky little man drew a deep breath. "And as for the guests themselves: Don't you think they would like to be invited?" he screamed.

"Emmmpyreal!" Blueboy always said whenever he described the party. It flickered and blazed for three days and nights, sometimes smoldering down to only a few partiers only to come to life with a roar again and again. Blueboy finally passed out after ten straight hours of drinking and they laid him out on a table, where he slept for his usual eight hours while the party raged around him. When he awoke, he raised his head and was delighted to find the party on an upswing.

The exact time of Cokey's departure is still one of the Ward's lesser mysteries. Dave had a fuzzy recollection of the grinning boy waking him up and asking for a loan of ten dollars and a "little godspeed." It could have been either the second or third day, but it was in the daytime. Dave was sure of that.

And the revelers had really torn up the house. Blueboy surveyed the damage, and it was his jubilant estimate that it would cost a thousand dollars to repaint and repair the interior and furnishings. Loudly and proudly he bore all the expense.

Of all the flamboyant figures at the wild gathering it remained for Delilah to be the center of attraction. In a way, her very presence stimulated the party, for she had never before been a guest at a social function in the Ward. No one had ever seen the girl in a party dress before. And because Delilah was the only atypical guest present, all the other guests took it to be their duty to see that she had a nice time. Cokey at best was co-guest of honor.

But Lila was also the hostess, a unique consequence due entirely to Lila's fatalism. The girl simply took it to be her duty to serve Dave and his guests. Effortlessly, and apparently invisibly, she saw to it that there was an everpresent supply of clean glasses, mixers, food, and whiskey. It never occurred to her to ask either Dave's or Blueboy's permission to reorder anything that was needed, and it did not occur to the two men to question her right to do so. In fact, Blueboy turned his bedroom over to Pig and Lila.

The unspoken bonds that were formed at the party, however, brought no amorous bliss. Three weeks after the party Dave and Delilah were still in the hand-holding stage of their romance, as

312

Dave acidly put it. They saw each other nightly, and on occasion indulged in torrid love making until at the climactic moment Lila would wrench away from Dave, faltering before her own ecstasy. And each time this happened Dave swore up and down that he would never date Lila again. One time Dave remained true to his word for three whole days; but this ended when Lila, small voiced and fearful, called him wanting to know if he was still angry.

Blueboy watched the fitful romance with fiendish glee. "You made her wait four whole years. Now see how long she makes you wait!"

It was Dave's misfortune to be not only determined, but a determindedly one-woman man. That is how he became trapped so helplessly in Lila's innocent clutches. And all the while he actually believed that he only wanted to seduce her.

He gave her presents and showered her with favors. He signed the handsome Cord automobile over to her and arranged for Kid Flick to give her driving lessons, reasoning that the gentle and considerate Kid would make an excellent instructor. Lila's quick proficiency proved him correct.

Dave, at least, had the comfort of being able to delude himself that he was only being denied a fair chance to get a dumb chick's cherry. He hardly liked Delilah, he thought. But to Delilah it was clear that her very life was at stake in this painful liaison. Body and soul she was endlessly Dave's, even as she believed that her stern God was outraged each time she enjoyed being touched by Dave.

Night before last they had spent the evening in Dave's front room, listening to the record player and chatting. Dave had not tried to kiss her all night. When she went upstairs to the bathroom she had procrastinated in Dave's bedroom, combing her hair twice. She had imagined that his bed was unevenly made up and so she had remade it. Dave had not bothered to find an excuse to come up and join her. His indifference terrified her far more than his kisses had ever done.

"You gotta, Lila, honey," Pig had said earlier this evening. "You gotta have a man sometime. And you thinks you is a Geechie what never falls in love but oncet; and you might as well admit that you're in love with Dave Greene. You're like a sick calf around here when he don't call. And you're sicker worse when you gets him all worked up for nothing. Dave's a grown man, honey, and you is a woman now. You can't expect him to sit around and hold hands with you until you is an old woman, can you? A woman is supposed to relax a man. Never tie him up in knots, honey."

In this state of tension Lila wondered how she had allowed her-

313

self to believe Pigmeat's advice that the surrender would be easy. With a sigh of determination she turned to face Dave. He was sprawled half on the bed, half off. As frightened as Delilah was she had only one real desire and that was to kiss Dave endlessly. But those hands. Those soon man's hands. They drove her wickety crazy. She got dizzy when his fingers touched her nipples. She imagined that it must be something like being drunk. And that was the trouble with all this, you should never let yourself get so high up that you don't care what is happening.

"You really must hate me if you can't stand to have me touch you." His voice was drained of bitterness; it was filled with a weary sadness.

"Ah doan hate yo, Dabe. Ah doan know. Mebbe yo doan do h'it right," she muttered.

Dave made an eerie sound through his nostrils. "Do it right?" he snarled. "We ain't done a damn thing. Not a damn thing, but kiss and make ourselves feel lousy as hell." He stood up and wondered why he had been so dumb as to ever try to seduce Lila in the first place.

He saw her nervously buttoning her blouse. He interpreted her motion as being furtive. Fury, love, and despair coiled like three serpents in his stomach.

"You ain't naked," he said, "can't you leave three lousy buttons alone?" He walked out of the room and Lila heard his footsteps going down the stairs.

She breathed more quietly as his steps descended. By the time he reached the front door she was not breathing at all, but when his footsteps passed the front door and went back toward the kitchen she opened her mouth and expelled her pent-up breath. Relief drenched her in a heavenly shower.

With Dave outside her line of vision her mind cleared once more and she knew that if Dave had walked through that front door and left her, she would have been doomed to dwell forever among the living dead. This, then, was the fated night. She knew that if she failed Dave tonight he would never try again. She knew this in the very bones of her body; her own fatalism had set the deadline. And now she lay stricken by the enormity of it.

She closed her eyes and prayed God to forgive her if it was a sin to enjoy your man more than the hope of heaven.

Silently.

Assured, in utter calm she got up and undressed, then turned out the lights and quickly got into bed.

Of all the conversations she had held with Pig about sex they had never discussed the crux of the thing. She was not even sure of the position she was supposed to assume. One Whinny Ilum and on the estates she had observed livestock, but this, she told herself, should be different. But, she decided, she was not supposed to know. That was Dave's business. Hers was only to serve.

But she did not rest easy. A lingering doubt still flickered in her mind, and she wished that Pig could slip into the room and for one minute whisper the secrets in her ear. She owed it to Dave.

But her wish was past the hour; Dave was climbing the stairs. She lay back on the bed and closed her eyes.

Dave went straight to the bathroom, disdaining to glance at the bed. Lila, fearing God but no coward before man, got up, flicked on the ceiling light and returned to bed.

Dave walked out of the bathroom and stared at her naked beauty. Pure cowardice kept him from rushing to the bed. He feared that Delilah was still Delilah and that she would flee once he touched her. He turned like a sleepwalker and started for the door.

"Dabe?" she whispered. "Dabe? H'it yoahs. Do what you want wid h'it."

Dave moved to the bed. And in one dizzy moment the world came screeching to a stop.

When it was over Lila gratefully murmured, "Done done 'um." Then she went to sleep.

In the morning Dave looked at Lila and wondered how he could have been so impatient with her. As she slept he convinced himself that a million years would not have been too long to wait. He looked at her black beauty alloyed in secret undertones of red, and promised himself that she would never regret last night. He kissed her lightly on the cheek.

"Thank you, Dabe," she whispered.

"I thought you were asleep."

She opened her eyes and looked very serious as she bobbed her head. "I wuz, kinda. But I guess you will never touch me again and I doan know it." She lowered her voice. "That was last night I wuz thanking you for."

"You're not sorry? Mad?"

She smiled shyly. "Ah be mad because you took so long. Whuffo you never beat me up and took it?"

"You nuts or something? Mad as I been I never thought about hurting you. Honest."

She bobbed her head again. "Ah knows," she said. "But you doan know how happy ah be now, Dabe. Caint exactly explain but we are free now, ain't we?"

Dave nodded and then kissed her for a long time.

Later she gave a little sigh of contentment and said, "Pig's gonna be so happy."

"You going to tell Pig?"

Lila studied the ceiling. "Ah doan hafta tell and Pig doan hafta ast. She gonna be able to look at me an' tell." She turned her face to Dave. "Caint you tell?"

"Lila," he asked, "what does done done 'um mean?"

She showed only the mildest curiosity. "It mean like when you got a hard task to do, and then you does it real good and finished." She shrugged. "Den you done done 'um. Thass all. Whuffo you asts, Dabe?"

"I don't know," he said gently. "I just asked."

They lay in bed and talked some more. To himself Dave tried to figure just how much was real and how much was love's imagination at work. But one thing was sure. This was not the same girl who had entered this bedroom last night. Her chin was firmer and so was her voice. And above all her accents had changed, were still changing. Lila's level gaze had never wavered, but now there was more than artless candor in her eyes. They held a light of supreme confidence, with nothing hidden, nothing veiled.

Positive proof that Delilah was a woman came later when she arose, still nude, and with carefree grace walked alone in beauty to the bathroom.

Days of both passion and revelation followed. Delilah permeated the lives of Dave and Blueboy. It was notably unlike what the two men had shared with Kelly. This was a more subtle relationship, at the same time as dynamic as life in the womb. When Lila walked into the flower shop, Blueboy did not rush up with quips and compliments, more than likely he would smile gratefully and hand Lila some work to do.

Dave and Blueboy accepted Lila as a part of themselves, and in a sense, they accepted her far more quickly than she accepted them. Perhaps she laughed a little more now, and certainly she walked more lissomely, as if she no longer had to worry about her hips being seductive and wicked-looking.

Lila's accent, always an enigma, changed perceptibly, or rather Dave perceptibly came to know and appreciate it. It was a constant source of information and amusement to Dave now. Delilah's accent fluctuated in direct proportion to her thoughts. Dave became quite adept in reading her mind simply by noticing the way she pronounced his name. Thus at times he was Dabe, Davit! (when she was displeased), Dabid, Dave, and David.

Dave found that the people around Delilah also influenced her

316

dialect. In the presence of people whose company she did not enjoy she was cryptic and all but unintelligible. In her lighter moods among friends she spoke in almost everyday English. Sometimes on these occasions she used better than average English. And at night in the delirium of climax she told Dave of her love in the fluid, beautiful patois of pure Gullah.

As time went by Delilah spent more and more nights with Dave. Blueboy begged her to leave her job at Booker's, pointing out that now that she was a licensed driver she could very well be his and Dave's "chauffeurette" if not more directly connected with the operation of the numbers bank. But Lila's everpresent sense of independence stopped her.

It was about nine o'clock at night of the day that 291 played, when Dave sauntered up Vessey Street. He was looking for something to do until Lila got off from work. He had virtually ceased to patronize Booker's since he and Lila had become lovers. It disturbed him to have to sit and watch Lila work. He preferred to drop in a few minutes before Lila's quitting time and chat with Mr. Booker until Lila was ready to leave.

The late August night lowered with a restive tension. The Block was thronged with testy, overheated loiterers. It was the kind of a night when the Ward would senselessly shed its blood. Earlier, Blueboy had remarked, "This is gonna be a night of 'chaud medley —the ritual dance of the Ward."

Dave wiped his face and hoped that Lila would feel like taking a nice cool drive in the country, but Lila was so eager to serve his whim that he was reluctant to voice any wish until after he was sure that she was not tired. The kid—he could never think of Lila in terms of mature womanhood—could be dying from fatigue, but if she had the slightest idea that he wanted to go for a drive she would insist upon driving him. A proud smile played around his lips. Nobody could love like a Geechie woman. Everybody knew that.

He turned into the Club Babylon and went up the stairs. Perhaps he would find someone in here with whom to kill time until Lila got off from work.

The first person he saw as he entered was Professor Blake, vice-president-in-charge-of-bullshit-at-the-Square-Table, the eternal booster, full-blooded white boy, and pain in the neck. Dave had never been able to make up his mind whether he disliked the man or only was irritated by him. Probably both, he thought. This Nordic-looking Negro was the epitome of so many things Dave hated that it was really inconceivable that the two could ever really be friends.

317

Professor Blake was a good-looking man, a handsome caricature of the service-club member whose bray is heard all over America. Dave swallowed his dislike or whatever it was and decided that the professor would make as good a drinking companion as any for the next half-hour.

"Fawncy meeting you heah."

Dave's eyes popped; the man was drunk. A chuckle started in Dave's throat and worked down by degrees into whooping belly laughs. It was too ridiculous. This was not like the breaking up of a session at the Square Table when the two profs were stiffly and correctly "high." Professor Blake was reeling drunk just like any other stupid cat on the Block.

"I own the joint, fella," Dave said between laughs. "Don't I have a right to come in my own joint?"

Professor Blake observed him with gravity. "Most apt. Very well put." He unfastened his collar and tie. "We shall proceed to have two or three drinks on me."

Dave motioned for the bartender to put a quart of bourbon on the bar. "Summer school's still open, isn't it?"

"I am positive that the idiot fact'ry is still in operation."

"Then what the hell you doing drunk? Suppose one of your students walks in here?"

"I am no longer connected with the fact'ry."

"You quit? Right in the middle of the session you quit?"

"The die is cast." Professor Blake had not been paying much attention to Dave, but now he turned to stare at him. "Why all the sudden emotion? Were you, by any chance, thinking of enrolling in one of my courses?" He leaned close and confided, "Terrible waste of time and money. Terrific waste."

At the moment Dave did not know why he was so upset by the professor's being drunk. But he was upset and worried. He thought of sending the bartender down to Booker's to see if Blueboy was there.

"But why in the middle of everything?" he asked, sort of sparring for time. "Why didn't you wait until next week when the whole thing is over? Somebody been riding you? Got your goat?"

"Because I wanted to," Professor Blake said petulantly.

"No resignation? No leave of absence? Just quits?"

"Without a mumblin' word!" And Professor Blake lost all interest in the conversation.

Dave saw the man pour three drinks and down them in as many minutes. Suddenly, and without malice, he was positive that the teacher was sick. He tried to decide what he could do for the man.

318

In view of the fact that Professor Blake looked like a white man, Dave reasoned that if enough money was passed he might be able to get the man into a local white rest home that catered to nervous breakdowns and alcoholics.

Whether or not he liked Professor Blake was no longer important. And anyway he was Blueboy's friend. But besides that, Professor Blake was a Negro and a teacher. He had a brain that was valuable to the Negro race. It was Dave's duty to save it.

"Since you quit like you did, can you come back next fall or next February?" he asked.

"I am joining the Army."

"Army?"

"I shall go to Spain."

"The goddam war in Spain is over."

"There shall always be a war, Mommy," the teacher said reproachfully.

Dave was sure the man was addressing a third and unseen person. "Cut it out," he said sharply.

"I walked out of class and walked straight to the railroad station, and bought a ticket to Chicago. Then I walked back to the Campus and quit. Then I walked home and packed my bags. You know something?"

"No. What?" Dave said.

"I didn't walk no more. I took a cab to the station and checked my bags."

"You go to hell," Dave mumbled. He glanced up sharply. "Were you sober then?"

"Certainly."

"You mean that you just got sick and tired of the same old thing? Got a yen to travel? All of a sudden you wanted to put a whole lot of air between you and the Campus?"

"Pre-shicely."

He clapped the tall professor on the back. "The only thing I hate is that you won't ever be able to come back to the University here. Blueboy and the Square Table is sure gonna miss you this winter. That Table will never be the same without you." And Dave was happy to find that he meant every word he was saying.

Delilah came up to them, and Dave glanced at his watch. Lila had been off for fifteen minutes. "Hi, Lila," he said apologetically. "Professor Blake is leaving town for good tonight and we were just saying the old farewells. I don't know where the time went to."

"That's all right, Dave," she said gently. "It's so hot. Want to take a ride?"

319

"Baby, I wouldn't care if you drove me to the North Pole tonight," Dave said. He turned and grasped Professor Blake's hand. "When does your train leave, Prof?"

"Two-ten. I'm going straight to the station. Bag's all checked you know."

Professor Blake had been sorry to see Dave go. He really didn't like the racketeer, but he did make a sturdy drinking companion. And somehow tonight he shirked the company of Blueboy. And Dr. White was out of the question. The doctor was one of the reasons he was leaving the Campus. The guy wasn't a fit companion any more. In fact he acted like he had suddenly come to know more than God.

Professor Blake had one good-by visit to make before he left town. He looked at his watch and decided that it was not too late.

To a man, the hustlers on the Block would defend the good name of Miss Althea Goins. Never, they would declare, would Pigmeat stoop to prostitution. But the estimable gentlemen of the Block were wrong; Pigmeat had been practicing harlotry for the past year and a half.

Even now she could not remember how the crazy thing had started, but it must have been like a game. That the game had ended in sex was not exactly distressing either. It was that she continued to play the game. And it was so crazy. It was just as if she enjoyed it, but she knew she didn't. She couldn't. It was too silly and . . . different.

Pigmeat put up with this eerie business, and her patron always put ten dollars on the dresser when he left. She had been sick with shame that first time, but the unneeded ten dollars had helped to rationalize the thing. And she never doubted that the sick man needed her. She did not understand, but her large heart made her suffer with him. And sometimes Pigmeat could rationalize the thing to the extent that she convinced herself that she acted only in the capacity of a nurse.

Tonight she was surprised to find her sole patron standing on the porch when she answered the doorbell. "Come in, Professor Blake. I sure didn't expect to find you here ringing my bell. How you been?"

"I had to come and say good-by," he stammered out. "I q-quit my job. I'm leaving town tonight."

Pigmeat shrugged. This was not the way he usually started the game, but probably he wanted to play it differently tonight. With

320

a haughty shake of her head she carelessly assumed her accustomed role in the charade.

"You bad boy," she scolded. "The idea. Come inside and let me take a good look at you." She turned on her heel and imperiously marched down the hall past Lila's room and into her own bedroom. Like a child the professor tagged along behind her. "And so you went and lost your job?" she demanded.

Professor Blake said nothing, although he looked about to cry.

Pigmeat sat on the edge of the bed, crossing her legs so as to deliberately show an expanse of creamy smooth thighs. "Tell me what you've done, you little idiot," she shouted.

Professor Blake still said nothing. He stared guiltily at his shoes. His collar and tie were unfastened, but he tugged at them as if he found difficulty breathing.

Pigmeat got up and crossed over to the dresser and picked up her hairbrush. Then she returned to her sluttish pose on the bed. The brush dangled loosely in her hand. It seemed to hypnotize the professor; it might well have been a snake.

"Little gentlemen don't come into a lady's room with their ties untied and their collars open like some tramp," Pigmeat snapped.

Professor Blake's eyes filled with tears. "I'm sorry, Mommy," he sobbed.

"And you've been drinking," she snarled.

The man sobbed louder and nodded his head.

"You drunken little snot," and now Pigmeat's voice became cold and cruel as she rose wholeheartedly to her role. "If you weren't my son I'd kill you. Do you hear that? I said that I ought to kill you you little half-white bastard. Now get out. Go away. I don't want you. Get out of my sight. I can't stand the sight of you," she screamed.

The thing that had been Professor Blake sank deeper in his chair. "I'm sorry, Mommy," he blubbered through his tears. "I don't want to make you mad, Mommy. I only wanted to come and sit and look at you, Mommy. Please don't make me go away, Mommy."

Pigmeat got up and went over to him, standing with arms akimbo. "You little liar. You just want to get on my nerves. Yes you did, you ungrateful little bastard. Get out of my room." She gave a fine imitation of maniacal laughter and sneered, "Why don't you go worry your father, pretty little pink boy? Why don't you go make a joke out of him? He's nothing but a poor white bastard like you."

She reached out and sharply rapped him on the hands with the brush. Then she suddenly smiled forgiveness.

Her hips moved lewdly as she returned to the bed. She stretched out one golden leg and dangled the other over the side.

Professor Blake suddenly sprang from the chair and fell to his knees beside the bed, his body racked with sobs.

"Mommy. Oh, Mommy," he said. "Please let me come home now. We're all grown up now, Mommy."

Pigmeat closed her eyes with a sigh. Her role was ended and she had earned her ten bucks. She felt the bed tremble as the kneeling man reached some sort of climax. But she would continue to keep her eyes closed, as she always did, until he left. She placed her other foot on the bed and demurely closed her housecoat. She wished he would hurry up and leave. She wanted to take a bath.

"Mommy?"

Her annoyance increased; he evidently wanted to continue playing the silly game. Pigmeat's anger gave way to a sad stillness. It crept through her body and she did not want to move or utter a word.

"I know why you hate me, Mommy."

And in the dullness of her flesh she heard, but she did not bother to cry out; she knew that she was going to die.

Lila awoke facing Dave. He barely snored, and his face was relaxed, less tired-looking. That long drive in the country had done him good, and it had also kept him from drinking. Already Dave looked better than when they had first started going together. Pig had said he would.

Now her battle would be to cut down Dave's drinking by half. In her mind she began to figure Dave's peak drinking hours. These, then, were the times when she must not leave his company, her job at Booker's notwithstanding. It all became very clear. Suggest a ride in the country, going to bed even. She pressed herself against Dave. Yes. When Dave looked as though he had had enough to drink she would whisper in his ear that she needed some loving right away. She smiled to herself as she pressed against him. She liked to do that. When he woke up all ready and things, he would think that it had been his idea.

She stopped the pleasant undulation. Someone was breaking into the house in broad daylight. They were making too much noise even to be Blueboy.

"Dave! Dave! Wake up, Dave. Pigmeat's dead and murdered. Somebody's killed her."

Far away and long ago Delilah could feel every muscle in her body tighten into a granite knot. Clenching her fists, she lay back and tried to wake herself up from his nightmare. She opened her eyes. One look at Blueboy's face told her this was no dream. Slowly, without thought, she got out of bed and, still nude, went into the bathroom.

Dave opened one eye and glared at Blueboy. "What in hell you screaming for? Can't you see we're sleeping?"

"Get up. Get up before the police gets here and go wash your face." Suddenly Blueboy stopped shouting and looked Dave squarely in the eye. "You two been together all night?" he said harshly.

"Sure we have, but what the hell's that got to do with anything? And what's this goddam joke about Pigmeat? You ain't funny you know. What'd she do?"

"Nothing goddamit, but get herself kilt. Strangled to death and nobody knows who done it 'cepting it had to be a crazy man and somebody she knew or she was asleep at the time it happened."

"Take it easy. You sound worse than Pigmeat."

"She's dead, I tell you. How she gonna sound?"

Dave stared. Blueboy was almost crazy with grief. "Okay. Okay," he muttered. "Lemme wake Lila up and . . ."

"She's already up, you fool. Can't you get nothing through your head this morning? And you pay Pig's rent. You think they ain't gonna ask why? You got a key, aintcha? Look lively."

"Well, where *is* Lila? She know? You tell her?"

"Yass. Yass. I tole her. She was awake. She got ears. She went in the bathroom."

"When? How long ago? She been in there all this time?"

"Yass. Yasss." Then Blueboy grew silent, catching the significance of Dave's questions. "What the hell."

The two friends stared at each other for one tense moment, then Dave leaped from the bed and rushed to the bathroom.

Lila was just getting up from her knees when the door flew open. "Ah awright, Dabe," she said gently. "Come, we got tasks tuh puhfoam." Lila seemed to flow rather than walk as she passed by him back into the bedroom. She dressed swiftly, completely ignoring the presence of Blueboy. When she began to comb her hair she spoke to him. "I wants to be at the bank when it opens."

"You don't need any money, little girl."

"Pig blonx to me. Ah tek cayh ob eberyting."

"As you say," Blueboy murmured.

Delilah glanced at Dave, who was frantically getting into his clothes. "Mek uh pace, blease, Dabe."

323

Their first stop was the bank, and they had to wait fifteen minutes until it opened at nine.

While Delilah was inside the bank Blueboy said, "I'd give a pretty penny to know just how much money that little girl has in her account."

"Theoretically she could still have every tip she ever made," Dave said slowly. "Considering how she lives. She could pay room rent and things out of her salary."

"Just room rent. Not clothes and things. Old Man Booker ain't Henry Ford."

"Yeah, I guess you're right," Dave said.

Delilah came out of the bank. "Where's de morgue?" she asked. "Ain't that where they got Pig?"

"Guess so. Morgue's in the hospital," Blueboy told her. "You sure you wants to go?"

"Ah want Pig home wid me as soon as pussable."

"Lila," Blueboy said softly, "you can't take Pigmeat home to Macon. Not the murder house."

"Ahm nevah goin' dere again. Ah brung um tuh Gay Street."

"You ask Dave?"

"Pig blox tuh me. Ah blonx tuh Dabe." She turned her eyes from her driving. "Why mek so you ast?"

"Okay," Blueboy said with a sigh. "So we go to the morgue, but something tells me that you are wasting your time. It'll be three, four days before they releases the body. Autopsy takes that long when there's been murder."

Abruptly Lila wheeled the car to the curb and stopped. "You mean they cut her up?" When neither man answered she said, "Dabe, who your lawyer man?"

"I don't have a regular one."

Without another word Lila savagely turned the car about and sent it hurtling toward the Ward. Still and composed as a carving she drove at breakneck speed. It was as if she had summoned all the devils and spirits from Wingate Island to help her spur the Cord in its mad flight. When at last she slowed the car to a halt in front of the residence on Gay Street, Dave and Blueboy expelled loud sighs of relief.

"Ah'll set in the house and wait for eberyting," she announced gravely. She left them in the car and walked swiftly to the house.

Dave and Blueboy slowly got out of the car. "I don't like this at all," Blueboy muttered.

"What?"

"That child acts like somebody in her family gets murdered every night."

"What makes you say that?"

"A damn Geechie can howl louder than a Banshee just on hearing of a stranger's death. It's like religion with them. They howls all night. I know. We were in Charleston many a time in the Navy. They can shriek like Africans. I tell you that gal is in a state of shock. Ain't no Geechie woman acted like this before."

"Lila don't ever get excited," Dave said. "When you ever seen her mad even? And when their best friend dies, you ever hear of anybody going into the bathroom and quietly praying all by themselves? Lila's okay."

"That what she was doing?"

"You should have seen her face as she was getting up off her knees. It was clean, inside and out. And lovely. Like heaven, I guess. Like she and Pig were both in heaven. You understand?"

"Then why you think she's so mad now?" Blueboy asked.

"When Lila asked me who my lawyer was and I told her I didn't have one, well, that was the first time she ever asked me to show any intelligence. And it was the first time she realized that mebbe I ain't too bright. Lila was alone in that car. Me and you? She didn't even know we was there. Not for real. I bet it's gonna be a long time before she asks me for help again. Lila's funny that way."

It was two days before the coroner released the body, but Delilah had everything prepared for Pigmeat's coming. The smallest detail was fitting and proper. Even the refreshments were exactly right. And it was during the laying out that Dave felt the impact of the obvious fact that Blueboy and Delilah were identical personalities. Both were small, compact and black with a diamond hard inner core of strength. Both were competent and both possessed a genius for management which was not evident in their acts, but in the results they achieved. The only concrete difference was that one was as noisy as possible and the other was absolutely noiseless. These realizations caused Dave to wonder how Delilah and Blueboy could be so compatible; he was prejudiced in his belief that people of similar traits were inevitably at odds. He was quite amused when the answer finally came. Lila and Blueboy were brilliant people; it is people with similar idiocies who cannot get along with each other.

The two days that the beautiful corpse rested in the house proved the depths and capabilities of love as Lila knew it. Every six hours she placed a fresh flower in the dead girl's hand. For two nights she sat facing the steel casket which the Ward had pronounced

325

"silver plated." Dave, Blueboy, Flick, Makepeace, and Blip spelled each other in keeping her company. During the early morning hours she would catnap, but she never left the side of her cousin unless it was absolutely necessary.

On the final night before the funeral, Lila and Dave were sitting together, holding hands. Dave gazed at the lovely face of Pigmeat, who in all her life had sinned against no man and wondered aloud: "Who could have done it?"

"Mek no diffrunce."

"Why do you say that?" he asked.

"See that beautiful chile laying there? No matter where he go, what he do, Pig's sperit gonna follow him and he gonna hafta look at that pretty face that he took. I feels sorry for him."

"Is Pig going to heaven?"

"Where else she go? You think Pig's like people in hell? You think God let this ting happen if He didn't want her to mek uh pace and come now?"

Invisibly directed by Delilah, Pigmeat's body was given the most poignant funeral the Ward had ever attended. The lovely waitress had so lived that comparative strangers, people she had served in Booker's only on rare occasions, felt a loss, and sent flowers and condolences. The casket did look as if it was made of silver, and for years the Ward was to debate the cost of the ceremonies, but none, including Dave, ever learned the expense. Only Delilah and the undertaker knew and no one dared ask either of them.

Until the very end, when the cortege wound the last twenty miles of misery to Jonesville, Pigmeat belonged to Delilah. Mourners gasped when they saw that Delilah had already caused to be erected a beautiful obelisk, evidently of pink marble, at the grave. After a brief hesitation, the mourners nodded approval, and said rather vaguely: "That's Lila's way."

Delilah emerged into full maturity after the funeral. A few days later she calmly told Dave that she wished to be married. The announcement startled, almost frightened, Dave. Perhaps it was because he was unable to conceive of their not already being married. The wedding date was set for Labor Day weekend, when the bank would be closed. They planned to slip out of town and secretly marry, thereby doing away with a big reception. In her tragic death Pigmeat Goins had accomplished that which she had so energetically conspired for in life.

It was after the funeral that the city detectives leveled their sights on Lila. They had questioned her and Dave in the beginning, but at that time their questions had been perfunctory. They had been confident of a quick solution then, but now they were baffled. No evidence of rape, assault, or robbery; a purely senseless crime, it would seem. The police sought to dredge some inkling of a motive out of Lila.

Upon their return the detectives were disconcerted by Lila's apparent determination not to help them. They asked Lila to go with them to the scene of the crime to see if she could detect anything missing or disturbed. She refused, saying that she had never entered Pigmeat's bedroom. When the officers mentioned force, Lila calmly stated that she would keep her eyes closed for as long as they forced her to remain in Pig's bedroom.

All but one of the detectives gave up in disgust. The one who remained was officially assigned to the Ward because it was well known that he understood Negroes and was their friend. The lone detective sighed and started all over again.

"Now see here, Lila, who was Pigmeat's boy friend?"

"She don't hab no juntlemon."

"Whadya mean by that?"

"She ain't hab none."

"She was a mighty purty gal." He sought to be fatherly. "Boys liked her, didn't they?"

"Yassum."

"Now if Pigmeat was a real purty gal and in good health she hada have somebody."

"Why mek so?"

"She hadda sleep with somebody."

"Dat a lil bed she got."

"It was not neither. Now see here, don't you want that murdering niggah caught?"

"He a nigguh?"

"She had a white man? Why didn't you say that before?"

"Say whut befo?"

"That she had a white man."

"Why mek so?"

"Because she did."

"She did?"

"Didn't you just say so?"

"Nossum."

"Well, what did you say?"

"Nuttin."

"She had to have somebody. How she get her money?"

"Whut money?"

327

"Money. Money! Live. How she live?"

"Wuk."

"Booker say she ain't worked in a dog's age."

"She go back iffen she need."

"Where'd the money come from when she didn't need?"

"Live on whut she sabe, I guess."

"Save? That was right much rent she paid there. Twenty, twenty-five dollars a month. That don't grow on trees."

"She paid twenny a month."

"That's right much for a single gal and you knows it. That's high rent in this town, black or white."

"Yassum."

"Yassum what?"

"Ah jes say: Yassum."

"How much you pay her?"

"Tree dollah a week."

"Even so, she got light and gas to pay. And heat to spend for and her clothes. Why that gal had more purty underdrawers and doodads than a white lady. Say, Pig ever work in the Heights?"

"Nossum."

"Them things look like they come from the Heights. Some black boy's got a job out there as butler or else, and he's been stealing the madam's clothes and giving them to Pigmeat. Thet's what."

He left so quickly he did not see the deadly venom in Lila's eyes.

The detective returned the next day. "I hear you and this here Pigmeat never been married," he began.

"Yassum."

"Why is that? Y'all got right smart age on yuz to be around so long and never marrying."

"Ah twenny, almost."

"Twenty? Why, gal, we got females here in the Ward having babies all over the place and they only fifteen, sixteen."

"Ah ain lak thet."

"Ain't like whut? Gal, I ain't said you wuz bad or nothing. I just say whut everybody knows. Colored gals starts out sooner than whites. Thass all I said."

Delilah had no comment.

"That Pigmeat went with a white man," he asserted.

"Nossum."

"You jes lying, cloaking for him. Thass mighty nice furniture she got there and she ain't had no bills due on it neither. Only a white man could afford that gal," he proudly stated. "Now what in the world she do to get him so mad?" he mused. "Maybe that colored boy that was stealing for her wanted to move in on that fine furniture and pretty yallar legs."

"Nossum."

"No sir, what?"

"Nossum everything you say."

"Wal, we're gonna get to the bottom of this thing yet. Who's this Dave Greene?"

"He my juntlemon."

"Juntlemon?"

"Friend-boy."

"You from South C'lina?"

"Yassum."

"How you come here?"

"Strain."

"I mean Why?"

"To go to collich." The answer once given surprised Lila. She had not realized that her yen for education was so near to the surface of her mind. The actual truth of the statement, or of any other statement that she gave to this man, was a matter of no consequence. Like all Gullah Negroes, Lila never thought of herself as lying to white people: she simply refused to share the truth with them.

"Thought you was a waitress?"

"Ah ain't sabed up enuff money yet."

"You a nice clean, intelligent gal; how come you ain't got one of them jobs out in the Heights? They got good jobs out there for smart colored gals."

A waitress in Booker's received four dollars weekly salary, plus tips that averaged well over three dollars a day. A girl in domestic service received eight dollars a week and no tips, and could not leave her job but one night a week. To inform this man of the true facts of life might anger him, Delilah thought, and so she said, "Ah doan got no refrunces."

"Smart gal like you is could get references easy. Why I'd be glad to say I knowed you."

"Tanky."

The man was perplexed; this girl did not fit, he was thinking. Not that she did not have manners and all. The girl was Vessey Street, and that made her available, but something was wrong. Upon reflection he decided that the girl, in many ways, acted as if she did not know that she was black. Gals like that cause trouble, he knew only too well.

"Who's Dave Greene?"

Delilah sensed that the man was intimidating her rather than questioning her. "He my boy friend. I tole you that one time already."

"What's he do?"

"He own the skating rink wid Kuhnul Eldrege." And that was Lila's form of intimidation. Poor white trash were reluctant to molest the Colonel and his close friends.

"Don't he own a gas station?"

"Yassum."

"Why didn't you say so then?"

"You doan ast."

Seeming to be inspecting the house for the first time, he asked, "He own this here house?"

"Ah dunno."

"So you don't know, eh? Where he get all this money from to be going inta business with? He's a young 'un ain't he?"

"Him twenny-nine. Him father a lawyer-man."

"Them lawyers gets rich sometimes. Everytime somebody die, the colored lawyer end up owning all of the property."

"Yassum."

"Ain't he in the nigger pool?"

"Wudda da?"

"That numbers game you people play."

"Ah doan gambling." Her eyes met the detective's. "Dave doan neider."

"Well, I know he got something to do with it, and it's gonna land him in a heap of trouble if he don't watch his step. Gambling's illegal."

"Yassum."

The detective nodded and walked out.

Delilah sat and pondered the ways of white folks. Colored folks, too, for that matter. Didn't folks know that they could not punish Pig's murderer? Human beings can only cripple and kill, but God can lay desolate a man's soul.

And He did.

26

The unforgettable summer of 1939 vanished into Labor Day weekend, and that Sunday morning Delilah was felled by an attack of appendicitis. In the hospital Delilah demurred any immediate wedding.

"I want to be strong and healthy, Dabe," she confided.

Lovestruck, Dave understood and tentatively mentioned Thanksgiving, but he insisted that then and there Lila was to start using his name. She agreed, and so from the day she left the hospital she was "Mrs. Greene" to the Ward. There was not a single snide smile on the Block; the Ward has never insisted upon inspecting the marriage license of its neighbor.

Before she was fully recuperated, Lila investigated the course of action suggested by Cokey. She found that she need pay only tuition fees to attend any classes of her choice at the Ward's topflight Catholic high school. She enrolled for typing, English, and bookkeeping. She dismissed all thoughts of attending college now. Lila was too honest to shelter delusions even about herself.

The Ward gradually forgot the tragedy of Pigmeat, and so did the police. Blueboy remained the benevolent despot of the Square

Table, having recruited new faces to replace the old. This fact alone dissuaded Dave from appearing at the table, although Lila never returned to Booker's after Pig's funeral. It was Dave's conservative nature that caused him to stay away. He disliked the idea of the new faces even if he had contemned the old. His virtual resignation, coupled with her own silent perseverance, enabled Lila to achieve her goal of reducing Dave's consumption of liquor by fifty per cent.

It was a pleasant morning in the pleasantest of worlds when Dave heard a familiar voice talking to Blueboy at the front door.

"Jes got back from the fair. Was you there?"

"Bout time," Blueboy grumbled. "The damn thing's been closed a month or more."

"Cokey." Dave bellowed and bounded out of bed and down the stairs.

Wherever Cokey had been, it was evident he had walked all the way back, but it was the same old Cokey, just the same.

"C'mon in the kitchen and rinse the dust of the road offen your tonsils, boy," Blueboy suggested. All three were asking questions without waiting for answers as they went back to the kitchen table.

"Cokey," Dave asked during a brief interval of silence, "did you know that Pig is dead? Murdered?"

The boy made an unearthly sound in his throat. Dave and Blueboy stood up, sure that Cokey had fainted, but somehow he regained his composure and weakly reached for a drink. "When?" he whispered. "How?"

"Blip passes by the house at two or so in the morning, and sees the front door open and the light burning in the hallway, but he don't think too much about it then. He's taking some chick home, see?" Blueboy said. "Well, about a coupla hours later he comes back the same way and sees the door's still open, at four in the morning. So naturally he gotta stop and see if things are okay. Mebbe there's sickness or something. Who knows?

"So he goes up and rings the bell and when nobody answers, he walks in, yelling for Pigmeat and Lila. He gets no answer, but Pig's room is at the end of the hall and the door is halfway open kinda. So he peeks in and there is the poor girl strangled in her sleep." Blueboy poured a drink to mark the end of his story.

"She told me," Cokey said in a whisper.

"Whaat?" Blueboy and Dave exploded in one volley.

"Graduation night. Remember, Dave? You and Lila went upstairs and for a while Pig got real philosophical and broody, but I thought I kidded her out of it, I guess. But it is just as clear as day. She

332

says to me: 'Cokey, I got a feeling I'm gonna need you one of these days soon. Real bad.'"

"Just like that?" Blueboy muttered.

"Yeah. And right out of the clear blue. And she said it was gonna be her own fault."

"What about Lila?" he asked. "Where was she?"

Dave smiled diffidently. "Here. We're on time now. She lives here. She never went back to the house on Macon. Won't even wear the clothes that was there. She's back in school now. We were supposed to get married Labor Day, but she had to have an appendix operation."

"Appendectomy," Blueboy informed them.

"Well, anyhow," Dave said, "you and Blueboy can fight it out to see who is gonna be the best man this Thanksgiving."

"I am the best man, but if Blueboy is gonna run out in the backyard and eat worms, I'll be only too glad to let him try to stand in my shoes."

"Boy, there ain't been nothing but peace and quiet around here since you left," Blueboy said. "You better watch your teeth. Ain't no sense losing 'em on my account."

With morbid realism Cokey saw that Blueboy had aged since his departure. His voice had lost its timbre and his complexion was dulled as if he had powdered his face with some ghastly gray substance. But for old times' sake he jibed: "Is you turning white, Blueboy?"

"I'm gonna lynch you yet, boy, and I ain't gonna do it quick and kind like a Georgia cracker when I do it either!"

"I just asked," Cokey drawled naively. "Seems like you is a shade or two lighter than when I left. Now if you is gonna turn white, I want to be the first to know. You hear me? I wants to *know* already. Because I don't want to come walking down the street and here comes this funny-looking little white man who says that . . ."

"Git him out," Blueboy screamed. "Git him out, I say." He stood up, trembling with joy and shook his finger in Dave's face. "He's your goddam buddy. Git him out. The last time he was here it cost me a thousand dollars when he done everything but chop a hole in the goddam roof. Git him out, or give him a goddam bath. He stinks."

"You guys really know how to serve breakfast to a guy with a headache," said Dave.

"What you want me to say?" Cokey asked. "That Blueboy is blacker than ever?"

"I'm gonna chop your goddam wig," Blueboy squealed. "It's a good thing I like you, boy. Or mebbe I would kill you."

333

"That makes me feel real good," Cokey replied. "That's awfully white of you, old man."

Dave burst out laughing. Cokey was just the tonic that Blueboy needed. He had not heard Blueboy yelling about the house for a long long time. It seemed that he had been so selfishly happy with Delilah that he had neglected his best friend.

"Go wash your face, boy," Blueboy said.

"Go in my room and get a pair of pants and underwear," Dave told Cokey. "Take what you want; makes no difference."

As soon as Cokey left them, Blueboy tried to look bored and unhappy. "So I guess we gotta give the tramp a room and a job?"

Dave grinned. "Hell yes. He's smart and everybody can use more brains around, but I'd hire the guy even if he was as dumb as you. I like him around."

"Lila's gonna be wild about it, too, I bet."

"Damn right. Only I hope she don't bug him with those lessons of hers."

"Lila never bugged anybody in her life; she don't know how," Blueboy said stoutly.

"I ain't nobody?"

"You don't count," Blueboy said with supreme candor. He went into the office that had once been the library and returned in a few moments with two canvas money bags. They were heavy and made a loud sound when he flung them on the kitchen table. He sat down and grinned.

Cokey returned, looking like a different person. They sat drinking and reminiscing until Blueboy said, "C'mon, boy. Let's take a ride. Bring them bags with you."

He got up and walked out ahead of Cokey. They went to Blueboy's huge LaSalle parked in front of the house. The little man handed the car keys to Cokey. "You drive, son, if you don't mind," he said, in an oddly unfamiliar sort of way. Cokey took the keys and walked around to the other side of the car. Once the big car was gliding down the street, Cokey turned his head to look at Blueboy, but the rocky little fellow was staring straight ahead, submerged in some thoughts of his own.

"You want this car?" Blueboy asked.

"What's wrong, Blueboy?"

"Nothing's wrong. You can have it; I don't want it. I never drove much anyhow and now I'm getting a middle-aged spread, I gotta walk more."

Cokey smiled dutifully, but he knew that Blueboy was a very weary if not sick man. "Tell you something, Blueboy. Now I can't afford this buggy, but as long as I'm in town, you got yourself a personal chauffeur. Okay?"

"Guess you win that one, boy."

"What bank we going to?"

"Turn right and go out Wall to Orange Street, and then park anywhere you can. I'll be okay after that."

Wall Street ran through a quiet white neighborhood for over a mile. After that it became the East End business district, with Orange Street being the main thoroughfare. But for half a mile or more between the houses and the business district there was an unpopulated stretch of roadway. The two friends were chatting aimlessly as they approached the empty stretch of road. A police car pulled alongside Cokey, and one of the two officers motioned for them to stop. Cokey braked the car to a stop on the grass shoulder of the road. The patrol car parked behind them bumper to bumper.

One policeman approached on each side of the car. "Hi 'ya, boy?" the one on Cokey's side said genially. "Nice fall day, ain't it? Seems like spring. You know, you forgot to stop for that stop sign back there."

Cokey knew immediately what was up. There were no stop signs on Wall Street.

"You know better than to turn into this street like that," the officer at Blueboy's window said.

Blueboy cleared his throat. "Now doan thet beat all?" he chuckled. "Bat dis ole eyeball one minit and this fool black boy done gone and broke the white capn's law."

Cokey almost burst into tears. This was a sad caricature of the old Blueboy. Blueboy wasn't even trying, he saw. Only six months ago, Blueboy would have been out of the car prancing about, laughing and talking a mile a minute, and the cops probably would have forgotten what they had stopped them for in the first place.

"Where you going, Blueboy?" the largest cop said suddenly. "This ain't your neighborhood."

Blueboy turned to Cokey. "See dat? See dat?" He turned to the policeman. "Now who'da thought that you folks woulda known old Blueboy, jes like that?"

"What's in them bags, Blueboy?"

Blueboy grinned. "Got money writ all over them, look like. What can I do for you gentlemen?"

The officer on Blueboy's side hitched up his pants. "Okay, Blueboy," he said at last. "Take them bags and put them in the patrol car."

Cokey gritted his teeth but knew better than to speak. He wondered why these cops were taking so long to carry out their intended theft. It made him nervous, and he reflected that they must be scared, therefore, dangerous. He tried not to look worried.

"I ain't moving," Blueboy said.

The declaration astounded all three of Blueboy's listeners.

"What you say, Blueboy?" the cop said.

"You want them bags. Take 'em yourself. You want to give this boy a ticket. Write it. But me? I ain't moving."

"Now you're under arrest."

Cokey looked at the officer on Blueboy's side and was frightened by what he saw. The man's face was the color of a beet except for a hard circle around his mouth where the flesh was a weird, putty-looking white.

"Arrested for what?" Blueboy demanded, staring through the windshield.

Without a word of warning the big officer opened the car door and grabbed Blueboy by the arm.

In a trance, Cokey saw it all in a hellish slow-motion movie. Blueboy left the seat and went into the air like a rag doll. Cokey heard the body hit the ground and then he saw the cop kicking Blueboy in the pit of the stomach. And now he could only see the head and shoulders of his friend who lay on the ground, retching violently.

A viselike grip on his own shoulder brought Cokey out of his trance. He turned to the officer and cried out: "Let me put the bags in the car. Blueboy's sick. He can't do it. Please, let me do it."

But the cops ignored him. It was too late. Already, curious motorists were slowing down to view the proceedings. When Cokey realized that the men's prize was lost, his terror returned.

Blueboy was on his knees now, still vomiting. And Cokey prayed that his friend would now be as cowardly as he was. Death was only a word or two away.

"Blueboy's too drunk for us to let him go," the cop told Cokey, who nodded mutely, knowing that for the rest of his life that he must live with his cowardice. But why should he and Blueboy die over a bag of money that did not belong to either of them? But he knew that that was only an excuse; he had been cut, and the whole world would soon know it.

"You go on home now and behave yourself," one of the cops told Cokey.

Shamefaced as he was, Cokey had to admit that there was wisdom in the command. Talk and threats of the NAACP could do no good;

336

Blueboy was under arrest. There was only one thing to do: Get Dav.
He prayed as he drove that, for once, Blueboy would remain silent.

Dave winced at the sight of Cokey. The kid's face was bathed
in sweat and tears and his eyes approached madness.

"They got him. They took him away from me and almost killed
him," he sobbed.

"Blueboy? Who? Talk sense." It was a cold and fatal voice that
Cokey never dreamed Dave possessed. It was the voice of a man who
would kill him instantly if he did not stop blubbering. This knowledge
eased Cokey's hysteria and between sobs, he told his story.

"Let's go." Dave took the wheel and decided to go directly to the
station house.

He entered the dirty brick police station with misgivings. It would
have been a whole lot smarter to have brought a lawyer along,
but this was a race between Blueboy's mouth and brutality. A desk
sergeant beckoned to him as soon as he entered.

"Over here, Greene," the officer called. He slid a printed form
across the desk and indicated the place for Dave to sign.

Dave was too used to cracker cops to even bother about reading
what he was asked to sign.

"That's twenty-two-fifty, and you can have the prisoner. He can
appear in court next Tuesday, and if he is found not guilty, you get
your money back. If he don't appear, then you forfeits this money
here."

Still not trusting himself to speak, Dave silently passed over the
money and picked up his receipt.

"That's a bad boy you got there," the officer said blandly.

Startled, Dave looked around to see if Cokey had followed him
into the station house. "Who?"

"Why that goddam Blueboy. Craziest nigger we had in here in a
long time. Never dreamed he was a bad actor. Nearly bit one of my
men's fingers off," he said proudly.

Dave moved over to a corner of the room and waited for them
to produce his friend. Vomit churned in his stomach at the sight of
Blueboy, bloody and defeated.

"The yellow bastards held me," Blueboy sobbed brokenly as if
to explain it all. "I wasn't even a man no more, Davey. They held
me."

"It's okay. Don't talk now. Don't worry. Everything's all right
now." He half carried the battered remains of his friend to the car.

Cokey took one look at Blueboy's eye and whispered, "My God."

It was Blueboy's left eye and it was a thing alive, darting about
in its own pool of blood.

337

"Hurry up and get us to a hospital," Dave said, "The colored one." He took the weeping Blueboy in his arms and held him like a baby.

They placed him on the critical list as soon as he was admitted, and it was ten days before Dave could bring him home. Lila silently rose to the occasion. She knew her task was to nurse her friend back to buoyancy.

Without fanfare, Cokey assumed Blueboy's duties as chief operator of the bank. What paperwork he was not able to perform, Delilah took home with her and did beside Blueboy's bed.

One day Blueboy said, "Why you sitting here all the time, little gal? I ain't dying."

"I like your company, Blueboy. Besides, it's just as comfortable in here as anyplace else. You don't mind me and you know it."

Blueboy smiled and closed his eyes for a few moments. A little later he said, "What you gonna do?"

"Do? Who do, Blueboy?"

"You and Dave," his voice was lucid and reasonable, but Lila could make no sense of his meaning.

"You're tired, Blueboy. Go to sleep. Just close your eyes and rest awhile."

"This is not the time to stint."

"Yes, Blueboy. Now you rest awhile. I think you're tired."

He chuckled as if to himself alone the joke was known. *"Quae nocent docent,"* he said just before he closed his eyes.

Delilah was concentrating on the fouled-up tally sheet she was trying to straighten out, and so it was a half hour later when she realized that Blueboy was dead.

338

27

Dave was betwixt and between. As much as he disliked the flamboyant manner in which the Ward buried the dead in the sporting life, he felt that the Block deserved a chance to have its last say over the remains of his friend. After all, Blueboy had been a leading citizen and the generous friend of the entire community. Dave also knew that Blueboy's mother was waiting in St. Louis to receive the body of her only child.

"Blueboy blonx to his maw," Lila said. "He blonx to the Ward, too, but not in death. You take him to his maw."

It never crossed Dave's mind to debate the issue once Lila had spoken. He nodded his head in assent and went downstairs to call the undertaker. Then he went into the kitchen and joined Cokey. Cokey was staring at the wall.

"Cut it out, fella," Dave said. He poured a drink and downed it.

"I got the heebee-jeebees. I can't stop thinking," Cokey complained. "All I got is crazy thoughts."

"Don't we all?" And Dave sat silent and succumbed to his own sad thoughts.

Cokey had been thinking about graduation night and Pigmeat's

339

ervation that the people in this house lived so easily. Now it
would seem that they were dying just as easily, but he did not
intend to upset others by airing his thoughts.

"I heard you on the phone," he said to Dave. "You taking Lila
with you?"

"You think you could manage the bank alone?"

"All depends on how you look at it. I sure in hell can keep on
doing what I been doing. Is that good enough?"

"What you been doing these past few weeks is good enough for
me, but mebbe I better stick to what ole Blueboy always said."

"What's that?"

"It always takes two to break the law."

"Come again?"

"Raid. Anything. You locked up, you want your right-hand man
on the outside. Pulling strings, raising bail, getting lawyers, watching
the dice—everything."

"Yeah. I see what you mean."

Delilah came in and sat down at the table. "Dabe?"

He looked up. "Yeah?"

"They nail him in a box or what?"

"To St. Louis? I guess so. I don't know much about these things."

"Ah been thinking, Dabe. This heah house blonx to Blueboy.
This ain't your house, Dabe. Not for sure. This house blonx to
Blueboy."

"What do you mean, Lila?" he said gently.

"It was a long, long time ago when you didn't used to lub me.
Ah remember him saying he gonna throw rocks at Mist Bookey's
windows."

And it did seem like a long long time ago. He placed his hand
on hers. "You want me to bring Blueboy home here?"

"Till he ready to go to his Maw."

"Tomorrow afternoon, I guess we'll leave." Dave went into the
hall to telephone the undertaker again.

"Come, Cokey. Help me fix the front room for Blueboy."

Cokey wasn't much help. Lila did things so swiftly and purpose-
fully that he felt useless just watching her. Something seemed odd
to him and so he asked, "How long you been planning this?"

"Planning what, Cokey?"

"You're putting everything exactly where you want it. Just as if
you'd already planned it."

"Oh," she said, understanding. "I did it once before already for
Pigmeat."

"Here? Here in this room is where they laid Pigmeat out? here?"

"Cokey, what is wrong wid you? She Dabe's fren. My cou Why mek you act this way?"

"Nuthin," Cokey mumbled and went back into the kitchen for . drink. He tried to make his mind behave in a logical, well educated way; but for Pigmeat's corpse to have been laid out in the very room she had prophesied her death was just a little too unearthly.

"Dave," he said. "Do you realize that Pig and Blueboy died unnecessarily?"

"If you're alive it's necessary to die. What the hell are you talking about anyhow?"

"Their deaths were so crazy."

"You're crazy. Take a drink."

"I ought to go help Lila," Cokey murmured.

"She knows what she's doing," Dave said with a morose kind of pride. "And she's stronger than you think; she don't really want no help."

"Dave," Cokey said desperately. "Blueboy didn't have to die. I mean he couldn't have got beat up at any other time. No. I mean that at no other time would those cops dared to have stopped us. Only on that kinda lonesome stretch. It was nobody's fault. Not really."

"Blueboy was murdered during a holdup. Don't try to tell me different."

"But he could only have been murdered at that particular moment," Cokey insisted. "It was only at that moment that he didn't feel like being pushed. Five minutes either way and he wouldn't have minded putting those bags in the policemen's car. Any other day."

"Sure. Any other day he wouldn't have been going to that particular bank. The whole thing was planned. Premeditated. They killed Blueboy because he threw a monkey wrench in their plans. When you're black you walk with death and there's no use trying to make a Square Table topic out of it."

The doorbell rang, and Dave went to answer it. Cokey sat and listened. They were bringing Blueboy's body in. He poured a drink to steel his nerves.

Lila came in, and he asked her, "Don't you have to show them what to do?"

"They knows," she sighed. "What'd Pig tell you, Cokey?"

"Dave told you?"

"Yes. What did she really mean, Cokey?"

341

on't you think she needed me when that guy was choking her
death?"

Delilah was silent for a long time. Finally she said, "You and
Dave 'fraid to die."

"Well, who isn't?"

"I'm not."

Cokey started. "Huh?"

"Come. The body be ready."

Hand in hand they went to view Blueboy. The embalmer had done
a masterly job. It was an ironic-looking Blueboy. His lips protruded
more than they had in life. He looked just on the verge of yelling
at someone. The casket was bronzed, and half the Ward would call
it solid brass, while the other half insisted it was gold.

When the hearse drew up in front of the house, word was passed
all over the Ward. Slowly, sometimes quietly, sometimes drunkenly,
sometimes in rags and sometimes in silk, the Ward crept to Blueboy's bier. The black granite of his corpse summoned them all.

Flick the Kid, weeping piteously, was the first to come. He was
followed by the two patriarchs of the Block, Colonel Eldrege and
Mr. Booker. They sadly gazed upon the remains of this young man
of almost sixty years. After that Makepeace, Blip, and Randy
arrived, and in no time at all, Dave and Delilah had a full-blown
wake on their hands. The Knights of the Square Table took over the
kitchen table, and soon even the upstairs rooms were packed with
mourners.

The Ward did not give Blueboy his final rites, but his wake
lasted for four days. It ended in the Lil Savoy at about the same
time Dave was watching his friend's casket being lowered into its
final resting place in St. Louis.

It had been finally agreed that Dave alone would accompany the
body home. Mrs. Harris was a wonderful surprise. She looked like
Blueboy masquerading in a long black dress. The mother and son
could easily have been taken for brother and sister.

"Thank you for bringing my son home, Dave," she had said in a
voice soft as Delilah's.

"He was my best friend. He was more than a brother or father to
me."

"I know. He writ and tole me so. He was a good son, Blueboy
was."

Dave spent most of that day sitting on the verandah of the
small home. The undertaker's men had been forced to remove the
front window to maneuver the casket into the parlor. Mrs. Harris

342

joined Dave from time to time, but their conversation was impersonal and slow. Dave was lonely and out of place.

It was almost eight o'clock at night, and the funeral would be held the next day. Dave and Mrs. Harris were again sitting on the front porch, almost level with the ground. It was hot and they both rocked slowly, companionably. Inside the house muted sounds made by Mrs. Harris' friends rose and fell.

"How come Blueboy never came home?" Dave asked. It was the presence of only Mrs. Harris' friends that had evoked the question. Where were the friends of Blueboy's youth?

"I thought you would have knowed. Blueboy thought he couldn't. I guess I kept him scared."

"But he had friends, didn't he?"

"Guess Blueboy was too young to have funeral attending friends. You see, Blueboy cut this white man something turble one day. It was on a trolley car. The poor man had to jump out the window of the trolley and it was still moving. Course Blueboy hadn't oughta done it. Bad talk never hurt nobody, but he was only a child. Fifteen. And he was trying to be manly, I guess."

"Are you sure Blueboy cut him?"

"Nobody thought to lay a hand on him and he come running home to me and he's justa crying. And I knowed there was only one thing to do. I give him three dollars. 'Twas all I had to my name. Don't know why I was saving it, but you never can tell when you might need. Then Reverend Jones, next door here—he's dead now—well, the reverend hitched up his horse and waggin and he drove Blueboy all night. He drove till that horse wouldn't take another step. And then Blueboy crawl outa that waggin bed and scoot. We never see Blueboy alive again."

"No?"

"It's the Lord's will for colored folks to love their children different from white folks. Never know when your flesh and blood gotta sneak away in the night."

"Did Blueboy write?"

"Yass, he did. Soon as he got to Chicago he had a young girl named Georgia Brown write and give me news."

Cruel memories flooded his mind and he was thankful for the dark. Smooth, handsome Georgia Brown. The touch of Didi's tiny hand in his. All the hell raised in all those devilish places.

"Georgia Brown," he murmured. "I know her."

"Yass. And she is a fine Christian, that chile. Cause a few years later Blueboy, hisself, writ—he was in the Navy then—and he tole

343

me how Georgia picked him up outen the street, and he all raggedy and dirty."

"Ummn. That's what Blueboy said?"

"Yass. After you and Blueboy started doing real good he sent me a registered letter with a thousand-dollar bill in it, and he say to mail it to this address he had in that letter to Georgia when he die so that she would be sure to come to his funeral."

"You did?"

"Why you just know I did. She shoulda been here 'fore now, but I jest know she coming."

In the dark Dave rocked and tried to recall past conversations. Never had Blueboy intimated any feelings of debt to Georgia Brown. Why? It was not like Blueboy, but neither was cutting a man. Blueboy had been a gentle man. Noisy? Yes. But nobody had ever been afraid of Blueboy. Respected, but not feared. That was Blueboy. He was not a knife man, and yet.

He did not want to see Georgia Brown. Her coming here would make everything final. Not only Blueboy's life, but his own. To Dave, the bank, success, the days of travel and fun, and Georgia even, formed a curious whole. Each belonged to the other. He and Blueboy had always planned to revisit all the wild old places in triumph. And that would be when they finally knew that they had lived a complete and successful life. But now the wild old places were sending Georgia Brown to tell him not to bother. All was gone.

Didi, Becky, Babylon, Pages, and Kootchies.

Even Kelly and Blueboy.

Georgia Brown was the messenger of Death.

Only Lila and Cokey remained.

Mrs. Harris rose and said that she was going inside for a spell. Dave stayed and brooded. A terrible agony of recall struck him and he ached with loneliness. He was back in the hospital and it was three days since Blueboy had been admitted, and his first day of real clarity.

"We did it all wrong, Davey-boy," Blueboy had whispered hoarsely. "We made a terrible mistake and we're gonna have to pay for it."

"What? What mistake?"

"Politics," Blueboy said. "We could have gone all the way. We was two-bit and didn't even know it. We could have paid everybody's poll tax. We could have owned the governor. We had the key."

"But we always agreed not to go into politics."

Blueboy raised his hand to silence Dave. "I was so glad to get away from white people, I plum forgot. I forgot that white folks

344

is still here. We forgot we was operating in America. You p
your freedom. Henry Ford never got a ticket for speeding,
Leastways, not in Detroit.

"We was chintzy, Davey-boy," Blueboy went on. "We forgot
had to live with crackers. And we never looked at the future." r
shot a long, hard look at Dave. "Niggers. Numbers. You realiz
they're forever?"

"No," Dave replied. But Blueboy was asleep.

A taxi stopped in front of the house. It was Georgia Brown.
Dave stepped off the porch to meet her.

Georgia's kiss was fond and warm. "Oh, Dave, I'm so sorry for
you," she breathed. "It was such a beautiful friendship."

"No more than you two."

"You knew we were friends for years, Dave."

"No, I didn't, Georgia," he said, fumbling for some words that
would take the jealousy out of his voice. "I only thought you were
like drinking buddies, not true friends."

"Dave," Georgia exclaimed. "We are standing here like two geese,
and Mrs. Harris is inside waiting."

They went through the house to the kitchen. "I'll look on Blueboy later," Georgia said.

"You are Georgia Brown," Mrs. Harris said. "My boy loved
you and I thank you for coming."

"Yes, ma'am," Georgia said. She bent and kissed the smooth
black brow. "Thank you so much for the letter. It has been a
long time since I've seen your writing, but I recognized it right
away."

"Time I got Dave's telly-gram I knew exactly what to do, and I sat
right down and done it. That was the very same bill Blueboy sent
to me, Georgia."

"You do your own writing?" Dave asked, mildly surprised.

"Yass, Dave, I can write pretty good." Her eyes were very kind.
"You see, I was only fourteen when the boy was born, and so I got
no schooling after that, but where others might forget their learning,
I had to write my boy cause I couldn't trust nobody else at first.
Later, when it didn't matter so much, I kept on doing my own writ-
ing."

"She has a lovely hand," Georgia said. "You two stay here and
talk while I go in to Blueboy."

The funeral was small and dignified and exactly the way Dave
wished it to be. He was glad that circumstances had robbed the
Ward of an opportunity to stage one of its circuses.

It was not until that night that Dave and Georgia had a chance

intimately. It was just after dark and the fall night was
ot, but Georgia was as cool and unruffled as ever.

lueboy left everything very tidy," Dave said, with a feeling
guilt. He knew that if he should die tomorrow his affairs would
a disgrace. No will, no insurance, businesses in fictitious names.
Nothing but money.

"What about the bank, Dave? Were you and Blueboy really
partners?"

"No. He worked for me." Would Georgia believe him? Now
that his best friend was gone it seemed impossible, wrong even,
that they had not been partners. "I wanted him to be," Dave said,
"but he absolutely refused."

"Know why?"

"No, I don't, Georgia. Sometimes I got the impression Blueboy
loved comfort and friends but was kind of leery of being rich.
Although he did leave his mother more than she'll ever be able to
spend."

"Are you really rich, Dave?"

"Yeah, Georgia," he said with a funny kind of a sigh. "I been
real lucky. Nothing but money in a way."

"I've been lucky too," Georgia said. "For a while there, I had so
much money I didn't know what to do with it." She lit a cigarette
and tossed the burnt-out match over the porch railing. "Dave, do
you know I own two apartment houses in Chicago, that if I was
crazy enough to move into either one of them it would cause a
race riot? Even the doormen are white."

Dave laughed and made a mental note to buy some apartment
houses in Chicago. "You still operating?" he asked.

"What else is there for me to do? My girls and my clients are
the only friends I have." There was a period of silence that they
shared equably. "God gave us the brains to make it," Georgia said
softly, "but he forgot about us enjoying it."

"I wouldn't say all that."

Georgia's laugh was an offhanded sort of thing, and yet there
was pure friendship in its notes. "I'll bet you a dollar to a doughnut
that neither you or Blueboy have been two hundred miles from
that hick town and its—what do you call it?—the Ward?"

Dave realized that Georgia was close to the truth. Save for that
waterhaul trip to Billy Bowlegs' town, and then later to Chicago,
he had not been fifty miles from the Ward. And with only the
slightest of exaggerations one could say that Blueboy had never left
the Ward since he arrived in the city.

To change the conversation he asked, "How did you and Bi
happen to meet?"

"It was the damnedest thing," she said. "Here was this di
ragged little black spasm, and his lips were poked out just as if
was saying: *'I ain't hungry! Mind your own business!'* He looked so
brave and, I guess, frightened, that I just walked over to him and
put my arm around his shoulder and led him into a real cheap
cafeteria."

She reached over and rested her hand on Dave's knee. "I don't
believe anybody else in the world could have done it. I can only say
that we must have recognized something in each other, loneliness,
maybe. The kind when you don't have anybody.

"You know, Blueboy wasn't much younger than I was, but he
was so tiny then that I thought he was a child. And, Lord, Dave,
you should have heard the whopper he made up to make me think
he was a man."

"You mean about cutting a white man? He wasn't lying."

"Blueboy never cut anybody in his life," Georgia said flatly.
"Twice Blueboy has just about saved my life. I knew that man.
He was a maniac with his fists, but not a knife man. I know
better than most."

"Were you and Blueboy ever real tight?"

"We loved each other. We were never lovers. I was a street-
walker then, Dave. When I got in after a night's work, I guess he
thought I was too tired." She closed her eyes as if in prayer. "I've
never had a lover. Neither has Blueboy, I think. Funny," she murmured.

They smoked and rocked awhile, each to his own memories.

"Dave?"

"Yeah?"

"Don't you really know why Blueboy wouldn't be your partner?"

"Hell no. Who does?"

"You would have made him sit around while you did all the work,
wouldn't you? If you were partners I mean."

"After all, I was the youngest. It would only be right."

"The other way, he had a good time running all over the place,
giving orders, bossing you even."

Dave had to grin in the dark as Georgia explained it.

"If you didn't like what Blueboy did you could always fire him,
or he could quit. But partners. Well, it's messy dissolving a partnership."

"So that's it," Dave murmured. "It's plain as day now. Funny
I never figgered it out for myself."

347

ueboy," Georgia said the name sadly. "You're going to miss
."

But there was Delilah.

Dave thought about her, and suddenly he wanted her desperately. He needed her. He had to get good and drunk. And then only in her arms could his tears wash away the ache.

He stood up and peered at his watch. "C'mon, Georgia, and walk me to the drugstore. I want to call up and see about the next train home."

Silently, Georgia Brown rose and took his arm. Together they walked down the brick paved street.

28

Dave did not drink any whiskey during his stay in St. Louis. He could not trust his emotions; it would have been so very easy to become messy, a disgrace to his iron-willed friend. But once the plane headed for home, he opened a bottle of whiskey and drank all through the flight. The pint was gone when he reached the city. He took a cab directly to the house on Gay Street.

Delilah was at school, as he very well knew, since he had not bothered to send a telegram telling her of his arrival. He found the empty house unspeakably depressing. To reinforce his feeling of being unwanted, he refused to call either the flower shop or the countinghouse, all the while knowing that one phone call would fill the house with companions. With whiskey glass in hand, he roamed the house, suffering in loneliness. Going into Blueboy's room he flung open the closet door and glared at the lifeless blue suits hanging there.

He left Blueboy's room in a hurry and went to the front room to the bar, downed a drink, and cursed Delilah for going to school today. He continued to drink and eventually began to appreciate the fact

e was not underfoot. He wanted to be alone and drunk for the
of his natural life.

e heard Delilah put her key in the lock of the front door and
found that he was too drunk to stand up. When she came into
ne front room her beauty mocked him as he realized he had
drunk himself impotent. His need for liquor had been far greater
than his need for her.

"Lo, Dabe." Her gentle voice was thankful.

"Hello."

She came and sat on the arm of his chair, and Blueboy's words
rang prophetically in his ear: It's a funny thing, but a man will
throw his wife out the window so he can drink in peace. Never in
hell has a real drunk ever thrown the bottle out the window and
grabbed his wife for a piece. Govern yourself accordingly, Davey-
boy. Dave shivered, but he motioned for Lila to refill his glass.

She did it wordlessly and then asked, "You want to talk about the
funeral now?"

"No."

"You want we should go to bed now?"

He reached down and picked up his glass. After a swallow he put
his free hand beneath her skirt and stroked the inside of her thighs,
but as her eyes still asked the question he pulled his hand away.

"Cokey moved," she said.

"Rats always leave a sinking ship, so what?"

"Dis ship ain't sinkin', Dabe. Nebah."

"Then what he leave for?"

"He's still working at the bank. And he stay wid me every night.
Only he heard about these four rooms and . . ." Her words dribbled
into silence. She saw that Dave did not wish to hear. And she was
glad that Cokey had moved and she would call him and tell him not
to come by this evening. Cokey was paid to run the bank, not to
humor Dave.

And in the days that followed it never occurred to her to bewail
her life's chosen task. She remained at Dave's drunken beck and
call twenty-four hours a day. She dropped out of school, never leaving the house. But her best was not good enough for Dave. Very
often her competence enraged him, and some days it seemed as if
his hand was constantly in Lila's face, spitefully punishing her for her
efficiency. Lila never flinched beneath the blows.

Once, after beating her, he was overcome with remorse and tried
to kill himself. Lila wrestled the bottle of Lysol from his grasp.
Another night he awoke screaming that Blueboy's mother had
tricked him when he was a boy. He decided to fly to St. Louis to

350

have Blueboy dug up and reburied in the backyard. He was
ing the police to ask their help when Lila coolly pulled the ▮
from the phone box.

The malady lasted three weeks and ended only because Dave
stomach rebelled. It refused to hold another drink. He would puke
up every drink he downed. The retching finally exhausted him and
he went to bed for good. Because his stomach would hold no more
whiskey, Dave succumbed to delirium tremors. Lila wept as she stood
and watched her man slip into insanity. She stared at him for a long
time before something ancient and sacrificial within her said to take
off her clothes and lie down with the raving man. She used her body
like a straitjacket, and for two days she held his sweating body in
her arms and scissor-locked his threshing limbs with her legs.

The delirium passed and he became a caged beast, longing for
a drink to quiet his raw nerves, but too weak to get up and get it.
Delilah used every trick God had given her sex to drain Dave of his
feverish energy. She tranquilized him with her entire body, not in
shame, but in the pride of knowing that she was at last conquering
his sickness.

Dave woke one morning and felt hungry, so he knew that he
was sober at last. It was a lovely day, and the sun's rays illuminated
Lila's sleeping face, making her more beautiful than ever. He
stroked her soft hair and wondered how any man, sane or mad,
could have made so gentle a creature suffer.

"Mawn, Dabe."

"I've been looking at you for a long time. I'm glad you woke
up."

"Dabe," she moaned. "Dabe. I thought you'd nebah stop dat
rotgut swilling."

"It's all over now," he soothed her. "Get up and put on your
clothes. You're going back to school today."

"Oh, Dabe, I lub you so."

Dave showered and shaved and was off to Booker's for breakfast. His next stop was the flower shop, where things looked exactly
the same only different. Since Cokey was a slightly more business-
like employee, he ran the bank more impersonally than Blueboy
had. There was a quiet air of efficiency about the place now, and
Dave was satisfied that Cokey was as fine a man as he could find
to replace Blueboy.

"Damn Sam. It sure is good to see you," Cokey said. "I thought
Lila had decided to keep you for herself. How is she anyway?"

"She's okay. Went back to school this morning," Dave said,
grinning.

351

nat's swell And now you just look around and see if everything
᠊ᴐ your satisfaction. And if it ain't, don't say a word. Fix it
urself."

The old routine with its new qualities engulfed Dave, and soon
even the passing of Blueboy receded into its proper perspective.
Lila never mentioned his debauch again save when she wished to
affix a certain date in his mind. Then she might say: "That was
right after St. Louis."

The money continued to roll in. One night Dave and Cokey
crammed one hundred thousand dollars in an old safe and buried
it in the cellar. Dave vetoed Cokey's suggestion to have a cement
floor laid over it. And one night while drinking in the Babylon
he explained: "Standing here in this bar, drinking, it might sound
silly, but we are in the Life. And as long as you're in the Life, your
own life ain't worth two cents. Now if anything should happen to
me I hope and pray that you're around to give Lila a hand. But no
matter what happens I want Lila to be able to put her hands on
that money without having to hire a damn blasting crew with big
mouths. That money is mine. And I don't want her to have to go
begging some white-assed revenue man for permission to spend it.
You follow me?"

"Yeah, I understand that completely," Cokey drawled, "but what
the hell's this crap about my life not being worth two cents? The
hell with your life. Just tell me why *mine* ain't worth two cents?"

As serious as Dave was trying to be, he had to smile. "You never
can tell when some nut is gonna take it inta his head that you are
the cause of his not hitting the numbers, and steps out of an alley
and starts blasting away at you. I hear that a damn fool killed a
banker in D.C. not long ago because his number didn't play one day."

"You know, as dumb as some of these darkies are, I don't think
I'm gonna advertise the fact that I'm Blueboy now."

"I been thinking. And I'm gonna assign you a bodyguard. You
want Blip-Blip?"

"You am crazy with de numbahs, boy! If a guy is crazy enough
to shoot Santa Claus, he only has to pull the trigger one more time
and shoot his bodyguard, too. Besides that," Cokey declared, "when
the shooting starts, that bodyguard is gonna be the lonesomest
sonofabitch in the Ward. Because *ah leffum!*"

This conversation took place the same evening that 967 came out.

29

They never knew what happened to their wedding plans. First, of course, was Lila's appendectomy. After that Blueboy's death made Thanksgiving inappropriate. Now a whole year had passed, and Dave and Lila were still unmarried. They simply forgot about it.

Fall 1940, and Dave Greene was no longer the boss of the Ward. Lila was. This amazing change took over a year, but it was during the summer of 1940 that the pattern became clear.

Never in her entire life did Lila ever ask Dave for money. She took what she wanted. And since theirs was a love without reservations, she could no more imagine Dave complaining abut the money she spent than she could imagine herself complaining if Dave took a sudden notion to kick her down the stairs.

Lila was a child of the Block. And her manner made her respected, and at the same time approachable by the lowest characters in the Ward. Whereas the numbers bankers in other cities did not allow their wives to mix freely in public places for reasons ranging from jealousy to a desire to raise the social standing of their spouses, Lila's love was unquestioned by Dave and he was tly satisfied with her social status quo, so the Ward's poor unfortunate felt free to approach her in public to plead their dition. Furthermore, Lila was increasingly more available and as absolutely dependable, while Dave became more and more unpredictable.

Never did Dave indulge in the drinking of oceans of whiskey as he had done upon his return from the burial of Blueboy, but he still was a tippler, and Lila had dissuaded him from carrying a huge and vulgar bankroll.

A person in need might ask Dave for a loan and he would be amenable, telling the person to meet him at a certain place and hour, but Dave was likely to get too drunk to keep the appointment, or he might forget about it all together. Far worse would be the times when Dave would feel sympathy for the borrower and would insist that the unhappy man drink with him for hours on end. As one citizen of the Ward put it: "Sure, anybody can borrow fifty bucks from Dave Greene any time you give him a good reason for need. But first you gotta get drunk with him. And who wants to stand around and help him lap up a quart of booze while your wife is waiting in the hospital, and they won't discharge her until you puts fifty dollars down on her bill?"

Lila did not drink, and her word was her bond, and so as time went by, she became the boss of the Ward. Take the story of Ernestine Boggs. Ernestine had a hard-working, weekend-drinking husband, who borrowed a friend's car one Saturday afternoon and was later arrested for drunken driving. It was a matter of one hundred dollars or one hundred days in jail. The Boggses did not have one hundred dollars, but they did have four small children who would be at the mercy of the Ward's charity if Jack Boggs remained in jail for one hundred days.

Jack had an employer who would fire him if he found out the true circumstances for Jack's absence from work, but Jack's job was secure if he returned to work within the next three days.

Julia Tucker, Ernestine's best friend, counseled her. "Ernestine, you ain't got no choice in the matter; you gotta go talk to Mrs. Lila Greene."

"Ain't no colored woman on earth gonna loan another colored woman money on just their word alone. And I ain't got no job. What I wants is for some man to go to the jailhouse and talk to Jack. And then Jack can show him how he's got a good job and all and can afford to pay back at five dollars a week or so. This ain't nothing no colored woman can help in. The women in this Ward what's got a hundred cash dollars you can count on your fingers and toes, and they ain't getting up offen it neither. Don't make no difference if she is some rich numbers nigger's woman. I bet she gotta account for every penny worse than I do. And you say she's young and pretty, too?"

"Listen, Teena, I know Lila. I worked with her in Booker's and she ain't got a soul in the Ward can say mean of her. Now I'm your best friend, why should I lie to you at a time like this? Now you go call her up and if you talk sense she'll arrange to meet you in Booker's."

"What's wrong with her fine house on Gay Street?"

"Lila's funny that way. She calls this 'she-she' business: just between you two women. You go to her house and Dave Greene's liable to have a houseful of men sitting around drinking and listening to the ball game. In Booker's it's just you and her sitting in a booth and drinking Coke. See what I mean?"

Ernestine's heart was not in it, but, as Julia had pointed out, she had no other choice. Her spirits rose a little when the quiet voiced and slightly foreign-sounding Mrs. Greene agreed over the telephone to meet her that very afternoon in Booker's.

Ernestine entered Booker's and her worst fears were confirmed; no one fitting the description of Mrs. Greene was waiting alone in a booth to meet her. Julia had said that Mrs. Greene was unmistakable. She would be the prettiest little thing in the restaurant. The only female sitting alone was a pretty little high school girl. It irritated Ernestine when the child beckoned to her, but worry had made her helpless and so she went to the child for no understandable reason.

"Come, sit," Lila said. "You must be Mrs. Boggs."

Ernestine sat down and burst into tears. If Mrs. Greene had not been able to make it, why had she sent her daughter to mock her?

"You gotta stop crying and tell me what you want," Lila said.

"You ain't no use to me," Ernestine sobbed. "I wants your Mawwwww."

"I am Mrs. Greene."

Mrs. Boggs astonishment bordered on terror. Mrs. Boggs knew from experience that children are not kind. She was convinced that this girl intended to play some kind of a joke on her. Of this she was certain and so she cried helplessly anew.

It was only after Lila had ordered two Cokes, one with spirits of ammonia in it for Mrs. Boggs, that the distraught woman finally came to believe that this was the woman she sought.

Ernestine Boggs got her one hundred dollars, and all was well. And Ernestine never tired of telling the story with the most artistic embellishments. This was only one of the many ways through which Lila gained stature as the true boss of the Ward during that hot summer of 1940.

It was during this same period that Lila fell in love with the voice of Marian Anderson, and this passion became her only real extravagance. In no time at all, Lila thought nothing of taking a plane flight to an Anderson concert more than five hundred miles away from the Ward.

This extravagance pleased Dave's vanity. In many ways it made his success a concrete thing. He liked to casually mention that his wife had left that afternoon for Chicago, but he expected her back before morning.

When Delilah took her sporadic plane trips she did not have the slightest idea that her appearance caused a flurry of comment and conjecture at the airport and on the plane. It was not her color alone that caused the curiosity. People always wondered how any little girl of any race could possibly be so impassive on what certainly must be their first flight unaccompanied by her elders.

It was impossible for these people to know that this was a twenty-year-old Geechie woman who lumped all manner of transportation together. Trolley, bus, train, private car or "Gawd hab mercy" (leaky rowboats that Gullah speaking Negroes use to get back and forth to the mainland) were all the same to Lila. She logically admitted that some modes of transportation were faster than others, but she refused to believe that one was any safer than another. When Gawd wanted you, you went and it didn't make any difference what you were riding in at the time.

That summer of 1940 was a mystery to Cokey. One year out of college and he was earning three times the salary of the white president of the University. Where the money went to was an entirely different matter. Undergraduates hit him up for money all the time, but their requests were minuscule. A quarter, fifty cents, six bits.

Another thing that worried Cokey was the sudden disappearance of all the pretty girls who had simply adored his company when he was a broke and carefree student. All were gone or married. In their places came working girls, hopelessly in debt, and teachers in possession of automobiles that needed expensive repairs.

Cokey's fertility had increased in direct proportion to his financial status. He must have financed wholly or in part, six abortions in the past twelve months. And like Dave before him, he was the target of crackpot entrepreneurs and inventors. He borrowed money to invest in a haberdashery, the first on Vessy Street. It lost money.

356

To recoup his losses he invested in a fish-fry restaurant. It burned down. A whole year had passed, but he was nearly as broke as the day he had returned to witness the tragic beating of Blueboy.

Cokey understood Delilah better and appreciated her brains more than anyone else in the Ward, including Dave. But even he was confounded to see the girl blossom into a financial genius of sorts. Lila's steely mind could not be distorted by wishful thinking. She recognized that the numerous small business ventures in the Ward were one-man operations and that it was not possible for two or more people to gain a livelihood from them. In view of this Lila would still back any and all ventures, but unlike Dave, she refused to accept partnership in any of them. Instead she demanded and got five dollars' royalty each week on her original investment.

"Cokey," Lila said one day, "we ain't gonna bury no more money even if we go to jail."

"What now, little girl?"

"I been thinking," she said slowly, "and if folks don't know what to do with money they ain't got no business with it. Remember Kelly?"

"Sure. Why?"

"I been thinking right much about her lately. I liked her. I truly did. She froward, but she nice. And she smart, that's the most impawtint thing. She was a chemist, wasn't she?"

"That's right."

"We gonna buy chemistry stocks and bonds from now on. And whiskey. In school they tell you what stocks is, but they don't bother to teach you how to buy them. You find out for me, Cokey."

"Okay. Will do."

"Before we is through we is gonna own stock in every chemistry company in the United States."

"As you like it," Cokey said absently. For he, too, was becoming immune to money as money. It was a bore. You had to count it, package it, and hide it, and yet you never had enough of it for your personal use. So what the hell good was money?

But even if he was not partial to money, he was curious. "You're investing money in chemicals just because you like a person who once studied chemistry and who might be working on the WPA now?"

"No. But there's a war coming, and them chemists makes everything that explodes, don't they? And they makes whiskey. Whiskey and war is always good business, ain't it? So I'm just glad that Kelly likes chemistry, too."

357

It was Christmas again before any of them realized it, and Dave and Lila still had not remembered to get married. Dave was simply unable to tear himself away from the Ward this particular Christmas. His college fraternity was holding its annual national conclave on the Campus. Dave had not made the fraternity, but he had been pledged to it at the time he left A&I to become a traveling waiter.

The local chapter of the fraternity had selected the Club Babylon as the downtown unofficial headquarters of the convention. This honor so pleased Dave that he had the club completely refurbished at a far greater expense than he could expect to profit.

In 1940 the Negro was still depressed, and a national convention of any Negro college fraternity was a pitiful thing to behold. But it did give the host city a chance to show off. For the Ward it meant an unending round of social affairs throughout the holidays.

Dave's search for respectability (Arkansas style) had been dormant since he first laid eyes on Kelly, but now the disease returned with a vengeance. Dave was secretly hoping that Nashville would send a delegate or two to the conclave. He hoped that they would be someone he had once known in Nashville, but that wasn't really necessary. The main idea was that he would be able to enter the festivities as a host. He could give predance dinner parties in honor of the Nashvillians as well as dawn breakfasts, teas, and whatnot. And not a damn soul in the Ward would be able to condemn his hospitality as social climbing.

And so it was that Dave impatiently awaited the twenty-seventh of December, but when the day arrived for the opening of the conclave, Dave was disappointed to learn that Nashville had not even sent a delegate. Down the drain went his secret plans of casually displaying his wealth. However, he did take to hanging around the Club Babylon more than usual in hopes that he would see some face from his A&I days.

It was the last day of the conclave and Dave wandered into the empty club about six in the evening. Joe, the bartender, poured a drink of Dave's favorite bourbon. He was accustomed to Dave's varying moods, and therefore did not attempt to start a conversation.

Two badge-wearing delegates came in and Dave promptly dismissed them as being college professors trying to relive their undergraduate days. These two were followed by a more likely-looking pair whose badges proclaimed the fact that they were from Chicago. Dave also noted that they were drinkers of bourbon, and so he motioned for Joe to place a quart on the bar, and soon the three of

358

them were in a friendly conversation that drifted from the Jones Boy.
to St. Louis Kelly, to Georgia Brown, to the race problem.

But of all the golden advice that Blueboy had lavished upon Dave,
the astute little fellow had forgotten to tell Dave never to ask a
stranger about a loved one. But even if he had, Dave probably would
have not heeded his advice this night, for he had been drinking all
day and now these two strangers from Chicago made him feel like
talking about Kelly. He asked if they knew her.

"Ole drunken Kelly Simms? You know her? That's right, I believe
she did say she went to school here. I know her well. Took her out
a couple of times. Pure juicehead. Works in a laboratory for the
state; plenty of free alky around." A sudden caution slowed his
tongue. "She's not a relative? I didn't think so," he said.

His companion said, "You should give the kid a break. After all,
she's got a lot of problems. Personally I admire her. She has guts
and cries on nobody's shoulder, or in their beer. Nor have I ever
heard of her bumming a drink from anyone. She and my sister
were damn good buddies until Sis got married, and I think I know
Kelly Simms just as well as the next man."

"You admire what? Her hollow leg?"

"Make up your mind, a girl with a hollow leg is one who drinks
and drinks and never gets drunk. You just said Kelly was a drunk.
So now just what is she?"

"If I owe an apology, she certainly has it, but I will never condone
the drinking habits of a dame who constantly has the smell of
whiskey on her breath."

"She does not drink all the time. That kid had a bout with TB
at one time, and her job demands that she take an X ray every six
months. I know that I would get drunk as I wanted to if every
six months I had to have an X ray and then sit around for ten days
waiting for a report to tell you if you're okay or if you've got to
spend the next four or five years in a sanatorium."

Dave wanted to tell these two men that they were not talking
about the same Kelly Simms he knew, but his lips were petrified.
He poured two drinks in succession and downed both of them

"Anybody that has TB has no right to touch alcohol" the first
man said. "And do you realize that she's going to lose her looks in
another year or so, at the rate she's going?"

"Sure. But the kid is mixed up. If Kelly would stop playing the
field and settle down in a good marriage she would be okay, but I
have a sneaking suspicion that Kelly is too proud to bring her
chronic TB to the bridal couch."

Suddenly Dave knew he was going to puke. He ran from the bar ıd down the stairs to the street, hoping the cold air would help ıim, but it didn't. He managed to make it to the curb before he started to puke his guts out.

Vomit arched out of his mouth in a seemingly endless stream. When the regurgitation finally stopped he was weak and badly in need of another drink. But he never wanted to see the inside of the Club Babylon again in his life. He would sell it to Colonel Eldrege in the morning, but right now he could only take care of finding another drink. He staggered across the street to the Lil Savoy, which he found to be completely empty. He ordered a pint of whiskey and began to sip slowly from the bottle.

He managed to sip almost half the pint without having another spell of vomiting. Then he began to use a glass. And somehow the glass reminded him that he and Kelly had drunk the last of their many farewell drinks right here in this bar. In his anguish he downed two drinks in succession and then let his mind dwell on Kelly.

But above all else he hurt. He hurt inside and out.

He alone had sent Kelly away.

No wonder a sheet of sadness covered her at times and took her away from him. And he had sent her away.

They had kissed, shared each other's food, and screwed all night long, and he was still as sound as a silver dollar.

Kelly had taught him everything else he needed to know, why the hell hadn't she taught him not to be afraid of TB?

But everything was clear now.

Kelly needed him.

And strangers in strange places were talking about her.

It was now necessary to make Kelly marry him to protect her good name.

His thoughts jarred against black granite: What the hell must he do with Delilah?

Delilah had to be made to understand.

But suppose she wouldn't understand?

She might even try to kill Kelly.

The crumbiest pimp on earth could keep two whores from fighting, but sorry-assed Dave Greene couldn't keep a slick little Geechie and a college bred genius from killing each other.

But the very idea of Lila harming Kelly filled Dave with a murderous fury. He picked up the remainder of the pint and walked out of the Lil Savoy. He had to find Cokey. Maybe he could get Cokey to marry Delilah. That was thinking. Yes. Cokey could marry Delilah, while he went to Chicago to save Kelly.

But Delilah was a selfish little bitch. Couldn't the little black fool

see he had to go marry Kelly? It was plain as day. But first he had t
go home and put Delilah out. No. First he had to go find Cokey.
Talk to him. And he hoped to hell that Cokey was sober. At least
as sober as he was. Funny how he had been drunk a moment ago,
but he was dead sober now.

And he was going to Chicago on the next plane.

Dave took the pint out of his pocket and drank from it until it
was empty, but it did not give him the lift that he needed. He
ordered another pint and put it in his pocket.

Funny.

He had just put a pint in his pocket and walked out of the Lil
Savoy, but now he was back and had just bought another pint.
Where had he been? He craftily took the pint out of his pocket
and furtively took a sip. He had to be careful not to get drunk. But
where had he been when he walked out of the joint a minute ago?

This time he made sure he knew what he was doing. He went
down to the street to the cab stand and took a taxi and gave the
cabby Cokey's address.

He had either finished the pint in the cab or left it on the seat
because Cokey took so long to open the door that he needed a drink
and didn't have one. And he was cold as hell.

This idea of being without a drink infuriated Dave so he tried
to kick Cokey's front door down, but all he did was hurt his toe.
Pain doubled his anger, and he yelled curses up at the second-floor
windows where Cokey lived. He spat on the porch and then went
down to the sidewalk, trying to make up his mind about the nearest
pad within walking distance, but he was too angry to think.

The hell with walking anyhow. Dave Greene wanted a drink, and
a goddam cab better hurry up and come by in the next two
minutes or else there would be hell to pay. He would call the police
and have every goddam cabby in town arrested and sued. And the
goddam police better give him a ride to a pad in a squad car.
They had an ass-kicking coming on account of Blueboy anyhow,
and now was just as good a time as any to give it to the mammy-
riding-white-bastards.

A horn tooted, and somebody called his name. He walked to the
car parked at the curb and saw it was Kid Flick. He got into the
car so clumsily that he struck his head against Kid Flick's shoulder.

"What's the matter, Dave? You in trouble?"

"Trouble? Kelly's dying and you sit here like a goddam dummy
and ask me if I got troubles? Take me to a goddam drink, you dumb
bastard. Move. Move this goddam car. How many times I got to
tell you? You deaf?"

Drunken hysteria carried Dave's words up into a high, womanish register, creating a weird effect that completely unnerved the Kid Flick. He sat motionless, staring through the windshield, making no effort to start the car.

"This is my goddam car, ain't it? Get the goddam thing moving before I kill you."

Flick the Kid nodded mutely, and the car shot forward on its way to the Club Babylon. Dave cursed all the way.

When they reached the club, Dave took the stairs two at a time.

"Gimme wisty," he yelled to Joe. "Gimme the bottle; I don't want no just one drink."

For the next thirty minutes Dave stood alone at the bar and drank. And during those thirty minutes Dave was not drunk; he was transported. Carried to some magic space just outside a world inhabited only by Kelly Simms. It was just as though he was standing outside of a house and peeping through the window at her.

She saw him and smiled. That roguish smile tore at his guts, and he cried aloud in pain. His broken sobs frightened Joe the bartender.

And Kelly's smile was so damn superior that Dave wondered how anybody could call her a juicehead. For a long time they stood looking at each other, getting to know each other again. And Kelly was lovely. Dave's throat and stomach leaped and plunged while he carefully studied every nuance of that devilish smile. He vaguely wondered if germs came out of her every time she breathed, but he knew that it wasn't important. He rather liked the idea of their gasping, choking, and dying together like in that movie with Greta Garbo. Only this would be more down with it. Real as hell.

When Kelly smiled provocatively and slowly swirled around in a circle so that he could see her shape with its pert little rump, he groaned like a madman and reached out to grab her, only to realize that she was in a different world. His genitals ached with emptiness and she smiled compassionately as if she knew it.

It was hard to say exactly what she was wearing, but it was made of gauze and was gorgeous like her face. And then she started to undress. Her reddish brown nipples were erect. A mad urge to kiss them made him gag and spit on the floor of the bar.

Looking at her, he decided to never have intercourse with her again. She was too delicate. He would bring her back from Chicago and keep her like a prized orchid.

Then she was gone.

Dave came back to this world filled with bloody fury. That was the same girl that drunks discussed in public. The bastards had been talking about his most prized possession and he had let the Later tonight he would hunt them down and kill them.

He hated all mankind; for all men hated Kelly Simms because they couldn't screw her. And he hated Kelly. What goddam right did she have to destroy her beauty with alcohol? It wasn't hers to destroy; it was his!

"Dave, you just dropped my drawers for now and evermore!"

With a cry of joy Dave looked about the bar. Kelly's voice had been right in his ear as clear as a bell. And he knew he had not imagined it. But why was the crazy little thing hiding from him? He giggled and started to search the bar. He went to a closet and opened the door, looking. He went into the next room and looked for her. He gave up and came back to stand at the bar. Suddenly his eyes slitted with suspicion. Joe was trying too damn hard to mind his own business. He had made believe he was not surprised to hear a woman's voice making a secret vow to Dave Greene.

The idea really frightened him, but he guessed that it had to be true. This bartender was a ventriloquist. A goddam black-assed Edgar Bergen.

But how did Joe know what words to say? Kelly had never told him. Never in a million years.

Or would she? After all, the no-good-whore was running all over Chicago begging for drinks. And all she had to do was to wire Dave Greene collect and he would send her a million dollars.

Two million.

Three even.

He could borrow money on the gas station, the houses, the houses in Nashville. He could sell the pickups' cars. He could pawn the bank itself if necessary.

Suddenly he was exhausted. He lowered his head and rested it on the bar. He tried to cry. He had a perfect right to cry. It seemed proper and fitting that he should cry. And so he rested his head on the bar, making horrible noises toward the floor.

Cokey entered the club, followed by Flick the Kid. The Kid was trembling from head to toe, but he resolutely stayed in step behind Cokey.

And Cokey was not in the mood for any drunks. Period.

Many of his former classmates were located in teaching jobs in nearby rural communities, and it seemed to Cokey that every damn one of them had come to town to spend the holidays. They were in abundance at all the affairs, and they had joyfully crucified Cokey.

In the beginning he had been able to smile away their barbed condolences, but the thing had by now grown into a battle of nerves.

.ghty-dollar-a-month teachers flocked to shake Cokey's hand, and .ll of them knew what Cokey was doing for a living, but they carefully asked just the same. And they tried to hide their jealousy of his big salary and his guts for realistically accepting a job in the numbers racket. They falsely congratulated him for doing what they did not have the courage to do, and they all thrust the same knife home: "Yes, but what are you going to do with your education?"

Then in funereal accents they spoke of the brilliant future he had faced when he had graduated. And it hurt in so many different ways. Most of all it hurt Cokey to find that so many Negro educators were capable of being envious of a racketeer. And some were downright angry. It was just as if Cokey had died and gone to hell on purpose.

Tall and homely, Cokey was a striking figure in his new tuxedo as he approached Dave at the bar. "Give me a glass, Joe," he said. Joe sprang to obey. Cokey was bigger than he was and younger and soberer, and Joe was convinced that Dave was going to get violent in a few moments.

Cokey poured a drink and sipped it while Dave, a crafty look on his face, watched him. Dave's tongue lolled out and up as if he was trying to touch his cheekbone with the tip of it. His head was cocked to one side.

"Pardon me, but did I offer you a drink?" he said to Cokey.

"Since I've already took it, you might as well. And while we're asking questions, what the hell are you running around, scaring the wits out of people for? What happened?"

"Who says somepin happened?" Dave said cautiously.

"Can't I look at you and tell? You want to go home and talk things over?"

"That goddam Lila's at home."

"What's that got to do with it?"

"S'Kelly," Dave whispered. "I got to go to her. She's got TB."

"So that's it," Cokey muttered. "When she get it? I mean, how long has she known it? Is she in bad shape? Gone to a sanatorium yet, or what?"

"I don't know nothin'," Dave sobbed.

"I know how you must feel, fella. Guess you're torn up as hell inside," Cokey said. "I'll fly out there in the morning for you. You can't go, I don't know how Lila would take that, but I know she wouldn't mind me going."

"She had it all the time; that's why she wouldn't marry me."

"Are you sure you know what you're talking about?"

"So help me. And she's drinking herself to death. She's ever running around bumming drinks like a whore. I promised Blueboy I would go."

"That's a goddam lie. Kelly begging drinks."

"Don't tell me I'm lying. Wasn't this club full of Chicago delegates ten minutes ago and they all talking about Kelly like she was a two-bit whore?"

"I guess this is serious," Cokey said slowly, still not knowing if Dave was being melodramatic or not. "What you want to do is go home and sleep on it. Tonight isn't the time to make decisions."

"I'm never gonna sleep again until I know she is okay and has everything that money can buy. Kelly comes first. I'm sorry about Delilah, but I love Kelly best. I can't help it."

All this was a whole lot more than Cokey had expected. Even if Dave was exaggerating, he was sure this was no time to take him home to Lila. He breathed with exasperation as he looked at his watch; he had a date to keep in less than an hour. This was all he needed to complete a lousy holiday. So now he had to call up the one sensible girl he had met all Christmas and inform her he had to wet-nurse his boss.

Already he could hear the clucking sympathy of the girl's friends and their sad voices, telling her that she should have known better than to date a man in the numbers.

He cursed aloud, but softly. Didn't those half-starving bastards know that not one single nigger had a brilliant future in June 1939? Didn't they really know that he had walked damn near all the way from New York to "throw away his education"? That he did not have one red cent and was ragged when he arrived in the Ward? That if it weren't for the numbers racket he'd still be on his ass? But why did Dave have to pick this particular night to pitch his drunk? He painfully decided to take Dave home to Delilah.

Cokey fished a nickel out of his pocket to call his date as Dave abruptly decided to take a walk. Tightly clutching the quart of whiskey, he soberly walked out of the club.

Cokey slammed down the receiver and followed Dave. Dave, it seemed, was not drunk at all; he jauntily strolled down Vessey Street. His gait reminded Cokey of Blueboy's famous strut, and he fervently wished that poor Blueboy were here now.

Flick caught up with Cokey. "Where's he gonna take and go, you think?" he asked.

"Dunno. If he turns the corner, he may be going home, I hope."

Dave did exactly that and so Cokey and Flick quickened their pace until they caught up to him.

"How's it going, fellas?" he said genially.

Cokey grunted and then said, "Fine. Fine. How's yourself?"

"Drunk," Dave said cheerfully. So cheerfully in fact that Cokey wondered if Dave's mind had not been affected by the news of Kelly.

"You don't look drunk," he said. It was a tentative kind of probing.

"Thass because I got lots to do," Dave confided.

Cokey shuddered.

Delilah opened the door in answer to Dave's ring and wordlessly admitted the three of them. Something had told her not to speak. Something was wrong or else Dave would not have rung the bell. He was always thoughtful that way; he would have used his key to save her steps.

But Dave looked unperturbed as he brushed by her, headed for the kitchen with the half-filled bottle of bourbon. Lila glanced at Cokey, but he shrugged noncommittally. They all followed Dave back to the kitchen. Lila leaned against the sink, arms loosely folded across her breast. None of the men sat down.

"I got a date in about twenty minutes," Cokey said, "but I'll take one quick drink before I leave you good people."

Dave had already poured and downed a drunk-sized drink and was in the process of pouring another when Cokey spoke. He stopped pouring to glare at Cokey. "Everytime you think this ship is sinking you run like a bat outa hell."

Delilah straightened up and opened her mouth to interject, but stifled what she was about to say so the sound that escaped her lips was a moaning gasp.

"Okay," Cokey said. "I'll call up the little darling and tell her I can't make it."

"Don't bother."

"Now leave us not get all hot and excited until after the fire engines come," Cokey drawled. "After all, who knows? Things might be worse than they seem."

A sudden rage distorted Dave's face. "You're stupid," he said to Cokey.

"Yes, very," Cokey said carelessly. He poured a drink for himself and wondered how long it would take before he got angry.

"You are a goddam yellow bastard."

Lila dully watched Dave as he harangued Cokey. Her man was mouthing curses like a deranged fishwife. His hands were on his hips woman-fashion and his voice was exactly like a girl's, high and hysterical. Even Dave's hips swayed girlishly. And for the first time in her life, Lila bitterly rebelled against what fate had in store for

366

her. She shook her head and stared in horror at the evil thing that was happening to Dave.

With arms still akimbo, Dave bent forward and screamed at Cokey, "Blueboy would still be alive today if you weren't such a goddam-stupid-yellow-cock-sucking-bastard."

Cokey stiffened. "Those cops had guns with bullets in them. What was I to do? We were two unarmed niggers in the heart of the South, now where does brains or the lack of them come in?"

"You could have took a lousy nickel and called me up. You think they would have beat him up like that if I'da been standing there in the station house to pay his fine?" His voice dropped to a ranting whisper. "Oh no, you goddam-ship-leaving-son-of-a-bitch. You didn't have the brains to call anybody up. I could have been at the precinct ten minutes before they got Blueboy there, but you, you educated jackass, had to drive to all hell and gone around town before you finally decided to come get me. You were only interested in Blueboy's job," he screamed. "You killed him. You killed him you dirty, murdering son-of-a-bitch."

Delilah gasped her shame. But the one grain of truth in Dave's assertions was too much for Cokey. He quickly left the kitchen and walked out of the house.

Lila heard the front door slam. "No, Cokey," she moaned.

Without turning his head, Dave struck her across the mouth with the back of his hand. His knuckles hit her lips and she instantly receded into her cool, impenetrable self. She leaned back against the sink, never once deigning to touch her bruised lips.

"Run. You yellow-bellied-little-bastard. Run," Dave shouted, as if Cokey could still hear him.

He picked up the bottle and drained it. Then he pulled out a chair and sat down at the table. It seemed like a ridiculously childish act after all his raving. He picked up the glass of whiskey Cokey had not touched. He drank it and mumbled, "How do I know he didn't call those cops himself? And they ought to ask *him* about Pigmeat." He shifted around in his chair and saw Flick, standing in a corner. "And what the hell you hiding for? You afraid to hear the truth? Stop shaking and siddown. You trying to ruin my nerves, too? What the hell are you anyway, a goddam epileptic?"

Flick was rooted to the floor. His withered hand danced crazily.

"Go home, Flick," Lila said gently, and when he did not move, she went to him and, taking him by his good hand, led him from the room. At the front door she put her arm around his waist and hugged him. "Jest stand out on de porch, Flick. You be awright in a few minutes. Den you go home. Tomorrow ebyting be awright."

The Kid Flick wordlessly stepped into the chilly night. Delilah closed the door and leaned against it to pray. When she had finished talking to her God, she went back to the kitchen.

Dave lurched through the kitchen door just as she was about to enter. She stepped back so that he might pass first. She presumed that Dave was only going to the front room for another bottle of whiskey, and so she took a chair at the table and waited, resting her head in her hands. In this position she appeared to be exceptionally childlike and weaponless.

She did not look up when Dave came back and sat down at the table facing her. She carefully waited until Dave had opened the bottle and taken a drink. When he had finished the drink she raised her head and looked him in the eye.

"Davit, do you hear me?"

"Whaddya want?"

"How drunk are you, Davit? Kin you remembah dis?"

"Go ahead and talk."

"Davit Greene, ah blonx to you," she said carefully. "And when dere is nobuddy around ah doan cayuh effen you kills me as long as it's just me and you. But, Dave, effen you ever strike me outside dis here house or in front of company like you just did, ah am gonna kill you."

Dave stared at his empty glass, and Delilah wondered if he had heard her. She rather thought he hadn't, but she decided not to repeat it. She would wait until tomorrow when he was cold sober.

Without a word or gesture Dave suddenly got up from the table and rushed to the front hall. Then Lila heard him stumbling up the stairs. She had been sure that he was rushing to the bathroom to vomit, but his footsteps seemed to be carrying him into Blueboy's room.

She got up and went in the hall to stand at the foot of the stairs. She heard Dave rummaging about in Blueboy's room, cursing hysterically, and she could not imagine what Dave was looking for, and at the moment, she did not dare to go up and ask him. So she remained at the foot of the stairs and waited, knowing that the night had not ended.

Finally Dave came out of the room and began to descend the stairs. He was carrying a pistol in his right hand. Lila pressed her back against the front door and wondered if it was her time to die but she was not afraid. She even told herself that if Dave was really crazy she was already dead.

At the foot of the stairs Dave looked at her and growled, "Move!"

"No. Dave, who you gonna shoot?"

"Cokey. You heard him."

"Cokey don't say nuttin."

"He didn't *'hab tuh say nuttin,"* Dave said, mimicking Lila' accents. Suddenly his words lost their polite sarcasm and once more were mad and delirious. "I was trying him out. He had his chance to deny everything. Did you hear him say a goddam word? Did you? Did you?"

"You kill Cokey, you gotta kill me fust time."

"So that's the way it is?"

Delilah struck him with her open palm. Dave stepped back and raised the gun to point at Lila's heart. She leaped forward, grabbing the heavy pistol with both hands and at the same time twisting her body so that her back was to Dave. In this position they both wrestled for possession of the gun.

Only their breathing could be heard as they struggled. Each summoned every ounce of their strength. They pulled and tugged for a long time, Delilah using all the muscle in her shoulders to try to twist the gun out of Dave's hand, but he was too strong for her.

Dave took a lunging step backward, but now Delilah was part of the gun and her frail weight came back with it. Dave lunged back again and fell in a sitting position. Lila landed on his legs and wondered why the gun hadn't exploded.

Dave was now flat on his back, still pulling and tugging. Delilah was also on her back, on top of Dave, wrapped in his arms. Both still gripped the pistol that was now pointed at the ceiling. Slowly she turned over on her side, pushing away from Dave, until their bodies formed a perfect cross on the floor. Panting and straining, Lila felt the muzzle of the gun pressed into her breast, but she never relaxed in her determination to straighten out her body completely, thereby breaking Dave's grip on the gun. The pressure her body was making brought the trigger to bear against Dave's finger.

Imminent death sobered his mind to a degree. "Quit. My finger's caught on the trigger."

"Yo doan leggo. Den shootit."

Those words defeated Dave. Lila did not fear death, but, drunk as he was, he did for her. Tears ran from his eyes as he released the gun. Lila, now in complete possession of the pistol, got to her knees, but it was not over.

Dave reached out and jerked her to him by her ankle. Lila came down on her face, but with all her might she threw the gun down the darkened hallway. Then she rolled over to face Dave anew.

And she now knew that Dave's momentary defeat had turned him into a beast, out to maim his conqueror. And she knew that

369

e future of Dave Greene—his life, his freedom from prison, ven his sanity—all that was the man she loved, depended now upon her strength and wisdom.

With one hand Dave held onto her ankle while raining blows to her body with the other. Slowly Lila bent her free leg until it was doubled, her knee almost touching her chin. Dave was still on his knees, seeking to pull her closer by yanking her by the ankle, wanting to have both hands free to beat her.

And at that moment Delilah did what she had to do. She slammed her heel into Dave's chin. Dave's head snapped back in semi-consciousness and he slumped against the wall.

Lila was on her feet and in the kitchen before Dave realized what hit him. She went to the kitchen cabinet and took a claw hammer out of the drawer. Then she closed her eyes and prayed.

She knew that God had never meant woman to be head of man. And she knew that the bank, the money, the luxuries were no longer at stake; they did not matter, were nothing, and so she told God. But she knew, as she knew God knew, that the defeated man who was her life, would soon stagger out into the street, seeking a lesser foe to murder. Taking the hammer with her, she walked back down the hall to the front door. Fate and her choice were one, there was no need to flinch.

"Dabe, git up and go to bed. Yo ain't leaving dis house dis night."

Dave didn't move. He stared at her with pure hatred in his eyes.

She brought the hammer down across his cheek. "Yo is goin' tuh bed, Dabe."

He reached out and grabbed her skirt, murder written all over his face. Without passion, Lila swung the hammer once more. It cracked Dave's jawbone.

He waved his hand before his broken face, palm outward in surrender. Lila stepped back and leaned against the wall. She was still leaning there, breathing in weary tortured gulps, when Dave got up on all fours and blindly started to crawl up the stairs. She watched her man reach the top of the stairs and tiredly pull himself erect. Then he lurched into the bedroom and she heard him fall across the bed. She closed her ears to the sound of his tears.

370

30

Just after lunchtime on the winter day that 176 played, Cokey bounded through the half-opened door of his apartment, and was surprised to see Delilah calmly sitting in the lounge chair. She was smiling.

"Lo, Cokey."

Cokey managed a grin. "Hiya, Lila. I knew that was your car outside, but since when you gone in for housebreaking?"

"Door's unlocked."

"Downstairs, too?"

She nodded. Cokey began to pace the floor, frowning all the time. He walked up to where she was sitting and looked down at her. "Not that I'm not glad to see you, but I guess I'm kinda sorry you came."

"I didn't come to beg you back to work, Cokey. I came to talk."

"Damn little to talk about now. I really came up face to face with the truth the other night. And it would have been such a little thing to do. So easy. Just make a phone call. I always said that Blueboy's death was unnecessary. It just so happened that he picked a damn fool to ride with that day."

"Did you have a nickel, Cokey?"

"It won't wash, Lila," he said softly. "I could have begged a nickel. Torn open the money bags. Must have been dozens of rolls of nickels in them."

"I guess I wouldn't be your fren if I tole you you did exactly right, but I know I never thought of no phone calling until Dave mentioned it. And I don't believe he did either until the moment he said it."

"Drunk man, sober thoughts."

"Dave did worse," Delilah said. "He was so mad at the white p'lice he went and took Blueboy to the colored hospital. Might just as well brought him home and called a midwife.

"We don't even know what Blueboy died from," Lila continued in her quiet voice. "He wasn't in no pain. I was with him; he just went away is all. But at the white hospital they would have took X rays and things. Dave's mad at the white folks helped kill Blueboy, too."

"I suppose that should make me feel better, but it don't."

"I understand, Cokey."

"Well, thanks for going to all the trouble to come up and talk to me, Lila. And in a way I guess I don't feel as bad now."

"That ain't what I came for."

"No?"

"I want you to go to law school, Cokey."

"Lila."

"I will pay every cent it cost."

"I could never pay you back," he said evasively. "No time soon anyhow."

"Dave and me are gonna need a lawyer all the time from now on, Cokey."

"I don't know." Cokey did not believe he could collaborate with the present Dave Greene, be the man drunk or sober.

"I ain't asking you to make up with Dabe. If it be Gawd's will, then you'll be friends again, but I ain't forcing nothing, Cokey. I could always come to the office by myself. It would be all right with Dabe."

The expression on Cokey's face was an amalgam of all that is bitter and sweet in the black man's life. It was a uniquely negroid dilemma that Cokey faced. Lila was offering him a chance to live a full and satisfying life, truly the chance of a lifetime. If a white man had offered this opportunity Cokey knew that he would be groveling with thanks, so why was the same gift unacceptable when it was offered by a little black angel?

372

"Okay, Lila," he said with a grin. "There is not one bit of sense in my sitting here, begging you to beg me. I am amazed to find that I am too intelligent to refuse."

Lila leaned forward in the chair and gravely extended her hand. Cokey stood up and went to her, and they sealed their agreement with a handclasp. Then they both sighed; they had done done 'um.

"How must I give you the money, Cokey?"

He grimaced cheerfully. "I really don't know, but I know that I can get by on way less than a thousand a year. That will be for three years."

"Can't you get into Howard right this minute? I don't want you brooding here alone like you been doing, Cokey. Don't the new semester start right now?"

"February. But I don't know if you can get in at midyear, I'll have to check. All this is so sudden, Lila, that I can't think straight, but there's a coupla of profs up on the Campus that will help me."

"Come. I'll take you to the Campus now."

Cokey picked up his coat and then hesitated. "Under the circumstances, riding around together might be kind of foolish."

"Me and Dabe blonx to each other for real now, Cokey. He won't care."

Later in the car Cokey said, "I see that Dave has a broken jaw."

"He was drunk and on the stairs," Lila replied.

She parked in front of the administration building and watched the tall form of Cokey bounding up the broad stone steps. To get his transcript would be the first order of business, Cokey had said.

Her gaze roamed the pretty Campus, and she wished that it was spring when the grounds were truly beautiful. The Campus grounds and her agreement with Cokey made her think of Pigmeat's grave. Idly, contentedly, she wondered what Pig was doing now. Tomorrow she must drive out to the grave. It was only right that Pig should have some share in helping Cokey. And she had to check on the grave and make sure it remained the most beautiful in Jonesville.

If I had never met Dave Greene I would be in one of those class rooms right now, she reflected. Then she reminded herself that she would be a very busy woman from now on.

Ever since that night of horror she had taken over Cokey's job. And now it looked as if she would have to keep it. Dave had come back from the hospital a new man. There was a docile tranquility about him now. And Lila knew that somehow he had gained a moral victory over himself that night, or soon after that night. Other than that, there was no difference in her man that she could discern. He dressed the same, talked the same, he even worked the same.

However, Lila was not too satisfied with Dave's tranquil air of submission. It showed a lack of determination; he refused to make a decision now. Already, "Ask Delilah," was becoming his trademark on the Block. That she must do something about this lack of self-reliance was Lila's only pressing problem. Lila's life was good, just as it had always been, and she thanked God for that.

She shifted her thoughts to Cokey. Sending him to law school might well be the true monument to Dave's and her success in this world, she mused.

She knew that Dave's conscience would one day make him apologize to Cokey, but now was not the time; the wounds were still too raw. But God knew that they were both men, and after today, Lila was convinced that the three of them had put away childish things.

After that she dreamed. She daydreamed as every human must. Without his dreams man would have long since withered and passed from the face of the earth. Dreams like Delilah was having are God's sole antidote for evil.

And it is well that God only permits us to dream of our future; for no man should know the exact times of his comings in and his goings out. Because this is justly so, Lila could not foresee that Cokey would be one of America's first Negro combat pilots; it was impossible for her to foresee Cokey's plane faltering, then crashing in the ocean, and the sharks off the coast of Africa eating his flesh. She could not dream in this January of 1941 that she would become not a "war widow" but a "penitenshus widow," while Dave spent two years in Atlanta for income-tax evasion.

The gods, in their mercy, refused to let Lila dream of what had already been decreed. And so Lila sat in her car, waiting for Cokey and dreaming pleasant dreams that would never come true. But it was best for her not to know that most things do not last always, and that only the things of black granite—like Delilah's own spirit, like the Numbers, and like the Niggers—are forever.

374